I0685347

CONVERGENCE 2012
Robert R. Ricks

A RAIMAZ Publishing Novel

RAIMAZ PUBLISHING
Published by RAIMAZ PUBLISHING, LLC.
RAIMAZ PUBLISHING LLC, 8346 S. Helenic Lane, West Jordan UT 84088, U.S.A.

First RAIMAZ Printing, March 2011
10 9 8 7 6 5 4 3 2 1

Copyright © Robert R. Ricks 2010, 2011

ISBN 0-615-50666-6

Printed in the United States of America

www.Convergence2012.com

www.facebook.com/convergence2012

www.RobertRicks.com

This book is a work of fiction. Names, characters, places and incidents either are a product of fiction or are used in a fictitious manner. Any resemblance to actual persons, living or dead, events, or locales are entirely coincidental.

PUBLISHER'S NOTE:

To my wife, Irene, who was by my side while undertaking this journey and my children, Angel, Maile and Zach, who have cheered me on every step of the way. I love you all more than words can ever express. A special "thank you" to my mom, Bobbie... Without you, I wouldn't be here. And, to those marked at the end of this book, your support means the world to me. Thank you all!

Chapter 1 – Arrival of a Watcher

The air was stale and thin, missing the freshness and vitality that Xanari was used to. It was hard breathing the foreign air, and the stagnant taste nearly made her vomit. She wondered how the humans could possibly stand such living conditions. In her mind, it was not living at all. She shook the thought away as she reminded herself of why she was there.

She was in a small structure, obviously a home. She felt constrained and the walls were far too close for her liking. She scanned the room and noticed that it was a bedroom of a young child who was sleeping just a few feet away from her. The child's breathing was loud and seemed labored to her, much too labored for one so small.

It must be the air she thought, again gagging.

She examined the small child, and she smiled as she noticed his vibrant aura. It was a pale blue with strong swaths of pink and yellow flowing around his entire little form.

She needed to understand her environment better and since the child was sleeping, she decided it would not harm her mission to adapt via his memories. She stood over him and positioned her long slender fingers just barely above his flesh. The warmth of his skin was surprising to her. Even though she was at least half an inch away, she could feel waves of heat radiating from his head.

Emotions and memories flooded into her mind. A jumble of wild fragments presented themselves to her, and she had to work hard to rejoin them into cohesive timelines. The child was named Jeff Hill, and he was 8 years old. He had lived in the house with his mother Diane his whole life, which made some things easy for Xanari. When she had enough information, she slowly moved back away from Jeff. She looked around again and everything was familiar to her, as if she had lived there her entire life. Looking back at Jeff, she motioned over him and a faint bluish mark appeared on his forehead. She had managed to find a suitable human and felt it was a good omen that the first human she had come across was worthy of the mark.

Glancing down she realized she would have to find some clothing and clean up. The shift had left her covered in an off-white glazed material that was beginning to dry and powder. She silently slid into the bathroom closest to her. Jeff's mother, Diane, was raising the child alone and only she, Jeff and a family pet, the cat named Sheba lived in the house. There was no threat near, so Xanari relaxed a bit, as she examined herself in the bathroom.

She was slim as many of her kind and had deep brooding eyes that rarely blinked. The eyes were the deepest blue that shifted as if an ocean roared within them. Her skin was smooth and soft as silk, pale in color a milky complexion that shimmered slightly. She had long flowing crimson hair that hung down to the floor and curled just above the surface almost as if it did not want to encounter the ground. Her build was closer to that of a teenager than of a full-grown woman, small breasts with a very athletic muscular build. When she moved it was with purpose and grace. Sheba, the cat, watched her from a window to the rear of the bathroom. The cat bowed its head as if to pay respect to the visitor.

Xanari examined herself in the mirror, and her gazed stopped at her necklace, which adorned her long thin neck. The necklace known as a Gak-lua-kuun had ten solid gold slender slabs each measuring around six inches long and a quarter inch wide. Off to either side of the gold were eleven smaller silver slabs roughly half the size of their golden brothers. Each slab had an engraving on it, which glowed softly. The engravings extended down the length of the slabs and wrapped around small stones of different shades at the bottom. They were bound together by an ebony thread, which seemed too fragile and delicate to hold the weight of the necklace. The black material was amazingly flexible and strong at the same time.

She gazed at the dust on her flesh and reached up to the center of her necklace and gently rubbed the third golden slab there and in barely audible phrases spoke. The necklace shimmered brightly for a moment, and the dust exploded off her form and simply disappeared. The air was suddenly filled with a floral scent a hundred times sweeter than anything on Earth. Sheba sniffed the air and began to purr in satisfaction.

"In a short while, this is what you'll smell all the time my dear friend." Sheba nodded and settled down to sleep still purring.

It was at that moment that Xanari heard the mother, Diane, stir from her bed and slowly walk towards the bathroom.

Diane stood for a moment in front of her bathroom and regarded the door. Her son never closed the bathroom door, which drove her nuts. She had scolded him many times, as she walked in on him doing his 'business'. She peered into his dark bedroom, and she could see his motionless shape sleeping. Then a smell came from the bathroom, gentle at first, but it grew stronger as each second passed. A scent she had never smelled before. It was so pure, so beautiful she had to take a step back. *What was that smell?* Her heart pounded in her chest. Someone was in her bathroom and regardless of how wonderful he or she smelled they were still in her bathroom. She slowly reached for the door handle, her hand was trembling. She paused a few inches away and examined the door again.

Damn it! Diane, get it together and open the door. She thought to herself.

She forced herself to turn the handle and flung the door open. It creaked and squealed sharply. She walked in and turned on the light. The air there was heavenly. "What could have made such a wonderful smell?" she wondered aloud. She slowly opened the shower, and nobody was there. "Jeff must have closed the door when he was done," she whispered to herself.

Sheba could see Xanari but Diane could not. Xanari thought about speaking with Diane, but after seeing how badly damaged her aura was decided against it. Instead, she stood and waited. Diane finished up and headed back to her bedroom. Flipping the switch on the way out she said, "Well if you find out let me know okay? Gonna go back to bed. Got a loooong day tomorrow."

A moment later, she was gone. Xanari waited until Diane laid down, and gently she placed her into a deep sleep. Within 3 seconds, Diane was snoring softly.

Xanari glanced at Sheba and nodded. "She will wake up in a few hours. Yes, I know the air purge was not needed to cleanse myself, but the smell was too much for me. I just needed a little more time to get used to this foul air."

Xanari knew most people would not be able to see her, but she did not want those that could, to draw attention to her. Because once she was pointed out, then the others would see her as well. Therefore, she decided to try to blend in as much as possible. She again reached up to the necklace and with her right hand; she softly caressed the last slab on it and began whispering. With her left hand, she motioned and a magazine floated slowly up to eye level. She motioned with her slender fingers, and the pages began to slowly turn. She regarded the images on the pages, and she shook her head. "Why cover their natural beauty with these material masks?" she wondered.

After the magazine had reached its end, she completed her ritual and the air shimmered around her. Her long flowing crimson hair began to snake itself into elaborate braids that formed a beautiful Celtic pattern and hung down her back. Clothing draped on her and her skin shifted a multitude of colors until she settled on a well-tanned complexion. Her body form shifted slightly, and her chest expanded outward. Her eyes and hair shifted colors and finally ended on a dark brown shade. She turned again and glanced at Sheba.

"What do you think? Will I pass casual scrutiny?"

Sheba stretched and hopped down and did three circles around Xanari's feet.

"Ah yes. The shoes. I forgot the humans need them yes?"

More whispering and shoes materialized around her feet as she lifted each foot.

Sheba meowed and Xanari smiled.

"Thank you for your help. I will not forget it. Yes, you are on the list as well as the child."

Sheba paused and stared at Xanari.

"The mother? I am sorry. I do not think she will make it past the tests. I'll make a note and follow-up on her, specifically though as a favor for your help. Will that please you?"

Sheba meowed.

"When? December 12th 2012 on Earth's calendar. One year from today, it begins. We'll have nine days once it starts."

Sheba purred.

"Until we meet again," said Xanari as she passed through the wall like a ghost to the sleeping world.

Chapter 2 – The Elder
December 12th 2011 - San Francisco 2:08 am

The park was quiet and when Kuthanaga shifted, there was no one around to witness his arrival. He stood there for a moment and collected his thoughts. Undoubtedly, the watchers had arrived, as he was the last to have shifted. Five thousand watchers were dispatched across the planet to mark the worthy and bear witness to his test. A single year to test and choose roughly one billion humans. It was a daunting task. He stood there and shook his head slowly. He knew it had to be done, and he was destined and prepared to play his role, a role, he had spent the better part of a thousand years preparing for. He paused for a brief moment and could feel the others. He was satisfied that they had all made it. The fact that the others had survived the shift unscathed was a testament to their training and preparedness. Still, he wondered if what they were doing was right. He knew they could not save all the humans. Most of that was the humans' fault, but still he wished there was something that could be less intrusive to gauge the ones who could be attuned.

He closed his eyes and placed his hand over the great necklace, which hung heavy around his neck. It was similar to the necklace that Xanari and the other watchers possessed, just three times as large, and one of the original ten that survived the arrival of the Annukai on the Earth. Kuthanaga had been on the crust many times during his training and knew how to blend in well with humans. He had already managed to secure several identities as well as amassed a large fortune, which would aid him on his mission.

Kuthanaga stood at five foot five inches tall and had a deep sea-green mane of hair that was wild and flowing. It gently hung to the middle of his back. On his face, there was a beard neatly trimmed into a v that extended two inches below his chin. His features were strong and bold and yet there was a soft sadness around his eyes. He had eyes of a man who knew his own destiny and was not afraid of it. His skin was a soft tan with a shimmering pale red set of markings that covered his entire body. These living fractal markings were identical on both sides of his figure forming an interconnecting tribal design that extended from the center of his chest outwards. His eyes were the deepest blue and the storm that raged within shifted and flowed constantly. Kuthanaga's build was very muscular with muscle bands not seen on humans. It was one of the distinct differences between the men and women of his kind. The women were almost identical to the human women, where the men were physically stronger with extra sets of muscles, which allowed them to easily outperform a normal human male twice their size by a factor of four.

He took a deep breath and with pure thought alone activated the Gak-lua-kuun that hung around his neck. The center stone flashed for a brief second, and his form shifted and grew outwards. He stood six feet six inches tall, with a deep brown skin complexion, heavy build to support half of his actual strength and no hair on his face or head. His eyes were piercing and he chose a dark green for the final color. He had the build of a linebacker and yet moved stealthily like a cat. In this form, he was known to the humans as Desmond Washington. He was wearing a silk suit, black in color with a slight green trim. The tie was green and had a pattern of a great tree with roots running the bottom length of the tie and branches reaching up through the top. He looked like he was worth a million dollars and if truth was told he was worth much much more.

He sighed and began walking. The sigh was not a sign of boredom, but more of pity. He could hear a short distance away several people sleeping in makeshift shelters and the frost on his breath told him it was cold out, cold enough to kill humans. In order to affect him, it would have to be much colder. He walked a few hundred feet and paused near a man who was passed out with a bottle tucked firmly under his arm and bundled as much as he could be. He shivered slightly.

Kuthanaga reached into his inside pocket and pulled out a wallet. Opening it revealed credit cards, IDs and a billfold filled with large bills. He examined the man briefly and after noting his aura nodded to himself.

"The morning will be much better friend. Sleep well."

His hand motioned over the sleeping form, and warmth passed from him to the shivering man. He could feel the cold pang of addiction, the heartache of lost love, the pain of the system treating this man like a piece of filth. The shivering passed and the man slept peacefully for the first time in years. He slipped the man five thousand dollars and took the bottle from him.

"You won't need this anymore. I wish your last year to be a happy one. So take this and start your path to happiness without any of these shackles."

He walked on a few more paces and saw another man. After reviewing his aura, he slipped the man the bottle and continued on his way.

He could see the street and there was light traffic flowing through the city like blood through the arteries of a concrete behemoth that refused to sleep. The stars were out and the sky was clear, which was unusual for San Francisco this time of the year. He knew all of this because he had sampled several individuals over the years to prepare for his Desmond persona.

The stars dully winked at him, and the moon's glow was a dim version of its natural radiant glory. He missed seeing things for what they really were, and he was anxious. His thoughts were interrupted as he heard footsteps quickly approaching.

Three thugs had chosen the wrong person to try to rob. Granted, two of the three were bruisers, and they were armed with knives. Normally, they would have easily taken out a human of Kuthanaga's size. However, they were dealing with an elite warrior of the Annukai, not a human. He waited until the last possible moment to slide to his left and spin. Using the momentum of the first man against him, he easily tossed him ten yards up and to the right. With a single punch, he broke the neck of the second assailant instantly. The final man had a pistol out and had Kuthanaga dead by right.

With a thought, time suddenly shifted and slowed, which allowed Kuthanaga to dodge right and roll under the gunman's outreached arms, which he effortlessly shattered as the gun fired. The bullet easily missed Kuthanaga but hit the first assailant between the eyes, as Kuthanaga knew it would. The gunman only saw a brief blur before the flash of white searing light flashed within his mind's eye, and pain filled his world. He fell to the ground screaming and Kuthanaga knelt and whispered a single word. The gunman was silent and staring.

"What the fuck?" he asked as he stared in horror at the bloody compound fractures of both of his arms.

Kuthanaga grinned perfect teeth at him. "What do you mean?"

"What... Why ain't I hurtin' no more?" blood ran freely from the bones which jutted out of his flesh.

"Because I want to talk with you."

Kuthanaga examined the man and peered deeply into him. He saw pain, death, drugs, brutality and other negative experiences. As he studied the man he saw something else as well. Something he had not seen in a long while and he smiled. Kuthanaga learned much about the human named Tim Christenson aka Big "T", and he decided he would be perfect.

"What about mother fucker?"

"Tim, how would you like a job?"

"W-w-what?"

"I said how would you like a job?"

"What the fuck are you talkin' about man? You fuckin' with my head or what?"

"No." Kuthanaga stared harder, lifted his hand, and placed a single finger on Tim's head. A faint bluish glowing mark appeared on Tim's forehead. The mark was there for the Watchers to see. Tim was now a marked agent of Kuthanaga and there were certain benefits to it, but also he would be on a very short leash.

"You will do what I say when I say when I call you on this phone." Reaching into his pocket, he revealed a HTC Droid cell phone.

"Um you're fuckin' trippin! Sorry man, but you broke my fuckin' arms... How am I supposed to take that? I can't do shit."

Kuthanaga paused, examined Tim's arms and nodded to himself. "Yes, let's fix those."

He closed his eyes for a brief moment and then abruptly slapped upwards on the base of Tim's arms lifting Tim to his feet. Tim was expecting more blinding pain and braced himself and instead, warmth passed along his arms and he watched as the bones snapped back into proper position and the skin healed up quickly leaving a large faint pink scar on both arms.

"W-w-what the fuck are you?"

"Never mind that. How much will you require to do my bidding?"

"You're what?"

"My work. How much? Tim... You can put your arms down."

Tim had not realized his arms were still stretched out before him. He let them fall to his side. His mind was reeling. None of this was possible. He felt dizzy. He opened and closed his hands slowly and bent his wrists. His arms were his again and he took the cell phone hands shaking, all the while trying to comprehend what was happening.

"$500 a day" he quickly blurted out.

"I'll make it $1,000 a day and will deposit it into this account..."

Opening his wallet, he handed Tim a debit card.

"The code to access is 6577."

"Serious?" Tim's eyes widened as he heard the numbers.

Kuthanaga paused and looked at him. "Do I appear to be joking?"

Tim shook his head slowly. "Dude that code is the..."

"Last four numbers of your social security. Yes, I know. That's why I chose it, so you wouldn't forget."

"Man, don't take this the wrong way or nothing, but are you the fuckin' devil?"

At that Kuthanaga laughed.

"That my friend is truly funny. I'm sure when everything is said and done, many of you will feel that way, but some will think I'm far from that. So do we have a deal?"

Tim looked at his fallen friends and then cautiously looked from his arms to Kuthanaga and swallowed slowly. His eyes darted to the pistol on the ground for just a brief moment. Kuthanaga retrieved the pistol and handed it to Tim with a grin.

"You were looking at this. Do we have a deal? Yes or no?"

He took the pistol from Kuthanaga making sure he held it in a non-threatening way and slowly nodded his head.

"Good, first things first." Kuthanaga motioned over Tim's body, the addictions to meth, cigarettes and alcohol were purged from his system, and Tim dropped to the ground as his body reeled from it. Black liquid dripped from his skin and eyes and with a great heave, a black mass ejected from his mouth and landed on the ground in front of him steaming in the frosty air.

"I could've made this painless, but I want you to remember it. That way, you will not go back to the poison. I will know if you do, and worse, *you* will know if you do. Therefore, your job for today is to stay clean and get your woman clean. If you cannot get her clean then lose her. I will call on you soon. Be ready."

Tim sat there for a few moments breathing deeply with a foulest taste he had ever had in his mouth. His head was pounding but for the first time in a long while, it was clear. He could think. He took a single long deep breath and was amazed that he didn't fall into a coughing fit.

"Sure thing man, any fucking thing you want."

"Clean up the language. You are working for me. I don't care for it."

"OK, no problem man."

Kuthanaga turned at that and started on his way again. Tim looked at his pistol, which suddenly felt very heavy in his hands and watched the tall man until he was out of sight. He slowly stood and glanced at his dead friends.

"Fuck guys. I'm sorry."

He started running then and didn't stop until he got home thirty-six minutes later.

Chapter 3 – The Tool
December 12th 2011 - San Francisco 3:10 am

Tim opened his apartment door and slammed it shut behind him. He was covered in sweat, and his breathing was fast and harsh. He doubled over and his face was red, and he fought to stay on his feet. Even exhausted he felt more alive than he had for a long time. After a few minutes, he pulled out the phone and examined it. It was a new HTC Droid phone with no contacts and no information stored on it.

He put the phone on the nearby table and stood up and looked around his tiny cluttered apartment. Through his front window, he had a decent view of the street and if the windows weren't covered with blankets some mornings he'd have a spectacular sunrise. He realized it had been a long time, since he'd watched a sunrise.

The apartment had a dank sour smell to it and he sniffed the air with a renewed awareness and he smelled himself.

"Aw fuck. Damn!"

He realized he was personally responsible for most of the hanging sourness in the air. He ducked into the bathroom, closed the door behind himself and turned on the light. It took a moment for the bulb to click on and it almost seemed the light resisted for a moment and then hummed and flickered in. Without a thought Tim had the shower on and he sat on the toilet to allow the shower time to heat up.

The bathroom was in bad shape, the paint had been peeling when he took it over the previous year as part of a gun trade, but neglect had continued the peeling until there were multiple shades of faded color. Obviously the landlord would just slap on a new layer of paint whenever someone moved out, and judging by the layers Tim counted at least six coats, each a different shade. There were cracks on the walls, lots of dark moldy mildew around the base of the shower and the mirror on the wall was cracked and the bottom edges of the mirror were rust-colored black. The tile on the floor was stained yellow and every so often there were drops of brown.

It always took a while for the water to heat up and when it was good and hot there was only four to five minutes of it. Tim saw the first signs of heat with wondrous steam. He stripped down and his bare naked feet craved the heat of the shower as the cool tile beneath his feet chilled him.

Tim pulled back the shower curtain and stepped in. The water felt like heaven against his weary flesh and he leaned into it and savored each drop as it soothed him and his nerves. He sighed a huge sigh and felt a weight lift from his shoulders.

Tim was an average sized guy standing roughly five feet eleven, he was a little on the chubby side with a gut that stuck out more than it should and it had been a while since he had been able to look down and see his lower regions. His face was rough and he needed a shave bad, his six o'clock shadow had become a seven-month-old beard. His brown eyes were angled and gave him a permanent doped up look. He had brown medium cut hair, which was cut a bit uneven. He thought the uneven cut gave him a cool vibe, which someone like Brad Pitt could pull off, but all it managed to do for Tim was make him look a guy who cut his own hair. His teeth were in decent shape giving the circumstances they were facing on a daily basis with the drugs and cigarettes. He had lots of tattoos, many of which he could not recall getting. There was no rhyme or reason to any of them except one. On his chest was a heart tattoo with barbed wire wrapped so tight that it cut into it and blood was spurting out of the top. This was his first and only tattoo that had any significance to it. When he thought about it, he'd feel an ache in his chest and it was this ache he tried his best to fight and forget.

He started to drift and noticed the temperature had started to drop.

"No, no, no!"

He quickly grabbed the bar of soap and started scrubbing like crazy. He scrubbed as if he was trying to wash away the past six years of his life. He scrubbed so hard his skin welted up. He washed his body, face and hair within twenty seconds and rinsed off. When he jumped out, he was shivering.

"I fucking hate this place." he hissed.

He grabbed a towel from the ground and it was damp to the touch. He dried off and he looked at himself in the mirror.

"Homie, you look like shit. We need to clean up a bit."

He opened the medicine cabinet, which had various empty pill bottles in other people's names, and he tossed them to the floor as he rummaged around until he found a pair of scissors and a razor. After cutting down the beard with the scissors, he was able to use the razor to trim it neat and clean.

"That's better."

Tim retrieved his purple toothbrush and brushed his teeth. He noticed the pink toothbrush that was lying on top of it was worn down and needed to be replaced. He had avoided thinking about her the entire time back in his apartment because he knew she was going to be a problem. Joy was more of a tweaker than he was and one of her things she'd get stuck on doing was brushing her teeth. She swore she wouldn't be one of those 'toothless bitches'. Both Joy and he had tried many times to clean up, but one of them would eventually bring the other down.

Tim recalled what the large stranger had said. Clean her up or ditch her. Both of those options almost seemed impossible to Tim. Joy was a pain in his ass and she drove him nuts, but in his heart, he knew she was the only person who really loved him for him. She'd have to clean up, that's all there was to it.

She must've felt him thinking about her, because she groaned from the bedroom. "Hon?" she asked.

He grunted and went into the bedroom. He sat on the edge of the bed and she leaned into him. Her check was warm on his back.

"Mmmm you smell good. How was the night out with the boys?"

He paused. What was he going to say about Rory and John? For that matter, what was he going to say about suddenly being completely clean? He shrugged.

"You know what? You'd probably wouldn't believe me if I told you."

Joy sat up in the bed and reached around to caress his face and her hand felt the neatly trimmed beard. She pulled back and turned on the small lamp.

"Wow, you cleaned up. And something looks different about you. What's going on?"

He looked at her long and hard. Joy was a petite little Asian firecracker. She was only four foot ten but carried herself like she was the queen bee. Her almond shaped eyes were a light brown in shade and when she was happy her eyes smiled, when she was pissed her eyes would pierce deeply. She had many tattoos as well, but hers were thought out and her "canvas" as she put it was a constant masterpiece being added to. She had various Asian inspired pieces. She was deeply tanned and even with all the months that had gone by with next to no daytime activities the complexion never faded. She was stacked for her size and it was her build that attracted Tim to her in the first place. Over the years, she had put on a little weight but nothing that was detrimental to his desire for her.

Tim thought about lying to her. Explaining a thousand dollars a day and mysterious phone calls and no more drugs could lead her assumptions down many roads, so he decided to just spill his guts.

"OK, so me and the guys decided to make a little extra cash by smashing and grabbing. Well it went bad."

She turned her gaze firmly on him and tilted her head and her mouth opened slowly with concern creeping across her face.

"How bad? The cops coming?"

He shook his head and extended his arms. The scars from where the compound fractures on his arms where the bones had jutted out were clear as day.

"Wait, were did you get those scars?"

"OK, Baby listen to me. These are scars from where the guy we were gonna jack broke em…"

She looked confused.

"Um OK, you must be fuckin' stoned cause you only been gone for a few hours. There's no way you could have broken your arms and healed up. That shit takes like months to heal."

Tim got frustrated. "If you'd let me fuckin' finish I'd explain what happened."

She crossed her arms and leaned back against the decaying wall that served as their bed's headboard. Tim explained how the night had gone down and she was silent until the end.

"Are you serious? You expect me to believe that bullshit? Who is she?"

Tim was floored.

"What?!"

"Who is she? Obviously, you're fuckin' some other bitch. I mean you come home and shower and clean up and expect me to believe that some big ass brother man killed John and Rory, snapped your arms and then offered you a gig making a G a day? Oh and healed you up like fuckin' Jesus Christ?"

Tim paused and looked at her.

"And cleaned me up from the shit. I'm straight. I don't need the shit anymore."

Joy looked at him.

"Bullshit. You know you want it."

She leaned over and retrieved a pipe and a lighter. She grinned at him as she went to put it in her mouth and Tim smacked it from her hands.

"I said I'm straight!"

He took her by the wrists.

"I want you to be too. Seriously, we don't need this shit. I need you though... I Need YOU!"

She pulled away and jumped out of bed to retrieve the pipe.

"What the fuck? What the hell did you do that for?"

Tim stood up and chased after her.

"Hey! I said fuckin' leave it. I'm not fuckin' no other bitch. I'm telling you the truth! Will you please just..."

Tim saw something out of the corner of his eye. He turned to look and nothing was there. Joy paused when she saw his body jerk stiff and looked in the same direction.

"What?" she asked in a whisper. "What is it?"

He didn't know why, but he felt they weren't alone in the room. His arms got goose bumps and he was frozen. Joy also felt something, but couldn't tell what it was. They stood there silent for twenty seconds until the silence was interrupted by a ringtone. Tim turned to face the kitchen.

"Whose phone is that?" Joy asked in a calm tone.

"Who do you think?" Tim walked over to the phone and answered "Hello." a pause and then he walked to Joy and handed the phone to her.

She slowly reached out to the phone and looked at Tim. "What?" she asked cautiously.

"It's for you," Tim said dryly.

She listened for a moment and could hear soft breathing on the other end of the line. "Hello?" she said.

"Hello Joy Tsia. Everything Tim has told you is true. He works for me now and I would like you to help him. To prove to you that what I say is true I'd like you to close your eyes for a brief moment."

Joy looked confused. "Close my eyes?"

The voice was deep and soothing. "Yes. Please."

She closed her eyes. It was then that she felt warmth pass from her head to her feet. Unseen by her or Tim, one of the watchers Azraeil was standing behind Joy. Azraeil pressed her hand firmly on Joy's head.

"Now Joy, this will be uncomfortable…"

The watcher started chanting and had her other hand caressing her Gak-lua-kuun. Joy dropped the phone and fell back into the watcher's arm. To Tim, she seemed to be floating in air. Tim grabbed the phone and started to freak out as Joy's eyes rolled back into her head and liquid oozed out of her skin.

"What's happening to her?!" Tim yelled into the phone.

"The same that that happened to you. It will be over in a moment. When it is done please hand her back the phone."

Tim waited and just as Kuthanaga had said, she was completely coherent. Tim handed the phone to her.

"W-what just happened? Why do I feel so weird? What am I lying on?"

She was shaking slightly and her head was spinning. She stood up and stared at Tim. She put the phone to her ear again.

"You were cleansed the same as Tim. Do not 'fall off the wagon' as they say, you will not get another chance at this. I now know why you do the things you do. To be treated as such by your own father. Such a horror. Such secrets you have. Many of which you have not shared with Tim like the suicide of your brother. You were there and could have prevented it. You were indirectly responsible."

Joy began to cry. How could this be happening?

"Enough! OK. I get it. I believe. I… Believe."

The voice on the other end paused.

"Good, then we understand each other. Help Tim for what he will need to do. He will need you and that means I need you. Do not disappoint me. Now let me speak with Tim please."

She sniffled and handed the phone to Tim.

"Hello?"

"Hello Tim, she is as clean as you are now. I expect you two to stay that way. Do you understand me?"

Tim nodded as he said, "Yes, I understand."

The line went dead and Tim stared at the phone. Looking around the room Tim could tell they were alone again.

Joy was hugging her knees and lying down in the bed in a fetal position.

"I feel so fuckin' dirty," she said between sniffles.

"I feel you. Water's cold though." Tim pointed at the bathroom.

"I don't care. I need to clean up." She got up, walked passed Tim and closed the bathroom door behind her softly. Tim heard the shower kick in and could faintly hear her sobbing increase. His chest ached and he wanted badly to comfort her. He didn't know what the man said to Joy on the phone, but it affected her in ways he had never seen before. He glanced at the phone again and wondered not who the man was anymore but more now, what the man was.

Chapter 4 – Preparation
December 12th 2011 - San Francisco 4:30 am

Kuthanaga was pleased with the way the watcher Azraeil was able to assist him with Tim and Joy. He had been in contact with all the watchers save one, the watcher Xanari, who had arrived shortly before he had shifted.

Kuthanaga was sitting in a large leather chair and was gazing out the window watching the Bay Area slowly wake up from its troubled sleep. Many were getting up early in anticipation of long commutes to jobs they desperately needed to keep yet despised to the deepest center of their cores. The economic situation in America had gone from bad to worse to desperate as it slid into a second depression. With DOW Jones barely scraping above 3,500 and unemployment at an all-time high of 37% it was no wonder, there were 'Tims' running around the streets. With California bankrupt, several vital agencies were operating with no money, one being the local police departments. They were stretched beyond their means, and the city streets were a scary place to be in the wee hours.

Within this chaos, the time was ripe for the tests to be implemented. He was in a condominium at the One Rincon Hill. He had a gorgeous view of the city and had managed to snatch his particular unit for a steal of a price at only $950,000. It was all for appearances. The humans were interesting in that they were driven by very primal urges and yet strived for higher level of morality all the while having two sides; an inner side which they shared with very few and an outer face that they wore for a variety of reasons. They could be the most charitable and caring person one day and modify a few variables and there was no limit to the atrocities they could commit. He paused and shook his head. It was a shame really because the argument could be made it wasn't purely the humans fault for their defects. After all, they were genetically manipulated before the usual time in their evolution. He wondered how the humans would have turned out if they weren't tampered with so early on. It was a moot point, as what was done was done and nothing could change the past. The humans for all their quirks and faults were distant relatives, which needed to be preserved. It was the correct thing to do.

Pondering human history, he wondered why they never deduced the simple truth. They were genetically engineered. They were bred for a purpose, and they surpassed the original plan and emancipated themselves. With the genetic manipulation they were now doing, he wondered how long it would have been before they could have proven it. The human's science was still in infancy, and yet they played with dangerous forces for mostly the wrong reasons. The man-made H1N1 virus would prove to be their largest mistake as a species. The natural flu virus was a creation of the Annukai meant to monitor the humans in their evolution and to watch for further genetic tampering at the hands of the Draconians. The influence of the Draconians it would seem was intense, and they looked forward to the Convergence to settle old scores with the Annukai. When the humans introduced the H1N1, it interfered with the data that was being collected and reported back to the Annukai. With flawed data, the Annukai would have to come to the crust and mark the chosen by hand instead of relying on the virus.

The Draconian bloodline was strong on the crust, and they had done very well for themselves amassing large armies ready to die at their orders. He knew when the time came, they would be a force to reckon with, and he was well aware of their intentions. The Draconians were a minor threat to Kuthanaga as another enemy was more dangerous than even the Draconians. An ancient foe that was more than capable of destroying a complete system if they knew the Draconians, the Annukai and the Quinuks were hiding there. Kuthanaga wondered if the Draconians even remembered their common enemy. With the Earth waking up and the galactic alignment, there was no longer anything to shield them from long distance scans and that fact alone scared Kuthanaga.

His thoughts were interrupted when he felt a slight tingling at the base of his skull. The sensation was similar to a foot waking up, minor pins and needles that was focused to a specific location. Telepathic pushing and receiving took time to master and get used to. He relaxed and the sensation was familiar. It was Xanari.

Hello Xanari, I was wondering when I would hear from you. How are you faring for your first time on the crust?

An image of Xanari faded into Kuthanaga's mind. He closed his eyes and focused in on her.

*These humans are interesting. It will take a little time to adjust to the sights and *smells*.*

Kuthanaga smiled.

Yes, the smell. Sorry did I fail to mention that when we were discussing the crust?

She nodded.

Yes. You did. However, I am now used to it. Now if I can get used to human shoes.

He examined her.

I see you have assumed a disguise. You will modify it again. You will still stand out as you look now. When you are among them, you will notice subtle things and will adjust. I would like to again thank you, and know you sacrifice much to be here.

She looked down and then after a moment looked up and stared deep into his eyes.

Yes, as have we all. I believe in this cause, even though my father may not. It is the right thing we do.

Kuthanaga nodded.

It is. We are responsible in part for the humans, and we must do what we can. You know what you are looking for yes?

She nodded and almost said something and paused.

You wish to ask a question?

Another pause. *I gave my word to a feral that I would recheck a human when the time came. Did I speak out of line?*

Kuthanaga shook his head.

No, you may make judgments like that. The humans we mark and protect are best guesses. The arbitrators will have the final say. We simply do the best we can.

Kuthanaga could sense some turmoil in the young watcher.

What is it Xanari?

I wonder if it is better to leave the questionable ones. I fear being an outcast would be a crueler fate for the humans we bring back that are not accepted.

He nodded. There were outcasts among the Annukai, and they rarely were heard from again.

Still, it is not our concern. We do what we can and that is all we can do. Does this satisfy your questions?

She nodded and a faint smile materialized on her face.

Thank you. I will check in soon.

Xanari.

Yes Kuthanaga.

You can also reach out just to talk you know. This is a strange place for you, and you will bear witness to many dark things. Never forget I am here for you. I am capable of cleansing you if you start to feel tainted.

She nodded.

I will. The invitation is also extended to you as well. And while I am unable to perform cleansing, I am capable of other techniques to offer relief.

She silently hoped for a reaction and all she received was a slight smile.

Noted. Good luck young one.

And then she was gone.

Kuthanaga leaned back in his chair and stretched. The Annukai had no need for sleep, which presented him with lots of time to think. He closed his eyes and began to meditate on what he needed to accomplish. He had a short amount of time, and his major fear was alerting the Draconians that they were among them, although there was one in particular, he wanted to find. If the Draconians knew, he was unsure of the success of the mission, but it was never assured of success in the first place.

Chapter 5 – The Dragon

December 12th 2011 – New York City 9:15 am

Richard Byington was doing his morning ritual of a four-mile run, 25 minute circuit training and light breakfast. He was nearing the end of his run when his phone vibrated on his hip. He retrieved it and glanced at the caller id. It was his brother Samuel.

"Yeah Sam, what's up. I'm in the middle of my run?"

A pause.

"Sam... you there?" Richard kept jogging in place as he spoke.

"Yeah. I just wanted you to know that Jessica died last night."

Richard paused and stopped jogging in place.

"What? Shit... Are you all right? What happened?"

"I'm fine, but the media is going to be all over this. Rich... She killed herself. The press is going to have a field day. They are going to draw a line between the economy and the job..."

"Sam. Pull it together. Have you called Sharon yet?"

"No. You're the first one I've been able to collect my thoughts and call."

"How did she do it?"

"Pills."

"You call the police yet?"

"No, she's in bed. I thought she was sleeping in."

"OK, did she leave a note?"

A long pause.

"Sam, did she leave a fucking note?"

"Yeah, she did."

"Did she mention *it*?"

"Yes."

"Destroy the note and call Sharon. She's your assistant. Get her there. Once she's over there make the call to 911. Do NOT call anyone else. I'll make the calls and get this all nice and tidy. I'm almost done with my run. It should work out perfectly

27

time wise. Now give Sharon a call. Cheer up man. Look at the bright side."

"Bright side?"

"Yeah, you're single. The President's financial advisor is on the market again. Do you know how much fun you're going to have?" He hung the phone up and continued his run.

As he ran, he knew his brother wasn't going to have any fun and while that was understandable, what wasn't though, was why his brother felt it was important to share family information with a human.

He sneered as he recalled how pretentious Jessica was. He never liked her and always felt she was too feeble to be allowed with the family. When he learned that she and Sam could not have any children, he breathed a heavy sigh of relief, as he knew the offspring would be weak, and he was thrilled that the family bloodline wasn't going to be muddled.

Sam was the eldest son and as such was granted certain privileges, which included the choosing of his mate. Richard, on the other hand, had to endure the choosing of his wife. Sam had wasted his choice on the human Jessica. As far as Richard was concerned, the death was a good thing as now his brother could find one of their kind to finally create a legacy.

Richard thought about his wife. He was matched with a very influential fashion magazine editor who wasn't half bad in his mind. She was easy on the eyes, smart, funny, great in the sack, very strong willed and dangerous. He respected her and they had triplets, all boys, which were a rare blessing and a very auspicious event. It was obvious they didn't want each other as mates as they rarely saw each other and had various conquests outside of the marriage that neither really cared about. The one thing they both shared though was a strong sense of discretion and obligation. They never lied to each other if a sensitive question was ever asked, which happened very rarely.

Sam told Jessica about the family and what they were only a month before her suicide. With the Convergence coming up, he wanted to prepare her for what was inevitable and explain how he had come to know so much about it. At first, she thought it was all just a bad joke until he shifted in front of her to prove his sincerity. The one thing that Richard knew for sure was his brother truly loved Jessica. It was this fact alone, which prevented the family from removing her when they found out about her. Sam was important to not only the family but to the Draconian movement as a whole. He advised the President directly and in doing so had a lot of influence.

Richard was nearing the end of his run, and this was his favorite part of the day. It was one of the few moments when he could really push himself. He'd get to his security gate run past Joe and after a few minutes was on heavily wooded private land. Once he knew he was out of prying eyes, he really poured it on. It was a short burst but enough to allow him to shift into his true form and give his flesh a break from being confined in the human form.

Richard took a deep breath and broke into a full sprint and with each step, his form expanded, and he could feel the ground give as his weight increased. Normally, Richard stood an easy six foot two, and had a very lean athletic build similar to that of semi pro long distance runner. He was handsome by anyone's standards and had a charming appearance with slightly chiseled features. He had a very light complexion, light brown eye and black hair, which was trimmed short and neat. Everything about him was perfectly balanced from his outfits to his neatly trimmed nails. As he shifted though, his height increased until he was standing just about eight feet hunched forward, arms extended well below his knees. If he stood to his usual height, he would be nearly twelve feet tall. His thighs were monstrous and while his arms were nowhere near the girth of even his ankles they were easily three times that of a common human. His face began to extrude outwards, and his nose shifted to something closer to a lizard than a man did, and the hair receded in until it was all but gone. His eyes were snake-like and sinister. The eyes in their natural state never blinked. His chest extended and delicate scales appeared on his flesh. The scales nearly absorbed the light and had no sheen to them at all which made his movements almost have a surreal unnatural appearance.

As Richard rounded the last corner to his house, he could see his sons through the kitchen window preparing breakfast. He was moving now and as he approached the door, the boys all looked in his direction as the vibration of his run was shaking the windows slightly. He came to an abrupt stop, which would be impossible for any Earth creature to make, and silently shifted back to human form as he opened the back door and walked in.

"One of these days you're going to teach me that dad," said his oldest son Richard Jr., who was the eldest by three minutes.

"In time. A full transformation can have some negative effects on one as young as you. Some get stuck and can't shift back to human form."

Junior sneered. "So what?"

Richard pulled a towel from the table where he left it before his run and wiped his face.

"So what? Do not underestimate the humans. They out number us. There are only a few million of us and billions of them. It doesn't matter what we own or how much money we have. If they knew what we were, they'd hunt us down."

The other two brothers finished the morning prep and started setting the table. Jacob the second oldest was silent and after a few seconds when he was sure his father was done speaking asked, "What is a suitable age to begin training?"

Richard grinned at him and replied, "You are old enough now, but I am being careful. In a year's time, it will not matter anyway and we'll be able to move about freely in the open. There won't be much to be concerned with the humans at that point. Their time is quickly coming to an end. So all I ask is you be just a bit more patient."

The youngest son, Christian nodded and said nothing. He set his father's plate and his brothers sat down. Once everyone had their plates in front of them he sat as well. They all closed their eyes and silently said a prayer and began to eat.

When Richard was nearly done, his phone rang again. He glanced down and saw it was Sam.

"By the way guys, you Aunt Jessica died last night."

They all nodded and seemed indifferent to the news.

"This is your uncle now. Hello."

"Rich. Jessica died last night…" at that Sam broke down into uncontrollable sobs

Richard could tell by his performance that the police must be there and nearby.

"Oh my God. I'm on my way."

He hung up the phone and looked at his three sons.

"I'm off to your uncles if anyone asks. Have you seen your mother?"

They all shook their heads.

"OK, I'll leave her a voicemail. See you guys later."

Richard ran out to the garage, jumped into his 2011 Iridium Silver SL65 AMG Mercedes-Benz, and started the thirty-minute drive to his brother's estate. As he drove through the gate to get back on the public road his phone rang again. He glanced down, saw it was his wife Melissa, and put his Bluetooth headset on.

"Hello Melissa. How are you?"

"I'm doing very well this morning how are you?"

"I'm on my way to Sam's. Jessica killed herself last night."

A brief pause. "Really? How interesting. It wouldn't have anything to do with next year would it?"

"Yes."

"Great."

The phone beeped letting Richard know there was a call waiting. He glanced down and saw it was Christy, a young voluptuous little sexpot who he had recently made the acquaintance.

"Yeah, tell me about it. Hang on a sec got another call. Don't hang up."

"That depends on how on long you keep me on hold."

"Won't be long I promise." he liked her fiery attitude.

He pressed the talk button and waited a moment.

"Hello, this is Richard."

A heavy sigh greeted him, followed by a purring noise.

"Hello?" he said again.

"Baby… I miss you. Why don't you come and sweep me off my feet and do those naughty naughty things to me again."

He chuckled. "You'd like that wouldn't you?"

He could feel her smile on the phone and desire rose in him.

"No, baby, *you* would like that. I promise."

"Yes, well I'm sure you're right, but I'm tied up at the moment. I'll be free around one-ish though. I'm sure you can occupy your time until then." His hearing was better than most and he could hear a slight vibration on the other end of the line. She moaned softly.

"OK, noon then. Enjoy yourself until then. I have to run."

"See you soon. Don't make me wait too long."

He pressed talk again.

"You there?"

A chuckle. "I almost hung up. You suddenly sound a bit more chipper. Why is that I wonder? Good news?"

Richard shrugged. "Nothing too exciting. So anyway, as I was saying, I guess Jessica took a bottle of pills and left a note."

"The press is going to love that. But then I'm sure the note is gone by now. Is Sharon there?"

"Yes."

Melissa seemed bored with the conversation. "Well then he's in good hands. Why are you going there?"

"To play the devoted brother. Care to make an appearance?"

"Why? I couldn't stand that bitch. Even I couldn't pretend to give a shit about her."

"So very true."

"But I am craving some husband time. I can fit you in around noon if you have time."

He grinned. "You wish you could fit me…"

"Ha! Stop it. Seriously for some reason I am craving your attention. Take it or leave it."

His wife's office was at least twenty minutes away from Christy's and his wife's idea of a 'quickie' took at least 45 minutes. He really wanted to release with Christy but something in his wife's tone excited him. Humans were a nice distraction but to be with a full-blooded Draconian in heat was something no human could ever hope to come close to. Christy would just have to wait.

In his native tongue he growled, "I will own you wife" which she replied in kind "You already do."

"Once I finish up with Sam, I will head your way and should be there a little before noon. Are we going to eat first or get right to it?"

"You can waste time eating with your little human toy after I'm done with you."

He grinned. "As you say my wife. As you say."

Richard hung up the phone and realized it was going to be an exhaustive day both physically and emotionally. He was not complaining.

The weather was bleak and cold outside. The rain came and went and a little while later Richard was driving up the driveway to his brother's estate. He could see several police cars and the standard security detail, which traveled with Sam.

The guards had let him in and had obviously called ahead because Sam came out with Sharon at his rear.

Sam stood six foot one and was a little heavy set with a small gut. He was salt and pepper with more salt in his hair than pepper, and he sported a full beard, which was neatly trimmed and almost all gray. He looked like a college professor minus the glasses. His eyes were red from crying and the bags under his eyes were swollen. He was wearing a gray jumpsuit. Even without the suicide, Richard knew his brother was under tremendous pressure from his job working with the White House. With the global depression in full swing there were many people who vilified Sam but there were just as many who viewed him as the chosen one to lead them to the promised land.

Sharon was just as tall as Sam with her heals on, and she was something to behold. Power suit, nails, body and all... She was simply perfect. She was tall for an Asian, which was not all too surprising since much of her physical attributes came from her Draconian blood. It was rare, but her human half had come to terms with her darker side, and they now worked well together. For a half-breed she was above average in all ways. Some would even whisper she was superior to many of the pure bloods, as she had next to none of the cravings and never had to be concerned with losing her cool and inadvertently shifting as some of the political Drakes had done in the past.

A detective followed a few steps behind them. Something about the detective bothered Richard, and he couldn't put his finger on it. He was a small man around five foot seven and he had a wide build to him. His tan overcoat and matching hat came straight out of old school cop cliché. He had a long bushy mustache and beard. He had a confident swagger as he followed. His eyes shifted constantly and Richard knew that nothing slipped past this detective easily.

Richard hugged his brother who was sobbing and as the tears came, Richard knew they weren't entirely crocodile tears. He held his brother for a few moments, and then he asked, "What happened?"

"I – I don't know. We went to bed last night, and I got up as I always do and started my day. Sharon came over and we were discussing the agenda for the day. I went up to see if there was anything she wanted special, since I was going to have breakfast made. And she… she wouldn't wake up."

He wiped his eyes and continued.

"I called 911 when I saw she wasn't breathing."

"Did she have a heart attack? What do you think happened?"

Sam shrugged and again hugged Richard. Richard was impressed with the performance but needed to make sure the letter had been destroyed or get the letter from Sharon and remove it from the scene. He had other more pressing matters he wanted to attend to.

The detective approached then with an outstretched hand, which Richard took immediately.

"Hello sir, my name is Detective Ramirez and we'll be handling the investigation."

"Thank you detective."

"If you don't mind, I'd like to continue talking with your brother. Ma'am, I'll need to interview you in a little bit as well so hang around."

She looked down at him and nodded. "There's no place I'd rather be than here. These folks are like family to me."

Ramirez led Sam into the living room, while Richard and Sharon went into the kitchen. They stood behind the island, and the police were milling about up and down the stairs with no one overly interested in either of them.

In Draconian Richard asked Sharon, "Was it destroyed? Where is it?" so softly only another of his kind could hear.

She glanced down at her brown Louis Vuitton Monogrammed Shearling Storm Handbag, which was near her feet. He could see a neatly folded letter written on pink letterhead just barely peeking through a small opening. He silently cursed. He'd have to scold his brother later for not listening.

He leaned on the counter and smoothly dropped a fork, which clanged on the marble flooring. A few of the officers glanced over and Ramirez diverted his attention from Sam to them for the briefest of seconds and continued his interview. Richard bent down, with one hand grabbed the letter, slid it in the sock of his right leg, and with the other retrieved the fork.

Ramirez saw Richard bend out of the corner of his eye and glanced over to see in the shiny stove's reflection Richard reach into the purse on the ground. Ramirez grinned to himself and continued talking to Sam.

Richard stood and put the fork in the sink. He continued talking with Sharon about how shocking the whole event was and waited for a little while.

He glanced up at the clock and saw the time was half past eleven. His wife would be waiting for him, and he knew better than to have her wait without a very good reason.

"Sam, I hate to run. Looks like you are in good hands. I have some meetings I have to get to. When you find out how she died, please call me."

Sam nodded and Ramirez stepped in front of Richard.

"So you're just gonna cut out like that?"

"Excuse me?"

"Give it up mister."

"What?"

"I know the girl there gave you something, when you dropped the fork you went straight in her purse."

Richard could feel his blood boiling. This human had balls.

"Look you rich fuckers are all the same. If the lady upstairs killed herself and left a note, that just helps us make the call it was suicide. No note, then we have to treat it as a possible homicide. So, if you have the note it'll save us all a whole shitload of paperwork and billable hours. You are aware we don't get paid anymore. We get vouchers. Vouchers don't pay for the kid's braces. We still do the job cause without us, there would be chaos and who knows what could happen to you all you rich folks. So, we do this one of two ways. Show me the letter or any letter so we can be on our merry fucking way with a small tip from you and your brother."

Richard started to sweat. "Or?"

"Or I get a few officers, and we search you." Ramirez glanced down and could just barely see the sock deformed slightly. "Not that I need to guess where it is Houdini."

Richard looked down and could see it himself. He cursed under his breath.

"How much?"

"6 cops and 1 detective. Hmmm that would be about eighty. Thousand."

Richard looked at Sam, who nodded. Sam started upstairs.

"Whoa whoa whoa. Hey Pierson!"

An officer came over.

"Escort this nice man upstairs. He's giving us a tip for our hard work."

Pierson's eyes widened and he nodded.

"So you gonna show me the letter?"

Richard glared. "You don't want to read it."

"Yeah I do."

"No, you don't. Trust me. If you need a letter Sharon will write one."

"Yeah, honey why don't you get started on that. In the meantime, while we're waiting. How's about, I take a peek?"

Richard stood there fighting all his urges to rip the small man to shreds as Ramirez retrieved the letter.

"Pink? Nice."

He unfolded it and started to read it aloud.

"Samuel. I am sorry but I cannot bear to live another day in this lie of a marriage. I wish you had decided to lie to me and keep me in the dark for the rest of my time left."

"Please stop reading."

The detective waved it away and continued. "Knowing that you are not human… What?" He had trailed off reading aloud on the 'human' part and read a few more lines.

Richard snatched the letter from the detective with such speed that Ramirez for a brief moment did not know what had happened. He reached for his gun, and it wasn't in its holster. Sharon was holding it from the barrel at her side.

"I told you not to read it."

Richard shifted his eyes to their true form, and he leaned in and whispered, "Your kids will be happier if they have a father and have braces yes?"

Ramirez realized he was in a shitstorm. No one would believe him, and he was terrified by was he was seeing.

"Take your money and leave."

About that time, Sam came back with Pierson, who had a small bag. Sam noticed the gun and the closeness, which his brother was standing to Ramirez, and he paused.

Several tense moments passed before Ramirez turned to Sharon.

"Could you please finish the letter, so we can leave?"

She nodded.

"Can I have my gun back?"

She again nodded and handed it back to him. His hands were shaking so hard he could barely holster it. A few moments later she had the letter finished and handed it to him.

Ramirez ordered the officers out of the house, and he stood at the doorway.

"Detective?"

He swallowed.

"I hope we'll keep this between us. It would be a tragedy if anything happened to your family."

He was sweating now. He slowly nodded. "I'm sorry", he said as he left.

Richard nodded and looked at the time. He was going to be late.

"Yes. Yes, you are."

Richard turned to Sharon.

"You know what has to be done?"

She nodded.

"All of them?"

"Yes. Every last one of them. Before the night is done."

"What about families?"

He grinned. "Only his."

He could hear the police leaving. The personal security men were handpicked drakes, so they would be solid witnesses as to what had happened at the house.

"He really shouldn't have made me wait. I warned him."

Richard ran out, jumped in his car, and sped to his wife's office. As he drove, he secretly wished he could dispatch the small man himself. Slowly tear him apart limb by limb or maybe take him for a special hunt. The anger rose in him, and he was relieved he was meeting with his wife because only a Draconian would be able to withstand the passion and rage he needed to unleash. Christy would probably die a bloody horrible death if she were the sole outlet for his savage frustration.

He arrived at the office only 2 minutes late and his wife was stabbing him with her eyes.

"You're late."

He crossed the room and saw the whole floor of her office was empty.

She retreated into her private office, and he closed the heavy oak door behind him.

"You're in a mood."

"Shut it!" he said as he ravaged her. He kept Christy waiting for two hours and when he showed up, all she could think was, "The wait was worth it…"

He spent the night working out his frustrations on Christy and across town Detective Ramirez enjoyed an uneasy dinner with his family. As they closed their eyes and said grace, a silent darkness fell on them, and their eyes never opened again.

Chapter 6 – First Day on the Job
December 13th 2011 – San Francisco 12:15 pm

Tim and Joy slept long and deeply. Both were plagued with dreams. There was a darkness, which invited them like a warm old friend calling them in from the bitter cold, but inside the darkness, they knew there was no salvation, there was no hope. Only pain and sadness.

Even though the room was cold, both woke up drenched in sweat. Tim had been lying there for nearly an hour when Joy finally spoke.

"It feels so weird."

"What's that?"

"Being straight. I crave it but I don't. Know what I mean. Wait no, that's not right. I feel like I should crave it, but I don't. Like a phantom craving, I guess."

He nodded. "Yeah, I feel you."

"What happens now?"

Tim had been wondering that since his eyes opened. He was filled with a sense of anticipation, and excitement mixed with a lot of fear.

"Let's get something to eat."

"You have cash?"

Tim shook his head. "Not yet, but something tells me I do when I get to an ATM."

They got up and dressed. Outside they could hear a huge mob chanting and yelling.

"Damn not again." said Joy annoyed.

Tim looked outside and nodded. "Yup another protest and holy shit it's huge."

Grabbing their bags, they left the apartment and walked in the opposite direction of the mob. Tim had his pistol at his hip tucked in. He was on edge. Walking seven blocks they found an ATM, and he slid the debit card into the machine and waited. It asked for his pin, and he punched in the code.

A menu presented itself and he checked the available balance and there was $2,000. He withdrew $300 and quickly hid the cash away. Joy smiled.

"Oh my God we get to eat something yummy!"

"What you want baby?"

"Dim Sum."

It had been ages since they had eaten Dim Sum and Tim had to agree it sounded perfect. He saw a cab and hailed it. He was surprised that it stopped for him as usually they kept going. He realized he looked a lot better cleaned up.

The driver was a wary looking man whose skin looked like it had been pulled tightly around his bones. The man spoke with a strong accent.

"Where you going man?"

"China Town."

"You got money?"

Tim pulled out four $20s. "More than enough right?"

"Yeah yeah. Hold on."

He got them to China Town in fifteen minutes. Tim and Joy laughed hard as he weaved in and out of traffic often times nearly hitting other cars or bikers. He would curse under his breath as he survived each near miss.

The fare was $47.50 and Tim gave the driver $60.

"Keep the change bro."

Joy jumped out the cab and spun around and Tim paused. He had forgotten how radiant and full of life she had been all the time before the drugs. He joined her and they walked hand and hand down the street. The eerie thing was normally China Town was full of tourist and many shops. Now there were only a handful of the stores open. Many were boarded up empty shells. China Town was a ghost town. A few gangsters were hanging out front of one of the shops and they approached Tim.

"What you want fool?" said one of the youths who couldn't have been more than twelve.

"Dim Sum!" Joy said with a giggle.

Something about her smile and bubbly attitude must have been contagious as the thug couldn't help but return her smile. One of the youths said, "Fine fuckers but you gotta eat at my grandma's spot."

Time and Joy shrugged. It really didn't matter where they ate.

The youth pushed past some of the other gangsters and pulled Tim and Joy.

"This way, come on."

Tim was nervous for a moment and then just relaxed. He followed and two blocks later, they entered a small shop. A little bell rang as they entered. The air was full of savory delights and an old woman came out from behind the counter. She moved slow and motioned for the two to sit. She looked at the young gangster and patted him on his head.

"What you want?" she asked plainly, as she turned to face Tim and Joy.

Joy proceeded to order pretty much everything on the menu and the old woman simply smiled and said "and?" after each item. When they were done ordering she wrote quickly and then disappeared into the kitchen. The young gangster pointed at Tim and said "you better tip fucker!" and he turned and left.

Tim grinned.

A few minutes passed and then basket after basket of steamed morsels of heaven came out. Joy and Tim ate as if they had never eaten before and after a little while; they leaned back in their chairs and sighed a sigh of complete contentment.

The front door opened again and the bell rang. Tim felt a presence. He leaned back to look and standing above him was Kuthanaga. Tim lost his balance and started to fall back. Kuthanaga snatched the chair and set Tim back into the right position.

"Careful now Tim."

Joy's eyes widened as she heard Kuthanaga's deep voice. "You?"

Kuthanaga nodded as he pulled a chair up to the table to join them.

"How's the food here?"

Joy looked at Kuthanaga and then at Tim.

"Yummy."

Kuthanaga smiled.

"Mind if I try some?"

There was a lot remaining on the table and Tim waved at it.

"Go for it. You paid for it."

Kuthanaga nodded and ate slowly savoring each bite.

There was an uncomfortable silence as he did. Joy took Tim's hand and she squeezed it to the point where his hand ached.

Kuthanaga noticed and placed his hand on top of theirs and shook his head.

"Children you don't need to fear me. I am here to help. I helped you already even though Tim tried to rob and kill me."

Joy relaxed her grip slightly and cleared her throat.

"Yeah, he feels terrible about that. But we were broke and were trying to find a way to not end up on the street…"

Kuthanaga again smiled.

"I know all of this. You do not need to explain anything. There are forces at work here, which are fueling the pain that everyone is going through right now. Know that this has to happen though. Also, know that everything you think you know is a lie. A lie which is going to be exposed very soon."

The old woman came out to check on Joy and Tim. When she saw Kuthanaga, she paused. Her eyes grew large.

In Cantonese, she asked him "Are you here to collect me? Is it my time?"

Kuthanaga looked at her and was amazed that she saw him for what he truly was. She must have been a half-breed. Only they had the gift of sight.

"You see the spirits of the fallen?" he replied in Cantonese.

"Yes." she simply said.

He shook his head. "No, your time is not yet Grandma. Soon."

He examined her and smiled. "I will be back for you though, I promise."

She gave him a small bow and a smile and went back into the kitchen.

Joy understood the exchange and asked, "What do you mean you'll be back for her? Why did you ask her about spirits?"

Kuthanaga waved her questions away. "Not everything at once child. There is a time and place for everything. But now is the time for us to begin working."

"OK, sure. What do you need me to do?" asked Tim.

"Simply drive. Joy you are welcome to come if you wish. Today is a special day."

Joy was curious and she nodded. Tim took the bill to the register and the old woman came out.

"No charge. Meal is free," she said.

Kuthanaga stepped forward and gently bowed.

"I'm afraid we cannot leave without paying for such a glorious meal."

"I said no charge." she turned and went back into the kitchen.

Kuthanaga smiled and turned to Tim and Joy. "Shall we then?"

Tim folded up $60, put it under his plate, and followed Kuthanaga.

When they had left, the old woman came out and began cleaning the table. She saw the $60 and smiled. The meal was only $45 and she was taken aback by the fact that the young man would leave money even though she insisted the meal was free. She put the plates in the bin and she struggled with the weight to get it in the sink. She slid the plates in the water and as they passed into the soapy liquid the plates shifted color. Every plate, which Kuthanaga had touched, turned into solid gold when she washed them. She stumbled slowly back and gently leaned against the wall. Her grandson yelled to her from the front door as she heard it ring.

"Grandma! Did they tip like I instructed them?"

She nodded. "Oh yes, yes they did. You leave them alone!"

He nodded and watched Kuthanaga and the couple cross the street.

Tim looked at Kuthanaga.

"Where are we going?"

Kuthanaga pointed at a 2010 Santori Black supercharged Range Rover and threw Tim the keys. "Santa Cruz."

Tim looked at Joy. He mouthed the words "Santa Cruz" and Joy just smiled. Joy got into the back seat and Tim got into the driver's side. He started the SUV up and he grinned as he adjusted the black leather seats. After checking the mirrors, they started the drive to Santa Cruz. The drive was relaxing and no one said a word for the first 20 minutes.

"I have a question." Tim suddenly blurted out shattering the awkward silence.

Kuthanaga faced him.

"I like, don't know your name."

Kuthanaga grinned.

"Would you like to know my real name? Or my human name?"

Tim paused. "Um, human I guess."

"Desmond. Is my name."

"Desmond. Cool. Should I call you 'Boss', 'Mr. Desmond', 'Sir' or what?"

"Desmond is fine."

"So… Desmond. What's in Santa Cruz?"

"Well not Santa Cruz exactly. Near it. There is a tourist attraction called the Spot. Are you familiar with it?"

Tim looked in the rearview mirror at Joy.

"Familiar with it? Hell yeah! That place is trippy. I took Joy there when we first started dating. I think it was our second date or something like that. Right babe? I totally know where it is."

Joy nodded.

"Good, we need to go there."

"OK, I can do that." Tim smiled as he had a course and direction. Joy could feel Tim's confidence and it made her happy to see him smile and relax.

It took another 25 minutes to get into Santa Cruz and as they drove Highway 1, the view was pleasant and nice. Early on as they had passed through Pacifica it was mostly gray and foggy, and they neared Santa Cruz the sky cleared and the ocean was wonderful to see.

Roughly ten minutes from the beach, the three made it to the outside parking lot of the Mystery Spot. There were people walking about and Kuthanaga smiled.

"What now?"

Kuthanaga got out of the car and motioned for them for follow him.

"Dude, are we gonna go through the tour?"

44

He shook his head. "No, we're going to take a private tour."

"Um I don't think they allow that."

Kuthanaga flashed Tim a look and Tim raised his hands. "OK, OK, I'm shutting up."

"Follow me closely and say nothing."

Joy and Tim followed and watched as Kuthanaga just walked in and no one seemed to notice the three. They weaved past the many visitors until they came to a game trail. Kuthanaga paused and closed his eyes. He started walking again and then stopped at a secluded area. The air was still in that place and Kuthanaga pulled out what looked like a large silver metal spike. Tim and Joy both could feel something was odd. It was quiet and sound almost seemed muted at the spot where they were standing. Kuthanaga took the spike, slammed it deeply into the ground, and pressed. A slight gurgling sound emerged and he muttered something under his breath.

"Thank you mother Earth. I hope you will understand why I must do this."

He pulled the spike from the ground and it was covered with a milky liquid. Kuthanaga used great care in catching the liquid with a small vial. He instructed Tim to hold the spike. Kuthanaga motioned for Tim to follow him a few steps, which Tim did. As he neared where Kuthanaga stood the liquid began running up the spike in the opposite direction towards Tim's hand.

"Turn the spike towards the sky please."

Tim did as he was told and Kuthanaga positioned the vial to capture all the liquid. Tim and Joy noticed a very sweet smell that drifted through the air.

"Wow that smells nice." Joy said.

"And tastes as just good." said Kuthanaga.

He capped the vial and smiled.

"Taste?" Tim had a few drops on his hand.

Kuthanaga pointed to the drops and said, "Try it." Tim paused and then licked. The taste was a pleasant mixture that tasted like banana and vanilla with a slight bubbly sensation that tickled his tongue.

"Damn! That is good. Tastes like…"

"Say no more. Let's let Joy try some."

Kuthanaga took the vial, opened it, and let a single drop fall on Joy's wrist. She tasted it and it was sour like a lime and immediately after a super sweet milky flavor filled her mouth and warmed her. She got goose bumps and giggled. "Oh my God. That was so intense."

Kuthanaga recapped it and asked them to describe the taste.

"Banana Vanilla that was very light tasting." said Tim.

"Like a super liquid lemonhead with warm milk." replied Joy.

Kuthanaga laughed long and hard.

Tim and Joy looked at each other confused.

"What the hell?" Tim asked as he stared at the vial.

"What is that?" added Joy.

"The Earth's Milk. It only found in a few locations on the crust… on Earth. It is a very special liquid as you shall see."

Both Tim and Joy wanted more of the liquid. They recognized the sensation.

"Is it addicting?" asked Joy.

"It is. However, with no withdrawal effects. Nothing negative. The flavor though, will never be forgotten. It is tuned into the taste you desire the most. If you needed to you could survive on nothing but it. As your cravings shift, the flavor will shift. It adapts to you."

Kuthanaga put the liquid away. Tim took Joy's hand, and they followed the large man as he walked.

"Hey Desmond, I'm kind of glad we met and want to apologize for trying to kill you. This is some next level stuff."

"Your apology is accepted and please, do not thank me. This is the beginning. There is a very high chance that when we are done, you will regret ever laying eyes on me. Nevertheless, enjoy the moment for what it is. Because good times cannot always last but we can cherish their memories."

Tim shrugged and followed Kuthanaga's advice. He held Joy and they walked in silence content and for the first time in a long while, they were at peace.

Chapter 7 – Decisions

December 13th 2011 – Salt Lake City 10:45 pm

Xanari had spent the better part of the day getting her bearings. The snow had begun falling around noon and recently stopped. The ground and everything was covered in fresh snow that seemed to glitter in the pale light. As the snow shimmered in the moonlight, it reminded Xanari of the Sands of Judgment near her home. The sands were warm while snow was cold. It was a new experience for her. She reached down and gently patted the ground.

Kuthanaga was right as usual. Her appearance was nowhere near, what the typical human looked like. She had shifted herself to add a few more pounds, shortened herself and added in imperfections that the typical human possessed. Her clothing also was changed as she discovered quickly that the dress she originally had on was not sufficient to warm her. She was now wearing appropriate weather-wear and snow boots.

The air was crisp and it burned slightly in her nose when she inhaled deeply. She exhaled and the steam from her breath frosted quickly. She smiled. It was always the simple things that pleased her.

She had observed large crowds of people at an area called the temple in the heart of the city of Salt Lake. The locations of the crust were interesting to her since the humans were never quite sure where they were they always needed directions to find their way. They would mark streets with signs and from what she could tell; they were based off a grid system. This was an odd concept to Xanari, since the Annukai knew where they were at all times even if blindfolded. Magnetism would provide feedback to the Annukai and with a heightened sonar-like ability; they would instinctively know where to go and where they were.

She examined the temple and read the people she came in contact with and the ones who showed potential she marked. She did this nonstop, most of the time the human in question would be easily identifiable based of aura, intelligence, and physical attributes. The ones who were too close to tell she would have to delve deeper and examine historical data to see what had brought the human to such a neutral level. So far, she had only come across twenty-six humans who were so severely polarized that she took pause and noted them. There was one child in particular that caught her attention and she was curious as to his living conditions, parents and other influences that would help foster such an outstanding human.

She preferred crowds since it was easier for her to blend in and not be detected, especially with snow on the ground. She always made a point to walk where others had walked. With the fresh snow on the ground, that would not be possible, so she would have to take great care and make sure no one would be able to see her footsteps on the virgin landscape.

The young human was named Wesley Roberts and he lived in medium sized home. The house was blue with white trim and smoke puffed from a chimney. The smell of the fire was distinct and Xanari was unsure how she felt about the burning of wood. Looking around she decided it was safe to enter the house. She walked through the wall and was in a formal living room near the front of the building. She could see a woman and two children in addition to Wesley. Scanning them, they all made the mark except the woman. Something was wrong with her aura. Additionally she seemed anxious and glanced at the clock on the wall.

"Hey guys. You should have been in bed hours ago. Your father is going to kill you."

Wesley laughed and looked excited. "Mom, it's dad's birthday. We want to wish him a happy birthday is all. We'll be able to get up for school in the morning I promise."

The mother didn't look thrilled about the idea but she gave in.

"Fine once you tell him happy birthday, you go straight to bed."

They all nodded. They were finishing a birthday card, drawing pictures and coloring it. Xanari wanted a complete picture and decided to scan deeper on each one of Wesley's family members. Wesley she had already gathered enough information, but his younger brother and sister were all but blank slates other than the cursory observation that Xanari had performed.

She focused on the younger brother who she learned was named Ricky. Ricky was carefree and full of life and energy. He had large ambitions, and dreamed of one day being a scientist. He loved his family very much and they did many things together.

The younger sister was named Anne and she wanted to be something special. She had dreams of being a doctor.

Xanari was about to examine the mother when the front door opened. Standing at the door was a man who stood six foot three. Very heavy build with a shaggy beard. His eyes were bloodshot and his cheeks were a lighter shade of red. He hurried in and closed the door behind him. He looked at everyone and then his wife.

"Why's everyone up still?" he asked.

Wesley stood and handed his father the card they had all made. "This is for you dad. Happy Birthday!" Anne and Ricky chorused in "Yeah Happy Birthday Dad!"

He hugged them all. "Thank you guys!" he growled.

The mother stood and cleared her throat. "OK guys, deals a deal. You said your Happy Birthday. Now it's bed time."

The father nodded. "You heard your mother. Bed!"

The children gathered up the craft materials, gave their dad another hug, went to their rooms, and prepared for bed.

A few minutes passed and Xanari was very interested in watching how the humans interacted with one another. She scanned the husband and was immediately confused. He was nearly polar opposite of his son Wesley. How could this be she wondered. His aura was black and had sprinkles of red and grays. She noticed also a smell coming from his pores that she could not recognize but was very pungent.

The man took off his jacket and threw it on a nearby chair. The wife was silent. She retrieved the coat and neatly hung it in a closet near the front door not more than two feet from the man.

"What did you guys have for dinner?" he asked as he gave her a slow once over.

She was nervous and for some reason her heart rate was increasing. Xanari watched as the husband stepped close enough to the woman that his chin was almost touching her forehead.

"We had chicken and mashed potatoes."

He hugged her and smelled her hair.

"Mmmmm you smell good."

She seemed more anxious and she pulled away and headed into the kitchen.

"I saved you a plate if you're hungry."

He stood with his arms stretched wide and then let them drop to his thighs with a whapping sound.

"Why you gotta walk away like that? I was telling you how good you smelled and you act like I said you smell like shit."

She looked at him and put her finger to her mouth quickly.

"Shush. The kids'll hear you. You know you shouldn't use that language."

"Sorry! Damn. I mean, hell, it's my birthday. Think I can get a little special birthday treat?"

She looked at him and anger swelled in her.

"I see you were out with the boys again."

He looked hurt. "What do you mean?"

She shook her head. "You've been drinking and probably goofing off. That's the only time you seem to be interested in me." she was standing in front of the microwave and was warming up a plate. The plate was spinning slowly and the room was filled with a low hum.

He leaned up against her and grabbed her hips. "Baby, you know that ain't true. I like it all the time with you. You the one that ain't never in the mood."

She pushed back with her butt and tried to shove him back to make room to slide to her left. He held on and pulled her close. His arms easily wrapped around her body. He squeezed and the air left her. She spun around and looked at him.

"Let go."

"You gonna give me what I want?" his voice was raised slightly.

The mother glanced past him and she looked back at him.

"The kids. I don't want them to hear. You're so loud."

He grinned a wicked grin at his wife. "Well then you gonna give me the sugar or what?"

50

She nodded. He let her go and she retrieved their coats. They put their jackets on, went into the backyard, and went into a small shed. Xanari made a point to walk in the trail they left behind. The shed door closed and Xanari passed through and watched.

The husband wasted no time spinning his wife around and pulling her sweats down. She leaned forward and closed her eyes. She didn't make a noise while he pleased himself. It was obvious this was not what she wanted and Xanari wondered why she would allow herself to be treated as such.

Xanari scanned the husband who she learned was named Bret. He would lie about everything, even things not important to his peers. His father abused him as a child and his mother never loved him. He compensated for these feelings by presenting himself as something greater than he was. Most of his relationships were violent including his marriage to his wife. Amazingly, he never really lashed out at his children mostly because his wife would always intervene and protect them. It was easy for Xanari to see how the human woman had become so dark.

Xanari examined the wife who she learned was named Jennie. Jennie was raised in a very religious home and her family was strict on her. They expected good grades and she excelled. When she met Bret, she fell in love with him quickly. The first time he hit her, he apologized and blamed it on his family and she forgave him. Many years would go by before it happened again. It would happen when he was fired from a job or if he had been drinking heavily. It was also a rare moment when they would make love. She had given up on that long ago. Now she would just silently do as he asked and she focused on the children. A deep resentment and seed of hatred was planted deep within Jennie and Xanari understood why Jennie's aura was so fragmented. She would suffer horribly so that her children would grow up never knowing the sacrifices she made for them.

It didn't take Bret long to finish up. When he was satisfied, he complained, "Damn woman, you were dryer than a friggin' desert. Must be too cold out here huh? I'm gonna eat that food and get to bed. Night."

She gathered her sweat pants up and dressed. She watched him go into the house and she cried silently. She looked up at the sky, which showed the clouds slowly breaking, and she could see some stars. "Why?" she asked quietly.

Xanari marked the woman and felt that she was strong enough to at least be judged. She suffered much to protect her children and to Xanari that was a true sign of strength. Xanari gently put her hand on Jennie's shoulder and warmth passed into the shivering woman. Jennie did not understand why but she felt better. Almost as if she had an answer. She wiped her tears away and went into the house.

Xanari watched as Jennie closed the door. She felt torn and angered. Not at the human Bret. He was just a product of his environment full of bad habits and a free reign to do as he wished. Xanari was mad at herself for taking the time to examine and get involved. She was one of five thousand who would have to observe and mark nearly 7 billion humans. It was time she got serious and got to the job.

She massaged the golden necklace on her neck and it responded immediately. It pulsed with energy and seemed eager to work. She held the fifth golden slab from the center and began to chant. Snowflakes slowed their decent and sound around her dimmed until suddenly there was nothing moving.

Sliding her hand until she was touching golden slabs three, four and five from center. She began chanting and her body started glowing. The air around her began for pulsate and there was a small explosion as air was displaced by another form. An exact copy of Xanari examined the original. The copy nodded and ran off. As she did two more appeared, and then four and then eight and so on and so on. This continued for twenty minutes where each would double until there were over a million Xanari images running at full speed. These were not actually complete copies, more like living cameras, which she could control from one location. She would monitor them every day for the next year and would be partly responsible for America. Only Kuthanaga, Azraeil and Xanari were on the American continent. The rest were in other locations. If one of the watchers finished their location, they would assist one of the others and this would allow them to finish before 350 days leaving them just over two weeks to prep the chosen 1 billion.

The mark would allow Kuthanaga to communicate with the chosen and explain to them what was happening. There would be signs of the coming shift well in advance of the 350 days, but the timing and normal method for choosing had been inadvertently destroyed by the humans themselves.

The mirror images of Xanari would spread out for another hour and would mark outwards. Xanari was the power source and if anything happened to a mirror, she would summon a new one to take its place. Maintaining mirrors of that quantity would take a toll on the watcher but she had spent most of her life preparing mentally for such rigorous tests and this was needed to be able to rise to the next spiritual level.

Not all of the watchers cared for the humans. In fact there were many Annukai who thought bringing the humans into the collective was a bad idea. Many of the watchers on the crust were earning their right to go to the next level of their teaching and the mission was deemed a severe enough test that it almost guaranteed any Annukai who accepted it a place within the council to begin their training, which was an almost unattainable goal for many.

Xanari was granted a seat in the council before she left because of her lineage and who her father was. She wanted to prove herself as an equal or superior to the others, which made her father very proud. Xanari felt the strain and it was severe enough she had to allow time to once again move. The Annukai could temporarily bend the time to give them the chance to complete a specific task but no one could or would attempt to modify what had happened as it was forbidden by penalty of death to any who was foolish enough to attempt it.

Xanari felt a cold wetness run from her nose. It was a deep purple in color and she had never seen her own blood before. That was a bad sign and it meant she had overworked her mind by performing the summoning as well as time bending. If Kuthanaga were there, he would have scolded her deeply for such reckless behavior. She wiped the blood away and grinned. Already she was getting information from the mirrors and hundreds of humans were marked. She would monitor her bleeding and if it happened again, she would tell Kuthanaga. For now, she was motivated and thrilled that she had accomplished such a huge summoning. She knew she was ahead of the others and this pleased her.

Chapter 8 – Roll Call

December 13th 2011 – San Francisco 10:00 pm

Kuthanaga was in deep meditation when he felt a wild vibration from the necklace around his neck.

"A time bend?" his momentary surprise passed when he figured out who it was.

"Xanari, you wild girl. What are you up to now?"

Kuthanaga created his own time bend and bent it heavily so that he could catch up and watch over the young watcher. Everything around him suddenly froze.

He closed his eyes and focused on Xanari. In his amazement he saw that she was mirroring at an alarming rate, one which was too fast and too many for such a young Annukai. He stared and was amazed. He studied her and saw that there was a back flow of energy forming around her. The mirrors were in too close proximity and the energy used to maintain them would cause a backlash, which he knew would destroy Xanari. While interfering with past and future events was banned this was a real-time situation, which he felt was acceptable to intervene on. If the elders had issue with it they would have to take it up with him later.

Kuthanaga reached up, caressed his necklace, and focused around Xanari he created a hole to allow the energy to pass to him. He pulled it to him and even though he strained some slipped through and he could see it snaking around Xanari's head. She had completed her summon and was struggling to maintain the time bend. It snapped on her end and to Kuthanaga she simple froze in place. He worked with the energy and pulled all he could to him. He was faced with a problem, where to channel it so that it would not cause any casualties. He blasted it out his window into the sky just as his own time bend snapped. The area that blasted simply did not exist anymore. No fragments of broken glass, no steel or brick. Nothing.

The sky above San Francisco had a glorious aurora, which no one had ever seen before.

Kuthanaga again examined Xanari and saw she was bleeding. She wiped it away and was still pulling in data from her mirrors. He felt his nose bleeding as was his mouth and he simply wiped it away. It was not the first time he saw blood and he knew it wouldn't be the last. He would have to have a talk with Xanari later, but for now, he was proud that she was bold enough to even attempt what she did and if she had paced herself and given herself the required time there would not have been any problems. She was strong and he hoped she would be strong enough to face what was coming.

He looked at his disintegrated window and wondered how he was going to explain the modifications. It was a good thing he was on the top floor, as any lower floors would have had dire consequences.

He started laughing to himself as he leaned back into his chair and continued meditating.

Chapter 9 – Loose Ends

December 14th 2011 – San Francisco 8:01 am

Tim and Joy had barely slept the night before. They kept trying to wrap their heads around what was going on. The "Milk" was also on their mind. Tim tossed and rolled in the bed.

Joy swatted him on his butt. "Hey, I'm trying to sleep here…"

Tim nodded. "Sorry. Been up and down all night. Let me ask you something. After you licked the milk, were you hungry at all last night? I mean yeah we ate a big ass lunch, brunch whatever you wanna call it. But we didn't eat anything after and I'm still not hungry."

Joy rolled on top of him and smiled.

"When I licked the milk? What milk are we talking about?"

He laughed. "Come on seriously. Are you even hungry now?"

She shook her head. "No not really. I mean I could eat if I forced myself. But I'm not hungry."

"Exactly! I wonder what Desmond is going to do with it."

She shrugged. "Who knows? I guess we'll find out. What I'm more interested in is what Desmond *is*. Obviously he's not a brutha from Hunters Point."

Tim had been wondering that as well.

"Well he's fast and strong. He's kinda magical. I mean he can do stuff you know?"

Joy nodded. "He seems kinda sad to me."

"Sad?"

"Yeah. Like he has a big weight on his shoulder."

Tim rubbed his head.

"He said his true name or human name. So, we know he's NOT human. So what does that leave?"

Joy sat up and grinned. She liked playing games.

"OK, how about this?" she started. "Monster, Alien, Vampire, Demon…"

Tim shook his head. "No, I asked him if he was the devil he just laughed at me."

"Or maybe an Angel. I mean he was all polite to the Earth and all that. Maybe he's an Angel. Plus, the old woman thought he was like the grim reaper or something. So I'm thinking he's an Angel."

Tim shook his head. "Then why does he keep saying shit like we may end up hating him?" Tim wasn't very religious and knew next to nothing about angels or demons other than what he had seen on TV.

"Oh well, I guess we'll find out in time yeah? I mean I think this is a good thing. I mean we're clean, we have cash, we've got each other and that's good yeah?"

She nodded. "Hell yeah fool!"

She wrestled with him and they laughed. He was actually feeling pretty optimistic and happy. So, he was grateful for that.

A loud knock came at the door. It wasn't a cop knock. It was forceful though. Tim had a feeling it wasn't Desmond and he gave Joy the 'be quiet' look. He slid out of bed and grabbed his pistol. He slid off the safety.

The knock came again. "Hey nigga open the door. It's Felipe!"

"Yeah hang on a sec."

Tim cursed silently to himself as he realized it was Rory's older brother Felipe. He motioned for Joy to go into the bathroom. He threw some cloths to her as she went in. He tucked his pistol within reach and unlatched the door.

Felipe was not as large as Rory, but what he lacked in the sheer size that his brother had, he made up with attitude.

"Yo man. You seen my brother?"

Tim shook his head. "Nah, not since night before last. We was bashin. We got paid and he took most of the cash and split. He mentioned Margie though." He hoped Felipe would take the bait and go looking around in Oakland where Margie lived. Especially since, she didn't have a cell phone.

"Nah man. I was over there last night. Bitch said she ain't seen him in a minute. So, since you the last mutha fucka ta see him. How's about we figure this shit out together. Ya know wad I mean?"

Felipe pulled out a chrome pistol and waved it at Tim.

"Yeah man, let me get dressed. Shit."

It was at that moment the cell phone rang.

"Nigga since when you had a cell phone? Thought you junkie motha fuckas sold everything," asked Filipe who picked it up before Tim could get to it.

Felipe looked at the caller ID and it read restricted. "Hello? Naw nigga he can't talk right now, cause he's in some shit. Call back later." Felipe turned the phone off and tossed it on the bed.

Tim felt a presence again and he quickly got dressed. If something was going to go down, he didn't want Joy caught up in it. He tried to get to the door when a faint gasp came from the bathroom.

"Nigga! Who you gots up in this bitch?"

"Wait man, it's just my old lady."

"Really well let's just take a little peeky peek yeah?"

He had his chrome pistol up and kicked the bathroom door in. Standing in between Joy and Felipe was a small woman. She was average in almost every way except one. Her skin shimmered slightly. Felipe met eyes with the small woman and he pulled the trigger. The gun misfired. The woman didn't even blink. Felipe reached up to discharge the faulty bullet and the woman stepped forward. Somehow, her hand suddenly held a blade and she thrusted upward and it penetrated his jaw and protruded from the top of his head. Blood sprayed everywhere but amazingly none extended past the small woman.

She released the blade and Felipe fell to the ground. She looked him over and simply said, "You've been marked as unacceptable."

Joy went to scream, the small woman simply waved, and Joy fell back and went limp.

The phone switched on and rang. Tim picked it up on the second ring.

"Hello?"

"Tim, I think you need to move to another location. The life you knew before is over."

"Um yeah it is. What the hell man? Dude who the hell is…"

Tim turned to face the small woman who was suddenly gone.

"Desmond, man… There was this chick here with weird skin and a knife. A big fuckin knife… And she like just killed Felipe."

"Yes I know. Tim calm down. Get Joy and meet me outside. We are going to take another ride. While we're out I'll make arrangements for you to be in a safer environment."

Tim shrugged and went into the bathroom where Joy was. All the blood was gone as was Felipe. He spun and looked at the door and it was still closed. Joy was there with a glazed look on her face.

"Babe... Joy!"

She focused on him. She looked around and smiled. "Wow I just had the creepiest dream." Tim looked around. "If it was about Felipe, it wasn't a fuckin' dream. We gotta go."

She suddenly was back in reality. "Holy fuck! Who was the girl?"

Tim shrugged. "I don't know but Desmond said he's outside. Let's go. We can't stay here no more. Felipe rolls fuckin' deep so his boys may be nearby."

She turned to go back to the apartment.

"What are you doing?!"

"If we're not coming back I need to get my stuff."

Tim grabbed her. "Leave it. Pretend we just had a fuckin fire and let's go."

She pouted.

"Fuck! Fine..."

She ran with him until they got to the front door. They took a breath and looked outside. Sure enough, Kuthanaga was waiting for them. They walked across the street and got into the Range Rover. Tim started driving.

"Hell of a way to start the morning Desmond."

"Well Tim. You ran with a pretty rough crowd."

Tim snapped back, "I bet not as rough as now right?"

Kuthanaga looked at Tim squarely in his eyes. "You would have rather me let him do what he would have? Or better yet killed you when I first met you?"

Tim shook his head. "Naw man, that's not what I mean."

60

"Careful the tone you speak to me human. I can always find another."

Tim felt hurt. "OK man sorry damn. I'm just shook up is all."

Kuthanaga understood and was quiet. He let Tim drive for a while and after a few minutes passed Tim calmed down.

"Thanks for saving my ass Desmond."

Kuthanaga waved it away. "Do not be overly concerned. We need to drive to Las Vegas."

"Vegas?"

Kuthanaga nodded. "Yes."

"OK… Vegas here we come."

As they drove, Kuthanaga meditated and thought about the coming months and what he needed to achieve. He wasn't happy about the timing of all of this, but then he knew it couldn't be avoided. The energy required to shift all the watchers and himself was immense and it took nearly a year of focus to channel it. If only the humans had not tampered with the flu virus things would have been much easier. However, fate was fate and he was now on the crust hoping to expedite the process of selection. Two tests were decided upon. Some of the elders questioned the morality of the tests, but with such a short amount of time, the job asked of the watchers was nearly impossible. Utilizing the results of the test would not only ensure the success of the mission but also clear up any markings of question.

Three hours had passed since Kuthanaga had said anything and Joy and Tim were silent the whole time. Tim was used to driving and did not mind the road that seemed to drag on and on. Joy slipped in and out of sleep and snored every so often. Tim liked her snore it was soft almost inaudible but every so often she would snort and that would wake her up.

Tim looked down at the gas and realized they were getting low. He also had to use the bathroom in a bad way.

Kuthanaga opened his eyes.

"Tim, please pull over at the next opportunity."

Tim nodded.

They exited and pulled into a truck stop. Tim noted that unleaded was going for $6.79 a gallon and shook his head. Joy woke up and stretched.

"How far out are we?"

Tim glanced at her and said "Hmmm probably another two hours."

She nodded and shivered slightly as she followed them inside. It was cold outside and she was still upset about leaving all her belongings at the apartment, but they would be in Vegas soon and she would have a great excuse to shop. Something she hadn't really done in a long time.

Once they were inside the convenience center Tim bee-lined straight to the bathroom and relieved himself. Once he was empty, he returned outside, found an ATM, took out $300, and then browsed the candy isle looking for a snack. Joy grabbed a bag of chips and a soda.

Kuthanaga grabbed three large bottles of water and stood by Tim.

"Hey man you want a candy bar or something?"

Kuthanaga shook his head and just watched as Tim kept browsing. Tim felt a little awkward as the large man stood over him.

"Desmond. You're kinda freaking me out man. "

Kuthanaga smiled. "I am sorry. I will wait with Joy."

Tim gave up and grabbed a pack of gum and a bottle of tea. He joined Joy and Kuthanaga at the counter. A young man with oily face and matching hair greeted him with a dry "Hello."

"Hey." Tim said with a grin. He slid all the items to the clerk. The clerk had a nametag with a white sticker over it that read BUD. He slowly grabbed and slid each item over the reader, which proceeded to beep. Beep. Beep. Beep.

Tim waited patiently.

Bud looked up when the last item had rang up and with lazy eyes asked, "Anything else?"

Tim nodded. "Yeah, I need to put $100 in the tank. Number three please." The clerk added that in and pointed at the register's display. "That'll be $121.86."

Tim paid Bud and shook his head. Prices were going through the roof. It was amazing how quickly it was happening.

They walked back to the car and Joy skipped and jumped in quickly. Tim noted also it was cold. Colder than he could have imagined it would be.

"Man it's fuckin' freezing."

Kuthanaga nodded. "Yes and it will get colder and hotter. Expect the weather to be a bit more… unpredictable."

Tim took off the gas cap and started pumping the gas. "Unpredictable? How do you know?"

"Because this has happened before many times. And it will happen many more times. The weather is the first indicator that the shift is beginning."

"The shift?" Tim asked. Kuthanaga was quiet.

A man in a red Honda got out of his car and started pumping gas behind Tim. Kuthanaga went and sat inside the car.

Tim decided he would play questions and answers once they were driving again. A couple of minutes later the gas pump finished and Tim recapped and jumped into the Range Rover.

"OK, we're ready to roll."

He noticed Kuthanaga had the three bottles of water out. He took the top off one and pulled out the small vial of milky liquid. He poured a single drop into the bottle and the liquid went from transparent to solid white.

"Wow." was all Tim could say.

Joy was leaning back and had not noticed what Kuthanaga was doing. "Wow what babe?"

She looked at Kuthanaga and saw the water bottle was full of milk. "Is that the same milk from yesterday?" Kuthanaga nodded and handed the bottle to her.

"Make sure you sip it slowly. When you are nearly done, pour a drop into another container of water or liquid and it will convert it to Earth's Milk as well."

Joy's eyes widened. "Wait you mean it can make more?"

Kuthanaga opened another water bottle and repeated. This time she watched and saw what he meant.

"Whoa. That is the coolest thing I've ever seen. So you can make unlimited Earth Milk?"

Kuthanaga nodded. He handed Tim a bottle.

"Here you are Tim. Let me see your drink. Tim handed his ice tea to Kuthanaga who opened it and put a drop in. It also shifted."

"Hey, I was going to drink that!"

"Try your bottle Tim."

Tim opened the water bottle and took a small sip. It tasted like ice tea. Actually, it tasted better than his ice tea would have.

"Wait it's different now."

Kuthanaga nodded. "Yes, whatever taste you are craving the milk will adapt to. That way you will never grow tired of the Earth's Milk. In addition, you will not need to eat, as all the vitamins and nutrients you need are in it. You should be able to sleep or stay awake as long as you like. It is the perfect liquid."

Kuthanaga put the vial away and started drinking from Tim's tea bottle.

Joy took a sip of her bottle as well and smiled. "Oh it's sooooo good."

She closed her bag of chips and leaned back again. "Too bad you don't have a food version of this. I like munching on different textures."

Kuthanaga smiled. "Oh we do have things similar. It's not here on the crust at the moment. However, it will be soon. I think you will like Annukai food."

"Ah noo kai?"

Tim started driving again as Kuthanaga spoke. "Yes, we are called Annukai. Just as you are known as humans."

"So what are you, if you don't mind me asking?"

Kuthanaga shook his head. "I do not mind. I guess you would consider me an alien. Some may call us elves."

Tim's mouth opened a bit. "Wait a sec. An alien isn't the same thing as an elf. I used to play D&D and elves are like mystical fairy folk type thingies."

Joy nodded. "Yeah, and I used to play online games. Elves are magical. Aliens are like all sci-fi with laser guns and stuff."

Kuthanaga waved away their comments. "It is easy to see how they might seem different but they are not, I assure you. We came to the Earth long ago. We were not alone. There were other races, which took refuge here as well. The Draconians and the Quinuks were also with us. The Quinuks were a race devoted to science and technology. The Draconians were a warlike species who excelled at physical combat. We Annukai were into the spiritual manipulation of the universal energies. We all wanted a new start and ended up stranded here on the Earth. We were unaware at the time that this was much more than a standard planet. It was one of the few fully sentient biospheres in this galaxy. With a rotating multidimensional axis with landmass materializing and disappearing every 26,000 years. When we arrived it was right when it was entering into it dark cycle. Once in the dark cycle if you were on the crust, manipulation of universal energies was difficult. The Quinuks used their science to manipulate their environment as well as the indigenous life on the planet to create workers. One of the worker tribes that were created was later to be known as humans."

He paused at that to let it sink in.

"Time passed and again another minor convergence. This time the crust was infused and suddenly manipulation of the universal energies was easier than ever. The Annukai were able to harness this energy and use it for many great things. The humans saw this and thus many of the legends were created. Fairies, gnomes, dwarves, etc. were all different forms of Annukai. It was also during this period that humans discovered the power of gold and silver. While the crust was in its awake period these metals allowed the humans to also tap into the universal energies, which allowed them to fight for their freedom. The Quinuks and Draconians did not want to let their slaves go so easily and many great battles were fought. The Annukai decided to remove ourselves from the situation and migrated to the spiritual dimensional plane of the Earth, which we called Nervanack. We knew there were more humans than the combined force of the Draconians and Quinuks. We trained some of the humans on how to defend themselves. "

Tim fought hard to follow what he was being told, but much of it was just too hard to understand. He would have to quiz Joy later to make sure he "got it". Joy was sitting up and listening intently. Nodding her head every so often.

"We watched the humans as time went on and when they were victorious we watched the Draconians slither into hiding their numbers severely reduced. The Quinuks eventually surrendered and the humans prospered. Then the next cycle arrived and the humans suffered greatly. You were almost wiped out, but each time somehow you managed to regain control and continue. The Earth is in its sleeping phase now. Soon it will shift again and we have determined this is the fifth phase. All of the dimensions will align on the Crust and humans again will be exposed to the living universal energies."

Something about the way he said the last part seemed ominous to Joy.

"What you call magic is simply a manipulation of universal energy. Therefore, you see, I am both an alien and the basis of much of your mythology. For they are one and the same."

Joy waited and asked, "So if I understand what you're saying, humans were created to be slaves?"

Kuthanaga nodded. "The Quinuks were too fragile to handle the hardships of the crust and it was their idea to create the perfect workers."

"So if we were created what was used to make us?"

Kuthanaga seemed to get a little uncomfortable at that question.

"You weren't made, you were engineered. The indigenous humanoid life forms here were your Neanderthal relatives. They were genetically modified with Annukai DNA. We were not happy to discover this, but what was done was done."

"So, you mean we're related?"

He nodded. "Distant cousins if you like."

Joy wondered something.

"You said your human name was Desmond. What's your real name?"

"I am known as Kuthanaga."

"Kuthanaga. I like it. So Kuthanaga, is this how you normally look?"

Kuthanaga shook his head. "I look very different than what you see before you."

Joy leaned forward and was grinning.

"OK, show us how you really look. If it's cool."

Kuthanaga closed his eyes and suddenly the glass in the vehicle started tinting darker and darker until it was jet black.

"Sure."

His form began to shimmer slightly and shifted to his natural form.

Tim kept the driving straight as he glanced over.

"Wow, your much smaller than I thought you'd be. Your skin looks crazy."

Joy cautiously reached out and touched his forearm.

"Wow, your skin is so cold but it's soft. Way soft."

Kuthanaga's eyes caught Joy's and she paused.

"Man, your eyes are intense. I've never seen anything like it. Makes it hard to tell if you're looking at me."

Tim glanced over and said, "Shit. Are they moving? It looks like whirlpools."

Tim continued driving and didn't like looking into Kuthanaga's eyes.

Joy though did not mind. "What's that?" With the shifting of his form, his traditional garb replaced the clothing he had been wearing and the large ornate necklace was now clearly visible.

"It is called a Gak-lua-kuun. It is one of the devices we use to manipulate the universal energy."

"So you can do magic with it. Is it what allows you to change the way you look?"

He nodded. "That and more. For example..."

He closed his eyes and focused on Joy. She felt a slight tingling on her scalp.

"What the...?"

Her hair started to lengthen and her short bob cut was now just beyond shoulder length.

She glanced in the mirror and smiled.

"You can modify us as well?"

He nodded. "Those are simple things to manipulate."

Joy ran her hand through her hair. "So, this is fake or real?"

"Does it feel fake?"

She shook her head.

"No, it feels like my hair."

"That's because it is. Even when I shift my form it's real."

Joy sat back in her chair and thought for a few moments. "So there are other aliens like you here?"

He nodded.

"There's Annukai, Draconians and Quinuks. The Draconians are very much among you. Quinuks can't shift so they rely on other means to hide their presence. They will modify your memory of the encounter so you do not remember. We Annukai are here but have not been here for a very long time. Draconians have been among you since the beginning. Manipulating and plotting."

He closed his eyes for a moment and shifted back to his Desmond form. The windows slid back to the normal tint.

Joy shoved Tim on his shoulder and he glanced back at her in the rearview mirror.

"Well Tim, now I know why you're so off. You must have a lot of alien DNA in you."

She laughed an uncomfortable laugh and Tim knew that this was just to let off some steam. What she had heard was bothering her. She had more questions but she could not bring herself to ask because she was too afraid of the answers. Tim also understood enough of what was said to know that many things were going to change.

Kuthanaga wondered if he had said too much revealing the history of the humans to them. He felt they deserved the truth. Soon enough the remaining humans would know it as well.

They continued to drive for another couple of hours and when they saw the city in the distance Tim grinned.

"We're almost there. Hey Desmond, what are we gonna be doing in Vegas?"

"We will be living there."

"Living?"

Kuthanaga nodded. "Yes, I promised you a safer location to live and I felt the San Francisco area wasn't going to be safe. Vegas, though will be."

"So you have a place out here?"

Kuthanaga smiled. "Yes, I have a small place I use from time to time."

Tim nodded. He glanced back at Joy who had a serious intense look on her face. He studied her and could see that the conversation earlier had really got under her skin.

"Hey Joy, we're almost there babe."

She simply nodded.

"You guys hungry?" Tim asked. He wasn't as he had taken a sip of his Earth's Milk earlier. He was amazed that it was always at the temperature he liked and always tasted perfect.

Joy shook her head and pointed at her bottle as well. Kuthanaga shook his head also.

Joy leaned up close to Kuthanaga and asked, "How old are you?"

He paused. "We do not celebrate birthdays as you do. Let me see. I am 36,732 of your years."

"Wow." said Tim.

Joy was going somewhere with her line of questions. "So you were alive during the manipulation?"

Kuthanaga nodded his head.

"I was but I was in hibernation during the engineering, my father told me firsthand what had happened."

"How old is your father? Is he still alive?"

"He would be close to 51,980 of your years. Yes, he is still alive. The Annukai choose when they pass. We can die from wounds. Aging though, is something we learned to control long ago. Once an Annukai has completed his life's journey if, he or she so wishes they may end the physical and move on. My father has never felt the desire to move on. As an elder, he has many responsibilities. I think he is waiting for me to rise to full elder status before he moves on."

Joy processed the information and continued to her next question.

"What about the Draconians and the Quinuks? How do they age?"

"The Draconians have always been jealous of our life spans and have wanted the secret to our longevity. They have a lifespan very similar to humans. They can live to be close to 500 years old."

Tim shook his head. "Dude, we're lucky to make it past 70."

Kuthanaga shook his head. "That is because you do not live balanced lives. Too much pressure, too much greed. Bad diet of eating filth. You are lucky to make it near 70. The human body can easily live to be 200 or more years if you lived your life as you were supposed to. Your bodies were designed for strength and hardship. The easy lives you live now are an insult to your ancestors."

Joy interrupted Tim who was going to launch a counter argument.

"And the Quinuks?"

Kuthanaga liked the fact that Joy was so persistent and on track.

"They do not age, but they cheat the process with cloning and memory imprinting. They will utilize a body until it starts to age beyond its youthful usefulness and they will then 'grow' a new body and pass their memories to it."

"So the original Quinuks who created humans are still around?"

Kuthanaga nodded.

"You seem very interested in this topic Joy. May I ask why?"

Joy nodded. "My whole life I've felt a little off. Never comfortable in my skin. There were times when I was using that I felt at peace, and then it would go away. I wondered why things never were completely right with me. Then I learn all of this and now know why I don't feel right. We were raped and forced to be something we're not. That's really fucked up. I mean I'm sitting here thinking about normal evolution and how we might have been. I mean the humans are fucked. We're not even natural. We're modified! We're fake! I'm just wondering if the original asshole who thought the shit up was still around. It would be nice to smash his face in as a way of saying thanks!"

Kuthanaga understood. It was a topic of debate even among his people. Many felt the humans were just abominations and should be allowed to go extinct. Others, including Kuthanaga and his father were of the opinion that humans had much to offer and were exceptional. They should be allowed to grow and find their own path.

"To answer your question. Yes, the original Quinuk scientist who did the DNA manipulation is still around. He is one of the thirty. Your anger is well deserved. I am sorry I have upset you."

She shook her head. "No, Kuthanaga. Thank you for telling us the truth. Even though it's shitty, it's who we are. I'm sorry I have an attitude and yelled."

He shook his head and put his hand on her shoulder. "You have nothing to be sorry for."

Tim knew Joy was smart but he was amazed at what he had just heard. Granted she had been in college and took some science classes and such but she really amazed him. Joy saw him looking at her in the mirror and she gave him a look.

"What?" she said.

"Nothing. I'm just trippin' on you. My girl is a super geek who is all edumacated. I kinda get what you guys were talking about and all that, but I think you're gonna have to baby step me though it in a bit cause my head is starting to hurt."

Joy grinned at him.

"Dumbass."

He nodded. "Yes ma'am, that's me, Mr. Dumbass. But, I am one handsome devil. And you soooooo love me."

"Yeah I do."

Kuthanaga felt an ache in his chest. It was painful to watch them and see how much they cared for each other. He knew by the time everything was done they might hate him and that bothered him. He had become fond of the two of them.

"Yo, Desmond. Where we going man?"

"Are you familiar with the Bellagio?"

Tim slowly nodded.

Tim continued driving and Kuthanaga examined the two of them. Joy was wearing daisy dukes and long socks with sneakers. She had an oversized tee shirt on with the neck cut out. Her shoulder protruded out of the tee as it hung at an angle. The design said "Freak U" on it. She had a white wife beater on under the tee. Tim was wearing a pair of blue jeans and a red shirt that said "Player" across the front of it in large white letters. He was wearing black slippers.

"Tim... Joy... I need to do something. Do not be alarmed."

Joy sat back and paused. Tim did not know what to expect and so he pulled to the side of the road and stopped the car as the windows tinted again.

Kuthanaga closed his eyes and Tim noticed a soft glow around him. Joy also watched as a golden sheen covered her and the light grew in intensity until both had to close their eyes. Even with their eyes closed, the light grew brighter. It only lasted for a moment. It took four seconds before they could actually see again.

Tim was staring at Joy when her eyes cleared.

"What?"

Then she noticed Tim was wearing a very expensive looking suite. His hair was styled nicely and he was wearing a cool blue shirt that almost shifted colors.

"Wow, you look hot honey." she said.

"Wait till you get a load of yourself mama! Damn!"

She blushed. She glanced down and saw she was wearing a very form fitting dress that actually worked well with her frame. The material was cool and soft to the touch and she got goose bumps. She liked the cut, the style and the color.

"Damn K. I really like it! Maybe I won't need to shop after all."

Kuthanaga raised an eyebrow when she referred to him as "K"

She smiled. "What? You like D better?"

He shrugged. "Now you will look appropriate for you lodging."

Tim looked at Joy again and gave her a wicked grin. He turned back around and continued driving as the windows returned to normal. They arrived at the entrance of the Bellagio and valet took the keys from Tim. There were lots of people from different areas standing in line to check in and there was luxury everywhere. Marble flooring and a huge Christmas tree in the center of the lobby caught Tim's eyes. He acknowledged it and then shrugged and followed a few steps behind Kuthanaga. As they made their way through the crowd of people, a beautiful tall blonde woman approached Kuthanaga quickly with a smile.

"Mr. Washington, so good to see you again. Your room is ready for you as always."

She barely glanced at Tim and Joy. Her attention was 100% on Kuthanaga.

"Hello Monica. Thank you." Kuthanaga motioned at Tim and Joy. "They will need to shop later. Please make sure they get whatever they need. I'd also like for them to have keys to the suite."

"Sure thing Mr. Washington. Is there anything else?"

He shook his head and kept walking. They walked for a little bit and passed poker and black jack tables. The air was filled with an oxygen-pumped scent with an occasional whiff of cigarettes and cigars. Nothing too overwhelming, which was surprising to Tim as he walked through a cloud of smoke that a small balding hairy man puffed out from his cigar. He thought for sure he was gonna catch a craving to smoke again when he passed a couple at a nearby slot machine, and yet there was none. Sounds of slot machines rang out and flashing lights were everywhere. Every so often they would hear the sound of a machine paying out and luring another sucker in to be taken by the one armed bandit. When they arrived at the elevators, the woman smiled and waited as the three entered it. She was still smiling as the door closed.

"Wow, they sure do like you here."

Kuthanaga smiled. "Yes, when you lose ten million dollars they suddenly are very friendly to you." Kuthanaga took out his key and placed it on the panel and pressed the top button and waited. The elevator started its accent and just as quickly as it began it ended with the elevator doors opening smoothly. They walked out and Kuthanaga paused for a moment and then placed his key on the door and a faint clicking sound filled the silent hallway.

He opened the door and Joy and Tim stood there motionless.

"This is your new home."

Tim could barely make his legs move. He shuffled forward and somewhere he could hear a scream. He realized it was Joy.

"Oh my God… Oh my God… Oh my GOD!!!!"

The view was amazing and the room itself astounded Tim. It was the largest thing Tim had ever seen. He looked around and luxury was everywhere from the 50" plasma screen hanging on the wall to the mosaic marble foyer. It was just too much for him to handle. He wandered into one of the rooms and sat on the bed. Joy walked in and sat next to him.

"Tim. I don't care what K asks you to do… You do it OK. He tells you to do a little old woman; you do it the best you can baby! This is off the chain."

Tim was nervous. Why him? Why Joy? What was so special about them? He was willing to kill Kuthanaga when they had first met. Why did Kuthanaga say they would regret ever meeting him? He was filled with so many questions and even more a small little voice in the back of his head said 'What the Fuck?' 'What's the angle man?'

"Tim you hear me?" asked Joy with a wild look in her eyes and a wide grin.

He nodded. He would wait and see what Kuthanaga wanted of him. He would do as he was asked. But, he wasn't about to be a slave. He was afraid of Kuthanaga but he wouldn't allow that fear to control him. For now, they were in Vegas and he was going to try to enjoy it for what it was worth.

In the other room, Kuthanaga was silently sitting in a chair. His eyes were closed and in his mind's eye, he watched Tim closely and he smiled. He was very happy that Tim was starting to wake up and ask the hard questions. He was optimistic for Tim and Joy.

Chapter 10 – Weird Coincidence
December 15th 2011 – New York 12:27 am

Richard sat in his office browsing emails of Google news reports when he was stumbled upon several reports in the San Francisco area describing an aurora over the city.

"Interesting."

He picked up his cell phone and pressed #2. A series of rapid tones followed and he waited.

"Hello?" answered a grumpy irritated voice.

"Sorry calling so late. It's Richard. Hey did you catch the news of an aurora in the Bay Area night before last?"

A pause. "No. We're not doing any testing of the unit. It wasn't us." Another pause, "You don't think they're here do you?"

"It's only a year away, you know? We knew eventually they'd start showing up. I want a team there checking it out. I want an answer to this question. How long before the unit is working?"

"We do a final test next month."

He nodded.

"Good. I'd also like to have a discussion with our other friends to see what they know."

"That may be a bit difficult."

Richard could feel his heart beating faster.

"Why is that?"

A pause.

"I said why is that?"

"Well I've left some messages already and they're not responding. No emails, text or anything. It's been a week."

"Never mind. I will contact them myself. Let me know once you know something."

"I will."

Richard hung the phone up. He leaned back in his chair and put his hand to his chin. He stroked his beard and smiled. "I wonder if you're here my old friend."

Chapter 11 – Special Markings
December 15th 2011 – Salt Lake City 9:01 am

Xanari was feeling the strain of maintaining the mirrors. She was making good progress but it was taking its toll on her. She moved very slowly when she moved at all. She was in a small building isolated from the world and she just mediated and focused.

She felt a slight familiar vibration at the base of her skull. "Kuthanaga?"

Do not waste your energy speaking young one.

She smiled.

It is good to hear from you. I am ahead of schedule and am about to send the mirrors further out.

How do you feel?

I am fine. Why do you ask?

Xanari, please do not insult me. I was with you during the time-bend.

She paused.

You were? I did not feel you.

No, you would not. You had your hands full.

She smiled.

Yes, I suppose I did.

Xanari, please be more careful. If you were to fall, I would be devastated. I am very fond of you wild one.

And I you, old one.

He smiled at her bold words.

When we see each other again, we will talk Xanari. Continue your efforts, I only hope the others can match your results. Be well.

As with you.

And he was gone again. Xanari was a little embarrassed that she was being watched but also flattered. The great Kuthanaga was monitoring her. She wondered if her father had anything to do with the extra attention, or was there something else happening? In any event, she was happy he had checked in on her. The mirrors were reporting constantly and she was getting lost with data, names, locations, auras, etc. Keeping it all organized and not losing herself was a task in itself, but pushing the mirrors out and keeping them from getting too curious was a serious issue that continued to arise since they were identical to her and shared her decision-making.

There were things she could control and things she couldn't. The best way to insure a mirror wouldn't go too far into a particular subject was to pause all the mirrors and divert her focus into the one in question. She then would do the marking, pull back to her haven, and allow the others to continue. This would not happen very often but it did happen a couple times an hour lasting no more than 15-30 seconds.

She was sensing a mirror's curiosity with a woman, Xanari focused on the mirror, and suddenly she was standing outside a large home colored maroon with white trim. The air was cool and a slight breeze was blowing. The heavy scents of roses hung in the air and Xanari notice lots of rose bushes neatly trimmed and of different colors lined the perimeter of the house. She saw the woman whom the mirror was so fixated on and saw why. Her aura was prismatic and shifted constantly. Xanari had never seen an aura like that before and was unsure why it would shift so drastically. The woman was asleep on her couch and Xanari passed through the wall to get a closer look.

The woman was in her late forties and was wearing flannel pajamas that were slate gray in color. The woman was starting to gray just a little on the sides of her hair and looked to be in very good physical shape. Her eyes were moving rapidly and she seemed to be deep in a dream of some sort. Xanari wondered why the woman wasn't awake like the majority of the other people in the area. There was no one else in the house. Glancing down at the coffee table in front of the woman, she saw mail addressed to a Rachel Jones. Xanari was curious as to what the woman was dreaming of and she closed her eyes and gently massaged the last golden slab of her necklace.

She was now visualizing what Rachel was seeing in her dream and it made Xanari pause.

The woman was watching as the ground heaved upwards as large shards of broken earth flew to the sky. The air was filled with and acrid smell and sounds of screams and chaos surrounded them. Hot smoke was everywhere and in the distance the ground smoldered and the faint glow of molten lava was peeking from the distorted waves of heat.

To the right there was a large group of humans who were not afraid. They were sitting and had their eyes closed. Sitting in the center of the group was Kuthanaga in his native form. Rachel ran towards the group as if to join them. Kuthanaga stood up as if he sensed something. He saw the woman running towards them, he extended his arms, a shimmering appeared around them, and a small hole opened up. Kuthanaga looked past the woman almost in the direction of Xanari and he pointed. Xanari could not hear what he was saying but Rachel glanced back and what she saw caused terror to fill her. She ran faster and when she was only fifty feet from Kuthanaga's protective circle Xanari saw a large form moving so fast it was nearly a blur and it was heading straight for Rachel. Kuthanaga pulled his Gak-lua-kuun from his neck and threw it back towards two humans who were on their feet. A small Asian woman caught it and the young man was hot on the heels of Kuthanaga.

Kuthanaga collided with the large form. The small Asian woman held the Gak-lua-kuun in her hands and she began to channel it. She knew some of the Annukai protection spells. The shield sprung back around the group and Rachel made it inside. Kuthanaga was battling fiercely in a way that Xanari had never seen an Annukai warrior fight. He was fighting with such blind rage. The creature he was locked in combat with was a Draconian, the largest that Xanari had ever seen. He easily dwarfed Kuthanaga, but it didn't matter. Kuthanaga was much too fast for the drake to hit and the tall human man had a pistol. He fired twice and both times, he hit the drake. The drake fought on and the human waited for a shot to present itself again. Just when it seemed that Kuthanaga was winning he exchanged words with the drake and his face showed a wide range of emotions from rage to pain. It hurt Xanari to see him so upset.

They continued fighting and the ground was breaking apart all around them. The human lost his balance and he fell to the ground. Kuthanaga didn't need to see it, he sensed the danger the man was in and jumped back towards him. He underestimated how fast the drake was as the Draconian launched himself as well and caught Kuthanaga before he could land.

Kuthanaga tried to twist and use the momentum of the drake against it, but the drake had locked its claws into Kuthanaga's thigh and shoulder. Kuthanaga screamed a silent scream and pulled the human up as he did. The beast tore a large section of his thigh off and blood sprayed everywhere. The man rolled, stood and shot a single and his aim was true. The bullet hit the drake in his right eye and he bellowed as he released Kuthanaga. The human went to shoot again and the gun did nothing he cursed and started reloading it. The drake motioned at Rachel and said something to Kuthanaga who was lying in a pool of blood that continued to grow around him. The drake laughed a long cruel laugh and he bolted away as the human started to shoot again.

Kuthanaga said something to the man who was sobbing. Then the great Kuthanaga took his last breath and went limp on the ground.

Rachel gasped and jerked abruptly, suddenly wide-awake. Xanari noticed she had been crying during the experience and she wiped away her tears and watched the woman.

Rachel sat up, pulled out a small book, and started writing notes in it. She paused suddenly and smiled.

"I know you're here. I cannot see you, but I know you are here. Aren't you Xanari?"

Xanari tried not to gasp, but she did anyway.

"Don't be afraid. I learned about you when you popped in to watch my vision. I've had that dream several times now. But, it changes constantly. Different places, different groups of people. Sometimes I die. Sometime the young man dies. This was the first time that Kuthanaga died. I feel your sadness. I wouldn't be too concerned. The dreams only come true sometimes."

Xanari marked the woman and decided she would have to come back another time. Her concentration was wavering because of her emotions.

"Come back anytime Xanari. You are always welcome here."

Xanari walked back outside, pulled back to her solitary sanctuary, and allowed the mirrors to continue. She was deeply troubled by what she had seen and what it could mean.

Chapter 12 – Evidence
December 15th 2011 – San Francisco 1:37 pm

Jeremy Masters stood outside of One Rincon Hill. He was in his mid-sixties, stood tall and had an air of importance about him. He was lean and his features were exaggerated with deep lines. His eyes were focused and had deep dark bags under them from lack of sleep. He was aggravated by the way his boss had treated him. He knew there was importance to the work that he did but at the same time, he wanted to actually live what was left of his life. It seemed he had always been under someone's thumb and at his current stage in life, that role was growing old.

Richard had been very specific about having a team on scene in San Francisco to examine an anomaly. The team arrived and their findings lead them to the spot where he stood. Looking up he could see on the top floor corner unit there was plastic sheets covering a large gaping hole. Taking out a small hand held computer and a sensor rod he pointed to the hole. The machine hummed loudly and numbers ran across the screen.

"Great."

He knew that the hole was the origin of the aurora and because of that fact alone; he could deduce that only one of two options could explain it. With the data he just collected, he narrowed it down even further and sighed. Neither of the answers would please Richard and so Jeremy stood waiting and pondering the best way to announce his findings.

Jeremy's phone rang and he took a deep long breath and let it out long and hard. He shook his hands quickly until they tingled.

He reached up to his Bluetooth headset and pressed a small button once. A beep and he could hear Richard's impatient breathing on the other end of the line.

"Well?"

He shrugged. "It's most likely Annukai. Slim chance it's a copy of our tech."

"Give me percentages."

He rolled his eyes and thought about it. "98% Annukai."

"Thank you Jeremy. That's all I needed to know. Take the rest of the day and enjoy yourself." Richard hung up the phone and Jeremy started walking.

"That went better than I thought." he said to himself. He walked on and whistled the Guns and Roses song Patience as he did.

Chapter 13 – Old Friends
December 15th 2011 – San Francisco 4:40 pm

Richard sat in his tall leather chair and wondered aloud. "Is it you my old friend?" The address of One Rincon Hill was of interest to Richard because he once had a condo in that same building himself. He really liked the location as well as the amazing view. Richard wondered if it were mere coincidence that an Annukai had a condo in the same exact building as he once did.

He regarded a laptop, which was closed on the desk in front of him. The desk was massive, made of Koa wood, and had black obsidian carvings of dragons along either edge, which lead to the floor. Black iron wrapped the edges and the desk has a brilliant sheen to it. The only things that sat on the desk were the Falcon Micro custom laptop and his cell phone. His office was perpetually dark as all of the windows were designed to auto tint and keep it the way he liked it. He preferred the dark to work in.

Flipping open the laptop he waited as the machine woke up. He typed in his password and waited. The screen popped up and he opened his Outlook program. A few seconds passed and he heard a familiar tone letting him know he had email. Scanning messages, he paused his cursor above an email with the subject. "Project Tiamat Status" from Dmitri Valdo.

He double clicked on the message.

Project is successful in basic trials. We will conduct the final test December 22 2011. Request test subjects of following specs:
Male – good condition – 25 to 35 years old. Blue Eyes preferred. QTY: 5
Female – good condition – 25 to 35 years of age. Blue Eyes preferred. QTY:5
Male – good condition – 3 to 5 years of age. Green Eyes preferred QTY: 5
Female – good condition – 3 to 5 years of age. Green Eyes preferred QTY:5
Looking forward to results. I think you will be very happy with them. Please advise when I can expect the test subjects.

Dmitri

He shook his head. More subjects? He had just sent subjects the month before for the trials. He pressed forward on the mail program and typed in **j.Christenson@harzalcorp.com**. He waited a moment and hit send.

Richard grabbed his cell phone, pressed, and held the number 5. A second later, various tones rapid dialed. The phone rang twice and then "Hello this is Christenson."

"I just sent you an email from our friend Dmitri."

"What does he need now?"

"It's in the email." Richard could hear a faint tone on the other end of the line.

"Yeah I got it."

Richard could tell Christenson was reading the message.

"Yeah this shouldn't be a problem. I think it'll take a day or so."

"Thank you."

Richard hung the phone up and slid it on the desk. He stood up and started pacing the office. If Annukai were on the crust, he wondered why. Was it the humans? The Draconians had worked long and hard to achieve the progress they had made on the crust and they wouldn't give that up no matter what. The Annukai had always been against the cultivation of the humans as slaves and test subjects with all their lofty moral objections. They were blinded by their righteous dogma so much that they had failed to see that humans were very special. Since they were part of the Earth, they shared many of the things, which made her special. It was the latent abilities, which the Draconians were after. The potential was there for them to be much greater than even the Annukai. It was this fact alone, which allowed the genetic manipulation of Annukai DNA, and human to be blended so easily. A secret which only a few high ranking Draconians knew. The Quinuks were the ones who discovered anddeserved all the credit. They learned early on that the spark existed within the humans. The humans called it the soul, but even they did not realize how strong it was within them.

Richard wondered if the Annukai knew what he knew and if that was the reason they were on the crust. Perhaps they were seeking the ones with the strongest souls. There were rumors that the Quinuks were playing both sides of the fence working with the Draconians as well as the Annukai. It wouldn't matter though, since the Draconians had been planning for a long time and had thought out all the possible scenarios. Richard had a separate issue. Should he report his suspicion to the great ones?

He shook his head. He would wait and see. There was time to alert them if it came to that, but for now, he wanted to focus on Tiamat and find more evidence.

He sat back down at his desk and reached to the bottom drawer. Inside was a small silver box that he withdrew. He pressed his palm on the surface of the box and the sound of sizzling flesh filled the room softly. He held it there and then he heard a slight clicking. He looked at his palm and there were several burn marks on the surface. He knew they would be healed by the next morning but it still bothered him he had to withstand it every time he wished to open the box.

He pressed down again on the still sizzling container and it slid open revealing a small black gem. He took the gem out, held it up to eye level, and concentrated on it. He could feel a tingling sensation over his body and the room was filled with the smell of ozone. The air shifted in front of him and he could see several small shapes sitting Indian style with their heads resting forward against each other's head. One of them leaned back and glanced in the direction of Richard.

The figure was short no taller than four feet and very thin. Its head was oval shaped wider at the top tapering off to a slightly pointed chin. It had two large almond shaped black glassy eyes. Its mouth was small and tight-lipped. The skin was a pale gray in color and the skin had heavy texturing to it. The being was naked and had no sexual organs. The legs were so thin that it was amazing they could support the frame of the being let alone move. The feet were forked and had only two large toes and a heel. It pointed a long gnarly finger in the direction of Richard.

What do you want Drake Lord?

Its mouth didn't move at all.

"I've got some questions for you. First and foremost is why have you not replied to any of the researcher's emails?"

The being paused.

We were distracted. We think we have discovered something very disturbing.

"Disturbing? Like the Annukai are on the crust?"

The being shook its head slowly. *No, we were unaware that Annukai had come back. That is not necessarily a bad thing.*

The others stood up and turned to face Richard.

"Well what has you all so spooked?"

This. they motioned and images of deep space materialized in between Richard and the group. Richard saw a star burning brightly and suddenly it went super nova. Another image of the same star from a different angle showed it collapsing in on itself and a brilliant explosion. The last image showed the exploding star in different shades of blues and greens and a blast shot outwards.

"What is that?"

That is a gamma blast aimed in our general direction.

"Wait, you mean?"

Yes, it looks like perhaps they have discovered our location after all of these years.

"Are you sure it's going to hit us?"

They shook their heads in unison.

*There are two black holes within its trajectory. We are unsure what those will do with the blast. We analyzed the collapsing star though and it was young and healthy. You are aware of the sister moon this planet used to have? *

Richard glanced at them. "Gama?"

They nodded. *Even if this is not them attacking, they are very close to us. It is only a matter of time. When this planet wakes, we will be discovered.*

They paused and continued. *When they detect us and use that weapon, we will not survive it.*

Richard nodded. "What if we were to use Tiamat?"

Not enough data to determine the answer to that question.

"Fine, well we have time. Next time let us know as soon as you discover something of this magnitude. One other question. You don't deal with Annukai do you?"

They shook their head.

We ourselves do not, but there are Quinuks who do. Is this an issue?

"Depends. I don't like finding out Annukai are on the crust, especially since we are so close with Tiamat. Additionally, I would hate to find out that Quinuks gave the secret of the humans to Annukai."

We Quinuks have a pact with Draconians. We have honored it all these years and still do. No Quinuks would reveal it that is within the circle. You can be sure of this. There are only two Quinuks who live outside of our circle. We do not speak for them. And we know for fact, those two have not revealed the secret either.

Richard nodded. The Quinuks were many things but one thing they were not was liars. They took their pride and honor very seriously.

"I meant no disrespect."

They all nodded. *None has been taken drake lord.*

Richard put the gem back into the silver box and it sizzled as it touched its padded lining. As he did, the images of the Quinuks faded from view. He closed the box and placed it back in the drawer.

He put his hands to his temples and he growled a low growl. His temples were pounding and in his chest, he felt a cold fear he had never felt in his life. He started a new email and addressed it to d.valdo@harzalcorp.com. The message read:

Dmitri,

Use all resources to bring Tiamat online as soon as possible. This is not a casual request. This is a revised directive. Something very urgent has been brought to my attention. Notify the whole team and set a meeting up. I will be sending more information shortly. Your requested materials are being sourced and will be available for you within 48 hours.

Richard

He set the priority to important and he hit the send button.

Fetching his phone, he dialed a number that he was hesitant to use. He dialed it slowly with a precise purpose and he waited. It rang once and a deep voice said in Draconian "Is this line secured?"

Replying in Draconian Richard said "Yes. I have a message."

"What is it?" the voice demanded rudely

"The Planet Slayers are near."

There was a low guttural growl on the other end of the line.

"You had better be sure of this."

"I have been informed by the Quinuk's high council."

"I'll pass the message. I pray you are wrong."

Richard hung up the phone and nodded. "So do I."

Chapter 14 – Working
December 17th 2011 – Las Vegas 12:40 pm

Kuthanaga had been in deep meditation for over two days and Tim didn't disturb him. Joy had been more than happy taking the time to do some shopping and taking in the sights. They danced and partied hard all the while avoiding a single drink and just enjoying the environment. After a whole day they finally had an appetite to eat again. They discovered a buffet at the Wynn that quickly became a favorite of theirs until Monica introduced them to the Bellagio's VIP buffet. It was almost as if Vegas had two worlds. One in which everyone was a part of and a second more exclusive reserved for only the most elite of the world.

Tim had tried gambling and discovered he was very unlucky. Joy on the other hand managed to win $35,000 by betting $1,000 on red 16. Tim almost fell when she hit it. They were enjoying themselves and Tim couldn't help but think it was the calm before the storm.

Joy was in the gym located inside the suite working out and Tim was watching the TV. There were riots in New York, San Francisco, Chicago and Los Angeles. People were on the street looting and grabbing food from where they could. It was surreal.

Kuthanaga opened his eyes and stood.

"Welcome back Des." Tim said as Kuthanaga approached him.

"Hello Tim. How have you and Joy been?"

"Joy's in the other room working out. I've been chillin' just waitin' on you. I figured sooner or later you'd get up and work would begin."

Kuthanaga nodded.

"I've been keeping an eye on the others. Now is the time for us to take care of a couple of things. Are you ready?"

Tim stood up and nodded. "I just need my jacket. Are we bringing Joy?"

Kuthanaga shook his head.

"No she will stay here."

Tim nodded. "Let me tell her goodbye then."

Tim walked into the gym and was still amazed that all of it was in a single suite. The room was huge.

Joy pulled her earphones out and looked at Tim. She stopped the treadmill and wiped the sweat from her forehead. Something on his face told her everything before he could even say a word. She walked over, nodded, and hugged him hard.

"Be careful baby."

He nodded. "I will."

He was scared and didn't know why. "I love you," he said.

Joy smiled and started to tear up. "Love you too."

Kuthanaga was standing there and he waited.

Joy wanted to ask what they were going to be doing but she decided against it.

"I'm leaving the card with you." Tim said.

Joy nodded and Tim turned and walked out of the room with Kuthanaga close behind him. Joy suddenly felt very alone as she heard the door latch on the front door.

Tim and Kuthanaga walked towards the elevator.

"Tim, I need for you to take off your right shoe."

Tim looked at Kuthanaga and almost said something and stopped. He reached down and removed his shoe.

"The sock as well please."

Tim did as he was told and Kuthanaga reached into his inside pocket and pulled out a slab of gold similar to what was on his Gak-lua-kuun. He motioned over it and a small slim sliver detached. He closed his eyes and muttered something and a black vein twined itself into the metal. The gold sliver shimmered softly and hung in the air as Kuthanaga put away the rest of the material.

Kuthanaga looked at Tim in his eyes and sighed.

"I am sorry for this Tim."

Tim looked confused. "For what?"

Kuthanaga focused and made sure the security camera was off and moved quickly and before Tim could tell what had happened he was suddenly upside down. Kuthanaga motioned, Tim's mouth clamped shut, and he couldn't say a word. Kuthanaga took the sliver and slowly inserted into Tim's heel.

The pain was intense and burned severely. A few moments later, the metal was penetrating bone and Tim saw flashes of light as the pain slammed him. No blood poured out of the wound. It was almost as if the sliver consumed the blood and didn't allow it to pour forth. After the sliver was deep within Tim's heel Kuthanaga motioned over it and then Tim swung back to his normal position.

Tim glared at Kuthanaga and suddenly he could speak again. He leaned in close to Kuthanaga and hissed, "Dude, you could've fuckin' warned me. What the hell is it?"

Kuthanaga simply smiled and patted Tim on his shoulder. "Insurance."

"Insurance? What the fuck do you mean insurance? Damn it feels funny. It doesn't hurt anymore but it tickles like a funny bone being bumped every time I put weight on it."

Kuthanaga nodded. "It is called the Martyr's Barb. It's there to help you. Through it I can be in contact with you under certain conditions."

Tim put his sock and shoe back on.

"Wait, isn't a martyr like someone who dies?"

Kuthanaga nodded as the elevator opened. He walked in and Tim followed him.

"I don't wanna die man."

Kuthanaga smiled. "And I don't want you to die. If things go the way they are supposed to you won't die."

"And if things don't go the way they're supposed to?"

Kuthanaga looked at Tim long and hard. "Then we're all dead and it won't matter."

Tim swallowed hard and didn't like the way he was feeling.

"So what are we doing now?" Tim asked.

"We're catching a flight."

"Where to?"

"We're going to New York."

"What's in the Big Apple?"

"A very special place. An old place. We need to bring the Earth's Milk to it."

Tim nodded. That didn't sound too bad.

"Where at?"

"The basement level of what used to be the Twin Towers."

Tim stared at him.

"Are you serious?"

Kuthanaga nodded.

"There's more than one reason those buildings were brought down. They were sitting on a vein. We need access to that vein."

Tim chuckled.

"What do you mean brought down? The terrorist did it with planes. I saw it all on the news."

Kuthanaga nodded. "You saw what they wanted you to see. The material used to bring those towers down was Quinuk technology. The Draconians needed to find a fear factor to push agendas through fast and it worked. The Draconians are after the same thing I am, but they do not know how to access it. The Quinuks as well are baffled by the living veins of this planet. However, as I said there were many reasons for those buildings to fall. Did you know there was a mountain of gold under the buildings? The gold is more important than you know, as the material is very conductive of universal energy as I explained before. When this planet wakes so does the gold."

Tim wasn't laughing any more. "So you're saying the twin towers were demolished by Draconian aliens to steal gold and to mind fuck us?"

Kuthanaga nodded and glanced sideways at Tim. "I believe I asked you to watch your language."

Tim nodded. "So we're going to just walk into the Twin Tower construction site and find this vein?"

"Yes."

Tim threw his hands in the air. "Whatever man, next you're gonna say the president is an alien."

Kuthanaga smiled. "You're learning fast. There have been a number of presidents who were Draconian. Your current one is not though. But, they influence him. They hide in shadows manipulating."

Tim jammed his hands into his pocket and rolled his shoulders in. The more he knew the more he wished he didn't know.

The elevator opened and they started to walk out of the Bellagio. The woman, who Tim had learned was named Monica Crawford, greeted Kuthanaga with a smile.

"Mr. Washington, is there anything I can do for you?"

He nodded. "Yes, Joy Tsai is remaining here. We have some business and will be gone for a few days. Please extend to her whatever she needs and bill my suite."

"That will not be a problem. Have a safe trip and we look forward to seeing you again."

Kuthanaga waved as he continued out. Tim followed close behind and when the valet brought the Range Rover around, Tim got into the driver's side and buckled up. Kuthanaga got in and motioned for Tim to drive.

An hour later, they were in line for security check. Tim still had his water bottle filled with Earth's Milk and he wondered how he was going to get through security. He also had forgotten he had his pistol and was getting nervous. Kuthanaga gave Tim a look and motioned for him to place his objects into the tan bin. Tim did as was instructed by the security officers and put his bottle, wallet and car keys into the bin. He found some loose coins in his pocket and he placed them in as well. He stood in front of the metal detector and he just knew he was going to get nailed. The security on the other end motioned for him to walk through and as he did he felt a slight tingle and he passed through with no alarms, no rush of guards, nothing. Kuthanaga followed as well and nothing happened as he passed through either. The bins passed through the small inspection booth on the conveyer and it was if no one saw the large water bottles filled with milk. A few steps more, Tim felt the tingling sensation again, and the weight of the gun was back. He glanced at Kuthanaga who simply nodded. A little while later, they were on a plane heading to New York.

The whole flight Tim was silent and he thought about Joy and what she was doing. Kuthanaga was also silent. He was wondering how Xanari was doing. He would check in with her and the others once they returned to Vegas. Tim wondered why they were traveling on a regular plane while Kuthanaga was fronting as if he was a huge high roller. Why not fly with a private plane. Why did they even drive from the Bay Area to

Vegas? They could have flown. One of the possible answers came to Tim suddenly. He realized Kuthanaga was getting to know him and Joy and wanted privacy. That would explain the drive to Vegas. But, why fly on a normal plane to New York? Was Kuthanaga afraid of the Draconians? Tim thought maybe he was and wanted to stay off the radar by doing things 'normal'. If Kuthanaga was playing it safe then Tim was grateful. If Kuthanaga was afraid then Tim knew he should be as well.

Chapter 15 – Follow Up
December 17th 2011 – Salt lake City 2:40 pm

Xanari had been troubled by the visit with Rachel. Something wasn't right. She had never seen auras shifting as they had with Rachel and the shared vision was more than troubling. It kept playing over again and again within Xanari's mind making it difficult to maintain her mirrors. She didn't know why but she kept one within the neighborhood of Rachel. Many of the mirrors had moved onto other states and they were making excellent progress.

Xanari knew she had to speak with the human and examine her closer. It was rare to find a human with such honed abilities anymore. In ages past, there were clusters here and there that were naturals. As Xanari and the other watchers prepared for the shift they were told the stories but also told not to expect much from the humans as they had become lazy and more obsessed with technology than nature and the vast majority of them would be unattuned. This would hold true in most of the industrialized countries of the planet. Yet there in one of the most heavily industrialized and gluttonous societies on the planet was a human who not only possessed the gift of sight but also a prismatic aura which seemed to intensify when Annukai were near.

She focused on the mirror that also seemed to be fixated on the human and within a moment Xanari's vision blurred a bit and she was once again standing outside Rachel's house. She walked up to the front door and went to knock. To her surprise, the door opened before her knuckles touched it. Rachel stood there smiling a warm genuine smile. Xanari couldn't help but smile back.

"Xanari. I was starting to wonder if I would ever actually meet you. I could feel your presence slightly but it would fade in and out."

Xanari nodded and Rachel stepped to the side and waved her arm back in a wide arc.

"Well come on in. Don't stand out there in the cold."

"Thank you Rachel."

"Well I see we already know each other by name."

Xanari walked in and waited. Rachel closed the door and hurried past Xanari. She rushed into the kitchen and poked her head out briefly. "Are you hungry? Thirsty?"

Xanari slowly shook her head and said, "No thank you."

Rachel came back with a small plate with sliced apples and cup that smelled of warm cinnamon and apples.

"I love apples." Rachel said with a smile. She sat down on the couch where Xanari had first watched her sleep.

"Do you dream often?" Xanari asked as she examined Rachel's aura again. It was the same. Whenever she was closest to Xanari the aura would react. It was perplexing to Xanari.

Rachel pointed to a bookshelf full of journals, some of which were worn down and looked very old.

"I write em all down. Takes a lot of time, but it's important I think to do it. Been doing it since I was a little girl. Dreaming that is. The journaling was something I started years later. I enjoy going back and reviewing the dreams and then seeing which version played out."

Xanari sat down across from Rachel and listened intently.

"I've been dreaming of you Annukai for a long time. I have seen your home and the forests. The trees that sing and the wind that carries the old."

Xanari's eyes widened. As far as she knew, no human was ever reported as being able to see beyond his or her own plane. So how was this woman able to do it?

"You've seen my home?"

Rachel nodded. "Yup not often but I have seen it five times. And the only thing that occurs as often was the dreams of Kuthanaga. He shows up in many of the dreams. You started showing up in my dreams roughly a year ago."

Xanari paused and considered what the woman was saying. It was interesting. There was only a few Annukai, which had shifted to the crust more than once. Kuthanaga was the Annukai with the most visits. Xanari concluded there must be a connection with shifting and Rachel's dreams.

"Perhaps you saw through a window left by our kind shifting."

Rachel threw her arms up and laughed a warm laugh. "Doesn't matter about the how and the why. I see and I write. You see and you mark. I've watched you doing some sort of marking on people in a couple of dreams."

"How far ahead are your dreams?" Xanari asked.

"Well they used to range. The furthest dream I had was when I was only 9. I saw my father die in a car accident and it was similar each time I dreamed it. It was ten years until that accident actually happened. Seems like the average is no more than two years. Most of them seem to be random though. I just lay down and go to sleep and they come to me. I have to admit though; lately the dreams have been mostly about you folks."

"Rachel do you know about the large creature which chased you in your dream?"

Rachel's smile faded quick at the mention of the drake.

She nodded. "Yes, I've seen his kind before. I believe Kuthanaga even knows that big fella on a personal level. I've seen them lock horns before and lately when they battle it out, it's been a tossup. Sometimes the beast wins and sometimes Kuthanaga wins. This is why I told you the other day to not get too upset with what you've seen. Nothing is set in stone. I'm not saying you can change anything. I know I tried everything in my power to prevent my dad from driving. I tried to convince him to walk everywhere or take a bus. Even take a cab, since my dreams were always of him driving. I tried to get my mom to drive us everywhere. Eventually though he died. Some things have to happen. I never saw my dad survive. He always died. That's why I'm saying there's hope."

Xanari sat and listened. The look on her face must have given away her feelings as Rachel reached over and held her hand.

"Trust me, if it's meant to be it's meant to be. No one can question what God wishes to happen."

Xanari nodded. The Annukai also believed in a divine being, which set the stage of life and allowed them to learn and grow. She smiled. "Yes, you are right. Still, it is troubling to see it."

Rachel took an apple slice and took a bite.

"This is where you leave in my dream."

Xanari smiled. She had begun to find an excuse to leave the human and did not want to be rude. She was relieved at the interruption and nodded.

"Yeah in the dreams you tried a lot of different ways of saying good bye without hurting my feeling. I know you have important stuff to take care of and I know I'll see ya again. Glad you decided to stop in and chat."

Xanari stood as did Rachel, she glanced across the room, and a small mirror was there. She caught the faintest flicker of her own aura and noticed it too was shifting rapidly as Rachel was near.

"Interesting." she said aloud.

"What's that?"

Xanari smiled and said, "It is nothing. I feel relaxed around you is all."

"That makes me happy. You looked like you had the weight of the world on your shoulder when I saw you earlier. Glad that you enjoyed our visit."

Rachel hugged Xanari and at first, she didn't know what to do. After a pause, she returned the hug and made sure she only gently squeezed. She knew the humans were fragile and did not want to injure one as special as Rachel.

"Thank you for inviting me in and talking."

"Anytime."

Xanari walked to the door and simply walked through it and disappeared from Rachel's sight.

"Wow, you don't see that every day." Rachel laughed and started to clean up.

Xanari released the mirror to keep an eye on Rachel from a distance. She was concerned that the Draconian from the dream was after the human and knew that Rachel played some part in the Convergence. She would have to council with Kuthanaga to discuss what had happened and what could happen. She returned to her solitude and wondered if she should be blunt and just tell Kuthanaga what she had seen or just avoid it all together. What would that do to someone if they knew a certain action could be their last? According to Rachel, no matter what you did, if it was meant to happen it would happen. So, if that were true she felt there was no harm in discussing the dream with Kuthanaga the next time they spoke.

Xanari examined herself again and noticed her aura was normal. Why did it shift as it did around Rachel? What could cause that? She now had a few more questions than she did before the meeting with the human and she feared more would present themselves to her as time went by.

Chapter 16 – Ground Zero
December 17th 2011 – New York 8:59 pm

Tim and Kuthanaga had made their way down to Chamber Street and even after all the time that had passed since 9-11 the area was still fenced off and protected with intimidating guards.

Tim looked at Kuthanaga who smiled and placed his hand on Tim's shoulder.

Do not speak. Simply think and I will hear your thoughts. As long as I hold on to you, no one should see us. We will still make noise though and need to be very careful where we walk for if we are careless and someone really looks at us they will see us. Do you understand?

Tim nodded.

Yeah, I guess. Don't be a dumbass and make a shitload of noise.

Kuthanaga nodded. He positioned Tim in front of him and gently pushed Tim in the direction he wanted him to go.

Wait there's a big ass fence coming up in front of us.

Kuthanaga kept pressing Tim forward.

Do not be concerned with the fence. We will pass through it as if it is not even there.

Tim walked and easily passed through the fence. The areas that made contact with him tingled wildly like an angry nerve ending being inflamed.

Man that feels weird.

Wait until we pass through a wall. The harder and thicker the material, the more uncomfortable it gets. Treat the fence as a lesson. We have a long way to go to get to the vein.

Tim nodded and carefully chose his steps. Even being careful, Tim made noise. It was hard for him not to. Kuthanaga on the other hand didn't make a sound. This made Tim wonder.

Can I ask you a question? Tim thought.

Yes.

Why do you even need me? I mean, you're stronger, faster, can do magic and shit. Why do you need me around?

Tim, I have but two eyes as do you, and you severely underestimate what you are capable of. But, if you need a reason, I enjoy your company. Also, when I am using the vein in the tunnels below I will need all of my concentration. It is then that I am vulnerable. I need someone to, how do you say, watch my back.

Tim nodded. *Cool, I can do that... I think. Wait, when you say you'll need all of your concentration are we still gonna be invisible?*

No.

And you won't be able to super ninja anyone who comes down there looking for us?

No.

So if someone comes down, what am I supposed to do?

I leave that for you to decide. I suppose knocking them out or killing them quietly comes to mind.

Wait, you want me to kill some Joe who might come in on us while he's working the job?

Kuthanaga paused.

Yes. You were eager to kill me when we first met.

Dude, that was different. I was fucked up on drugs and just trying to score. I don't think I could do that straight. Don't get me wrong, I've done a shitload of bad things in my life. But it all feels so wrong now, you know?

Kuthanaga nodded. He knew this could be a problem.

Tim, anyone is capable of doing anything if the right pressure is applied. I need you to help me and if that means killing someone in the process then you have to do so.

Desmond, man... I don't know. I'm fuckin' scared man.

Kuthanaga looked Tim in the eyes. *Tim, if you fail me, Joy will die.*

Tim's mouth dropped.

What?!

If you fail me I will kill Joy.

What?!

This is more important than you or me. We need to succeed. I need to know you can do this.

Tim's mind was racing. His heart pounded hard against his chest.

Fuck it. I got you man. Let's just get in and out. Fuck, you're a cold piece.

Kuthanaga was quiet and he continued to direct Tim.

Ground Zero was for the most part was finished. The building jutted up into the sky and was all dark. It was like a lifeless monolith. All the glass was in and standing at the base of One World Trade Center formerly known as the Freedom Tower was something else. The building was over 1,700 feet tall and resembled a giant hypodermic needle made of stone and glass. Tim thought everything looked done until they were inside. There were still lots of vacant walls and wires' hanging in bunches.

Kuthanaga directed Tim to stairs and they went to the subbasement 2.

This is where it gets uncomfortable.

Kuthanaga gently pushed Tim towards a solid wall and Tim hesitated. He had subconsciously ducked down as they passed through the wire fence to protect his eyes, but as he approached the solid wall, his heart pounded.

How thick is it?

I do not know.

How do I breath?

You will not be able to. Also, you will not be able to see. This is going to be uncomfortable and I imagine very scary for you. Take deep breaths and let me know when you are ready.

Tim calmly took six deep breaths and he nodded as he inhaled deeply.

Kuthanaga started pushing Tim in a direction and Tim walked. As his feet hit the wall it wasn't uncomfortable, it was excruciating.

Fuck! This hurts.

It will pass, just focus and keep moving.

Tim's legs and lower torso entered the stone and he wanted to scream.

Keep moving!

Tim's head entered into the wall and the world went black. He saw flickering lights in his eyes as if he had spent ten seconds pressing on his eyes. He couldn't tell if he was still moving and he couldn't feel Kuthanaga. The fact that he was still thinking let him know that Kuthanaga was still with him. Tim feared what would happen if Kuthanaga let go of him and Tim pushed forward. He was pushing with all his might and he felt his heart pounding heavily and the sparkling flashes of light in his eyes were intensifying.

* We are near Tim. Just a few more steps.*

Tim felt a huge tug and suddenly his feet felt no resistance and his legs followed. A second later light poured into his eyes and he gasped. He fell and was instantly lifted by Kuthanaga.

You will get used to that sensation. You did well. I feared you would pass out and yet you did not. Be proud.

Whatever. Where the hell are we?

Looking around they were in a large room roughly 100' by 100'. Tim couldn't see any doors.

What is this place?

Kuthanaga pointed at the center of the room and there was a small hole in the ground.

I knew it. They have the vein exposed and are trying to figure out how to tap into it.

Great so this is good?

Kuthanaga shook his head.

No, this is bad. The Draconians have learned a lot. They know about the veins. That means they know much more than I feared. When I am in the hole, you must be very careful. If a drake finds you, I am not confident of the confrontation. If you are faced with a drake, you must aim for its eyes. That is the only spot on its body, which is vulnerable to your gun. Anywhere else will hurt it but will only serve to upset it more.

Tim got nervous at that. He fired guns lots of time and was a decent shot, but the idea of shooting something in the eye while it was coming at him didn't sit well.

The eyes huh?

Yes. Do not miss.

Kuthanaga examined the room and after walking the area twice positioned himself over the hole in the center of the room. The hole was roughly 5 feet wide in diameter and Tim couldn't see how far down it went.

OK, Tim I will attempt to make this as quick as possible.

Cool… Sounds good.

Kuthanaga released his grip on Tim and he pulled out the small vial with the Earth's Milk in it. Tim watched as Kuthanaga closed his eyes and Tim swore he saw a ghostly version slide out from Kuthanaga's body. As it slid away, the vial faded from Kuthanaga's hand.

Tim looked around and had his pistol out with the safety off. He listened hard and heard nothing. He scanned the room a third time around and he started getting nervous. He didn't know why but he felt like he was being watched. Reaching in his inside pocket, he slid three clips onto his belt. He noticed the temperate was rising and he began to sweat.

"What the fuck?"

He walked over to Kuthanaga and whispered, "Dude hurry up. I got a bad feeling."

Not seeing any reaction from Kuthanaga Tim decided to put his back against the wall as opposed to standing in the center of the room. He started backing up and as he did, Tim heard something and he turned to see what it was. A quick blur and Tim realized he was in the air. He slammed the far wall hard and he couldn't catch his breath. He knew he had cracked a rib or two and maybe punctured a lung. Looking up he could see his assailant. It resembled a man with exaggerated muscles and scaled skin.

"Fuck…" he coughed and blood came out.

The hulking man was moving fast. Amazingly, Tim still had the gun in his hand. His knuckles were white as he swung the gun up to eye level and fired.

Chapter 17 – The Deal
December 17th 2011 – New York 11:59 pm

Kuthanaga descended quickly for twenty seconds, slowed, and stopped in a small alcove. He entered it and was covered in light. There was something there in the alcove with him a being that emitted power. That was something he had not expected. He realized it was a guardian of some sort. It was made of light and moved like smoke and it glowed with such intensity that it made it hard for Kuthanaga to gaze upon it.

"Who are you?" it asked Kuthanaga.

"I am Kuthanaga of the Annukai."

"What is your intention Kuthanaga of the Annukai?"

"I want to return this Milk of the Earth."

"Do you know what will happen to this vein if you place the Milk into it?"

Kuthanaga shook his head. "I can only guess at what will happen."

"This vein extends to many smaller veins which lead out into the world of the humans. If you place the Milk in it, it will replace the water within the veins. That will then flow Milk to the humans. They cannot be trusted with the sacred liquid. You are forbidden from doing this."

"Does the Mother forbid this?"

The being shook its head. "No, *we* forbid it. The humans are petty, wild and savage. The milk would drive them mad. We will not be responsible for this."

"I will be the one who carries the burden. My people know the risks involved, but as the Mother awakens, many of the humans will die. By using the milk we can quickly determine who is worthy of protection."

The guardian thought about what Kuthanaga said and replied, "And if your calculations are wrong? It will be known that the Annukai were solely responsible for the extinction of the humans. Know this outsider, we represent the Mother herself and her will is law. The humans have done much to her and as such have no love from us. If you are wrong and the Mother is unhappy, you will be made to pay. The worst will come to you Kuthanaga."

Kuthanaga was unsure. He was taking a great risk. The guardian came closer.

"Why do you hesitate? Do you not have faith?"

"I do, I am just weighing what you have said and am giving it the respect it deserves before making a decision."

The guardian nodded. "Also, there will be a price to pay for this, Kuthanaga of the Annukai."

"Price?"

"Yes. There will come a time when the Mother may be in need. When that time comes, you will assist her guardians with no question."

"That goes without saying. We Annukai respect the Mother and would gladly defend her."

"Then you have our permission to use this vein."

Kuthanaga took the vial and opened it. Taking the silver spike, he pressed it into the soft earth. Gently he poured the liquid into the spike. The liquid bubbled and a few seconds later, there was no sign of it.

"You have done what you requested; now you must leave."

Kuthanaga knew better than to argue. Something told him that the guardian was very old and very powerful. He left without a word and slowly returned to the surface. He slid into his body and instantly he smelled blood and gunpowder.

He spun around and saw a drake lying down in a pool of blood a few inches away from Tim who was crumpled up in a fetal position. Kuthanaga motioned over Tim and focused. Tim had several broken bones, severe internal bleeding and a punctured lung. After a few seconds, Tim opened his eyes and groaned.

Glancing down at the drake on the ground Kuthanaga grinned. "Looks like you're a better shot than you gave yourself credit for."

Tim shrugged. "Had to do it for Joy. I knew if I missed she would die."

Kuthanaga grinned a toothy smile at Tim.

"You know Tim; I was telling you a lie. I wanted to illustrate a point. I am fond of Joy and want nothing bad to happen to her or you. You need to look within to find the strength. Tim, I chose you for a reason. I chose you because I know you can do what I ask."

As Kuthanaga spoke, he motioned over Tim, the familiar warmth passed into Tim, and he was able to breathe again without effort or pain. Kuthanaga grabbed the drake on the ground and slid his body towards the large hole in the ground. He rolled the body over and could see that Tim's shot had indeed hit its mark. Rolling the body once more and it fell down the shaft.

Tim stood up and slowly stretched. "You're lucky you can kick my ass."

"Why is that?" asked Kuthanaga with a slight grin.

"Cause I would love to kick you in the ball for that shit. I really believed you was gonna kill Joy if I didn't make it."

Kuthanaga held Tim's shoulder again and pushed towards the wall.

Actually, if I failed, it would have been a nonissue. We fail and the human race will cease to exist within a year. You and I need to have a long discussion soon about what it is that I just did and what it will mean soon.

What do we do now?

Take a deep breath.

Tim did and the second time through the wall wasn't as bad as the initial attempt. As they came out the other end, Kuthanaga continued.

We go back to Vegas and wait. We listen for the news.

Tim shrugged. He was happy to be heading back to Vegas. He thought of nothing else but Joy, as he lied broken on the floor bleeding.

Sounds good to me. What about the drake we left back in the hole?

Wishful thinking. Let us be positive and deal with that problem if it arrives.

Tim and Kuthanaga continued on their way and later that morning they were on a flight back to Vegas. Tim slept the whole flight. Kuthanaga silently worried. Much had changed on the crust since his last visit and the Draconians were more organized and had nearly limitless resources. He hoped luck was on his side.

Chapter 18 – Trespassers

December 18th 2011 – New York 7:35 am

Richard was stretching and preparing for his daily run when his phone began vibrating. Looking down he saw it was Raymond Oakes head of security for Tower One.

"Yes?"

"Sir there has been a breech in sub level 2. The core room."

"When?" Richard didn't like this. The full week of bad news just kept getting worse and worse and he was aggravated to no end. He would need to blow some steam off and a run was exactly what he needed. But, he also knew that the core room was one of the potential treasure troves that was to be protected at any cost.

"Last night. One of our guards never checked in and a thorough search has been completed."

Richard knew it wasn't a case of a guard stepping off his post as the guards for the core were pure bloods who would protect the core room with their life.

"Lock it down and make sure all the videos are collected and sent to me. I'm on my way."

"Already working on that sir."

Richard hung up the phone and changed his clothing. He would have to find an alternate way to relax after the breech was investigated.

Walking down the stairs to the main foyer Richard called his brother. Three rings later and Sam picked up the phone breathless.

"Morning brother." Richard said as he exited his house and headed for his long black limo.

"Hey Rich. What's up?"

"What's up with you? Why you so winded?"

Richard could hear moaning in the background and recognized it. "Um, just working out is all."

"Just working out Sharon. You should know better than to lie to me. Be careful with that one. She leaves marks."

"Ow! Yes, I know. Careful. Please."

Richard smiled. It was good to see that Sharon had taken it upon herself to help Sam with his broken heart. He may have been truly in love with his wife, but no pure blood could resist the seduction of another Draconian if she wanted him, even a half-breed would have her way. Sam's blood must've wanted Sharon for a while and everyone knew Sharon was a beast so it was just a matter of time.

"Sam, I'll check back with you. I'm on my way to the core room. We've had an incident there. So if you need me, you'll have to use a landline."

Sam was moaning. "OK."

Richard hung up and regarded the driver. "Tower One, please."

The driver simply nodded and they were off. Richard pulled out a sliding tray that was on the seat next to him, it swiveled out, he flipped a display that was the top part of the tray and a small keyboard, and mouse was revealed. A login screen popped up and he entered his credentials and waited. A second later there were many icons lined neatly on the left hand side of the screen.

He double clicked an icon called "Security Logs" and inside that folder, there were thirty-two more icons of different projects. He found the folder named Tower One and he double clicked.

There were 24 video files twice as many audio files and three special files. The three special files were what he was looking for. They were room measurements of temperature, air consumption and room weight. The Draconians had been looking for the vein for a long time and knew it would help them locate other access points that would provide project Tiamat with additional backup energy. They wanted to protect the room and so they designed it to only have one access point at the roof level and made sure there was always a guard posted there. The room had many sensitive sensors in place to record and if they were tripped the guard would investigate.

Richard brought up a query dialog box and typed in a search for any alarms. He saw all three alarms were tripped at 12:21AM. The audio revealed a short battle, which ended with a single gunshot. Groans of pain could be heard. The labored breathing went on for a while until he heard a man's voice. Listening to the conversation, he learned of Tim, Joy, and the fact that Tim had been the one who killed the guard. In addition, there was some coercion towards Tim. A threat against Joy's life. Also some sort of mission.

Analyzing the weight sensor showed that 556.056 pounds suddenly appeared in the room and then fluctuated to 235.025. Richard wondered where the extra 321.031 pounds disappeared? The weight jumped to 647.099 and Richard deduced that must have been when the guard showed up. It reappeared in the room a few moments before the conversation was recorded. The room was at 968.130. Then the weight dropped down to 556.054 again near the end of the conversation. Richard noted they left with .002 pounds less than they had entered the room with.

The air consumption showed similar results. There were three things, which bothered Richard. The first was how these strangers had known about the core room. The second was how they got into it and finally what were they doing there?

He played many possible scenarios in his head and as they drove along the streets, he had a good idea where the missing guard was. The only problem was going to be extracting his body if it was where he thought it was. The core hole to the vein was deep and it got hotter as you reached the bottom. To make matters worse there was some anomalies in regards to recording video in the room itself. Whenever they attempted to film the video would just be pure white. It didn't matter how they tried to record. Audio and everything else would record, just not video. They had probed the shaft many times and could detect different energy pockets but hadn't figured out how to tap the vein. The Quinuks had promised they would solve that mystery after they had completed the Tiamat project's first trial run.

Richard grinned. He was almost certain an Annukai was involved. They had many tricks to get in where they were not welcome. He wondered why risk a mission with a human and not another Annukai. It was obvious the human had been nearly killed by the Draconian guard. It was just luck that he was able to hit one of the few weak spots on him. Annukai knew the weak spots of drakes especially a very special Annukai.

"Why Kuthanaga, it is you isn't it old friend?"

Richard smiled. If it was indeed Kuthanaga he was certain they would meet face to face before everything was said and done. After all Richard had taken something very precious from Kuthanaga and even though he was Annukai, he knew he wanted Richard's head more than anything in the world. He wondered if somehow Kuthanaga knew about the Tiamat project and was trying to somehow sabotage it.

It didn't matter by the end of the day the core room would be cleaned and searched from top to bottom and what Richard didn't know he would know more of by then.

He called Raymond and waited.

"Sir?"

"Yes, I am getting a team down there. Please make sure no one disturbs the room. Are there any guards in there now?"

"Yes sir. Officer Gould has been down there since shift change."

"Good. I am only about twenty minutes out. My team will be there soon."

"Understood."

He hung up and focused his attention on the screen in front of him. He selected an icon called "Clean up" and he double clicked on it. A box came up with a simple dropdown menu and a submit button. He dropped down the menu and selected Tower One Core Room and clicked submit. A message window came up stating that the message had been sent.

Richard knew that it would take the team ten minutes to get to front lobby. He decided to follow up on the status of Tiamat and the materials requested by the Quinuks. He double clicked on another icon called projects and a security screen popped up. He placed his thumb on the tray in a slightly curved section on the bottom right. He barely felt the needle slid into his thumb. A moment later the security screen passed and several projects that he was responsible for popped up on his screen. He located Tiamat and double clicked.

A chat screen opened on the right hand side and the left had a series of jobs assigned to various people. He saw that the materials that Dmitri had asked for were delivered earlier that same day.

"Well, I hope that makes Dmitri happy."

He double clicked Dmitri's name in the chat side of the screen and it had an icon next to his name saying he was away from desk.

Richard quickly typed:

You have your supplies, I expect results ASAP. Please let me know when you are to do first full test. I would like to be there to witness results.

He pressed <Enter> and it showed up in the chat window. He shut down the terminal, pushed it back into the housing unit, and poured himself a drink.

The remainder of the ride was uneventful and quiet. He stared outside the window and watched all the humans as he passed them. After four security checkpoints they finally ended up where he needed to be. Walking to the front desk he could see all the guards on duty and he was satisfied that they were competent and fully charged up. His team was there as well. He motioned and his team followed while the human team stayed at the front desk. Raymond knew the drill and didn't mind. The job was stable and paid very well. He had great benefits and his bosses were strict but fair. With a family of five and bills to pay, he would scrub toilets if they asked.

The team moved quickly and quietly as they made their way to the subbasement. When they got to the secured area Richard punched in a code on a keypad and waited while his retina was scanned. The door slid open and they entered a smaller room than the core room. Jumping down they landed quietly and smoothly.

Richard looked around and canvassed the room. He got to one of the walls and he could see a small series of blood droplets. He motioned to the team, which had been checking other areas. They came over and instantly began collecting evidence. While they did, he examined the shaft and peered down it. It was dark and a low rumble could be heard deep within it. Near the shaft, he could see some blood smears.

"I think our lost guard is down there. You'll have to gear up and go down to verify. I am done here. When you get the blood analyzed look for a match with the name Tim."

A couple of the team nodded and went back to work. Richard walked to the exit and with an effortless jump was out of the room.

"Sir, what should I do?" asked Officer Gould.

"Stay posted here until relieved."

He nodded and Richard exited. As he got near the front desk, he received a text message from Christy it simply read.

I'm hungry.

Ne nodded to himself. Her timing was perfect. Raymond acknowledged Richard as he walked back to his limo.

Richard jumped into the limo and instructed the driver to take him to Christy's.

He knew it would be a few hours before the results from investigation would yield anything of more use than what he already knew and Christy was just the diversion he was looking for.

Chapter 19 –The Stage is Set

December 19th 2011 – Las Vegas 2:10 pm

The flight back to Vegas had been delayed twice, once because of mechanical issues and a second time due to bad weather. On the flight back, Tim was silent and Kuthanaga knew the encounter with the drake as well as his own methodologies had left a bad taste in Tim's mouth. He also knew Tim was concerned about the Martyr's Barb and unfortunately, there was nothing Kuthanaga could do to alleviate his anxiety. The barb would have to stay as it was vital to the mission.

When they got back to the Bellagio, Joy jumped Tim and hugged him. She had been sitting in the suite with the couch rearranged so she could see the front door when it opened. Tim was happy to see her and all his stress almost seemed to melt away. Kuthanaga was glad that Tim had Joy, as he knew the human would have to lean hard on her in the upcoming months.

"Wow, you weren't gone that long. I thought you guys were gonna be like away for a month or something."

Tim shook his head. "Nope, in and out quick style. Whatcha been up while we were gone?"

She shrugged. "Just watchin' a lot of TV and ordering room service mostly. I didn't want to be out and you guys show up or need me. You know?"

Tim nodded and walked over to the couch. A blanket and leftovers were on one of the tables.

She grinned. "Like I said, I didn't know when you guys would be back, so I seriously just vegged. I was watchin' the news, but things are getting way out of hand and it was starting to depress me. Did you hear about Washington?"

Tim had heard other passengers talking about some protestors who were gunned down, but not the specifics.

"Just bits and pieces. What's up?"

"Well there were protestors who were really just peacefully sitting there and not moving. The army came in to move them along and one guy kinda lost it and was kicking the shit out of two soldiers like he was Jet Li or something and the next thing you know they opened fire. They killed over thirty people and the worst part was there was kids there."

Tim might have been shocked at some point if he wasn't still reeling from the fact that an actual alien tried and nearly succeeded in killing him.

"Damn, that's messed up. So what's happening now?"

"A lot of riots in all kinds of places. There were ten cops who died and a lot of fires. Some was in New York, San Francisco, Los Angeles… you know pretty much where protests were already going full swing. Now there's fires and looting and lots of gunfights. The president had to declare martial law and now there's strict curfew in a lot of the cities."

Kuthanaga was listening and then he sat on a couch in the far corner of the suite, which faced out over the strip and he closed his eyes and began to meditate.

Tim leaned back on the couch and watched the television. Joy continued, "So with the curfew a lot of people have been arrested for being out after it. In Oakland, a group of teenagers was being rounded up and one shot a cop. The cops fired back and killed six of them. So, you know what happened there. Giant fuckin' riot broke out. Still going on last I heard."

Tim nodded. "Sounds way fucked up."

Joy glanced at Kuthanaga and then looked at Tim long and hard.

"You ok?"

Tim shook his head.

"Nope, but you know what? Doesn't matter. You wanna go downstairs and grab something to eat and chill?"

Joy nodded.

"What about Kuthanaga?"

"He can grab his own food when he's done or he'll drink more of the milk."

Joy glanced at Kuthanaga who hadn't moved at all and his face showed no emotions. He was obviously in his own world and once he was in it, there was nothing that could be done to break him out of it. She had tried before.

"Cool, let me put on some makeup and we can go."

"Baby, you're already the most beautiful thing in Vegas, why you gonna fuck with perfection?"

She shrugged. "Fine sweet talker, let's go."

Tim glanced once at Kuthanaga and then opened the door. Joy went first and he followed.

Kuthanaga waited for the couple to be in the elevator. He could hear their footsteps and the motor of the elevator. Its doors opened and they got in. When it began its decent, Kuthanaga opened his eyes.

He stood up and motioned and the furniture moved across the room out of his way. The floor was empty and he motioned again. A ghostly bluish flame danced its way around in a circle on the floor burning a pattern into it. He focused and more little flames danced until the center of the circle was filled with numerous sigils. He took a deep breath and all the windows blackened. The room was dark except for a dull blue glow that filled it. The center of the floor shimmered softly and Kuthanaga nodded to himself.

Reshnogga. Reshnogga are you there?

Kuthanaga could feel the contact and at first, it resisted and then relaxed.

Kuthanaga? How goes it?

The stage is set. Where are you at this point?

I am in Mexico City with the mirrors spreading fast. I have mirrors as far north as Juarez and as far south as Guadalajara. Why?

Kuthanaga motioned and the circle in front of him took on the shape of the Earth. Veins stretched all along its surface, he focused on veins around New York, and one vein lit up and glowed brightly. He followed three small veins. One went down to small island near Florida called Bimini and one to a small town in Canada called Maniwaki the final branch worked its way to Mexico to a small town called Don Martin.

I want you to take up residence at a town called Don Martin. That is going to be an important area within the next six days.

OK, I will take up haven there. How goes it with the others?

It's going well everyone has mirrors working rapidly, in fact we are ahead of schedule.

116

Glad to hear that. It is good news indeed. Kuthanaga nodded.

Let me know once you start to see activity there.

I will.

Kuthanaga felt the connection with Reshnogga fade and he focused on Xanari. The connection came easily and he could almost see her. He realized their connection had grown very strong in a short amount of time and that startled him somewhat.

Kuthanaga, there's been some interesting developments here in Utah.

On my end as well. The seed has been planted and I may need you to relocate and monitor your mirrors from another location.

Is there another watcher that can take that assignment?

Yes, but few that I trust with the task. Why? What has got your interest in Utah?

A human with extraordinary gifts. She has the gift of sight and I observed it. You were there and a drake was involved?

A drake? What did he look like? Do you have a clear image in your mind of him?

Yes...

Focus on it.

Xanari did as she was instructed and it was as Kuthanaga feared.

Yes, I know this drake. His human name is Richard Byington. His real name is Zygriel. He is a highborn drake. He is the descendant of Azmieodius the Cruel. He and I have a history. The last time I shifted the crust I encountered him. He...

Kuthanaga paused and regained his composure. Xanari could feel a wave of emotions pour through their connection. She knew something very bad had happened between Kuthanaga and the drake. Kuthanaga continued.

* He killed my wife.*

Wife?

Xanari had never heard of Kuthanaga having paired with another Annukai.

Yes, her name was Sani; she traveled with me even though she knew it was wiser to stay behind. We were here gathering information about the Convergence. When we encountered the drake I was unaware of him and when he attacked she saved me. Her act of heroism came at a great cost. I fought with him and he mocked me terribly. His strength was more than I could handle and when I thought for sure I was done he simply stopped attacking and walked away laughing as his humans surrounded us. I was able to pull us back before any more of us were hurt. Sani, though, never woke again.

Xanari was stunned. Why had she never heard of any of this? Annukai were not private about their loss, in fact they shared so that the healing could be more beneficial. The only thing she could think of was he did not want to forget. He did not want to forgive. He wanted vengeance.

Yes young one, your thoughts are correct.

Xanari was angry with herself. Try as she might to shield her thoughts from Kuthanaga, it was no use. He was simply too powerful.

Do not be angered. I will not jeopardize the mission. We will do what we shifted to do. Tell me more about the dream this human of yours had.

*The drake seemed very interested in her. He pursued her and you and another human came to her aid. You threw your sacred Gak-lua-kuun to a human woman and you fought the beast. The human man used a gun and wounded him a couple of times. The ground was giving way and the human started to fall. You jumped to save him but the beast was faster and he wounded you badly. The human shot again and hit it in the eye and he fled. You... You died in the humans arms. *

Kuthanaga swallowed.

Show me the humans you saw in your dream. The woman and the man.

Xanari focused and Kuthanaga nodded. It was indeed Joy and Tim.

Yes, these two humans are with me now. They are important.

Kuthanaga considered the news and came to a decision.

Have you been in contact with the human who dreamed this?

Yes.

And did she recognize you for what you were?

Yes. She knew me by name. She had dreamed our meeting before it had happened.

So she is accurate?

Yes, but she mentioned that she has had the dream of you and the drake battling many times. Sometimes you win and sometimes he wins. She is unsure of the final outcome.

He smiled weakly.

Well then, it is not all bad news. Xanari, I want you to see if the human will go with you to Bimini. I agree with you that she is very important and if she does not want to go then you will stay where you are. Please let me know of her decision the minute you know. I would prefer to have you assisting me with the situation I have set in motion, but if I need to grab one of the other watchers, it is fine. You have come across something I was not expecting. Her insight will be very much needed. So please let me know.

I will Kuthanaga. One last thing before I go.

Yes.

I am very sorry for your loss. If you need me to help with the mourning process when you feel the time is right, I am there.

Thank you. I will keep that in mind. Do not be concerned for me. It happened a long time ago. I just did not want to forget anything so I kept it all alive inside me. Again, do not be concerned and thank you.

You are welcome.

Her connection faded slowly and he took a deep breath. This human Xanari found was very important. She had a role to play and Kuthanaga wasn't sure what it was but he knew somehow that she was instrumental. The one thing he suddenly knew was Joy also was to have a larger role in things, more so than he originally thought. She would have to undergo some basic training if he was to trust her with the usage of his Gak-lua-kuun and he wondered if she would be able to manipulate her environment before the Convergence happened. He silently hoped that Xanari's human's ability wasn't as keen as she suspected because if the situation she described to him unfolded then he wouldn't have his vengeance and worse the humans' fate was uncertain. He knew from the beginning that things would be difficult but he maintained his hope that things would turn out for the best. He would have to wait to hear back from Xanari if she would be able to hold down the Bimini location to report to him what was happening. Kuthanaga considered relocating Tim and Joy to Canada but wondered if it was better to handle that location on his own.

Glancing at the ground and the ghostly image that floated there, Kuthanaga knew there was no going back. He had set things in motion that could not be undone. He sat down and again meditated.

Chapter 20 – Commitment
December 19th 2011 – Las Vegas 3:30 pm

Tim was glad to be alone with Joy and he wondered what he should tell her. His foot still throbbed with each step and he still didn't know what it did. Kuthanaga had said it would allow him to keep in touch. Did that mean he could read Tim's mind and know his every thought. The idea that nothing was private not even his own thoughts bothered Tim.

Well at least he was doing something good. The thought came at him like a thunderbolt. He was helping right? On the other hand, was he? What exactly were they doing with the Earth's Milk at the bottom of Tower One? Another thought plagued Tim. He was taking the word of a complete stranger that he was one of good guys. Tim thought about his encounter with the Draconian. He obviously was trying to kill Tim and that was proof enough that what Kuthanaga had said about them was correct.

Tim realized he needed to have a very serious discussion with Kuthanaga and see exactly what was going on. He knew that the chances that Kuthanaga would tell him everything he wanted to know was small, but he vowed that he would at least try.

Joy had been staring at him for a while and she knew he was somewhere else and she didn't want to disturb him. He glanced at her and gave a fake smile. He was trying to ease her concern but it wasn't working. She cleared her throat and took his hand in hers.

"Tim?"

He nodded. "Yeah."

"What the fuck?"

"Excuse me."

"You've been acting funny since you got back. What's wrong babe?"

He shrugged.

"Some crazy shit went down in New York."

"Yeah? Like what?"

He pulled up his shirt and she could see pink scars along his ribs.

"What happened?"

"I ran into one of those fucking dragon things. Draconian. Thing was fuckin' huge and fast. I got real lucky babe."

He took a deep breath and realized that a single tear had fallen from his eye. It hit the table and he swore he could hear its impact. He wiped his eye.

"I was fuckin' dying. All I could think about was you."

He was looking her deep in the eyes and she was speechless. Her heart ached at the thought of losing him. She could not imagine a world without her man.

"Tim. Let's get married."

His eyes got big.

"What?"

She shoved him as she grinned at him.

"What you don't wanna have me as a wife?"

He quickly shook his head. "No, I didn't mean that."

She enjoyed shocking him. She hoped it would pull him from his darkness to her. It was working.

"Fuck it. Let's do it. I'm kinda bummed you beat me to the punch though. I wanted to do it all romantic and surprise you."

"So is that a yes?"

"Yep. When you wanna do it?"

"Right now."

"Now?!"

"Yes now. Let's get some rings and get hitched!"

Tim stood up and shrugged. After nearly dying, he liked the idea of taking their relationship to the next level. He always knew he'd be with Joy forever and he'd take her as wife for as long as he could.

"Fuck yeah baby!"

He took her by the hand and they made a mad dash for Tesorini, which they had noticed when they had first arrived and had passed every day since they had arrived. They entered the jewelry store and it was brilliant to the eye. A few people were milling around wide-eyed examining the display cases which glittered with all forms of jewelry from ultra-high-end watches to necklaces and rings. There were two men in the store, one was dealing with a woman and the other a tall man in a neatly pressed black suit greeted them as they entered.

"Hello there. Can I help you?"

Joy was bubbling. "Yes we need wedding rings. Nothing too fancy but something nice."

The man seemed not at all surprised by the request and he led them to a specific display and stood behind it.

"What kind of a budget are you working with?"

"Price is not an issue." A deep voice said from behind them.

Joy spun around and saw Kuthanaga and Tim didn't move. He had almost felt Kuthanaga before he had said anything.

"Desmond." Joy waved.

"It is customary to have a witness when one gets married. Correct?"

Joy nodded.

"I would be honored if I could help."

Tim shrugged. It was obvious to him that Kuthanaga was going to keep a very watchful eye on him. As long as Joy was happy, Tim didn't care. They spent ten minutes looking through various rings until one ring jumped out and caught Joy's eye. She took a deep breath and held it. She looked at Tim and he smiled. Kuthanaga gently put his hand on Tim's shoulder and smiled.

"I believe we have found the ring that has taken the voice from her."

Tim nodded.

"How much is it?" asked Joy cautiously.

The man glanced at something behind the counter and said "36 thousand."

Joy's jaw started to open and before she could say anything Kuthanaga interrupted. "That is fine. We need to find a ring for the husband-to-be now. I think I see one which is suitable for you Tim."

Kuthanaga walked with purpose to a heavy solid white gold ring that had a thick black band around the center.

Tim followed, part of him was irritated, and the other half was flattered. Tim's father had died when he was a young boy and his mother brought many new 'dads' home. He realized Kuthanaga reminded him of some of his early memories of his father. He looked at the ring and was impressed with its size and design. It wasn't gaudy and it was classy. Tim scanned the other rings and had to admit it would have been the ring he would've picked out.

"Yeah that's hot. Whatcha think babe?"

Joy smiled as she examined it. "How much is that one?"

Kuthanaga waved it away. "It is my gift to you two."

Joy smiled and was excited. Kuthanaga leaned over to the merchant and said, "May I see the two rings side by side?"

"Of course."

The man already had Joy's ring with him and he placed them down on a white silk swatch.

Kuthanaga slowed time and focused on the rings. They rose and hovered in front of him for a moment. He reached into his inside pocket, took his nail, and slid it on the small gold slab. A small sliver snaked off, danced around Joy's ring, and melted into its surface. He slid again and a thicker piece snaked off and danced around Tim's ring. The rings pulsed for a moment and the glow faded.

The rings settled back into their normal position on the white swatch and time again flowed normally.

Kuthanaga pulled out a wallet and handed the man a credit card. The man regarded the card for a moment and looked Kuthanaga over briefly.

"I'll need to size the rings. It'll take a little bit."

"That won't be necessary. I'll take care of them." The merchant shrugged and entered the information into the machine and the total popped up. He slid the credit card and waited. The machine came alive and kicked out a paper receipt and a second slip.

"Please sign."

Kuthanaga signed the slip and the man boxed up the rings and handed small bags to Joy and Tim.

"Good luck you two!"

"Thanks!" Joy was smiling a toothy smile, which lit up the room.

Kuthanaga was leading them on the way out. "Let's go to the suite for a few minutes to complete the rest of your wedding preparations."

They nodded and followed Kuthanaga back to the suite. When they exited the elevator in front of their suite a low hum could be heard emanating from within the room. Tim glanced at Joy and Joy looked back. They were holding hands and Tim's grip tightened. A glowing blue light seeped from the corners of the door as Kuthanaga opened it.

"Do not be concerned. I am just working. There's nothing to be afraid of."

Tim's grip didn't ease as they entered. They passed through the door after Kuthanaga and both of them paused.

"What the hell?" Joy said barely audible.

The center of the room was now completely clear of any furniture and the walls were shimmering and reflecting the contents of the center of the room back and forth infinitely like an ever-shifting hall of mirrors. Directly in the center of the room was a tree stump and around it was a glowing band of blue symbols and a circle. Around the circumference of the stump, various other symbols drifted in seemingly random patterns as if caught in currents of energy. Directly above the stump was what appeared to be a map of North America. There were glowing lines that formed a complex matrix that reminded Tim of a spider's web. To Joy, it looked like a vascular system.

"Yes Joy, it is veins we are looking at. Tim, it may look like a web at first glance, but notice not all of the lines are connected completely together. They may seem to connect but they actually overlap. Some run deep underground while others are close to the surface. We were accessing a vein closer to the surface in New York."

Joy ignored the fact the Kuthanaga was reading her mind and Tim had just stopped caring and took it for granted that any thought was up for scrutiny by his Annukai task master.

"What's that?" Joy asked pointing at three veins, which were glowing a pale pink.

"That is what Tim and I accomplished in New York."

Joy was about to ask another question when suddenly the room flashed and everything was back to normal.

"We're getting off track," said Kuthanaga.

"Where's the map and all the glowing stuff?"

"It's still here. But we have more important things to discuss than the map at this moment."

"We do?"

He nodded.

"Yes, your wedding. Do you have any ideas on what you'd like to wear? I'd like to try something. Can I see the rings?"

Tim and Joy handed the bags to Kuthanaga who motioned and the rings floated out into his hand.

"Tim may I see your hand? Joy, yours as well."

They extended their hands and Kuthanaga placed the rings on both of their fingers. Joy was about to make a joke about how large hers was when suddenly it moved and she watched as the ring sized itself to the perfect fit. Tim's also changed. He thought he saw the faint glow along the rings surface but said nothing of it.

Kuthanaga placed his hand over the rings and closed his eyes.

"I want you to close your eyes and picture the clothing you want to wear. Do not just see how it looks, but picture the fabric, the weight. Try to be as specific as possible."

Tim and Joy closed their eyes and Kuthanaga noted that Joy was able to easily picture the dress within her mind where Tim kept getting distracted. He was all over the place. He pictured the shoes and the pants and then would shift to the jacket instead of all the details at once. Joy's outfit shifted and slowly it took form and there were pieces on it that Kuthanaga realized there was no tailor Earth who could make it. He nodded to himself as he saw how easily she was manipulating her environment. Tim's clothing shifted back and forth and Kuthanaga smiled. He caught the individual pieces that Tim was envisioning and he helped.

"Well done. Open your eyes and see your outfits. I have masked them from each of you. When the wedding is about to begin I will reveal them. But you can see your own outfits and make whatever adjustments you wish."

Tim looked down and he grinned. He was wearing his tuxedo, but the cut was comfortable and stylish. It was perfectly pressed and had a slight gray tint to the black that shifted in the light. The shirt was a soft blue and his shoes were black with blue flames.

Joy also examined herself and her dress was white but it had a silky strip of baby blue that almost seemed to flow like water.

I got the idea of moving water from your eyes. she thought to herself knowing Kuthanaga would hear.

He nodded and smiled.

The dress was mid cut just above her knees and the tail was long and almost floated behind her. Her heels were stiletto with ankle straps and her legs were covered with an airy almost translucent sheen that had a slight hint of blue. Her veil was a similar material and she had even gone as far as manipulating her hair and makeup without even fully consciously thinking about it. She had thought about some jewelry but decided to go with something simple.

"I believe it is a good thing we mask you two until just before the wedding as it would be impossible to not get noticed."

Tim tried to imagine what Joy looked like and was getting very excited.

"Please hand me back the rings. I shall give them to you shortly."

Tim and Joy removed the rings and Kuthanaga placed them in his inside pocket.

"Where we gonna do this?" Tim asked.

Joy shrugged. It was at that moment a knock at the front door startled them. Kuthanaga walked over and opened it. Monica Crawford stood there with her eyes bright and a grin from ear to ear.

"Someone told me you were planning a wedding for today?"

Joy nodded.

"We just need something nice and pretty and someone to marry us. Nothing too formal or extravagant."

Monica smiled.

"Well we are the Bellagio and we have a couple of locations. Would you like to do this inside or outside?"

The weather had remained cold and to make matters worse the wind was blowing fiercely.

Joy shook her head as she recalled the bitter chill.

"Inside please!"

Monica nodded.

"I agree. How many people are going to attend?"

"Just us and Desmond and a priest I guess…"

She nodded. "OK, well we have a brilliant location which I think will be perfect for you. We call it the East Chapel. I'll make sure it's ready for you right now."

Joy was smiling.

"Well Mr. Christenson," said Joy still smiling. "Last chance to back out."

"Fuck that! Let's do this."

Monica used a headset and after about three minutes, she turned to face them.

"OK, everything is ready. Is there any special religious ceremony you'll need? Do you want to do your own vows? Follow what the priest says etc.?"

Joy looked at Tim and smiled. "I know what I'd like to say. Do you have anything?"

Tim shrugged. "I got skills ya know. I can do freestyle baby."

Joy turned to Monica and said, "I think we'll do some kind of hybrid if it's OK."

Monica nodded and relayed the information into her headset.

"Religious affiliation?"

"Catholic." answered Tim.

"Spiritual." answered Joy, "I believe in God. I just don't have any formal religious leanings." she added.

Monica nodded and started walking to the elevator. "What about your clothing?"

Kuthanaga smiled. "They are on the way as are the flowers."

They walked for a while and eventually made their way to the East Chapel and there was a waiting room for the bride. Kuthanaga instructed Joy to stay put until he sent for her. After Joy had been tucked away he told Tim to go "change". Tim grinned and nodded. He knew that once Kuthanaga was ready for him he'd let him know to come back to small chapel.

Kuthanaga bent time, created three mirrors, and quickly morphed them into various human approximations to make everything seem normal. He waited until they were outside the rear of a building three blocks away, he had them gather flowers from some nearby bushes, and they modified them until they were hybrids of roses and lilies that were a brilliant white with a tint of blue. They started walking to the chapel and he allowed time to flow. He removed the disguise on Tim and Joy's clothing and once the mirrors showed up with the flowers they quickly decorated the chapel, which took fifteen minutes. The priest showed up and smiled at Kuthanaga.

"Who are you?"

Kuthanaga smiled. "I am the witness."

Monica poked her head in and caught her breath. The chapel looked beautiful and the flowers we unlike anything she had even seen. The smell of the small flowers tickled her nose and she waited until Kuthanaga nodded to head over and inform Joy that the room was ready.

Tim, you can come now.

Tim nodded and headed back towards the chapel.

Monica saw Tim as she was going to get Joy and she nodded at him.

"It's almost time. The room is ready. I'm on my way to get Joy. You know where it is right?"

Tim nodded. "Yup. I'm on my way."

She examined Tim as he walked past her and noted his outfit was a little too edgy for her taste but seemed to suit him.

She walked a little more and knocked on Joy's door. When Joy opened the door Monica's eyes widened and she was shocked. The dress was one of the most beautiful she had ever seen.

"Oh my. Wow, you look beautiful. You have to get me the name of your tailor. That dress is amazing… The chapel is ready if you'd like to follow me."

Monica put the stopper on the door to keep it open and Joy followed her.

When Joy saw the chapel, she almost cried. It was small but perfect. There was a pair of double doors, which was open to reveal the chapel, and the floor was covered with a floral design of blue and pink. At the far end of the room, the priest was standing there waiting with a warm disposition. Kuthanaga was there standing behind Tim who was wearing an outfit that was all him. She laughed when she saw the flames on his shoes.

The chapel had three rows of seating on both sides of the isle. Situated on the sides of each row were beautiful flowers that made the air smell sweet and floral. Behind Tim and the priest were two large mosaic glass windows shaded in blue. It was amazing when she noticed that all the blues matched up perfectly.

When Tim saw Joy he was speechless. The dress was amazing and fit her like a glove and he was overwhelmed with emotions. He felt butterflies in his stomach and his pulse quickened. He realized next to her the dress was nothing; it was her radiant glow that made the dress.

She walked up to him and it looked surreal to Tim. Something about the way the dress moved seemed unnatural almost as if he was watching a film that was rewound. A few moments later, she was standing next to him.

"Hi." she said.

"Hi." he replied.

The priest was a short man a little on the heavy side, dressed in black except for the small white square at his throat. The lines on his face were long and deep. His eyes though looked alive and alert. He had a warm fatherly smile and he waited until Joy was in position.

"OK, so which of you wishes to go first?"

Tim grinned and had been thinking of what he was going to say and had even tried to put some of his thoughts down on napkin to practice. Thoughts were jumbling through his head and he tried to rein them in to create the words that came from his heart. Kuthanaga could sense the rising elevation of fear in Tim and he closed his eyes while still creating the illusion that they were open. Focusing on Tim he helped him calm down and forced his mind to focus clearly.

"I'm ready." Tim said and he knew he was.

He took Joy's hand in his and stared deeply into her eyes.

"Joy, we've been through a lot together and you are my everything. I can't imagine a world without you. Cause if you weren't here I'd be empty, sad and without the one person who really and truly understands and loves me. I love you more than anything. There are no words that can truly express to you what you mean to me. I stand before you ready to love you for the rest of my life. I would gladly die for you if I needed to and just want you to know how deep my love for you is. I will be the husband you always have hoped for."

A pause and Joy responded.

"Tim, there's many things I love about you and even when you are at your craziest, you are still the man I can't stand to be without. I never get bored hanging out with you and can honestly say I have never loved anyone as much as I love you. You are my everything and I am yours forever. I want you to know that I know you love me and I feel it. We've already experienced bad times and I can't wait to make a lot more of the good times! I love you so much and can't wait to be your wife."

The priest nodded and realized these were words that were unrehearsed and from the heart. It made him smile and filled him with happiness.

"Now that you two have exchanged your dedications to each other, may we have the rings?"

Kuthanaga handed the rings to the priest.

"Tim, do you take Joy to be your wedded wife to live together in marriage? Do you promise to love, comfort, honor and keep her for better or worse, for richer or poorer, in sickness and in health, and forsaking all others, be faithful only to her so long as you both shall live?"

Tim nodded. "I do."

"Joy, do you take Tim to be your wedded husband to live together in marriage? Do you promise to love, comfort, honor and keep him for better or worse, for richer or poorer, in sickness and in health, and forsaking all others, be faithful only to him so long as you both shall live?"

Joy nodded. "I do."

The priest looked at Kuthanaga.

"As witness to these promises will you do everything in your power to uphold these two in their marriage?"

Kuthanaga nodded.

"I will."

"Excellent. Tim, please repeat after me. I, Tim, take you Joy to be my wife, to have and to hold from this day forward, for better, for worse, for richer, for poorer, in sickness and in health, to love and to cherish till death do us part."

Tim paused for a second and cleared his throat.

"I, Tim, take you Joy to be my wife, to have and to hold from this day forever, for better, for worse, for richer, for poorer, in sickness and in health, to love and to hold…"

"Cherish." corrected the priest. He ignored the error on forward and liked the forever replacement.

"Oh yeah, cherish… Till death do us part."

"Joy, please repeat after me. I, Joy, take you Tim to be my husband, to have and to hold from this day forward, for better, for worse, for richer, for poorer, in sickness and in health, to love and to cherish till death do us part."

Joy smiled and she squeezed Tim's hands.

"I, Joy, take you Tim to be my husband, to have and to hold from this day forward, for better, for worse, for richer, for poorer, in sickness and in health, to love and to cherish till death do us part."

The priest did not know why, but the room felt as if many eyes were on him and the couple. He glanced up and all the chairs were empty but he couldn't shake that something else was in the room.

Kuthanaga sensed a strange sensation in the room. Some force was among them and he glanced around. The room was empty except for the four of them. He saw that the priest had noticed something as well. The priest focused again and continued. He held up the rings so that Tim and Joy could see them.

"From the earliest times, the circle has been a symbol of completeness, a symbol of committed love. An unbroken and never-ending circle symbolizes a commitment of love that is also never ending. As often as either of you looks at this symbol, I hope that you will be reminded of the commitment to love each other, which you have made today."

He handed each of them the rings they were to give each other and he continued.

"Will each of you repeat after me? I, Tim, give to you Joy, this ring, as a symbol of my commitment to love, honor, and respect you. With this ring, I thee wed."

Tim nodded and repeated the sentence perfectly. He slid the ring onto Joy's finger and she noticed the ring was warm.

The priest looked at Joy, "I, Joy, give to you Tim, this ring, as a symbol of my commitment to love, honor, and respect you. With this ring, I thee wed."

Joy repeated and placed the ring on Tim's finger.

"Before God and the honored witness, Tim and Joy have promised each other their love and have given each other rings to wear as a sign of their deep commitment. Therefore, I declare that they are husband and wife. You may kiss the bride."

Tim pulled Joy to him and he kissed her with such passion that Joy felt as if it was the first kiss that they had ever shared. A shock of energy filled them both as they kissed. She could feel his love so profoundly that she felt tears roll down her cheek.

Tim wiped the tear away and gently caressed her face.

"I love you so much Mrs. Christenson," he said.

She smiled.

"I love you Mr. Christenson."

The priest smiled and put his hand on Tim's shoulder.

"There's some paperwork on the table there I need you to fill out."

Tim and Joy worked on the paperwork as Kuthanaga walked the room straining to see what else was among them. The priest watched him and walked over to join him.

"You feel it too?"

Kuthanaga nodded.

"Yes I do. What do you think it is?"

The priest shrugged.

"Some would say angels. Maybe the Holy Spirit. I couldn't say. But something *is* here."

Kuthanaga nodded. He didn't know what it was and he couldn't pinpoint it. Whatever it was it didn't want to reveal itself.

Once the paperwork was done, the priest congratulated the couple again and he left. As Kuthanaga and the couple exited the chapel, Monica was waiting for them.

"Congratulations Mr. and Mrs. Christenson."

"Thank you!" Joy said with a smile. She liked being called Mrs. Christenson.

Kuthanaga handed Monica a small envelope and she quickly tucked it away.

She radioed a few instructions and headed into the chapel.

Kuthanaga started walking and Joy and Tim looked at each other.

"I am heading back to the suite and then will be gone for a few days. Please enjoy yourself and when I return we will discuss what needs to happen. We will talk more then. Oh yes, one more thing before I leave you…"

He motioned and they were in their original clothing.

Monica turned and saw them barely turn the corner out of her sight. She had caught a momentary glimpse of the clothing shift, waved it away, and explained in her own mind that it was another couple that she saw.

"You two have fun. I will be back."

Tim reached out and gently grabbed Kuthanaga's arm.

"Thank you for this."

"You deserved it Tim Christenson. Please enjoy."

Tim nodded and watched as Joy hugged Kuthanaga.

"Yeah, thank you so much!"

He embraced her back and then he walked away. After a few moments, he was lost from their sight in the sea of people.

"So Mr. Christenson what would you like to do now?"

He grinned at her.

"Well, we are married now! Shall we shop for toys?"

She made a face and punched him in the arm.

"Wow freak-a-zoid! Didn't take you long to go there."

He shrugged.

"Come on don't be that way. It was only an idea."

"Well, we could always go look. I don't see any harm there."

She smiled at her new husband and he hugged her. They walked off arm in arm with an almost visible glow.

Chapter 21 – Travel
December 19th 2011 – Salt Lake 2:10 pm

Xanari was anxious to speak with Rachel. She shifted to the mirror's location and walked up to the door. She knocked and there was no reply. She waited for a few more moments and knocked again. A few more anxious moments passed and she walked through the door into the house.

The couch was there and the house was silent. She walked the halls and after a few minutes she was sure no one was home. She took a seat on the couch and waited. She meditated and continued to monitor the mirrors and finally a few hours later she was stirred by the sound of the front door opening.

Rachel had her arms full of groceries and was fumbling with the door. Even though Xanari was obscured from sight, Rachel addressed her.

"Can you help me please Xanari?"

Xanari stood and grabbed a few of the bags and shifted into focus.

Rachel smiled at Xanari.

"Let's put the groceries on the kitchen table."

Xanari followed her into the kitchen and noticed the front door was still open. She focused on it and it silently slide close.

"So Bimini huh? Never been near Florida before."

Xanari was amazed. "How did you… Dream?"

Rachel smiled. "Yup. That's why I went and grabbed some supplies for the trip. Also, you'd better let Kuthanaga know soon your answer. If you wait too long you won't get him for a few days. He's traveling somewhere north. In a couple of the dreams he was unavailable and the others he was available."

Xanari nodded and set the bags on the kitchen table. She closed her eyes, massaged the sixth slab on her necklace, and pictured Kuthanaga. After a few moments, she could feel his presence. Not mentally but physically. She opened her eyes and he was standing in front of her. Rachel dropped a glass she had been filling when he materialized.

"I wasn't expecting a visit." Xanari said.

Kuthanaga looked stern and he examined Rachel who looked surprised to see him.

Has she accepted the offer?

Xanari nodded.

Good. I wanted to meet her myself and I can see you were not exaggerating. Her aura is very interesting.

As is ours Kuthanaga.

He looked at Xanari and noticed her aura was also shifting.

"Hello there Kuthanaga. It's nice to finally meet you."

He nodded and took her hand in his and shook it gently. "You as well. I'm glad you have agreed to go with Xanari."

She grinned. "I didn't dream any of this. How interesting."

He looked at her closely. "What do you mean?"

"I've dreamed of talking with you, but not now, not here. Not a single dream. There is something different about you. Something I can't quite put my finger on."

He smiled. "So maybe there is hope for me after all. Maybe I'll survive all of this."

She nodded. "Maybe. Well I'm sure it'll all work itself out somehow. Things always seem to anyways. Somehow someway."

"So you have all of your affairs in order for you travel?"

"The only bill I have is the house here and the utilities."

"Those will be taken care of."

Kuthanaga closed his eyes, read Rachel, and found all the information he needed. It took him some effort but everything he needed was there. It was obvious to him that she could have put up a fight and resisted him but she had sensed him and allowed it.

"I'm sure it will be. But you and I both know in a year it won't matter much anyways."

He nodded. "True, but I still want to make sure you are compensated in all ways for your agreeing to travel with Xanari."

She studied Kuthanaga and noticed something was troubling him.

"What's going on big guy? You seem troubled. What brought you here? You normally wouldn't be here. So what's on your mind?"

She was observant if nothing else. He was troubled. The presence at the wedding was something he couldn't explain and it was an experience he was unfamiliar with. Annukai believed in a celestial deity who created all from nothing but he was hands off. He simply set the stage and allowed life to run its course. The notion of angels or a Holy Spirit that could visit and watch after humanity seemed alien to him.

"What is your understanding of angels?"

"Depends. I've never dreamed of angels. At least have never seen them. I have witnessed miracles but have always felt those things were supposed to happen. I always kinda thought angles and demons were you guys to be honest."

Kuthanaga nodded. Many of the exploits of the Draconians and a few rogue Annukai had created various legends. Some of the well know demons and angels were named directly from drakes and Annukai.

"Yes. I thought that as well. Something happened to me today. I could sense something I couldn't see and yet I knew it was there."

"Well you know, I know when you are around even though I can't always see you. Maybe it's something else? Maybe another alien?"

Kuthanaga doubted that another species of alien would be foolish enough to make the same error that they had made so many years before.

"I suppose it matters not. Whatever it was, it was content on simply watching us."

Rachel was interested.

"What was it?"

"What?"

"You said it was content to watch. Watch what?"

"A wedding."

"Wedding huh? Was their family there?"

Kuthanaga shook his head. "No just the priest and me in addition to bride and groom."

"Where were their families?"

"The mother and father died long ago for both bride and groom. The brother of the bride has also died. Sister of groom has not spoken to him in a long while."

"I wonder."

"What?"

"Maybe the family showed up after all to watch and pay their respect."

"Ghosts?"

There was much speculation about the humans and ghosts among the elder Annukai. What happened when the humans died? Did they pass onto the next phase? Rachel had pointed out an option he had not considered and it helped him. He sighed and felt relaxed.

"I am grateful for your wisdom. Thank you."

She shrugged. "No biggie. Glad to help when I can."

Kuthanaga looked at Xanari.

Make sure you protect this human.

Xanari nodded.

"I will leave you with Xanari. There are things I must attend to. I will see you both soon. Xanari, here is the location I need you to go to. The resources you need to get there are here."

Kuthanaga dropped an envelope on the kitchen table and placed his hand near her and she could sense the location.

She nodded and he closed his eyes and faded. Xanari was alone again with Rachel. There was much more she wanted to say to Kuthanaga but she knew there was a time and a place for everything.

Xanari opened the envelope and inside it was cash and IDs. Xanari knew she would have to mask Rachel as they traveled to match the credentials and that would mean potentially losing contact with mirrors and losing a few. Nevertheless, Kuthanaga deemed it necessary and he knew better than anyone else what was at stake.

"I guess I'll finish packing for our trip."

Xanari waited and thirty minutes later, they were on their way to the airport.

Chapter 22 – Revelations
December 20th 2011 – New York 1:20 am

Richard sat in the bed staring at Christy, the moon light illuminated the curves of her back and he sighed. She was becoming a bore to him and he was torn, should he just leave her or kill her. She knew a lot of information and he didn't want any of it to become public knowledge. He wondered if she was worth life or if she was just another human plaything to be discarded when he was done with her. He decided to have some fun.

"Wake up."

"Come on baby. Three is enough. I can't handle it anymore. I'm getting sore."

"No not that. I want to ask you something."

She rolled over and stared into his eyes. She was no stranger to rich powerful men and something in her told her his tone was serious. She wasn't about to be on the receiving end of a half ass attempt to leave the relationship. She laughed at herself for even thinking the word relationship. No, they were bed buddies. She knew that. She knew he was married and could never end up being with a woman like her. She decided to take matters into her own hand and try to keep what little pride she had left.

"Yeah, I've been meaning to talk with you too. So maybe this heart to heart you want to share with me will work for both of us."

He was interested in what she was getting at.

"Really? You had something to tell me?"

She nodded and rolled over. Her voluptuous breasts caught the light and the cool air made her nipple erect.

"I was thinking this is fun and all that, but I need to break away from you. The sex is phenomenal, but I need more and you can't provide that."

"Hmmm, go on."

"So after tonight I don't think we should see each other anymore."

"Fascinating."

He traced his finger along her stomach and was smiling. She had somehow sensed that he was going to give her bad news of some sort and wanted to be the first to act. He liked that. It showed she had instinct and brains. Something that many humans seemed to lack.

"Why is that interesting?"

He sat up and held her legs.

"Well, I was going to tell you what a monster I am and see if you could keep a secret. But if you are sincere and this is what you want, I won't stop you."

She smiled. "Monster?"

He grinned a big grin.

"Yes a wicked, evil monster."

"And what if I couldn't keep the secret?"

"Well then that would be very bad."

She detected a tone in his voice and something in her screamed 'get the fuck out…'

"Well, I think I'll pass on the secret then and just keep things nice between us."

She rubbed his chest and postured that she was relaxed. He could smell the fear on her and it excited him.

"Well how about one last romp in the hay for old times' sake?"

"No, that would be a bad thing for both of us."

"How so?"

"Well it would just make me want you more and also make you want me more. And since we're trying to make a nice clean break, let's just do that."

She went to slide out of the bed and he shook his head.

"I'm sorry. But I think it's time we talked about my monster inside."

Her heart started racing.

"No, let's not. Seriously. I just want to take a shower and dress up. Would that be OK?"

Richard reached out his hand and placed it around her fragile neck. He was getting very excited now and she could see it through the sheets. She realized she was in a very precarious position. She would have to figure a way out of the situation or she knew her life was going to end. She went to jump out of the bed but she was moving in slow motion for him. He tightened his grip and slammed her back against the wall. The air escaped from her and her eyes widened. She realized he was going to kill her.

"Christy, I gotta tell ya. I've really enjoyed our time together and you have been a blast. I really am going to miss you. You knew how to get me off so well."

She punched hard and connected with his face and it seemed to have no effect. She tried kicking with all her might and the kick landed on his chest. Again, it seemed to have no effect other than exciting him more.

"Yes, fight it. Fight for your life!"

She went to scream and he slammed her again. She went limp in his hands and he cursed. He hoped he hadn't accidently broken her neck. He felt her pulse and could hear her breathing.

His phone rang and he debated killing her while she was unconscious.

"Where's the fun in that?"

He answered the phone.

"Yes?"

"You wanted the results as soon as we had them."

"Yes. What do you have?"

"The blood belonged to a Tim Christenson located in San Francisco California. We found the guard or at least what was left of him in the shaft as you suspected. Our team went to get the subject and he wasn't at his last known address. What we found out also is the woman Joy is Joy Tsai. She was the name on the apartment and the phone for the location. The last anyone saw of them was weeks ago. They were described as junkies."

"A junkie could not do what was done unless he was very very lucky."

He turned away from Christy to continue his conversation. She was coming too, realized where she was, and saw Richard on the phone. Christy kept a small knife in her purse, which happened to be on the nightstand near her. She could see the blade in it. She reached over slowly and managed to get it. Richard could hear her breathing change and knew she was awake. He would deal with her after he was finished with his call.

"Anything else?" he asked.

"No sir."

"Well I have to get back to what I was doing. I'll check in with you in the morning."

He hung up the phone and Christy knew her time had come and she struck out with the blade and she punctured deep on the left side of his chest. He allowed the blade to penetrate and then he shoved her back.

"Wow that actually kinda hurts. I like where you stabbed me. Under normal circumstances that would actually be a death strike, but you see we Draconians have a slightly different anatomy than you humans."

"What?" was all she could manage to say.

Richard reached out and grabbed her again by the neck.

"Here's the secret."

He shifted and her eyes widened as he did. He studied her. When he was done, he towered over her. His jaw was open and inside were rows of teeth. Christy tried one last time to shove him away and he just shook his head.

"I'm in the mood now. You penetrated me."

He glanced down at the blade, which was still sticking out of him.

"My turn."

He pushed her down and his massive form enveloped her. The pain she suffered was unimaginable and he completely used her up. When he climaxed she had long since been dead. He slowly walked into the bathroom. He pulled the blade free and dropped it in the sink. He glanced back at the bloody mess lying in the bed.

He shifted back to his human form and turned the shower on. Within a minute, he was in the shower cleaning up. By the time he was done, the cut had almost completely healed up. He walked back to the bed, grabbed the comforter and the sheets, and rolled her body up in it. He placed the roll on the floor and dialed a number on his phone.

"Hello?"

"Yeah it's me. I need a cleanup. I will text you the address. Make sure it's thorough."

"OK, on my way."

He hung up the phone and texted Christy's address. He knew within ten minutes the crew would arrive. He dressed up and popped in a couple of sticks of gum. He was always discrete when he met with Christy and she had been more than accommodating in keeping their arrangement private.

He waited and soon he heard a gentle knock at the door. He opened it and two men stood before him. He motioned at the roll on the ground.

"There's the body. Make it disappear. Also, I would like the room to be searched and if you find anything let me know. Clean it all up. I'm heading out. You know what to do."

The men nodded. It wasn't their first clean-up job, so they knew what they were doing. Richard gathered his belongings and whistled as he walked out the apartment.

Chapter 23 – Honeymoon
December 23rd 2011 –Vegas 3:30 am

Tim and Joy had been enjoying relearning each other in the privacy of the suite. With Kuthanaga gone, Tim felt more in control and with Joy by his side, he felt alive. His near death experience made him appreciate the little things in many ways. It was noticeable to Joy who was constantly amazed when Tim would point out things like flowers and the sunset, things that he never seemed to pay any attention to before. She knew his run in with the drake had severely affected him.

They spent their time exploring each other and it felt fresh and new again. Tim made love to her and sex had become very passionate and deeply emotional between them. They had been together for years and Joy realized they had never maintained eye contact. Now as husband and wife, the lovemaking was like nothing she had ever experienced. It was a beautiful thing as they shared and focused on pleasing each other.

The pillow talk had also elevated to new levels and they were talking about deeper topics then television or the best drugs to score. Substance had crept into their relationship and it was good. They talked all night long and slept in late. When they would wake up they were ravenous and would eat large and retire back to their bedroom.

Tim had discovered the jacuzzi tub and was relaxing with Joy sitting next to him.

"So you know Christmas is coming up."

Tim nodded. He despised Christmas. It was a hard time for him and he wondered why Joy was suddenly bringing it up.

"I know you don't like it. I know why. But, I think since things are going so well maybe we should make a clean break of everything if we can and try to start over totally clean. This time last year I don't even really remember what we were doing."

Tim did. He was robbing a couple for their money, the husband had tried to fight back, and Tim had shot him dead with a bullet to his face.

"Yeah, I don't really want to talk about this. Christmas is bullshit anyways. I mean why wait till one fucking day to let the people around you know that you love them and care about them?"

"Tim. Babe. Come on. Don't be so negative. I was just saying maybe we should get something for your sister. You know bury the hatchet?"

Tim was turning red. He could feel the anger rising in him.

"What? Fuck her! I don't ever want to talk to her again."

He was jonesing for a fix and it scared him. He hadn't really wanted anything since Kuthanaga had cleansed him.

"I was just saying. At least you still have some family left."

He started to get out of the jacuzzi and as he jumped out, he started to slip. He saw the floor rising up to bash him in the face and suddenly he froze midair a few inches from the ground. He heard a gasp and turned his head to see that Joy had her hand raised towards him and her ring was glowing a dull blue. The anger left him and he just stared at her.

"How the hell are you doing that?"

She shook her head.

"I have no idea. I saw you falling and I reached out to catch you. Then the next thing I see is you floating."

She calmed down and envisioned him on the ground softly, he floated the last couple of inches, and he quickly stood up.

Tim looked at her ring, which stopped glowing, and he saw a black strip snake quickly out of sight. It reminded him of the barb in his foot.

"Son of a bitch."

Joy carefully got out of the jacuzzi and got them both towels.

"What?"

"Kuthanaga."

"What?"

"He did something to our rings. Or at least yours."

They quickly changed into dry clothing and sat on the living room couch.

"OK, so how do you think this works?" asked Joy.

"Got me. You did it not me."

"Let's experiment." Tim could hear the excitement in Joy's voice.

Tim saw a pizza box on the counter and he pointed at it.

"Pizza come!" he said as he pointed.

Joy waited and when nothing happened, she pointed and closed her eyes. She pictured in her mind the pizza box floating in front of her. She heard Tim grumble and she opened her eyes. The pizza box was floating in front of her.

"Aw man. What am I a retard? How the fuck are you doin' it?"

"I just closed my eyes and pictured the box moving to me. I imagined it."

Tim's eyes widened. "Oh."

He closed his eyes and he thought about the pizza box and imagined it back at the counter. He opened one eye and could see the box skittering across the floor. It slammed into the base of the counter.

"Fuck."

"Hey you moved it at least."

He nodded and smiled. It was something. He would have to practice. Joy was smart he knew and he was fine with her being better at using the ring.

"I wonder why Kuthanaga put the mojo on the rings." Tim wondered aloud.

Joy shrugged. "Who cares? Now we got some fun stuff to play with. Imagine what we could do at the crap tables."

Tim nodded and thought about it.

"We'd better not. I mean we have a shitload of money as is and pretty much anything we want here. Plus, Kuthanaga would probably shit a kitten if he found out."

Joy nodded. She was proud of Tim. He had come a long way and to hear him taking the moral high ground was weird but Joy liked it. She hugged him and she felt guilty about bringing up his sister.

"About earlier…"

"Forget it. I know how you feel about family and it's cool. Thanks by the way. I would've bashed my face in if you hadn't figured out the whole ring thing."

She squeezed him.

"That's what I'm here for! I got your back. Literally."
He smiled.

She kissed him.

"I'm tired." Tim said.

"I'm not! Go ahead and get some sleep. I'm gonna practice with the ring." He shrugged. He would practice on his own when no one was around. He knew he could figure it out but he didn't want to be embarrassed if he messed up.

He walked into their bedroom and sat on the bed. He saw the remote next to the TV and he could see the power button. He closed his eyes and took a deep breath. He pictured the remote, the texture and the buttons. He focused on the power button and imagined he pressed it. A second later, he heard a clicking noise and a low hum. He opened his eyes to see that the TV was on.

"Easy Peasy." he said.

He propped a pillow under his back and zoned out watching an infomercial on gold coins. He drifted off and dreamed.

Chapter 24 – Decisions

December 24th 2011 – Maniwaki, Canada 9:13 am

John Chabot walked outside his house and breathed in the winter air. It was cold and fresh and he felt alive. He walked to his truck and started scraping off the ice that was on his windshield. He didn't mind it. His breath puffed little clouds as he worked the glass. He had the day off and he wanted to get some ice fishing in. There was a spot his father had showed him and it was always a good bet.

The windows cleared of ice, he jumped in and started the truck. It roared a loud roar and lurched forward as if it were excited to get going. He didn't know why, but he felt as though he were being watched. Glancing in his rearview mirror, he didn't see anyone and after a few anxious moments, he relaxed.

He arrived at the large stone, which was his marker and parked the truck. Getting out he gathered his gear from the back and started walking. The ground was smooth and there were no footprints in the snow, which was a good sign. Tourist had been getting closer and closer to his spot each year and he knew it was only a matter of time before his favorite hole was taken over.

Even though the land belonged to his people, the Kitigan Zibi, they didn't mind the tourist. In fact, the increase in the tourism allowed the Anishinaabeg to stay and work on maintaining their cultural heritage. The tribal ways were still acknowledged but the fact remained many of the Kitigan Zibi held regular jobs and had their kids in regular schools. It was a real effort getting the children to maintain a working knowledge of their culture.

Each step he took crunched in the ground and he pushed on with an excitement growing within him. He always loved fishing the spot. It was more than just a good yielding fishing-hole. It had a history to it. His grandfather showed his father and he in turn shared it with him. There was a large rock nearby that his father told him was special. The rock was the first place he had heard the story of the Seven Fires.

John approached the rock and smiled as he recalled memories of him and his father fishing and talking. Most of the time the conversation was light and fun. Occasionally though his father would speak of the seven prophets and the history of his tribe.

He leaned his gear against the rock and stood there listening. The air was still and he could hear his breathing. He took out his ice chisel and started to work a hole in the ice. When it was large enough he retrieved his ice saw and worked it to the size he wanted.

He returned to the great rock and put the gear away he wouldn't need anymore and was about to bring the remainder of his gear to the hole when he heard a sound that made him pause. The sound of dripping. Drip. Drip. Drip. It was faint but clear. He worked his way around the rock until he was behind it and he saw a sight that made him pause. There was a small hole and it had a smooth groove. A white liquid was coming from the hole and it dripped down to a large bowl-shaped depression on the rock.

John wondered what the liquid was. It was clean and smooth and had a pleasant subtle scent to it that he couldn't quite describe. He marveled at the fact that it wasn't frozen.

"How strange."

He placed his finger in the shallow pool and smelled the liquid on his finger. It was cool to the touch but not as cold as it should be. It had a very strong smell that reminded him of vanilla and mocha. His stomach grumbled and he realized he was hungry. He didn't know what the strange liquid was but it didn't seem to be dangerous as far as he could tell and his gut instinct told him it was OK.

He shrugged and tasted it. His eyes widened and he smiled. It tasted better than he thought it would. He cupped his hand into the liquid and sipped it and as he swallowed he felt warmer and his hunger was gone.

"What the?"

He squatted down and examined the liquid closer. His heart was beating. This wasn't normal, this was something else. His mind started reeling. He grabbed a canteen and dumped it out. When it was empty, he filled it with the liquid. He was filled with a sense of urgency and he knew he had to speak with the tribal elder as soon as possible about the strange liquid. He quickly gathered his gear and headed back to his truck.

Unseen by John, Kuthanaga was crouched on the top of the rock and watched silently with extreme interest as he started to drive off.

John drove back into the center of town and saw the Chief Gilbert Tallbrother. Tallbrother walked with purpose and pride and his shoulder length hair gently swayed as he moved. He wore glasses that glinted in the early morning light. He had deep lines around his mouth and none around his brow signifying a man who had balance in his life. John respected the elder greatly and knew if anyone could understand what the mysterious liquid was it would be him.

"Excuse me." John said as he parked and quickly approached Tallbrother.

"John. What is it?"

"Sorry to bother you. I came across something I think you should see."

Tallbrother nodded and motioned for John to follow him. They entered a small building and sat at a old weathered round table. John explained how he had come about the liquid. He handed the canteen to Tallbrother and waited.

Tallbrother opened the canteen and smelled it. To him it smelled like warm syrup and butter.

"You said this smelled like vanilla and mocha?"

John nodded and the Chief got up and retrieved a small glass. He poured the liquid into it and examined it. It looked like milk to him and yet it smelled nothing like it. He was hungry and decided he would test the liquid. He took a small sip and he felt the warmth as John had described and the flavor was amazing. He sipped a little more and his hunger vanished just as John had said.

"Please try this again." The Chief grabbed another glass and poured a small amount into it as well.

John smelled it and it still smelled like vanilla and mocha. He sipped and smiled.

"It's warmer now. It tastes good yeah?"

The Chief nodded. He walked to a coffee pot, which was nearby, and grabbing a third glass poured coffee into it. He then poured the milky liquid from his glass into the coffee and watched in amazement as the coffee shifted color and looked like the milk.

"Did you see that?!" John asked.

The chief nodded.

"John, when I drank the liquid it tasted and smelled like syrup and butter to me. To you, it tasted and smelled like vanilla and mocha. Why the difference? And now it changed the coffee."

Michael Grayson entered the building and walked towards the two men.

"Whatcha guys doin?"

Tallbrother smiled. "We're guessing the flavor of this drink. Would you care to try?"

Michael shrugged. "Sure why not?"

Tallbrother grabbed another glass, put a small amount of the liquid in, and waited as Michael sipped it.

"Damn, that's good. Tastes like a mixture of vodka and strawberries. I love it. What's it called?"

Tallbrother and John looked at each other.

"It's a recipe we're working on," said John quickly.

"Well when you guys put it out let me know, because I'll buy it!"

Michael turned and walked out of the building whistling.

"John, how do you feel?"

"I feel great. I was tired earlier but now I feel really energetic and excited."

Tallbrother nodded. "I also feel it. I don't think this is anything man-made. We all seem to taste something different in the liquid. I wonder if this has anything to do with the Seven Fires prophecy? Is this a test? Could you imagine if someone were to sell this? A liquid that tasted good to whoever drank it?"

John hadn't even thought about selling it. He was more concerned with what it was. They tested the liquid in the coffee glass and it was the same as the canteen's liquid.

Tallbrother smiled. "This is a good thing John. We should have this tested by those closest to us and see if they can determine what it is. Once we know for sure, we can get others involved. Something tells me that this liquid is much more than an accident. I'll need to take some of the liquid for testing and then I want you to put the rest in a safe place."

John nodded.

"Where was the spring at again?"

"The great rock where we fished a few winters ago."

Tallbrother smiled and nodded. He knew the exact spot.

"Did you see any tourist there?"

John shook his head. "No. I didn't see anyone out there."

Tallbrother nodded. He needed time to test the liquid and talk with other elders as to the next step. If this was indeed part of the prophecy, he wanted to make sure the correct action was taken.

Tallbrother gathered small samples of the liquid and when he was done, he thanked John and he left the building. John sat there for a while and had a profound sense that change was coming.

Kuthanaga watched from outside and anticipation filled him.

Chapter 25 – Christmas Miracles
December 25th 2011 – Don Martin, Mexico 2:14 pm

Reshnogga had done as Kuthanaga had asked and changed his location to Don Martin and it wasn't a bad location to monitor the mirrors from. The humans were celebrating Christmas and many were at neighboring churches. Reshnogga marveled at the religious devotion in which the humans in Don Martin had.

He wondered what was supposed to happen in the town of Don Martin. Why had Kuthanaga instructed him to come to this location? The area was arid and warm. The landscape was bleached and barren. Cactus's and pelicans seemed to dominate the area. The town had once flourished as a fishing haven before the enormous damn was opened sending the town's livelihood to the Rio Grande.

To say the residents were poor and barely making it was an understatement. The few remaining fishermen ate what they caught and had little extra to even think about selling. The Mexican government had abandoned them and they were bitter. The tension was running high and Reshnogga saw many deeply damaged auras. There were some that stood out as exceptional and they were marked. It didn't take more than an hour to examine the entire town.

In a dry patch of what used to be a moderate sized lake was a shallow depression. A small child name Enrique was playing there with his little sister Anna. Enrique had a stick and was pretending to be a warrior with it while his sister giggled and cheered him on. He stepped forward near the center of the depression and his foot sank an inch. He stumbled to the ground and cried out. His mother Maria heard him and she hurried to his side. He was sitting down staring at the depression, which had started to fill up with a milky white liquid.

"Are you all right?" His mother asked him.

He nodded. Maria noticed he had stopped crying and that Anna was quite. She followed her son's gaze and noticed the milky liquid.

"Lord in heaven." she said and carried Enrique back to the shoreline. Anna followed her mother.

"Javier." called out Maria. Her husband Javier was tending his nets and patching a few broken lines. He turned to face her and walked calmly to her.

"What is it?"

She pointed to the depression, which had filled up and created a small white pond. Javier stared at it and scratched his stubbly chin. He had lived in Don Martin his whole life and was a third generation angler. He had never seen anything nor heard anything that looked like the white pond. He walked towards it and a faint smell of apples filled the air around him. He knelt and examined the liquid. He cautiously put one finger in and the liquid was icy cool to the touch. He smelled his finger and it smelled strongly of apples. He tasted it and was amazed at how wonderful the flavor was. He smiled.

"Get something for us to collect this."

"Is it safe?"

He shrugged. "It tastes good. I feel fine. I feel great." Indeed he did. He suddenly felt more energy and somehow knew the liquid was safe.

He nodded suddenly. "Yes it's fine. Hurry. I want to get as much as possible. Soon there will be other here. We need to get as much home as possible now!"

His wife ran off and his son and daughter cautiously approached.

"It's OK. You thirsty?"

They nodded and he gathered some up in his hands and they tried the liquid and smiled.

"Peppermint!" said his daughter.

"Milk and cookies!" cried his son.

Both kids looked at each other and then back at their father. He reached in and took a deep drink and it still tasted like apples with a touch of vanilla ice cream.

"So it doesn't taste like apples to you?" he asked his children who both shook their heads.

Maria was back in five minutes, the white liquid had filled up a large section, and Javier was now standing in shin deep. She had brought several bottles and buckets with her in a small wagon. They worked quickly and as they were finishing a couple walked up and noticed them.

"Hey Javier, what is that?" asked the old man who Javier recognized as Neil Lopez.

"I do not know. But, if I were you, I would get as much of it as possible. It's amazing."

Neil could detect a sense of urgency in Javier's tone and he motioned for his wife to follow him as they quickly headed home to get containers.

Within two hours, the whole town had heard of the miraculous liquid and word of it reached Reshnogga who quickly went to observe. When he arrived, people were all around the edge filling all sorts of containers and others waited patiently as no matter how much people walked away with the small pond kept filling up.

Reshnogga watched and smiled as he saw the people helping each other. He monitored their thoughts and was amazed that each person had a distinctly different experience with the liquid and it seemed to have healing properties of a sort. Many felt it was a Christmas miracle and as the evening approached prayers were heard as the entire town converged on the location to give thanks and marvel at the liquid.

Reshnogga understood why Kuthanaga wanted him there as he saw small thoughts of monetary gain started to filter though several of the people who were in the large crowd. He couldn't blame them as they were starving for the most part and were barely surviving. He wondered how the 'miracle' was going to play out.

He found a remote spot and closed his eyes. A brief moment passed and he could feel Kuthanaga.

Yes, Reshnogga.

I see what you have set in motion here. It will be interesting to see what the humans do with this liquid. What other propertics does it possess?

It can self-replicate in any liquid it comes in contact with.

Really?

Yes.

What would happen if it were to be dumped into a river with fish or one of the oceans?

It would depend on the size. It will replicate roughly one thousand times its volume before dissolving into the large liquid. As far as life, it will act as normal to them with the only adverse effect being the opacity it would add to the normal water. Even that would pass after some time as the physical contact with the creature would change its composition based off of base desire and need.

You mean it can change?

Yes. It is really amazing. I learned of it after we arrived here from my father. It took me a long time to actually locate it and get a large enough sample. How are the people reacting to it?

They are treating it like a religious miracle. They are all sharing it. For now. I am sensing some have other ideas for it.

Perfect. It is going as I had hoped.

Are there other locations?

Yes, America and Canada. The Canadian location has already showed. I am here watching it unfold. I am waiting to hear from Xanari on the other.

So you'd like me to maintain my position here?

Yes.

As you say.

Thank you.

Kuthanaga faded from his mind and he headed back to observe the humans.

Chapter 26 – Mending Bridges
December 25th 2011 – Las Vegas 11:11 pm

Tim watched as Joy sipped from her drink. The glass originally had champaign in it, but when she added a drop of the Earth's Milk to it, it shifted and he understood that only Joy knew what the flavor was. They had been sober and clean since Kuthanaga's appearance. Tim was proud of Joy and himself for not giving into any of their cravings. He was happy and he felt warm throughout his body. He realized this was entirely a new feeling for him. Usually there was always something that would ruin his mood, especially on the holidays. He studied Joy and saw she wasn't there with him. She had a glossed gaze that was staring in his general direction but wasn't really fixed on anything. He had his suspicions of where she was in her mind and he didn't want to interrupt her. So, he sat and ate quietly.

They were sitting in a lavish restaurant, which was amazingly empty. They had been getting phenomenal service and been living large. The ambiance was romantic and mellow. A fire pit was nearby and it illuminated the room with a soft flickering orange tint.

Joy was thinking of the last time she had a "happy" Christmas and it was the year before her brother died. Noel had large dreams of being a famous writer and he was sharing with her the plot of his next book. He had published a novel before but it didn't really elevate his position within the sea of wannabe writing stars. The book was decent but was a bit too abstract and artsy for the masses. Noel took it in stride and kept at it. He had been using many drugs and was the one who initially introduced Joy to crank. He raved how it allowed him to work for days and be much more creative and focused. Crank wasn't the only drug he was fond of; he also enjoyed heroin and meth. Joy was content with just the crank and as her brother slid further and further down into his private hell, she was slowly trying to break out of hers.

Noel and Joy were very close, she enjoyed his company and shared with him the most intimate of secrets, and he was always there for here when she had good news or bad. She would see him crashing hard, she helped him however she could, and when he was at his lowest level, she even tried to convince him to clean up with her. He had sold almost everything that wasn't nailed down and the only thing he owned of value was a shotgun that their father had given him. He tried to convince Joy to take it down to the local pawnshop and score for him and she refused because she wanted to help him clean up. Little did she know that the shotgun she refused to pawn for him would be the instrument which would end her brother's life and forever scar her.

A tear rolled down her check and as it trickled down it snapped her back to Tim. He was watching her and when she focused her gaze on him and wiped the tear away, he quickly looked down and acted as if he did not see the tear.

She smiled.

"Sorry. I was…"

He nodded and said, "I know, you were thinking about Noel. It's cool don't trip."

She sipped her drink again.

"Sometimes I think all of this is just a dream. I mean a couple of weeks ago we were trying to figure out our next score and now we're living like top notch royalty."

Tim took a bite of his filet mignon and the juices flowed through his mouth as he chomped on it hungrily.

"I feel you. I keep waiting for Kuthanaga to show up to yank me away on the next mission. I wish I knew what the hell we were doing. I know it has something to do with the milk. Other than that…"

He shrugged. He thought about the milk and decided he would drink some before he went to sleep. It wasn't something he wanted to drink at the beginning of the day because it would fill him up and he enjoyed the feasting they had been doing since Kuthanaga had left.

"Yeah, I worry about you. I think it must be important though. Things are getting crazy you know. Maybe all this bad stuff is a sign."

"A sign?"

"Yeah, apocalypse, end of days, etc…"

"I thought you don't believe in that stuff?"

"Well I didn't really believe in aliens before either and now we know for sure right?"

Tim nodded. There had been increased specials on TV about 2012 and the Mayan calendar. They had even heard a couple discussing it as they rode in an elevator a few days earlier.

"Well we don't have to wait very long right? I mean it's less than a year away. I don't really care what happens as long as you're with me, I'm cool."

Joy smiled and he couldn't help but smile back. He wondered, if when they were old, would she still have that magical effect on him? Tim continued his ravenous consumption of his steak and washed it down with his Dr. Pepper.

Joy didn't eat much as she loved the Earth's Milk. She swore by it and claimed she had toned up and had a ton more energy. Tim was of the opinion that working out two hours a day would accomplish the same thing.

Joy brought her milk everywhere with her and would put a single drop in whatever she had ordered and would smile as she sipped it. Her glass was almost empty and Tim shook his head.

"Man you can really put that away."

"What this?" she motioned with her glass.

"Yeah. I can drink about a shot glass worth and I am full. How can you drink so much?"

She grinned at him. "You always were a light weight."

"Yeah?"

She nodded. "Seems like I need more of it now, since I pretty much just drink it and not eat or drink anything else. Plus with all the working out I do, it just feels normal to me now."

Tim nodded. He would drink some milk every night but he enjoyed eating and his sodas, so would avoid it during the day. He didn't work out and he knew he should. Kuthanaga would be back at some point and if the last mission was any indicator of what he might be up against, he realized it would be in his best interest to get in better shape.

"I'm gonna start working out with you tomorrow."

Joy nodded. "Good."

"So Mrs. Christenson, did you get everything you wanted for Christmas this year?"

She smiled sweetly at him. "Oh yes, and much much more. And you Mr. Christenson. Did you get everything you wanted?"

"Yes ma'am, I did. Although I'm hoping for a special little present when we get back to the room."

She flashed him an evil grin. "Oh my, Mr. Christenson. You're so bad."

He nodded and wiped his mouth clean.

"Shall we retire to the room my dear?" he said in his best English accent.

"Why yes we shall…"

Joy went to stand up and her glass toppled towards the ground. Tim instinctively reached for it but was across the table. Suddenly the glass stopped and floated back to within Joy's reach. She snatched it up and looked around quickly to see if anyone saw. No one noticed and she exhaled slowly.

"Damn, you're getting good with that."

Tim nodded. Something bothered him. He didn't think about it, the ring just responded to his thoughts and it did the work. He had been working with the ring every day but he was still having a hard time making it do what he wanted. So why then did it work so flawlessly this time? He shrugged it off and focused on the more pressing issue.

"Pretty soon, I'll be able to do some seriously naughty things…"

"Yeah right. You try anything with the ring and I'll kick your ass."

Tim put both hands up in mock surrender. "OK, no ringy ring for sex."

She motioned for him to hurry along and they walked out hand in hand.

A few minutes later, they were inside their suite and Tim sat down on the couch and sighed. He had been thinking about his sister and watching Joy made him soul search.

"Penny for your thoughts." Joy said with a smile as she noticed his mood shift.

"I was thinking about Judy. Maybe you're right. I mean if we are gonna be fucked in a year or who knows what, why should I stay mad?"

Joy smiled and plopped down next to Tim.

"Well you know, she does live in Hawaii and they are behind us on time. It's still early enough to call and say Merry Christmas."

Tim nodded and stretched across and grabbed a cordless phone, which was nearby.

"Do you know the number?" Tim nodded. His sister had been at the same house for over ten years and he knew she'd never change her number unless something really weird happened.

He dialed and waited. On the third ring, he heard a young female voice answer. "Hello?"

"Yes, hey is your mom there? It's your Uncle Tim."

He heard a lot of distortion and what sounded like the phone dropping. A few moments later, he could hear the phone being picked up.

"Hello, this is Judy."

"Hey button nose. It's your baby brother." A long pause before he heard her breath again.

"Tim?"

"Yeah. I know, last person you'd expect to hear from right?"

"What do you want Tim? I don't have any money for you."

"No! I don't need that. That's not why I'm calling you. I just wanted to let you know that I'm clean, married, and happy. I wanted to say sorry for being an asshole all these years. I just wanted to say Merry Christmas."

He could hear her breakdown on the other end of the line and she sobbed. He felt his chest ache and as he glanced at Joy, who he noticed was beaming with pride. He wiped away the tear forming in his eye and he continued.

"So I don't want you to worry about me anymore. I'm a big boy and am handling things like you wouldn't believe."

She regained some of her composure. "Tim, are you serious? Is everything OK?"

"Yes, I promise everything is cool."

"I'm so glad. I've been worried about you. I love you and I miss you. I'm glad you got your life back together. How did you do it?"

He paused. "I saw the light. I hit bottom. Joy and I help each other stay clean now. I even have a pretty good job if you can believe it."

The front door made a noise and Tim stood up as he looked at Joy who shrugged.

"Hey sis, let me call you back. I need to take care of something real quick."

He hung up and stared at the door. He wondered who it was and suddenly he was afraid.

The door swung open and a thin man stood there with a wicked grin.

"Hello. You are Tim Christenson correct?" he had a pistol at his side and his eyes were wild.

"Nope. Afraid you got the wrong person man."

"Really? And she's not Joy Tsai? Or, should I say Joy Christenson? You know when you get married it's public record. I represent someone who is very interested in meeting you both. We can do this very quietly and painless or we can do this very loud and painful. Your choice."

Tim stepped in front of Joy cautiously.

"I don't know who you are, but leave her out of this."

"I really don't need to bring her. She wasn't on the list. You are the one I needed, but after seeing her, I think I'll bring her along for some fun. You look like you enjoy a good time don't cha babe?"

Joy flashed him a look of pure range and before Tim could say anything the man flew back and slammed through the wall. Tim turned and faced Joy.

"Did you?"

She grinned and nodded.

A low growl came from the hole in the wall.

"OK, fine by me. Let's play humans."

Joy looked at Tim. "Did he just say humans?"

Tim nodded and motioned for Joy to move back away from the hole.

"If he's one of them, they move fast."

The growl faded and suddenly the room was silent. Tim's heart was pounding in his chest and he heard a thunderous drumming in his ears. Joy was anxious as they waited. Time seemed to slow to a crawl as the anticipation mounted.

"Where is he?" asked Joy.

A crash again and Tim saw the drake easily stood eight feet tall hunched over tearing straight for Joy and Tim threw a punch wildly. He was ten feet away, but he felt contact with the beast who immediately flew back towards the new hole in the wall and suddenly he was suspended in the air. Joy had her hand up and Tim knew she was controlling him.

"What should we do?!"

Tim's head was racing. He was unsure if a fall would kill the drake and he knew they were very tough. Kuthanaga had told him a head shot would do.

Joy decided to toss him out the window and as she motioned towards it Tim reached out to try and stop her. He focused on the drake's head and Joy felt resistance. She pushed with everything she had and Tim felt a huge jerk and suddenly the drake's body flew through the window with a loud crash and they both heard a sickening thud as its head landed a few feet away from them. Tim had accidentally tore its head free.

"Fuck me!" he yelled.

"Wow! Great idea babe."

Tim looked at her in complete shock.

"Man o man. We need to get the hell out of here. If one of these came then there could be a whole shitload. I mean how will we know who is who. They can look like us."

Joy had a thought.

"Remember what Kuthanaga used to do to us with the clothing and everything?"

Tim nodded.

"Let's change the way we look and sneak out."

"Man, I don't know. It's one thing to grab shit and move stuff. How the fuck do we make ourselves look different?"

Joy thought about it.

"Let's try. I mean do you have any other ideas?"

Tim glanced down at the drake's head and shivered slightly.

"Fuck it, let's try."

Joy nodded and closed her eyes. She imagined her eyes a light shade of blue and after feeling what felt like a slight electrical current flow from her finger to her head, she opened her eyes.

"Did it work?" she asked.

Tim looked at her and grinned. "Wow, blue eyes…"

"Ok, come on. You try."

Tim's mind was a blank he couldn't think of anything.

"I don't know what to do. How'd you do it?"

"I just imagined my eyes were blue. Picture someone and imagine that you look like that person."

Tim nodded and thought and thought. He concentrated and he felt a strong electrical surge though his body and he convulsed slightly and shook.

"Ow!"

Joy's eyes widened and her mouth opened a bit.

"Dude, are you shitting me? What are you imagining?"

"Fuck, I don't know, I couldn't decide between Bruce Willis and Brad Pitt. How do I look?"

"Um, well I guess I can see some of that in there. At least you don't look like you."

She closed her eyes and Tim watched as she shifted forms and suddenly she was a slender well-built man. He looked somewhat familiar to Tim and he couldn't put his finger on it.

"What the fuck? A guy?"

Joy nodded.

"Yeah, since they are looking for me and you, they won't be looking for two dudes."

Tim nodded.

"Who is he?"

"Who?"

"The guy. You made yourself look like someone. Who is it?"

"One of our old neighbors."

Tim nodded. He knew exactly who it was.

"They guy you were attracted to?"

"Are we gonna go all jealous now, or can we just go?"

Tim shrugged.

"Fine, let's go. But we're gonna talk about this later."

Tim hurried for the front door and Joy followed him. They avoided the elevator and took the stairs. They calmly walked down the seemingly endless flights of stairs, which felt like it took forever until they hit the main casino floor. Tim noticed a few guys that were watching the front door and police were entering and making their way to the elevators. Obviously, the body had made some kind of an impact since the casino was buzzing more than usual.

Tim walked cautiously to the lounge area and Joy followed at a safe distance trying to look like they didn't know each other. They sat in different parts of the lounge and casually watched as the police disappeared. Joy struck up a conversation with a woman and Tim was amazed at how quickly Joy had managed to get in good with her.

Tim wanted a drink bad and realized he had left his supply of the Earth's Milk in the room. Joy had done a good job with her disguise and even her purse had shifted into to a backpack. He hoped Kuthanaga would understand the situation and not be too upset about leaving the milk behind.

A few people would pass by and look at Tim and there was always a mixture of expressions on their face. He glanced at the large mirror in front of him and nearly spilled his drink. To say he was ugly was an understatement. Obviously, the worst features of Bruce Willis and Brad Pitt had made their way into his Frankenstein disguise.

"Fuck me."

A man who was also sitting at the bar near Tim noticed him and grinned.

"Down on your luck too?"

Tim nodded.

"Yup."

"Well you know what they say?"

Tim shook his head.

"No, what's that?"

"What happens in Vegas, stays in Vegas. Just leave that bad joo joo behind you my friend and stay positive."

Tim nodded. He saw Joy get up and walk with the woman. As they headed out the front door, Tim noticed two men glanced at them and then looked down at their phones. One shook his head and they kept scanning the area. Tim decided to make his move.

"Hey man, you know any good strip clubs?"

The man nodded. "Fuck yeah I do. I know one that's even open tonight."

"Show me and the first two lap dances are on me."

"Deal!"

The man got up, dropped a twenty on the bar, and headed towards the exit. Tim walked with him and as they got closer to the two men, Tim could feel his chest ache. He was sweating and he made eye contact with one of the men and for a brief moment, he swore the eyes flashed reptilian. He played it off and said, "Man I need a lap dance like you wouldn't believe."

"Well I have a spot that is killer!"

They walked a few more steps and they were outside. Tim could see Joy a couple blocks down waiting for him. She had obviously ditched her friend who was nowhere to be seen.

The man started to walk in the opposite direction and Tim quickly reached into his jacket and pulled out a hundred.

"Oh shit man. I forgot I need to do something. Here's for the lap dances. Enjoy bro."

"Cool man. Hope your luck picks up. Merry Christmas."

"Me too. Merry Christmas."

Tim walked on calmly until he was next to Joy. They then walked on for another twenty minutes until they felt safe.

"What do we do now?" asked Joy.

"Well, I think we need to find us a spot to lay low and wait for Kuthanaga to call."

Joy nodded and they found a motel room, which Tim paid cash for and they sat on the bed and Joy leaned into him.

"Well at least you made up with your sister."

Tim nodded. Joy had shifted back to her normal appearance and it took Tim a few minutes to figure out how to go back to his normal look. Once he did, he realized he had a huge headache.

"I'm thrashed. Let's get some sleep."

Joy hugged him and they laid down.

"I love you."

"And I love you."
Tim kissed her and then they drifted off together.

Chapter 27 – Personal Matter

December 26th 2011 – New York 2:07 am

Richard waited until the man was finished.

"So what you're telling me is that somehow two humans took out Briel? Not only one of our best hunters but also my fucking nephew?"

A long pause.

"I asked you a question."

"Yes sir. We were able to get our men into the room and clean up the body before too many people saw it. There were a few with camera phones but nothing we can't handle. We have all of their belongings that were in the room as well."

"Why was Briel alone in the room with them in the first place? That isn't standard procedures. Any ideas on how they were able to take him out?"

"It was his orders. We were to maintain control of the lobby and outside perimeter. When his body landed outside we sent a team up. The police arrived and we had to move quickly. We have his head and will send it to the Quinuks to have them record his ending."

"Fine. I want to know the minute you have any information. Please, do not let me down again."

He slammed the phone down and anger roared in him like a star set to go supernova. He checked himself, took a deep long breath, and slowly exhaled. His wife was standing there silently and he faced her.

"Did I hear correctly that Briel is dead?"

He nodded.

"Who did this?"

"Humans. Possibly Annukai as well. I'll know more once the memories are downloaded."

She nodded. He studied her, no emotions were visible, and that alone gave him pause. Briel was one of her favorites and the lack of emotion was troubling. When a female drake was without emotion, it meant one of two things. Either she was very close to causing a lot of property damage as well as physical to him and anyone near or she was emotionally shut down. Both were bad.

"I shall deal with this matter personally love. Do not be too disturbed by it. Briel brought this upon himself in a manor. He did not go with a team as he should have."

She nodded.

"I will leave it in your capable hands husband. For now."

As she walked away he noted and filed away her threat. It was a telling sign that she was closer to the blood bath than shutting her emotions down.

Richard picked up his phone and dialed a number.

After one ring. "Yes."

"It's me. I need to get to Vegas now. Please make sure the plane is prepped and ready when I get there."

"It will be ready."

He realized the human was more of an issue than he had been the day before and now it was personal.

Chapter 28 – Discoveries

December 27th 2011 – Las Vegas 12:45 pm

Tim woke up and saw Joy staring at him.

"Finally awake?"

Tim didn't know why but he felt tired and drained. He reached to his side where he normally kept his Earth's Milk and realized he wasn't at the Bellagio.

"Shit."

"What?"

Tim sat up slowly and rubbed his eyes. The memories of the previous night came back into clear focus.

"Nothing I was just hoping that last night was some tripped out nightmare. Guess not huh?"

"Nope. It happened. All our stuff lost. *Again.*"

Tim grinned. "Yeah. Well it could've been worse."

Joy nodded and walked to the bathroom and ran the water for a moment. Tim stood and stretched. He was thirsty and was going to ask joy about her Earth's Milk when she walked back to the bed with a water bottle shifting to the familiar white liquid.

"Figured you'd want some. I went out earlier and grabbed some supplies. Nothing special, just some water and a couple of breakfast burritos from a roach coach."

Tim nodded and realized he was upset about not having access to the Earth's Milk and it must have been obvious to Joy as well.

"I wonder what would happen if we stopped drinking it? I mean go straight cold turkey on it."

Joy shrugged and took a sip and handed it to Tim.

"Who knows? All I know is, it tastes great and I don't have to eat if I don't want to and I have energy for days."

Tim nodded and something inside him was nervous. He suddenly knew he was addicted to the liquid and he didn't want to find out what kind of withdraw symptoms he'd get if he quit. He had been addicted to many different kinds of drugs and each had their own form of hell he'd been to. The last thing he wanted was to add another painful experience to his lengthy list. He would have to find a way to keep a small amount on him at all times, especially now that he knew they'd be on the run until they met back up with Kuthanaga. He knew Kuthanaga had said there were no withdrawal effects and yet he wasn't sure.

"So what now?" Joy asked.

Tim thought for a moment and was at a loss. He wondered where Kuthanaga was and he knew he should stay somewhere near and also needed a way to warn him. It was more than likely that the suite was being watched and Tim didn't want to put Kuthanaga's skills to the test.

"We need to make sure Kuthanaga doesn't go to the room. We need to leave a warning somehow."

"Maybe Monica at the front desk can help?"

"Couldn't hurt to try."

"We're gonna jet out of this room after we call though, so get ready to bail."

Joy smiled and pointed at a small plastic bag and then her purse.

Tim nodded.

He walked to the phone and dialed the Bellagio. A couple of rings and he heard.

"Thank you for calling the world famous Bellagio, how may I help you?"

"Yes, I'd like to speak with Monica Crawford please."

"One moment."

A few seconds went by and a familiar voice spoke.

"This is Monica."

"Hey Monica, it's me Tim Christenson."

"Tim! Are you OK? Was anyone hurt?"

Tim paused for a second to figure out how to handle the question.

"Hurt? What are you talking about?" He decided it was best to lie.

"Your suite was demolished and it looked like something really crazy went on in there. We reviewed the tapes and saw you and your wife enter and some strange man forced his way into the suite. Then the tape went blank. It was the weirdest thing. We had a lot of complaints and when security went to check it out they discovered the destruction. Then the police showed up and locked it all down and wouldn't tell us anything."

172

"Well we're OK. I think he was looking for Desmond. We talked and took off. Listen that's why I'm calling. I'm worried about Desmond. Are there still two guys dressed all in black with earpieces and red ties on? One white guy and one black? They're pretty big."

A brief pause and a hushed "Yes. They've been here since I got in at 7am. Who are they?"

"I think those guys are looking for Desmond. I know this is probably not cool, but could you make sure if Desmond comes back that you tell him that his employee is sick and called into work. Don't use my name, just say that."

"Do I want to know why these guys are looking for Desmond?"

"I wish I knew. But I'm worried and hope you can help us out."

"If I see him I'll pass the message on for you. So you guys are OK?"

"Yeah, we're cool. Thanks. We owe ya."

"Be careful."

"We will."

Tim hung up the phone and he looked at Joy.

"So we gonna go disguised again?"

Joy shrugged.

"Up to you Mr. Bruce Pitt…"

"Damn, that really sucked. OK, I have a better idea now."

Tim focused and closed his eyes. His form shifted and he aged. He was bald at the top and had gray sideburns and a wild beard. Tim's clothing shifted as well.

Joy rubbed her chin and waited until he opened his eyes.

"OK, I give up. Who are you supposed to be?"

"My uncle. Joe Christenson. We called him Goat."

"For obvious reasons."

Joy's face frowned a bit as she concentrated. She didn't close her eyes and her transformation was much faster and smoother than Tim's was. She suddenly was an older woman with solid white hair rosy checks and a warm weathered tan.

"Who?"

"Don't know. Some woman I used to see gardening outside my brother's house all the time."

"Works for me. Let's hit the road."

Joy nodded and they opened the door and walked outside. "Where to?"

"I want to withdraw the max for today and try to get as much cash on me as possible so we can get completely off the grid. If they were able to track us with the wedding license, then it shouldn't be too difficult for them to get to the bank account. The card might get us busted, but we need to hit it at least once more."

"I know a way we can get enough money for us to hang with for a while."

"Gambling?"

Joy nodded.

"I don't know. I think we can lay low easy enough. I know I have about a G on me right now. I can get another $300 from the machine. Thirteen should last us for a bit. If we don't hear from Kuthanaga when it starts running low, then cool. Otherwise, I'd like to just keep moving and lay low."

Joy took his arm and smiled warmly at him. "OK. We'll play little old couple for now and just chill."

"Hey do you know where the nearest ATM is?"

"I saw one a couple of blocks away from the Bellagio. There's got to be a ton of them. All the casinos have em."

Tim smiled at her.

"That's the last place I want to bring you. The one you saw was outside?"

She nodded.

"Fucker."

He smiled. They continued to walk back towards the Bellagio and they made sure to slow their pace. Joy even threw a little twist in her step, which almost made Tim burst out in laughter.

"Dude, that's not how old people walk. You look gimped."

"Shut up! Maybe that's how I walk you know."

They arrived at the ATM and Tim slid his card into the machine and entered his code. He waited and the screen went blank for a few seconds and then displayed his balance. He had $17,537.98 and he shook his head. He had never had spare money laying in an account before and it frustrated him that he wasn't going to be able to get out all of the money. He tried to withdraw and suddenly his card ejected.

"What the fuck?"

He slid the card in again and punched in his pin. The menu came up again and he tried to withdraw $300. It waited and a small hourglass spun on the screen.

"Damn thing is laggy."

Joy was keeping watch, she noticed a black Cadillac Escalade with black tinted windows slow down on the end of the block, and quickly looking on the other end of the block, she saw another matching SUV. She grabbed Tim's arm and he knew what it meant. The cash came out as did his ATM and he jammed it into his pocket and slowly turned to face Joy. As he did, he glanced at the end of the block and saw that the vehicle hadn't moved. Why were they waiting?

"What do we do?"

"Looks like you get you casino wish. Let's get inside and mix with any crowd and change real quick."

She nodded. She looked up and saw a man get out of the vehicle in front of them and he slowly approached. They made a quick right into the casino and it was almost empty.

"Fuckin' economy sucks!" Tim hissed. They walked deeper into the casino and Joy glanced back and saw the large man walk in behind them. He was a good hundred feet behind them and she recalled how quickly the drake from the previous night moved. She was ready to strike.

"What now?" she asked.

"Play a slot machine."

Tim sat at one and slid a $20 in it. Joy kissed his baldhead. "Good luck honey." she said as she did the same at the machine across from him.

The man walked over and stood next to Tim. He was close enough for Tim to hear his breath. Tim was calm, unnaturally calm as he turned to face him.

"You need something big boy?" Tim asked the man. The man stood nearly seven feet tall and his hair was a brilliant red. He removed his shades and stared at Tim.

"Yeah, what's your name old man?"

"Joe is my name. People call me Goat. Why?"

"Well Goat you have an ID on you?"

"Why? You the police or something?"

"No."

"Then fuck off. Unless you the police or the law you don't have the right to see shit."

At that moment, two more large men walked through the entrance.

Joy was starting to get nervous and she glanced quickly at Tim who seemed so calm. What was he was doing, she wondered.

"Fuck the ID. Let's go old man."

The drake went to grab Tim's arm and Tim was ready. He swung and connected hard with the man's chest, which sent him flying towards the two men who had just entered.

He saw them easily dodge his body and he transformed and flipped in midair and landed easily. He grinned at Tim and set to charge.

Joy had a feeling of what Tim was going to do next. She didn't know how she knew but his plan was in her mind. She focused on the slot machine next to him and strained. As the large man streaked towards Tim, he screamed out in pain as he suddenly collided with a machine that Joy had launched at him. Tim's leg was nicked by a piece of cable, which trailed behind the machine, as he stood in between the row of slots.

The two men watched as their college was slammed across the room with the machine lying on top of him. His body didn't move. They set to charge and one pulled a gun and fired a single shot so fast that Tim didn't see him move. He heard Joy scream out in pain and saw her fall to the ground.

"No!" He felt rage well up within him and he glared at the man who suddenly was moving in slow motion. Tim didn't know what he was thinking but suddenly the room was in motion and it seemed like everything was exploding towards the men. The room was suddenly lit up like the sun itself was shining

176

inside. Dust filled the room and Tim struggled to find Joy. He lifted her up and saw that she was unconscious. He glanced at the front of the casino, there was a huge gaping hole, and he was standing in a large empty room. Everything that was around him a few seconds ago was now outside.

He carried Joy towards the rear of the casino and something told him that there would be more. He made his way to the kitchen and Joy moaned. He saw blood on her face and his heart was pounding.

"What happened?"

"You've been shot."

"I what?"

"You've been shot."

Tim pushed on and saw an exit. There were many people now scrambling around. The explosion had brought life to the casino.

"Can you stand?"

Joy stood and wiped the blood from her face. Tim could see the wound and it looked like a cut.

"I think it missed you."

"I'm fucking bleeding! It didn't miss me."

"No, I mean it didn't kill you and it looks like a cut."

Joy looked around and saw a towel hanging and she held it to her head.

Sirens blared in the distance.

"Do you think you can shift again?"

Joy closed her eyes, her form slowly shifted, and she groaned.

"My head hurts."

"Hang tight baby. There's a group heading out the back. Let's go with em."

Tim saw a man which he focused on, and shifted his clothing similar to him, Joy noticed the clothing, and she shifted hers as well.

Tim held her arm and he could feel her weight on him as he gave her support.

They mixed with the group who went outside and when they made it out Tim could see a few more of the men just watching their group. A few tense moments went by before an ambulance and two police cars arrived. Some of the crowd pointed at Joy who was still bleeding and Tim noticed he was also bleeding. Tim looked up and saw that the men had disappeared.

The police asked a few questions, Tim, and Joy both gave similar stories that they were working and heard a loud explosion and suddenly realized they were hurt. The paramedic examined Joy and told her she would need stitches and may have a concussion. When he examined Tim, he also said Tim would need stitches.

Tim and Joy were loaded up in the ambulance and as it drove off it passed Richard who was standing outside the casino with six men. He watched the ambulance drive by.

"Should we follow it?" asked one of the men who watched the ambulance pass.

"No. If they are on it, it will not matter. I will get to them later. But this…" He motioned to the large hole in the front of the casino and turned to see massive amounts of damage to buildings across the street.

"This is downright interesting. I want my men found and I want to see the tapes as well."

The men split up and started working.

Richard frowned. A mess this large was going to be difficult to hide. He shook his head and scanned the area. He saw a shimmer in the corner of his eyes and he spun quickly to examine it. A small beautiful woman was there just standing. She was looking around and their eyes met. He watched as her eyes widened as if she recognized him. He walked towards her and she bolted. She moved too fast to be human.

"Annukai."

He was gaining on her and a moment before he could lock his hands around her she simply vanished like a misty apparition.

"This just gets better and better. Who were you? Not Kuthanaga. He wouldn't have ran."

Chapter 29 – Fear
December 27th 2011 – Bimini 4:16 pm

Xanari had relocated with Rachel and done as Kuthanaga had asked. Everything worked out well and there were no incidents with the travel. They had been in Bimini for a few days and Xanari had been keeping her mirrors working hard. She had made it, as far west as San Francisco and Seattle and the furthest point east had been Colorado. Some of her mirrors were flying to the east coast while others were doubling back and double-checking specially marked humans.

Rachel seemed to be enjoying the weather and her dreaming continued on a daily basis.

Nothing out of the ordinary had occurred in the small town. Xanari was wondering why Kuthanaga had selected that particular town for them to be in. She was about to contact Kuthanaga when one of her mirrors interrupted her thoughts and Xanari focused in on what it was seeing. The mirror had come across a bizarre scene where several drakes were entering a casino. She could see the shimmer of their true forms that looked like ghostly faint outlines. The mirror took great care to not be seen. Suddenly a large crash and a gunshot. A single moment passed before a large explosion rocked the area. The casino entrance had been blasted open and a small bald man was standing alone she noticed his form shimmered slightly and watched as he lifted an elderly woman up who Xanari noticed was also shimmering slightly while bleeding from her head.

A few minutes passed and another group of drakes showed up and one man stood in front of them. Even though he was disguised, she could see his true form and there was no doubt as Xanari's heart tried to jump out of her chest when she recognized who the man was. It was the drake from the dreams. He motioned and the majority of the drakes entered the building. He was about to do the same when he suddenly spun and faced her. The mirror ran and Xanari knew she only had one chance to remove just the single mirror without disrupting the others. The strain was great but she was able to do it just as the drake overtook the mirror.

She was breathing hard and noticed that Rachel was staring at her.

"Xanari? Are you OK?"

Xanari shook her head.

"I just saw him."

"The beast?"

"Yes."

"I just had a dream about it and was trying to tell you. Sorry, there wasn't more warning. I dreamed about the skinny man and his lady friend as well. The beast is after them and he'll catch them if we don't do something."

Xanari was confused. "I thought we saw them with Kuthanaga when the Convergence happens. Why then should we be concerned this early if you've already seen the future."

"Correction. A *possible* future. Things are changing very quickly and I don't know why. Something is happening and making the dreams more chaotic. I have a very strong feeling though that if we do not act; something bad is going to happen."

Xanari nodded and focused on Kuthanaga. She could feel his presence and she tried to connect.

Yes Xanari. Have you witnessed an event yet?

No, but there is news. Rachel has had a vision about the human who is aiding you as well as the Draconian. I have also seen with my own eyes his pursuit of two elderly humans, which shimmered. Something very intense is going on in Vegas and my mirror was almost slain. I barely pulled her back in time.

Are you sure? There was a sense of urgency in his voice.

Yes. The drake saw my mirror and gave chase. Before that there was a large explosion and an older human stood alone in the wreckage and then carried the human woman.

Did you see the explosion?

Yes.

Share it with me.

Xanari focused on the memory and as Kuthanaga watched, his heart pounded in his chest as he saw the familiar form of Richard. Anger welled in him. He cursed and blamed himself for being careless. Xanari could feel this through their connection and didn't say anything.

Did you notice anything odd about the explosion?

She thought about it and realized there weren't any flames or fire from the explosion.

I would say the old man did it. Though how, I cannot say.

I can. He used Annukai energy.

How?

Kuthanaga wondered how Tim could generate so much energy. It more than surpassed his wildest expectations.

The human is Tim and the woman is Joy. I added in Beyandee to their wedding rings. I expected them to discover how to use the rings to manipulate simple things and communicate between each other, but not anywhere near the level you saw. It seems we have underestimated the humans' abilities. They are closer to us than we thought. What of the vision?

Xanari reached out and held Rachel's hand.

"Rachel can you show Kuthanaga your vision? Just close your eyes and think about it."

Rachel could sense a strange sensation of different thoughts in her mind and a wild electrical sensation at the base of her skull with a cool tingling running the length of her spine to her tailbone.

"S-sure."

Rachel did as she was told and Kuthanaga saw a hospital.

Chapter 30 – Closing In
December 27th 2011 – Las Vegas 1:25 pm

The ambulance brought Tim and Joy to the local emergency room where they were admitted and attended to. Tim was stitched up quickly and he waited impatiently while they examined Joy.

The Nurse Practitioner, which examined Joy, was a tall skinny man with dark skin and deep purplish gums. His breath smelled winter-fresh as if he had just brushed his teeth. The teeth were too white for Joy and his dark skin made their whiteness even more brilliant. His hands were cold and strong. He was gentle with her but her head felt like it had been hit with a mallet.

"My name is Jeffry Singh and I'm going to be taking care of you. So what happened to you?" he asked while he cleaned the wound.

"I really couldn't tell you. One minute I'm working and the next I'm outside with a friend who told me I was hurt in some kind of explosion."

"Well, you have a nasty little cut here. I am going to need to numb you up and stitch it up. You Ok with that?"

Joy slowly nodded. "Yeah."

He worked quickly and was done suturing her within twenty minutes. The twenty minutes felt like an eternity to her. She was more than paranoid and she watched the NP like a hawk, ready to strike out if she needed to. The name she had given to them was Jamie Grant, which was the name of her first grade best friend.

Joy wondered how Tim was and she was still trembling when the NP finished.

"There you go. Good as new. How are you feeling? Any dizziness? Headaches?"

"No, just was sore around the area." Joy lied. She wasn't concerned about any headaches. She wanted to find Tim and get out fast.

"OK, well usually we like to keep head trauma in for 24 hours for observation."

"I'd rather not. I don't have any insurance and I need to take care of my kids at home. They'll be home from school soon and I need to be there."

He shrugged. "That's fine. If you understand you are waving treatment, you are free to go. Do you have a ride?"

She nodded. "Yes my friend will pick me up."

"Fine, I see you have paperwork still to finish filling out. I'll have another document for you to sign as well. Hang on a sec; I'll have one of the nurses bring it to you. You take care OK?"

Joy smiled and watched as he walked out of the room. She could see a couple of police officers down the hall and she wondered again, where Tim was.

A few minutes passed and the door opened. Tim walked in quickly with a slight limp looking like the little old man.

"Ready to blow this joint?" he asked with a grin.

She nodded.

"OK, shift and let's slid out."

Tim closed his eyes and suddenly he was a younger man with strong features and nice clothing. He opened his eyes and looked at Joy.

"How's this?"

She smiled. "You're getting better at it."

He nodded.

She focused and her head throbbed badly. She shifted into a young girl with features similar to the ones that Tim had.

"Ah you're my daughter? Who's yer daddy?"

She flashed Tim a look.

"I can't believe you're still cracking fucking jokes."

Tim nodded as he helped her get off the gurney. When she stood up she nearly fell to the floor. Tim grabbed her and lifted her slightly.

"I got ya. Take it easy."

Tim quickly glanced out the door and saw that the coast seemed clear. They walked outside and headed for the exit. As they got near it Tim saw several large men approaching the sliding doors. He leaned against the wall and held Joy there. The men walked past them and Tim avoided eye contact and focused on his breathing and heartbeat. He worked at staying calm.

When they passed he turned to head to the door. A man was there staring intently at Tim. The man was wearing an expensive suit and a deep blood red tie. He saw that the man noticed his slight limp.

The man sniffed once and smiled. Tim looked at the man and something inside of Tim screamed for him to run.

"Tim? Is that you Tim?" asked the man.

"No, my name is not Tim. I don't know who you think I am. I'm here with my daughter."

"Joy." The man regarded both of them with a grin. Tim thought for a moment of lashing out and running when suddenly he felt the icy cold end of a pistol on the back of his head.

"Let's not do a repeat of the casino. You try something like that here and a whole lot of innocent people are going to get hurt."

Tim was confused. How could this man know who they were?

"I can tell by the expression on your face that you're wondering how I know it's you beneath those disguises? Well one thing is the same. You scent. Your blood scent to be more specific. Once I know it, I know you. You left enough back at the casino."

Tim wondered if he was fast enough if he could get the gun to shift off his head and aim it at the man.

"Tim we have much to discuss."

The man behind Tim lowered the gun to the small of his back and pressed in hard. He could see another man who took position behind Joy. Tim glanced at Joy who was pale and breathing heavy.

"Yeah? Like what exactly?"

"Well for starters. How does a human shift his form? How does a human do the type of damage you did back at the casino? And finally how did a couple of humans manage to kill Briel?"

"Briel? You mean the guy who attacked us?"

"Yes."

"Tell your butt-boys to drop their guns and I'd be happy to show you."

"Tsk, tsk, tsk… And we were just starting to develop a dialog. Threats? Tim, I think you should really take notice of the precarious position you are in. Where is Kuthanaga?"

"Kutha what?"

"Fine Tim. You want to play games? Good. I like games. I have a bunch I can't wait to play with you. Let's go."

He turned to lead the way when he saw a faint blur. He turned to look at Tim and Joy who had simply vanished.

A low growl filled his throat and he bit so hard on his mouth that blood filled it instantly.

"What the hell?" One of the men said.

"Where'd they go?" asked another.

Richard shook his head and motioned for the men to follow him.

"What are your orders?" one asked.

"We're done here. I need the inventory of the Bellagio suite examined immediately. I want this checked out as well."

He pulled a water bottle filled with the Tim's Earth's Milk in it.

The larger of the two men collected the bottle and walked back outside. Richard took a couple of breaths and shook his arms quickly.

Several miles away a confused Tim and Joy stood on the side of a highway and quickly shielded their eyes from the bright sun. Kuthanaga stood there examining them.

"What happened?" asked Tim.

"I caught up with you and brought you here."

"How?"

"I carried both of you as I bent time."

"You bent time?"

Kuthanaga nodded and positioned his hand over Joy's head. He examined her memories of the time that he was gone and glossed over their intimate moments and just focused on the confrontations. One fact Joy was unaware of was that the bullet was flying true. Somehow, she had managed to block the bullet and send it on a different trajectory, which caused only minor injury to her. He nodded and motioned over her wound, which quickly healed, and only a faint pink scar was barely visible as the hair filled back in quickly.

Joy sighed and was happy the pain had passed.

Kuthanaga also scanned Tim and when he arrived at the conflict in the casino, he paused and stared at Tim.

"Amazing."

"What?" asked Tim.

"What you did at the casino should not be possible. In fact, your confrontation with the drake in the suite should not have been so easy for you. The modifications I did to your rings would account for some of the object manipulations. But, even the camouflage you created should not be possible. There's something I am unaware of going on here."

Tim shrugged.

"Man, this is your gig. We just stumbled onto how to use the rings and to honest. Most of the time I don't even know what the hell I'm doing."

Kuthanaga motioned over Tim's leg and Tim felt the warmth spread across his leg and knew that it was healed good as new.

"Well we have time to figure it out. For now we need to get across country to Bimini."

"What the hell is Bimini?" asked Tim.

"It's an island near Florida," answered Joy.

"She is correct. And since I see that our position here is compromised, I need to move you to a safer location until the next mission."

Tim nodded. He noticed Kuthanaga was studying him.

"What's up?"

Kuthanaga waved the question away and motioned for them to walk with him.

"Hey Kuthanaga."

Kuthanaga turned to face Tim.

"Yes."

"Thanks for doing what you did with the rings."

Kuthanaga nodded. He was troubled. The rings were modified, that was true, but they were modified with only a small amount of the conductor. The rings were of the right material, but there should have been no way the humans were doing what they were. He had put the material in so he would be better able to communicate over great distances regardless if the phone was working. He was perplexed by the sudden rapid advancement of the manipulation of energy. He wondered what the drakes were thinking about the humans.

"Oh shit!"

Kuthanaga again faced Tim.

"What?"

"The Earth's Milk… It was either destroyed or they have it now."

Kuthanaga smiled.

"It doesn't matter. It was only a matter of time before they got their hands on it anyway. Do not be alarmed. I have more for us all to use once we get to Bimini."

Tim was relieved. He was doing the best he could and felt completely exhausted.

They walked on for another few minutes.

"Hey Kuth, sorry to keep interrupting your thoughts."

"You are not. What is it Tim?"

"Why we walking? Where's the ride?"

"We are almost to her."

"Her?"

Kuthanaga smiled as he saw a slight shimmer.

"Yes, her…" Kuthanaga pointed at the shimmer, which Tim hadn't seen, but Joy had.

"I wondered what that was." said Joy.

Kuthanaga noted that Joy was becoming very sensitive and was impressed.

Xanari materialized and she smiled softly.

"You were able to save them?"

Kuthanaga smiled back. "Yes, thanks to you and Rachel. The timing was a little close for my liking. But yes, we were successful."

Xanari examined Tim and Joy and looked confused.

Kuthanaga, I can understand the woman, but why him?

Young one, it doesn't completely matter the aura. Some humans can be measured by their actions as a whole. This one reminds me of a human I knew long ago. That human was a dear close friend of mine and I have a feeling this one will not let me down. He has already come a long way in a short time. I'm sure there are some you have come across which defy the superficial scans?

Xanari thought of the woman who protected her children.

Yes, you are correct.

Tim walked forward and said, "Hi, my name is Tim Christenson and this is my wife Joy."

"Hello. My name is Xanari."

Xanari regarded Joy and smiled. Something about the human felt familiar and comfortable.

"Kuthanaga, we should be going. I am uncomfortable this close to drakes in pursuit."

"You have nothing to worry about. They will not be trying to pursue. They are not foolish or wasteful. But, I do need to get back my mirror is reporting that something is happening and I want to be there. Tim, Joy, please take Xanari's hand. I will be with you soon enough."

Kuthanaga started to fade out. Joy looked at Tim and he shrugged. They took Xanari's hand and Tim was amazed by how smooth her skin was. Joy also noticed this and was about to say something when suddenly the air seemed very thin and Joy fought to take a breath. Tim had felt a sensation similar when he phased with Kuthanaga in New York and was getting used to it. Joy was lightheaded, her eyes were filled with brilliant flashing lights, and she was afraid she would pass out. She looked around and the place she was previously at was no more. They were in a misty blackness with shades of colors shifting in from all sides. Brilliant shades of blue swam around them as if it were a living thing. Light broke through, distinct shapes started forming, and Joy felt herself slipping out of consciousness. Suddenly she felt the grip of Xanari tighten and it was all she needed to snap back to focus. A few seconds passed and suddenly the three of them were standing on a beautiful beach of white sand. The water was the most amazing blue that Joy had ever seen.

Tim whistled and looked around.

"Man this is crazy."

Xanari smiled. "Wait until the Convergence. You haven't seen beautiful yet."

"Convergence?" asked Joy.

Xanari caught herself and wondered how much Kuthanaga had told them.

"What do you know of it?"

"Well I know what the word means. I'd like to know about what your definition is."

Xanari looked down and felt foolish.

"It is not my place to discuss it. I have said too much already and I must speak with Kuthanaga before I can say anymore."

Tim laughed.

"No worries. I'm smart enough to know that somehow you were able to let Kuthanaga know we were in trouble. So I ain't got no problems. Thanks for that by the way."

Xanari liked his spontaneity and nodded. "It was my pleasure to help."

Rachel walked up and examined Tim and Joy.

"It was my pleasure as well! It's good to finally meet you in the flesh. The lord knows I've been seeing a lot of you lately in my dreams."

Tim had seen and been through too much to even begin to question what the cheerful woman said. He took it completely at face value where Joy paused and said.

"Dreams?"

Rachel nodded. "Yep. Been dreaming about you folks for the better part of two weeks now. Never knew who you were before meeting Xanari and Kuthanaga."

Joy smiled.

"That's cool. So you're kinda psychic then?"

Rachel nodded.

Tim was exhausted and he looked at Xanari.

"Is there somewhere we can rest? I'm really tired."

Xanari nodded and motioned for them to follow.

"So what are you guys doing here?" Joy asked as they all walked. The wind was warm and the fresh ocean breeze lifted Joy's spirits.

"Waiting for some event to happen." Xanari made a point to walk slowly as she could see that both Joy and Tim had been through a lot. The fatigue was apparent on Tim. Joy, on the other hand was very good at hiding her feelings.

"Like what? If you don't mind me asking?"

They passed colorful brightly painted houses and Tim couldn't help but smile. They seemed so vibrant and happy.

"We don't know. Kuthanaga relocated us from Utah to here and told us to keep an eye out and we'd know when it happened."

Joy nodded.

"Kuthanaga is like that huh? He asks you to do something and then you find out when you find out. How long have you known him?"

Xanari approached a small purple building with the paint showing some wear and tear from the elements and opened the front door. It creaked and groaned slightly.

"Hmmm. I've known Kuthanaga for a little over two thousand human years."

"Human years?"

"Yes, you're counting and time tracking is very basic to Annukai. We have a universal time that is more abstract than your linear form. For example, we Annukai have ten stages of our life. I am just entering my fifth cycle. Kuthanaga is on his ninth. The tenth is when we make preparations to rejoin the universe. We do not track these stages by days, years, or hours. They are by spiritual growth. Some take longer than others do and they stay for long periods. Annukai rejoin the universe either by choice or accidentally."

"So then you guys don't have birthdays or holidays?"

"We do have celebrations on predetermined times, but they usually coincide with celestial events and we prepare well in advance. The parties can last for what you would call months. We have three large celebrations, a birth of a new Annukai, the joining of two Annukai and the merging of an Annukai with the universe."

"Wow."

Xanari had entered the building and inside was a little small but when Tim saw a couch he was content to collapse into it and immediately he started snoring.

"I see Tim sleeps easily?"

Joy nodded and smiled.

"We've had a rough day."

190

"I am sorry for your pain. Is there anything I can do?"

Joy shook her head. "No. Kuthanaga already healed us up."

The sun shone through the window, the light reflections danced around on the walls, and ceiling and Joy scanned the room and saw there was a small wind chime hanging on the far window dancing in the breeze. The shifting shells reflected the sunlight and she noticed her arms at her side were so heavy. She sat next to Tim and hugged him.

Xanari watched over them until Joy too began to snore faintly.

Rachel was quiet the whole time and she saw Xanari head back outside. She followed and when they were far enough where it was safe to speak and not disturb Tim and Joy Rachel asked, "So what do you think?"

Xanari took a deep breath.

"I think this is a calm that will soon break into a maelstrom."

Rachel nodded.

"You have good instincts. I also feel the same."

Rachel and Xanari stood there looking at the horizon and the only sound was the faint whispers of the wind as it gently played with their hair.

Chapter 31 – Initial Results
December 27th 2011 – Maniwaki, Canada 5:47 pm

John had been diligent in keeping the area clear of anyone and patiently waited for Tallbrother to let him know when it would be OK to share the liquid discovery with others. He had been drinking it for days and he was amazed. The taste never grew old and it always changed. Additionally, he felt stronger, warmer, and more alert and had an overwhelming sense of wellbeing.

John was just arriving back in town when he saw the chief and made eye contact with him. Tallbrother waved for him to park and talk with him. John was excited. He hoped it was information from the scientist friends of Tallbrother.

He jogged over to the chief who had a serious look upon his face.

"John. I have heard back from my friends."

Something in his tone and posture made John uneasy. He suddenly realized he had been drinking a lot of the liquid and hoped the chief wasn't going to tell him that it was toxic.

"Bad news?"

"In a manner of speaking yes."

John's heart was beating.

"Please tell me. Is it poison?"

The chief shook his head.

"No, no. Nothing like that. The scientists have no idea what the liquid is. It changed constantly depending on who was looking at it. They have determined one thing though. It is alive."

"Alive?"

"Yes. That is how it changes its flavor. My friend Stacy thinks the liquid has some sort of intelligence and knows what we desire and changes itself to match that."

John didn't know how to respond. It wasn't poisonous. He did not see anything wrong with it being alive. He suddenly shrugged.

"Well it's safe then?"

"As far as they could tell, yes."

"So why are you scared?"

"Not scared. Concerned. I don't know what this liquid could do. Then Stacy also told me it has more nutritional content in a drop than a bottle of the vitamin drinks. It contained substances in it that they had never seen before. It was almost alien she said."

"It came from the Earth."

Tallbrother nodded. He had been to the site many times while waiting for the results and the liquid seemed to come from deep within the rock. A rock, which had been there for as long as the chief could remember.

"Yes. The question before us now is this. Do we share this discovery with the outside world? Or do we keep it for the tribe and other tribes? You know what they will do with it if we give it to the outsiders."

John thought about it and stared at the chief.

"I would think we should share with all. The more we share the better."

The chief thought about it and it seemed like the weight of the world rested on his shoulders. He knew it was just a matter of time before it got out. He was fearful of what it would mean. The Kitigan Zibi didn't mind tourists and outsiders visiting, but he knew this would bring waves of greedy vile people who would flood the area like hungry wolves.

"I think you are right. We shall call everyone together and discuss this as a group. Whatever we decide shall be the path we'll walk."

Kuthanaga sat nearby and listened intently. He watched Tallbrother and he nodded to himself. He understood why the chief was apprehensive and he had good reason to feel that way. Human nature was far from what it once had been and Kuthanaga knew that the serene environment that the Kitigan Zibi had fought so long and hard to maintain was about to get the hardest test it had ever faced.

Kuthanaga watched the chief and John walk off to gather the town elders to call the meeting. He was about to follow them when he felt the slight tingle at the base of his skull. He felt the contact of Reshnogga.

Yes Reshnogga. What is it?

Chaos. I have never seen such a display of wanton violence and brutality. Madness. Why are we even thinking about allowing the humans into the collective?

Kuthanaga could feel the pain and anguish that the young watcher was feeling.

Relax Reshnogga. Share with me what has happened.

As you wish.

Kuthanaga could feel a rush of emotions, almost as if the floodgates to a thousand tortured souls filled his mind.

Control, please. Control.

Reshnogga caught himself and calmness filled him. The presence of Kuthanaga had an effect which helped him deal with the situation.

Kuthanaga could see everything unfolded as he expected with the town's people hording and sharing with no problems. The liquid would replicate so quickly that there seemed to be an infinite amount. Word spread quickly and twenty four hours had not even passed before military trucks showed up. At first, the military didn't do anything to upset the people; they just took samples and set up a few tents nearby. The people were questioned and everything seemed to be calm and nonviolent.

The second day more military showed up and they blocked off the area leading to the liquid. The town priest tried to reason with the soldiers that the liquid was a miracle sent by God to help the poor. The prayers were ignored as the soldiers held their lines and would not allow anyone to pass.

This too didn't seem too problematic as word spread that you could put the miracle liquid on any liquid and it would make more. The entire town had its supplies and another day passed peacefully.

The morning of 27th though would bring a dark specter of death. Someone had starting shooting and many of the town awoke to the smell of burning flesh and the sound of assault rifles. Another group of outsiders had heard the story of the liquid. These outsiders were part of the Blood cartel and they wanted the liquid. The military soldiers were ambushed and taken by surprise. The attack was quick and brutal. The soldiers were out manned and out gunned.

When the men started collecting the liquid in barrels and loading it on trucks many of the town people stayed away and tried to hide within the confines of their homes. They sat quietly and prayed.

One of the thugs took a small group and went door to door. They would burst into the houses and take what they wanted. A few tried to fight back and that was the spark that caused the violence to escalate. The town priest pleaded with the leader of the criminals and again tried to explain that the liquid was a miracle and all could take from it. There was more than enough for everyone.

The leader a cruel high-ranking foot soldier of the cartel was called the Vulture. A name well deserving of one so dark and cruel.

He laughed at the priest and shot him once between the eyes. The priest's body fell back and rolled towards the liquid. His blood flowed freely and mixed with the white liquid. A few seconds passed and the blood shifted to white. The vulture motioned and the priest's body was retrieved and tossed away like trash.

The men saw the killing of the priest and it spurred them on to darker desires. The few young women in the town were rounded up and gang raped. When the men were done, they executed them. The rest of the town was systematically executed. There was no exception. Children to the elderly were wiped out. The road ran red with blood and Reshnogga watched and did nothing. He knew he alone would have been more than capable of killing the criminals.

The cartel spent a few more hours loading up what they could carry and as the evening fell, the town was silent. The only sound was the occasional flapping of buzzards, which wasted no time feasting. Kuthanaga broke the link when he saw a small girl badly burned being eaten by one of the raptors. Reshnogga knew the girl. She was the daughter of the family, which had discovered the liquid initially. She had been one of the few which Reshnogga felt were worthy of the mark and she was gone.

I am sorry. I understand how you feel. I wish I could say I didn't expect this, but I did. This is necessary in a way. We cannot save all of them brother.

You knew this would happen?!

There was a tone in Reshnogga's voice. Kuthanaga had forgotten that many of the watchers had never seen violence in its basest form. They had read about it and trained in combat, but had never seen it up close and personal. Never felt the searing heat of the flames or the stench of rotting flesh.

*This is part of the humans. This is in their nature. We have an almost impossible mission to do. Trust me Reshnogga, if I thought there was any other way, I would have pursued it. There is a method in this madness. I only ask that you do not carry the burden on yourself. The weight of this lies on my shoulders. The humans are exceptional and it is usually in their darkest hour that the truly remarkable ones reveal themselves. The auras only give a brief glimpse. I have seen with my own eyes the darkest of them shine with such brilliance. *

Reshnogga listened in silence. He knew out of all of them Kuthanaga had spent the most time among the humans and knew them the best. He felt as though his heart had been darkened by the senseless violence that had happened. The true irony was that the liquid still poured out. There was more liquid now that when the slaughter began.

Kuthanaga, I accept your offer to take this burden. I do not wish to carry it the rest of my life. When we are done, you shall take it?

Yes, Reshnogga. I will honor that request. I will ask you when we are done if you wish to learn from this event. If you do not, I will take it as my own. I swear.

Reshnogga nodded.

Thank you. Do I still need to be here or can I find another location to continue my marking?

You may leave if you wish. I can see where the rest of this is going.

As you say.

Kuthanaga wiped a tear from his eye and sighed heavily. It was hard and he knew it was only going to get worse as time went on. He knew it had to be done and yet he was tormented by it at the same time. The weight was already becoming unbearable for him. He took a few minutes to regain his composure and focused on Xanari.

Kuthanaga?

Yes young one. How is Tim and Joy?

They are sleeping. Are you OK?

Yes. I am fine. I am going to be checking with the other watchers to gauge their progress. I am almost done here. I don't anticipate me being here for longer than two more days. I will then come to you there. Have you seen anything new yet?

No. Nothing yet to report. I do have a question though.

Yes?

How much have you told them about the Convergence?

Not much. Feel free to explain to them if you wish. It is not a secret.

Is there anything I'm not to speak of?

Do not discuss my personal past or the dreams that Rachel has had about the drake and me.

OK.

Thank you for your help Xanari.

You are welcome Kuthanaga.

He broke the connection and watched the sun slowly start to set. The sky was a deep burgundy with shades of orange and yellow stretching high. He closed his eyes again and slowly reached out to the watchers to check in.

Chapter 32 – Tiamat Rising
December 27th 2011 – Los Vegas 11:59 pm

Richard had waited patiently as the testing was done and the information was gathered. He was sitting in the Bellagio lounge and slowly ate his meal in silence. A young drake named Antonio was near him waiting patiently. He savored the last bite of his meal and next to his plate, his cell phone vibrated wildly. He swallowed the bite and sighed.

"Hello."

"Well husband. Did you find out how Briel was killed?"

"Yes."

"Did you find who did it?"

"Yes."

"Are they suffering a long slow death?"

"No."

"Why not?"

"Annukai."

"What?"

"An Annukai helped them escape. I believe it was Kuthanaga. It does not matter though. We have their blood."

A pause answered him. The hesitation on his wife's part was telling.

"Did you say *Kuthanaga*?"

"Yes."

"Are you sure it's him?"

There wasn't a drake who hadn't heard of Kuthanaga. He was legendary, as was the last encounter Richard had had with him.

"Not 100%. But I know it is him."

"You said you have the human's blood?"

"Yes."

"So you are thinking of using the trackers?"

"Yes."

"Do you think it wise?"

"Does it matter?"

"I suppose not. You do recall what happened last time they were released?"

"I do."

"I have faith in you husband and will leave you to your task."

"Thank you."

He hung up his phone and motioned for Antonio to come closer.

"Antonio, I need for you to get me a sampling of the blood we got earlier."

Antonio nodded and lumbered off.

Richard rubbed the temples of his head. He did not want to use the trackers, as they were notoriously unreliable. As smart as they were it was always difficult to tell if they were actually after the target of choice or if it was a target of their choice. He was unsure if there was another option. He wondered.

He took his phone out again, pressed a single key, and waited. Rapid tones were barely audible.

He waited as the ghosted ringing rang once, and then a familiar voice answered.

"Richard? What do you need?"

"Dmitri, please give me an update on Tiamat."

There was a mixture of excitement and irritation within Dmitri's voice as he quickly answered.

"We are ready for final tests. Why do you ask?"

"I wonder. If I had the blood of a certain human what is the chance that Tiamat could locate that specific person?"

"Well… I suppose with some slight modifications, it could be made to target an individual, which could be used as a tracking device. It depends on how much blood you have. Why?"

"I'm considering using the hunters to track them…"

"Are you serious? You must want them badly if you're considering that."

"Yes."

"Well I can't promise this will work. Tiamat wasn't designed for tracking."

"Yes, I know. When are you testing primary functionality?"

"Tonight. We are recording and streaming to level one servers if you want to watch."

"I think I will. I'm very interested in seeing the power levels it generates."

"I will have one of the techs text you when we are 30 minutes out."

"OK. After the tests, see if you can modify the code to allow for tracking. It would be a nice feature to add to the weapon. Remote tracking."

"Agreed."

Richard hung up the phone and took a sip of his drink.

"Another day or so won't change anything."

He stood and stretched.

Walking out of the lounge, he walked to the front desk. A pretty girl was entering information into one of the terminals. She looked up as he approached.

"Can I help you sir?"

He nodded.

"Yes, you have my room key I believe."

He showed his ID and she nodded. A few minutes later, he was sitting in a couch, which was large enough to support his size and weight. He had a large black bag with him and he opened it. Inside were various tools that he always traveled with. He retrieved a small laptop and set it on the table in front of him. He opened the lid, a few seconds passed, and a login screen greeted him. After logging in, he opened a web browser and read the world news. One article caught his attention. It was a breaking story of a massacre in small town in Mexico called San Martin. He grinned as he read of a mysterious white liquid.

"White liquid? Interesting."

Richard flipped his phone open and called Antonio.

"Hello?"

"Antonio, I also want some of the white liquid which was found in their room. I need it quickly."

"OK. I'm here now and have the blood. I'll be there within 20 minutes."

Richard hung up and continued reading. Nearly three hundred men, women, and children were dead as well as thirty-five military. The article didn't explain why they were dead and he rubbed his chin and wondered why there was military there in the first place.

He dialed a number and waited. Two rings and a woman answered.

"Hello this is Brooks."

"It's me Richard. You following this massacre in Mexico?"

"You mean the one in San Martin?"

"Yes."

"I am. Why the interest?"

"White liquid."

"Yes we have a team there now investigating it. The Mexican government was kind enough to allow us to help. Why are you interested?"

"I'm not sure yet, but I think I may have some of it as well."

"So it's a mystery to you also?"

"Yes. What has your team discovered so far?"

"Well there are some rumors that it is some sort of miracle."

"Miracle?"

"Yes. We have some samples and are running tests now. You are interested in results?"

"Yes, I am."

"Well we can play a game then. What do you know of a project Tiamat?"

Richard paused. How could this human have even heard of the project?

"There is a mythological story of a Tiamat, but I am unsure of what you mean by a project Tiamat."

Richard knew he had to be careful. He didn't want to let anything slip with such an influential human and yet he needed to know just how much the woman knew.

"Richard we go way back. You know I have people everywhere. You know there are many among us who would have nothing to do with Draconians. I'm not one of them. I figure there is enough of the pie to go around. I share with you and you share with me. It's worked well in the past and I don't see why it'd be any different now."

"Roberta, you act as if I actually know something. I don't know of a project Tiamat. Maybe if you told me what you think it is I can look into it and find out some answers."

"OK, play dumb. I know it's a weapon and my source says it's close to being tested. I just want to make it clear that we know where we stand with each other."

"A weapon?"

Richard was furious. Someone was going to die a slow painful death for this leak.

"What kind? We are always working on weapons. Weapons make lots of money. You know your military wouldn't be so impressive if we didn't share our development with you. What kind of weapon specifically?"

"Some kind of particle beam."

Richard relaxed a bit.

"Yes we have a weapon like that. We have been working on it for a few years now. Not sure what the name is. It may be called Tiamat. Not sure though. I'll have to look into it."

"I appreciate that. We'll let you know what we come up with the white liquid."

Richard hung up the phone and sighed. Someone leaked Tiamat and some misleading information. Or, perhaps it was a misunderstanding of what they were seeing. Tiamat looked like a particle ray and could destroy solid matter. It was easy to see how someone would think that was all it could do.

Only a handful of people were present during the early testing of the unit and Richard knew most of them personally. Of the few he didn't he'd have to initiate a watch list and find out who was talking. It was too close to completion to let the cat out of the bag.

He shrugged and stood. Walking to the bathroom sink, he continued to weigh his options. The humans had gotten away. How he wasn't sure but he had his suspicions. He remembered his father telling him about a time when an Annukai moved so fast that he must've been manipulating time. If that was what was happening this time, then the Annukai who was doing it was very powerful. Richard again smiled to himself. He knew of one who was strong enough to be able to perform such a task.

"Kuthanaga, my friend, your tricks won't work next time we meet."

He knew that time manipulation was a loaded gun with a hair trigger. Many things could go wrong with any form of manipulation. He realized that the humans were important in some way and in that realization, he had power. Kuthanaga's feelings for them would be his downfall. He walked back to his laptop and grabbed his phone. He dialed and waited.

"Yes Richard. You know I am trying to finalize the tests for Tiamat?"

"Yes, I am aware. If it wasn't important I wouldn't interrupt you. And as hard as it is for me to say, you're probably one of the smartest people I know."

"I understand." There was a tone of satisfaction in his voice.

"Earlier, I had the humans and before I could place hands on them they vanished. I don't believe it was teleportation. I do suspect it was time manipulation."

"Impossible. No one can do that…"

"Except Annukai."

He let the word sink in.

"Annukai. It has been rumored they can do that. But there are strict laws they follow about modifying the natural balance of things. I would think that would be forbidden even if they could do it."

"Regardless, I suspect it. What I need to know is how."

"Annukai possess the natural ability to modify their environment with force of will. They do this by working with the natural flow of energy, which surrounds us all. On the crust they were severely limited, something to do with too much noise that the planet generates. On the other dimensions, they were able to do many extraordinary things. I don't see how they could be of any threat on this plane."

"So they use energy. Is there a way we could somehow strip them of their abilities or the energy itself?"

"I suppose there is. But, without having an Annukai to test on, it would be pure speculation. I do know they need to concentrate when performing their manipulations. This is very well documented. I don't know how an Annukai manipulated time and made off with your targets. That would require a great deal of mental discipline."

"And if it's Kuthanaga."

"What?! You've seen him? He's back?"

"No, I haven't. But I'm sure it's him."

"He's the only one I would bet on to be able to do what you've said. The only Annukai I know of who was more able was his father. Why are the Annukai here? Do you think it has something to do with Tiamat?"

"Doubtful. But, I do think it has something to do with the Convergence. Now I am learning of a white liquid. I'll get a sample to your team once we've checked it out. I also have one more question for you. A human just asked me about Tiamat and he described it as a particle weapon. We have a leak."

A long pause and a deep sigh.

"I have my suspicions. I will check with a few of the brothers. When I know for sure, I'll let you know."

"Fair enough. I'll let you get back. Keep the time manipulation in mind. I really want to catch whoever it is and I want to surprise the hell out of him when his tricks don't work."

"I'll look into it."

Richard hung up just as a solid knock came to his door.

Antonio was standing there with two small black cases. Richard took them and nodded. Antonio turned and stood guard outside the room as Richard closed the door.

Sitting down at the table again, he opened both and laid them out. There were two small vials of blood labeled in Draconian. The woman's had much more in it, but the vial for Tim had more than enough for the hunters to work with. The other case had a vial of the white liquid.

"Let's see what you are."

Richard carefully opened the vial and gently smelled it. The smell of fresh blood excited him.

"What the hell?"

His pulse raced. He hadn't smelled such a pure strain of blood in a long while and his hands shook with anticipation. How could the liquid smell like blood of someone he had long since killed?

He cautiously tipped his pinky in the vial and put a drop on his tongue. His eyes rolled back in his head as the taste filled his mouth. It was warm and perfect.

He capped the liquid and placed it back in the case. He rose and opened the door where Antonio was.

"Please come here."

Antonio followed him back to the cases. Richard motioned to the white liquid.

"Open it carefully and smell it. What does it smell like to you?"

Antonio did as he was told and when he opened it and sniffed his eyes widened.

"It smells like great white shark blood."

"And is that your favorite?"

Antonio nodded. He stared at the liquid.

"Get a small cup and taste a bit."

Antonio grabbed a small glass and place a few drops of the liquid into it.

"Go ahead."

He sipped and smiled as a deep chill filled his body. When the chill reached the base of his spine, he shivered uncontrollably for a moment.

"What do you think?" asked Richard.

"It's perfect."

Richard nodded.

"I want you to contact the team and make sure a good sample of this liquid and the blood gets to Dmitri. I want it there via personal transporter. Get the best and make sure nothing happens to it."

Antonio nodded and Richard packed the liquid back up and closed both cases. He had made his decision to not use the trackers. He was going to wait for Tiamat to get to Tim and Kuthanaga. The white liquid was interesting and he knew that somehow Kuthanaga was involved with that as well. It would take some time he knew and while time was something he didn't have a lot of, he knew that rushing the situation and making brash decisions would not yield the results he was after.

Handing the case to Antonio, Richard watched the large man leave.

Chapter 33 – Council Decision
December 28th 2011 – Maniwaki, Canada 9 pm

Chief Tallbrother sat at a long table and patiently waited for the people to respond. He had poured a small amount of the liquid in everyone's cup and when they were all done sipping and smelling he simply waited. It didn't take long as people slowly realized that the milky liquid was something special.

A woman named Sarah Raincloud was the first to speak. "You said this liquid came from our land?"

He nodded.

"It is limitless?"

He shrugged.

"I do not know how much is in the ground, but what I know is this."

He had a pitcher of orange juice in front of him. He took the liquid and poured a small amount in with the orange juice and it slowly shifted to white.

"We can make as much as we need. I have had it tested and even though I trust the people at the lab I am sure they have kept some for themselves and it's just a matter of time before others gain access to it. They will not need to enter our land. I vote we keep this among our people and share with the other tribes and let them decided what they wish to do with it. I do not want to see our land ravaged by corporations. I don't know if we'll be able to hide such a large secret for long, but I think it is wise."

Many of the council nodded in agreement. A few seemed deep in thought.

"This could be a huge boost to our community. The revenue we could make from harvesting and selling this liquid is unbelievable. A liquid that tastes like your favorite drink? The money could help us in ways we never dreamed before."

The Chief nodded and rubbed his eyes. He had not slept well and the pressure was visible to anyone with eyes. There was a huge weight on his shoulders.

"Yes, but what I fear is what others will do to control the liquid."

The door opened up and John was standing there with a concerned look on his face.

"John what is wrong?"

"Chief, I have news of other places with the white liquid. A location in Mexico has a pool as well. The entire town was butchered. Even military from what I heard. There are a couple of stories on it. I did some research on the internet."

The Chief nodded and the weight seemed to increase on him. He stood and looked at everyone.

"It is exactly that which I fear could happen here. I would be more than happy to push the liquid out to the other tribes but no amount of money is worth the risk I see."

The others were silent and deep in thought.

"Shall we vote now?" He asked. They all nodded.

"All in favor of keeping the liquid a secret?"

The whole room raised their collective hands. He nodded.

"So it's decided then. We shall share with the other tribes and tell no one of the sacred rock. We need to find a way to hide the area from the tourists. I thank you all for your time. With your cups you can make as much of the liquid as you need with just a drop. If you run low check with each other or come see me."

He walked towards the exit and paused. He felt something was there with him and he looked around. Just outside near the window he saw a man who wasn't there and was there at the same time. He wondered how he could have missed such a large man. Tallbrother went outside and greeted him.

"Hello stranger." He said to Kuthanaga.

Kuthanaga smiled at him. "Hello Chief."

"Do I know you?"

Kuthanaga shook his head. "No. But, I know of you and I also know of the liquid. So you've decided to keep the secret safe?"

Tallbrother examined the man and something told him the man was more than what he seemed.

"Yes. We will share with the other tribes. However, we will not share it or sell it outside. What the other tribes decide is up to them. We can't risk it."

Kuthanaga nodded. "That is the wise thing to do I think."

"If you don't mind me asking. How do you know of the liquid?"

Kuthanaga smiled a wide grin.

"I'm afraid we all have secrets we need to keep. Suffice to say, I am pleased with your decision and know we will meet again. Stay safe and well."

The Chief nodded as the tall dark man walked away. The man had a weight on his shoulders, which made the chief's seem infinitely smaller by comparison, and yet he carried it almost as if it were a badge of honor. The Chief was relieved by what the man had said. Validation was a rare thing and something about the man put the Chief at ease.

"You too, stranger."

Kuthanaga walked a little further and suddenly shifted out of view. The Chief rubbed his eyes and smiled. It seemed to him that a great storm was building but for a while at least, it would be in the eye that the tribe would reside in. He knew with certainty that they had done the right thing. But, just as the sun rose every day, the time would come when change would crash upon them and he was fine with that.

Kuthanaga was pleased with the decision of the chief and he knew that they would be a positive source of the Earth's Milk. He wondered about Mexico. Why would a criminal cartel want it? It cleansed people, made them whole, and balanced, which would be counterproductive to the very nature of their business. Also, if someone had a sample of the liquid they could make as much of it as they wanted without having to buy any more ever again. If the cartel was trying to gather it all and ransom it, then why kill all the people? The questions plagued Kuthanaga and he felt pain for the watchers, as he knew they were bearing witness to thousands of horrors such as the massacre in Mexico. He knew he'd have to follow up on the cartel and see what their intent was with the Earth's Milk.

The air was still and the sounds of the evening were subdued and almost seemed to be hiding something. Kuthanaga realized he was on edge and knew instantly why. He hadn't allowed himself time to heal from the rescue of Joy and Tim. They were unaware of the price he had paid to time bend so heavily. He had seen Richard and wanted to slit his throat while time was slowed. He could have done it but the moment he would have attacked the bend would've been broken and the rest of the drakes would have been on him. He didn't want to risk Tim and Joy and he knew he had an obligation to get as many qualified humans ready for the Convergence as possible and he knew somehow they were instrumental in that task. Still, the thought haunted him. He was sure he could have probably taken Richard out and reestablished the bend before the others were on him. He shrugged and grinned. There would be time to take care of his old enemy and he would settle for nothing less than total obliteration of him.

He sighed and focused on himself. The bend had caused serious damage and his temples throbbed terribly. He needed to heal. Breathing deeply and slowly he focused and drew the air in. As he breathed, he concentrated on the central slab of his Gak-lua-kuun. He could feel the heat rising inside him as well as the golden artifact. Energy began to build within him and he let it fill his entire being. He was glowing brightly and when the energy was threatening to consume him, he exhaled and energy tendrils flowed in all directions out from him and he watched as they snaked away. Some were tinted in red and some were a shade of gray that shifted darker to lighter as it moved away from him. Seeing the reds and grays lifted his spirit slightly, as he knew he had managed to cleanse himself from the distortions that were growing inside him. He realized if he had waited longer than a day, he would have been in very bad shape. Time bending was a dangerous thing to do alone, but to start and maintain one while transporting two humans was reckless and suicidal. He was acting more like Xanari and that thought made him laugh aloud. He wondered how she was doing as well as Tim and Joy.

Chapter 34 – Tweaking

December 31th 2011 – Las Vegas 1:11 pm

Richard was sitting in his suite staring out the window deep in thought. The Tiamat project was bearing fruit, much more than initially expected. The tests had exceeded Dmitri's wildest expectations and Richard also was very impressed. The amount of energy generated was off the scales and Dmitri had worked what remained of the night to recalibrate all of his equipment to compensate for the increase.

Dmitri was also working on the tracking protocol that Richard had asked him for. He was making progress quickly and Richard knew it was only a matter of time before he was going to see the humans as well as Kuthanaga again.

He looked out the window to the busy street below. The humans were scurrying around going about their normal lives preparing for one year to end and another to begin, blissfully ignorant of the violent change that was to come. Many of them would be preparing their New Year's resolutions to lose weight or quit smoking. In little less than a year they would have more basic goals in mind such as eating and surviving. He watched them with detached interest and suddenly wondered what his wife was doing. He was about to call her when his phone rang. He answered quickly and simply with a "Hello".

"Richard. It's me. I think I have a rough working version of the tracker for you."

Richard recognized Dmitri's voice and he detected a faint hint of excitement in the normally cold and dreary mannerism of his lead scientist.

"How so?"

"I used a small sample of the blood and the tracker is pointing towards Florida."

"Florida? Interesting. How accurate is it?"

"It'll point you within 10 miles."

Richard considered this and smiled.

"That will do just fine. Have you given any more thought to our other topic of discussion?"

"Time manipulation?" asked Dmitri.

"Yes. It occurs to me, that knowing their general whereabouts would do us little good, if our Annukai friends simply stopped time and vanished again."

"Yes. Tiamat can track but there is a delay, as well as resources. As far as the Annukai, I have a couple of ideas which might work. And even if they don't we'll still collect data and have a better idea of what's occurring when they manipulate time."

"Well get ready and send me the information where they are. I'd like to wish them a special happy New Year."

Chapter 35 – Changes
December 31st 2011 – Bimini 9:13 pm

Tim had slept restlessly on and off since they had arrived in Bimini. Joy had slept almost two days straight. Tim would wake up and check on Joy and then would rest more all the while sitting near Joy watching over her. He felt drained and exhausted. He was sore to his core and his head ached horribly. It reminded him of a hangover multiplied by a hundred. He would sense Xanari more than see her and for some reason she kept her distance from them.

Xanari was concerned. They had seemed fine when they arrived. Granted they were worn out, but this was something different. Their auras were shifting and changing hues drastically and the heat they were generating was alarming. She mentioned her concerns to Rachel who had had no new dreams of the couple. Xanari was concerned that they would die. Several times, she had stepped in to heal them but when she placed her hand on either of them, she could sense nothing wrong with them. She had been concerned enough to reach out to Kuthanaga who was also very troubled. He had promised her he would join them before the New Year was upon them.

Then abruptly Joy woke up ravenous and soon after Tim too was up eating his fill as well. Xanari was relieved and made no mention of the event to the couple.

Tim had a mango in his mouth and the juice ran down the corners of his lips as he hungrily slurped it up. The sweet flesh of the fruit seemed fresh and new to him.

"Damn, this is good."

Joy had her own plate of fruits and she was a bit more reserved in her consumption then Tim, but not by much.

"Hell yeah it is."

"How you feeling babe?"

"Better. My head doesn't hurt anymore and I'm not so tired."

Tim nodded. The headaches were the worst for him.

"What do you think it was?" he asked.

"No clue. For me, I was shot in the head."

"Grazed. It looked worse than it was. Besides Kuthanaga healed ya up good."

"True. What do you think?"

"I think we over did shit a bit. Just my gut feeling."

Joy nodded.

"But we kinda had to right?"

Tim shrugged as he took another bite, savoring the flavor.

"Man, all I know is, we were just trying to survive. I'm feelin' better. Stronger. Yeah. I feel good."

Joy nodded.

"What day is it?"

"New Year's Eve."

"Serious?"

"Yup."

"Damn, already?"

"Uh huh."

"Remember last year's?"

"No not really." Tim thought back and for him that night was a blur of random images.

"Yeah, well you know why that is don't you?"

"Was way wasted. Don't even remember what I was drinkin' or anything."

"Well when you start the night out with a bottle of Jagermeister, that's what happens."

Tim vaguely recalled the icy cold bottle in his hands and the strong wonderful flavor of black liquorish and grinned.

"Damn, I do remember that!"

They both laughed a bit. Tim took the last bite and leaned back in his chair.

"What was our New Year's resolution?"

Joy shrugged.

"We didn't do any. I don't think we really cared what the new year was bringing. I know I didn't really care."

Tim nodded.

"Yeah. I know what you mean. I can't believe how different everything is now. I really think about the future a lot now."

"So do I babe." Joy got up and stood over Tim and kissed him gently on his forehead. He smiled at her and sensed a familiar presence in the room.

"We don't bite." Tim said.

Joy looked around and just barely saw Xanari phase in.

"I am sorry to interrupt." she said softly.

"No worries." answered Tim.

"Something happened while you were sleeping."

"Something?" asked Joy.

Xanari nodded.

"Kuthanaga had us down here because something was supposed to happen here and for a while we were unsure what he was referring to. This morning an event happened on the island which left little doubt as to what he was referring to."

"What was it?" Tim asked cautiously.

"The ocean turned white."

"White?"

Tim and Joy looked at each other.

"White like milk?"

Xanari nodded.

"The entire ocean?"

Xanari shook her head.

"No, a small section to the south of the island. It is right off the beach. It extends outwards and then stops."

Tim smiled.

"Well if it's what I think it is, I know what I'm drinking this evening!"

Joy laughed and they left the room and headed to the beach. Xanari followed closely behind them curious as to their sudden excitement.

It took them only 15 minutes to get to the beach and as Tim and Joy approached they paused. The beach was full of people and the area was roped off. There were all sorts of people around the ropes and there were spotlights shining on the water and there were men in hazmat suits sampling it.

"Well fuck. That sucks."

Xanari was puzzled. "What is the problem? What is sucking?"

Joy smiled.

"No, not sucking. He means this is unfortunate."

"Why?"

"Because they're not going to let us take any of the water."

Xanari understood and smiled.

Tim looked at her and shrugged.

"Why are you smiling?"

"Because I already have some of the liquid. Kuthanaga had instructed me to gather some of it when we first heard of it."

Tim grinned. "Oh! Well then, I guess we don't really need to be here then."

Joy took Tim's arm and squeezed gently as they turned to walk away.

Xanari had turned also to return to the house when she saw Rachel running towards them. Joy went to wave hello but something in Rachel's eyes conveyed the urgency in her mind. Rachel was looking beyond them as she approached almost as if she were looking for something.

Joy released Tim's arm and she turned as did Xanari.

Instinctively Joy shoved Tim to the side and as she did he grunted and a whistling sound passed near Joy's head and she knew all at once they were under attack.

Xanari was also moving, faster than Joy could see and she was uttering harsh sounds and her necklace glowed brilliantly.

Tim stumbled and caught himself and he spun around quickly. What he saw made his heart stop and then squeeze. The drakes were on them and moving quickly.

"How the fuck?" was all he could say as his vision exploded with a brilliant flash and his mouth was suddenly filled with a salty warm sensation.

"Hello Tim. Miss me?"

Tim faded quickly into oblivion as he fought to regain consciousness.

Joy glanced back and saw Richard lifting Tim and flinging him over his shoulder with next to no effort. He made eye contact and winked at her.

Rage welled within her and something began to happen. She started to shimmer and she swung as she saw Tim do before and energy flowed from within her and snaked towards the large man. It hit him in the center of his large chest and he flew back. He spun in the air and made sure the he landed on his back and he pulled Tim with him all the while careful to not have his unconscious prey take any unnecessary damage. Richard's chest felt as if it were on fire and rage fought to release itself from within him.

The other drakes were quickly surrounding Rachel, Joy and Xanari. Within moments there were thirty drakes around them all heavily armed. Xanari examined them and her heart was pounding. She crouched and allowed the energy to fill her. She wondered for a brief moment how Joy was able to assault the large drake. She pushed the thought away and when the energy was peaked she focused and bent time as energy blades extended from her hands. She sprang upon the drakes and removed their heads before they knew what had happened.

Joy saw a shimmer and Xanari's muscled tensed up and suddenly there was a blur and the beach sand filled the air. The Drakes were suddenly standing there with their heads gone and their guns aimed upwards. The air was filled with random sounds of gunfire and the remaining people who hadn't fled when the Drakes first arrived now tried and their screams were mingled with the gurgling sounds and Xanari stood there with steam rising off her body and she was staring where Richard had been.

"Where's Tim?" asked Joy.

"When I was dispatching these I turned to face the one who had him and he was already gone. I don't know how. I searched up and down the beach and he wasn't there." Xanari looked ashamed.

"What?!"

Xanari did not have an explanation. Drakes were fast, but with a time bend she should have been able to catch up to him with no effort.

"Where's Tim?!!"

Joy was sobbing now. Fear had taken firm hold of her heart.

"He has him." said Rachel in a barely audible whisper.

Rachel was sitting and she had a dazed look on her face.

"Who?" asked Joy.

The air shimmered and suddenly Kuthanaga was there with an intent look on his face. He surveyed the scene quickly and his eyes met Xanari's.

"Xanari. What have you done?"

"Not enough. Zygriel has Tim."

Kuthanaga paused and contemplated.

"You did this while time bending?"

She nodded. He was impressed but also terrified. She had broken a vow that all Annukai lived by.

"Xanari."

She looked away and knew the price would have to be paid and she wasn't concerned about it. She was upset that she failed in protecting Tim.

"I am sorry Kuthanaga. I failed you."

He shook his head.

"Do not be sorry. I should be the one apologizing. I should have been here sooner. I got here as quick as I could when you reached out."

Rachel stood then.

"I wasn't fast enough. I dreamed it. I know where Tim is. I wanted to prevent it. I wasn't fast enough."

Joy's fear increased.

"Prevent what?"

Rachel was silent and she searched for the strength inside to utter the words which Joy knew before she could even say it.

"They're going to kill my husband aren't they?"

Rachel's eyes answered as they filled with tears.

"Oh no they aren't. You said you know where he is. Kuthanaga, let's get him."

Kuthanaga paused and considered. It was obviously a win/win for Richard. If Kuthanaga showed up, it was very likely he would be killed. If he did not, Richard would take great satisfaction in torturing Tim and would send what was left back to Kuthanaga in pieces.

Calmly Kuthanaga reached out to Joy and nodded.

"I am already prepared for a solution to this problem. Rachel. This is the first time you have dreamed of this?"

She nodded. Kuthanaga closed his eyes and he could feel Tim, but the connection was different. Something was causing interference. He was still alive though. Kuthanaga smiled weakly and took Joy's hand in his.

"Joy, I still sense Tim and can tell you for certainty that he is alive. I promise you I will get Tim back. You see, I anticipated something like this happening. The only problem is, Tim will have to be very near death for me to pull him to me. The drakes have many techniques they will use before going to that extreme. We need to find him before that."

Joy looked Rachel in the eyes and Rachel could feel the pain in her heart.

"I'll show you what I've seen." she said to Kuthanaga.

Joy looked around and saw the beach was empty except for them and the dead drakes. Kuthanaga and Xanari stood in front of Rachel and they closed their eyes and the beach was silent except for the sound of the waves gently crashing against the shoreline. Joy felt so alone and she silently cried and prayed to God she would see her husband alive again.

Chapter 36 – Breaking
December 31st 2011 – Florida 11:55 pm

Richard was breathing heavily and even though Tim was next to nothing as far as weight was concerned the small man was becoming increasingly heavier. They were in Florida but the view was heavily distorted and the air was stale and didn't move. He grunted with each step. He'd have to have a long discussion with Dmitri about his 'solution' to the Annukai time manipulation. Shifting dimensions was risky and also painful. He wondered what the effect would be on his captured prize. It mattered little as he knew Tim would be valuable beyond comparison for the short time he'd be alive. He needed something to give his wife for the loss of her nephew and Tim would fill that need nicely and he was sure that Kuthanaga would come looking for his human pet.

The air around him had a faint purple tint to it and he could see what was happening on the prime and he was thankful he had shifted when he did because not more than a second after he did, he saw his drakes falling to the ground. Thirty good men killed in less than a second. He knew he would have to bear the weight for that sacrifice but he also knew if he hadn't done what he did, he would have undoubtedly been killed.

Tim began to stir and Richard dropped him to the ground. Richard took out what looked to be a leash and strapped it to Tim's neck and waited. When Tim groaned again Richard pressed a small button on the side of his watch. A gentle beep filled the air and even though there appeared to be lots of people and cars driving around there was no sound which made the faint beep unnaturally loud.

Tim groaned and opened his eyes. He immediately regretted the decision. Richard was smiling down at him.

"Where's Joy?"

"Who cares? I wasn't after her specifically. It was you."

Tim sat up and anger welled in his heart.

"I asked you a question."

"And I gave you an answer. And, before you try to finish what your wife started…"

Richard revealed his chest to Tim and the blast was still fresh. Tim could smell the burnt flesh and see the charred wound was still oozing. The sight and smell of it made him ill.

"Two things. Number one, you'll be stuck here and will never figure out how to return to your own dimension. Number two, and this is the important one, if I die, you die. Feel that collar around your neck? It'll blow your head clear off. Understand me Tim?"

Tim felt the collar on his neck and he glanced around. People were passing through them as if they were ghosts.

"Where are we?"

"Florida."

"Florida?"

"Yes. We have a ways to go before we shift and then we'll head home."

"Home?"

Richard nodded and grinned. "Oh yeah. You'll love it. We'll hang out a bit and really get to know each other. And after that... Well, after that my wife would like a few words with you."

Tim swallowed. "I don't suppose we can just go to a strip club and hang out like homies?"

Richard reached down and lifted Tim to his feet.

"No, we have a lot of walking to do and we need to get started."

Richard's watch started to beep and he spun around and a shocked look was on his face.

"What did you do human?!"

Tim's heart pounded.

"What? I didn't do shit man."

They both paused and Richard stared from his watch to Tim's neck and Tim froze.

"Dude, seriously. Get this fuckin' thing off. I didn't do anything!!!"

Richard backed up and then closed his eyes.

"Fuck!"

Richard opened his eyes and started laughing.

"Relax human. I am only joking with you. Happy New Year. The alarm was to remind me so I could call my wife."

"A fucking joke? Dude you're killing me."

"Not yet. Start walking. Go that way."

Richard shoved Tim in the direction he wanted him to go and Tim saw ghostly people hugging and kissing. Everything seemed so surreal. He wondered if Joy was OK and he silently prayed that he would see his wife again.

Chapter 37 – Pain
January 1st 2012 – Florida 4 am

Tim and Richard walked for hours and finally Richard grabbed Tim by the shoulder and leaned to him close enough that Tim could smell his breath. It wasn't foul or sour or anything sinister. In fact it smelled rather nice and Tim couldn't help but comment.

"Dude your breath is like a scope bottle."

Richard was taken aback for a moment and smiled.

"Just because I'm a drake doesn't mean I don't take care of my hygiene. You live as long as we do and you learn real quick to take care of the basics. Now that we have that out of the way. We're going to shift back to the prime but before we do, I need to know how you're feeling."

Tim was feeling pretty worn out and every movement was five times harder in the strange purple dimension then on the dimension he was used to.

"My head hurts from you cold cocking me and this purple place really sucks ass. I'm alive and breathing but I feel like shit."

"I'm sorry to hear that because this is going to hurt. A lot. If you'd like I can knock you out again so you won't have to go through it. You were out when I brought you in earlier. It almost made me pass out when we got here."

"Wait aren't you gonna fuck me up anyways? So why do you give a shit how I feel now?"

"Tim, I'm not working on you right now. That fun is for later. I can at least extend some basic niceties for the time being. From a mutual respect platform. I am impressed with what you and your woman are able to do and the fact that Kuthanaga has chosen you as his pet means something special about you. So that's why I am offering you a way out."

Tim thought about it and decided he would be better off awake then totally knocked out.

"Well I appreciate that. But I'll try to hang."

"Up to you."

Richard pulled out a small device and after pressing a few buttons a low whine started to rise in volume.

"Prepare yourself as best you can."

Richard grabbed Tim's arm and suddenly there was an intense whooshing sensation and Tim's skin felt like it was being peeled from the muscles and his muscles felt like they were being ripped from his bones. He tried to scream but he was silent. His mouth opened and he exhaled and tried to scream through the pain and there was no sound. He saw Richard was also in intense pain and it was obvious that Richard was trying to maintain his grip and not rip off Tim's arm. The intensity rose and suddenly everything was black and the whooshing sound sounded like a hurricane and suddenly Tim felt an icy sensation on his back and he was suddenly drenched to the bone with ice cold water. He gasped and felt strong hands lifting him off the ground.

Richard motioned for the drakes to place Tim in a large van which was a few feet away. The purple haze was gone and sounds were filling the void that the silence had occupied for the hours of walking that they had done.

Tim grumbled something that Richard could barely hear.

"What's that Tim?"

"I should've had you knock me out."

Richard laughed.

"Sorry things have to be rough going forward. I rather like you. You make me laugh. But we do what needs to be done."

Richard motioned for two Drakes to sit next to Tim and he stepped into the van.

"Take us to the airport. I want to be home as soon as possible."

A lean lanky Drake nodded and started to drive. Tim sat there shivering and his muscles ached and he fought to sit straight. His body screamed to go into a fetal position and he fought that impulse with all his will. Richard noticed this and he felt very similar and he smiled.

"You have spirit. I'll give you that."

Richard's phone began to vibrate wildly in his chest pocket. He retrieved it and saw it was his wife.

"Excuse me. It's the wife."

Tim nodded and motioned for Richard to answer the phone.

"Hello."

"Hello husband. Happy New Year. Did your hunt go well?"

"Yes. I have the human."

"The one I want?"

"Yes, the one we both want."

"Where are you?"

"I'm on my way home. Should be there before the evening."

"And the Annukai?"

"There was one there. Not Kuthanaga. But she was ferocious. She took out the thirty men I had on her."

"Thirty?"

"Yes." He could hear concern in her voice.

"How is that possible?"

"She manipulated time."

"How did you escape?"

"I'll go into that later, suffice to say, I am alive and have my human which should answer the many questions I have."

"Fine you ask the questions and I choose how we dispose of him once I am done playing with him."

"As you wish my love."

"See you soon."

He hung up the phone and looked at Tim. He shook his head. He knew his wife well and knew that once she got her claws in him, Tim would know the sweet pain that she was known and feared for. He wouldn't be able to offer him salvation. He remembered she once kept a plaything alive for three months while she tormented her for ten hours a day. The screams slowly shifted into soft whimpers until one day there was nothing left of spirit and in boredom she killed her. Richard knew she could've kept it going longer and with a strong will like Tim's who knew how long she could keep him in agony.

"Tim. If I were you, knowing what I know, I would get as much rest as you can now. When we get where we're going you're going to beg me to kill you. Rest now."

Tim swallowed.

"I can't."

"Why not?"

"Too scared."

Richard nodded and grabbed a small bag which was near him on the floor of the van. Inside he found a vial and an injection gun. He placed the vial in and looked Tim in his eyes.

"This is the last act of kindness I can bestow upon you. I hope your dreams will be pleasant."

Tim clenched his jaws and Richard injected the liquid into Tim's neck. Tim didn't fight it, and within ten seconds was gently snoring.

The Drakes watched this and knew that Richard was indeed trying to offer some peace before the living hell was to begin. Richard's reputation was legendary and if he was disturbed by the thought of what his wife was going to do to the human, they knew it was going to be bad.

Tim slept. For how long, he had no idea, but when he was waking he found himself naked and shivering on a cold slab of metal. His skin was covered in goose bumps and no matter how hard he shivered there was no relief and his muscles ached. He was stretched spread eagle and he was upside down at a slight angle. It was far enough back where his head was pounding and he couldn't move his head at all. He was shackled. His eyes darted around the room. It was completely white everywhere he could see. There were several white leather chairs covered in plastic and a medical tray with easily twenty or more sharp sinister devices which almost seemed to glow with an unnatural hunger.

He blinked his eyes and cleared his throat. The acoustics in the room were odd. There was a distinct echo which added to the sinister quality of the room. He realized he had to urinate and he fought to hold it in.

"Um hello. I know you're gonna torture me and everything. Do you think maybe we could timeout for a bathroom break? Hello?"

He saw a bedpan just out the corner of his peripheral view and he wondered if he could still manipulate things. He closed his eyes and the urgency increased. He realized at the angle he was in, if he did urinate it would run down him and hit his face.

"Come on..."

He focused on the bedpan and he felt its icy metal surface cover his privates and he relieved himself. Careful in his focus he pushed the bedpan to the ground within his view.

He was suddenly startled by clapping from behind him.

"That was impressive." said a sultry woman's voice.

"Yes and disappointing. I was so hoping to see him wet himself." said a voice he didn't recognize which held a strong Russian accent.

"Bravo Tim. Really. We need to figure out how you are doing that."

He recognized Richard's voice instantly. The table spun around and he realized they were watching the whole time.

As the table spun, Tim saw a large machine which filled the whole wall which was behind him. There was another table inside of it what held restraints in it as well. It had a clear glass-like substance which covered the chamber and Tim wondered what it was.

Richard was there relaxed in a chair wearing an expensive suit and the woman next to him was both beautiful and terrifying all at the same time. She was one of the most fit women Tim had ever seen and was symmetrically beautiful. It was her eyes which caused the fear. Something in her eyes hinted at the evil which lurked behind them. She had on simple clothing all in black and she had a thick plastic garment that Tim had seen before on TV and the movies when someone was doing messy work and didn't want to get bloodied. She had black latex gloves on and her demeanor was all business.

A tall man sat near her and he was stone cold. Something about him appeared totally fake. He looked like his skin was plastic or synthetic.

"Glad you enjoyed the show. To be honest, I have no idea how I do it. I close my eyes and concentrate. That's it."

Richard waved it away.

"Tim, we know about the Annukai, and specifically Kuthanaga. What's he doing here? How did he manipulate you and Joy? How many other Annukai are here?"

Tim thought about it a second and tilted his head towards Dmitri.

"Dude. Are you meat gazing me? I can understand honey there checking out the junk. But you? What the hell?"

Dmitri simply smiled and said nothing.

Richard shook his head.

"OK, my love. He is yours to play with. Please do not kill him."

She grinned.

Richard looked at Tim as he rose.

"I'll see if you're more into talking after my wife warms up with you."

Tim swallowed hard. He had seen movies where the hero was tortured and images of James Bond getting his royal jewels slammed repeatedly with a knotted rope was playing in his head. He shivered a bit more as he imagined what was to come. For all his bravado he was terrified and his eyes watered a bit as he watched the tall woman rise and move to him. She caressed his flesh and even though she was wearing gloves he could feel the warmth tickle his goose bumped covered flesh.

"You know I am going to take my time with you Tim. I want us to be very intimate. My husband wants information. I could care less you see."

She massaged his chest and she rested her hands over his heart which was beating strong and fast. The metal slab he was on began to move and as his head rose upwards the blood from his head flowed back to normal and his head pounded and he felt lightheaded.

"You killed my nephew and I was very fond of him. So I am torn. I can play with you and then kill you, but then that won't bring him back. In fact, that wouldn't even begin to address the pain in my heart. You'd be dead and I'd go on hurting. On the other hand I could allow you to live. Take away things that you love and make sure you don't die. That way, you could share my pain every day."

She was massaging his shoulders and went along his arms and rested on his left hand and traced around his ring finger.

"Maybe find your wife and have another plaything that I can abuse to the point of death?"

Anger welled in Tim and he swung with all his might at the woman as he concentrated. All the while he was unaware that Dmitri was standing behind him with a device. As Tim lurched forward he felt a searing pain in his head as the device was slammed down.

"Oh. Looks like I hit a nerve with Tim Dmitri."

Dmitri nodded.

"Yes, it would appear so. Well since it appears that there needs to be a level of concentration needed for him to use his abilities, the helmet will prevent that."

Tim moaned as the helmet sent waves of electricity down his skull. He relaxed and the surge stopped. Melissa walked over to the table with all the blades and took one which was long and wicked. She smiled.

"Tim, Tim, Tim. Were you going to do something nasty to me? I'm hurt. Well enough of the pleasantries. Shall we begin?" She gently ran the blade down from the center of his sternum to just under his bellybutton. A thin line followed but it didn't break the skin. He could feel the cold blade and he tried to pull his stomach in away from it.

"Where shall I begin?"

She glanced down.

"Meat gazing. I have to tell you Tim, not much meat to gaze at there…"

He groaned and flashed her a look which made her smile.

"Shall I begin there?"

"Let's not and say we did."

Again she smiled. He maintained humor even when faced with the possibility of castration.

"Yes, let's save that area for later. For now, I'll just start with your hands. Did you know that the human hand has many specialized nerves in it? Some of the densest areas of nerve endings in the body are there. Let me show you."

Dmitri grabbed his hand and turned it palm down. With speed unimaginable Melissa had removed a single finger nail and for brief moment Tim felt nothing. Then the pain quickly blasted his finger.

Tim screamed and Melissa continued on the one hand for more than two hours and the pain rose and fell constantly and eventually he passed out.

As Tim passed out Kuthanaga searched frantically for more clues on where he was. The images that Rachel was showing him was more than troubling and he knew it could be a long time before Tim was near death. The Martyr's Barb would only work near death or death itself. It seemed that Melissa was set on taking her time and that wasn't a good thing. The modified wedding ring would allow him to communicate with Tim, but the instant he did he knew the helmet would send electricity into Tim and he'd lose contact as there was a level of concentration needed.

Kuthanaga cursed. He needed more information. In frustration he almost disconnected from Rachel when he saw Richard return to the room.

"How is our guest?"

"Resting uncomfortably."

"Dmitri, I want to make sure your device is working. Take him through some basics and even though he won't say what he's thinking about, he'll be thinking. I want as much information as possible."

Dmitri nodded.

"When we have the information, may I have him for Tiamat? He seems very strong and I think he may be the one."

Richard looked at Melissa and she shrugged.

"When my wife is done and I have extracted my information, you may have him."

Dmitri smiled softly.

"So how long do you think you'll be here?" asked Richard of Melissa.

"I'll be here for another five hours at least and then will head home."

"Fine. I have a couple of meetings with Sam and will be busy until late."

She nodded and noticed that Tim was waking.

"Enjoy yourself. I know I will."

He nodded and walked away.

Chapter 38 – Hunting the Hunter
January 1st 2012 – Bimini 1:13 am

Kuthanaga opened his eyes and glanced at Joy who was stern and silent. Her eyes were red and swollen. Her jaw was clenched tight.

"I know where Richard will be, and I have seen that Tim is alive. Rachel's visions have been fairly accurate so we'll work from those."

"How is he?" asked Joy.

"He's alive. I won't go into what they will be doing to him."

Joy growled. "Tell me! Otherwise my mind will imagine the worst of the worst."

Kuthanaga gently placed a hand on her shoulder. "I'm afraid your fears will not be too far from what will happen. Which is why I am going to do something I fear is reckless."

Xanari stood nearby and she tilted her head slightly. Reckless? Kuthanaga doing something reckless? She was listening intently.

"The Drakes get a lot of their technology from the Quinuks and I happen to know a few who are friendly to the Annukai. I am sure they know where Tim is. I saw a large device where Tim is at and I'm sure it's Quinuk technology. If they helped build it then they might know where it is. Also I know where Richard will be and fortunately for me it is close to where my Quinuks are."

He turned to face Xanari. "Have you gotten to the east coast yet?"

She nodded. "Yes I have roughly forty mirrors along the east coast. Where specifically?"

"New York."

"Yes, I have one in Newark."

"That will be fine. I will join up with her."

"Kuthanaga is the risk worth it?"

He nodded.

"Yes it is. He is important to me."

"You know that the Drakes will be expecting you. Somehow Zygriel was able to escape even though I bent time."

"He escaped because he shifted slightly. Your time bend affected him, you just didn't see him."

She nodded. "He took a great risk in doing that."

"Yes he did, but it worked. He is very smart and resourceful. I know my fate and you yourself have seen a confrontation which is supposed to happen after the Convergence begins. So, let's take that as I am successful in this effort and go from there."

"I wish you success Kuthanaga."

"And you too Xanari. Please look after Joy. I fear they will be looking for her as well soon."

Joy's eyes widened a bit and she remained quiet.

"I shall make sure nothing happens to her."

Kuthanaga closed his eyes and focused on Xanari. Xanari reached out and brought her mirror into focus and Kuthanaga slowly faded out.

Rachel had been silent the whole time simply listening. She didn't have the heart to mention she hadn't had the confrontation dream of Kuthanaga and Richard since she had shared it with Xanari. She didn't know what it meant but she didn't want to add anything to the heavy air of sadness. She would allow them to hold onto the hope they had and she prayed Kuthanaga would be successful.

Kuthanaga materialized and looked around. The street was empty and littered with debris. The mandatory curfew was in effect since the massive rioting which had been going on for months escalated in the deaths of six police officers. He focused and made sure he was barely visible as he started running. He knew roughly where he'd find his Quinuk contact.

A couple of hours later he was outside the New York University facing the Tamiment Library. He walked through the walls and headed to the basement level. He walked through a wall and there was a hidden room. Inside a small Quinuk was reading quietly. The Quinuk glanced up.

Kuthanaga. Been a long time. How did you find me?

"I kept tabs on you old friend."

So the humans have tampered with the reporting mechanism? Which is why you are here?

Kuthanaga smiled.

"Yes. They did. I am also here because I have seen something which troubles me."

The small being closed the book and regarded Kuthanaga directly.

What would that be?

"Tiamat."

You've seen it?

Kuthanaga nodded.

Swear on your father.

"I swear it."

The Quinuk was silent for five seconds.

And what do you want of me?

"I need to know where it is. A human under my protection is to be placed in it."

Then he is as good as dead.

"Yes, I understand. I'd like to prevent that."

How many Annukai do you have with you?

"Just me."

Forget about it then. The area is guarded by at least a hundred Drakes.

Kuthanaga laughed. "Is that all?"

Kuthanaga as a friend I warn you against this. It is impossible.

"My friend, you forget we can manipulate time itself."

The Quinuk looked away for a moment.

"What is it?"

That will not help you there my friend. We have made a recent breakthrough on time manipulation ourselves and earlier this day my brothers have delivered a device which will counter any time fluctuations you may create, which basically negates that ability.

"Well that's not good."

As I said, there's no chance of success.

"Again, I disagree.   Your devices are mechanical? Electrical?"

Biomechanical and Electrical, yes.

"So then I would imagine they are susceptible to EMPs?"

Yes to a small degree but they'll self-repair. The amount of energy needed to affect all of them would require a large release. Are you telling me you can tap that much energy now?

Kuthanaga shook his head.

"No, but I only need to affect a small area for just a second or so."

I see. Yes you may be able to buy yourself a second or two, if it works. You'll need to find a way in and get to your human. That will be difficult. Almost a month ago we were instructed to add detection capabilities to the facility. It was then I suspected Annukai were on the crust.

"I just need to know where the facility is, I can get to where I need to get easy enough."

Kuthanaga. I know the loss of Sani has affected you. I'd hate to lose two friends. Please consider what you are doing. Is the life of one human worth the risk?

"He's not just one human. There is something special about him and his wife. They are able to do things I have never seen before and do not understand."

The Quinuk was silent and a look appeared on his face for the briefest of moments..

There are things you do not understand about the humans.

"Such as?"

They are more complex than you realize. Have you not wondered why it was so easy to meld the Annukai DNA and the human DNA? The humans are very adaptive and in all the years of analyzing them we finally understand why.

"Yes, we Annukai have wondered and debated how the humans were so easily accepting of our DNA. What have you learned?"

Their souls are powerful. The flesh is nothing more than a vessel to store that energy. The humans are unaware of the power they possess.

"And Tiamat harnesses this energy."

Yes.

"Humans are destroyed in process?"

Yes.

"Hildreath, Tim is a valued friend who I have sworn as my protected…"

Yes, I know where you are going with this. Damn Annukai and your honor. Here is the location of the human.

Images swirled in Kuthanaga's head and he smiled.

"They have it under Ellis Island?"

Yes.

"Thank you old friend. You will not be forgotten."

If you die, I will be.

Kuthanaga left the Quinuk alone surrounded by his books.

As he ran on he realized that the fortress he was going to try to infiltrate was going to be nearly impossible to crack. The Quinuks were many things but one thing they were not was exaggerators. It was the opposite. They usually were very conservative in their estimations. The fact that they had provided Drakes with detection capabilities specific to Annukai meant that there would be no stealth involved. Brute force was also not an option as a single Drake was more than an equal to a normal Annukai. Kuthanaga was more than confident that he could take ten or more Drakes but more than that and he'd be overwhelmed. His options were quickly running out.

There was one option. He knew doing it would mean almost certain death for him. He and Xanari had already come close to violating the Annukai code of time. It was a fact that wasn't lost on him. He knew they'd have to face the council later and welcomed the chance to present his case then. He realized all at once that there was no option that wasn't available to him in regards to Tim. He knew that Tim was special and that he had a fate to follow.

Chapter 39 – Facing the Hunter
January 1st 2012 – New York, Ellis Island 2:22 am

Richard had been wondering about the information he'd get from Tim. He glanced at the back of the boat and he saw that Tim was still stacking Zs. He knew that in a few hours Tim would be in the most pain he'd ever experience in his life. Richard knew his wife was very persuasive with her abilities and even with his strong will, Tim would break beneath her onslaught. His phone vibrated and he glanced down and saw it was his brother Sam.

"Hello?"

"Rich. I need some help. We're under a lot of fire about the economy and I'd like to run some of the agenda past you and see what you think."

"I'm a little busy brother. Can it wait for a bit?"

"Sure. How about later this morning around 9am?"

Richard thought about it and nodded. "Yeah, that should be fine." Melissa should be pretty deep into Tim by then he thought to himself.

"Great see you then."

The air was cold and the sounds of the splashing waves against the side of the small boat rhythmically soothed his nerves. His phone vibrated again and glancing down he saw it was his wife.

"Hello Melissa."

"So where's my plaything?"

"I'm nearing the island now."

Peering ahead he could see the dock, missing though was his security detail.

"Melissa, did you send the guards like I asked you?"

"Yes of course why?"

"No reason, just checking. Let me call you back."

He hung the phone up and growled in native Draconian. "Be prepared. Annukai are here."

The six men who were with Richard on the boat snapped to attention and readied their weapons. Richard turned to grab Tim when he felt an odd tingling over his entire body. He spun around and felt the icy touch of a long Annukai blade at his throat. Glancing around he saw all six of his men sliding down where they stood all gutted and headless. Kuthanaga stood there with a grin.

"Hello Zygriel. Been a while."

Richard sat back down all the while keeping his hands in plain sight. He knew if Kuthanaga wanted him dead he would've been. The fact that he was still breathing was an exciting mystery to him.

"I'm curious as to why you have decided to spare me."

"I figured it was time we had a talk." The boat slowed down and came to a halt. Richard realized Kuthanaga had taken out the men and also the driver of the boat and turned it off.

The sound of the waves continues to splash against the side and there was an uneasy pause as both men sized the other up.

"You took my human and for that reason alone, I should kill you. Not to mention what you've taken from me in the past."

"Which in my defense I was unaware of until after I had killed her."

"Would it have made any difference?"

"To be honest, I'm not sure. And as far as your human goes, he killed one of my blood. My wife really wants his head. And to be honest I'd rather face death then her wrath. I found him once and I'll find him again. What I do not understand is why he's so important to you Kuthanaga?"

"You wouldn't understand."

"Fine, I can get beyond your fascination with him. What are you doing here?"

"Cleaning up the mess the drakes and Quinuks caused with the humans. You are aware of the Convergence?"

"Yes."

"Well we can't sit by and allow them to all die."

"So let me get this straight. You are here to save humans?"

"Yes."

"Well why didn't you say so. We don't care about them."

"OK, so let's talk about Tiamat."

Richard clenched his jaws and squinted his eyes at Kuthanaga.

"What about it?"

"I've told you why we're here. What's the deal with Tiamat?"

Richard threw his hands up.

"Well if you want to ruin the surprise, we were building a weapon to wipe you Annukai out. After the betrayal of the slave revolt, we never really forgave you. We knew when the Convergence was done we'd all be on the crust and didn't want to have to deal with your unwavering morality. We figured if we'd wipe you out we'd control the planet."

"Nice."

Richard nodded.

"Yeah I thought so. We'd been planning it for a very long time. But it won't matter."

"Really? Why is that?"

"Do you remember them?"

Kuthanaga took a step back for a moment and paused.

"You don't mean?"

"Yes I do."

"I figured they would find us all eventually. How do you know for sure?"

"Quinuks."

Kuthanaga lowered his blade off of Richard's neck.

"I will still kill you Zygriel, but not now."

"You sure? I'm not sure I'd like to face my wife without the human."

"Does she know what he looks like?"

"No. But his blood will reveal who he is to my scientist. Plus once she gets started with her toys he'll spill his guts."

"Grab another human on the island and I'll imprint him with Tim's memories. She'll never know the difference. I'm sure you can handle your scientist. This one is coming with me. It's a trade for sparing your life. You do recall the honor pact between our races?"

Richard bowed and nodded.

"Of course. I am a bit shocked you'd sacrifice one human to save another one. That's very anti Annukai."

Kuthanaga looked him deep in his eyes.

"Some of that man died with his wife. You'll see how different I am the next time we meet. Now drive the boat so we can get your replacement."

Richard cautiously passed Kuthanaga and started the boat again. A few minutes later they were on dry land and they found a guard and Kuthanaga quickly knocked him out and focusing on him altering his appearance and imprinting Tim's memories on him.

"Kuthanaga, if you don't mind me asking. Why didn't you just do this and slip aboard the boat and just swap them out?"

"Because I wanted to talk with you and see if what I suspected was true. Plus I wanted you to know for sure that I could have killed you… Rest assured that I will kill you eventually."

"I see. Well I thank you for this small token. I hope you'll understand if I do everything in my power to kill you first."

Kuthanaga got back in the boat and started it up.

"I expect nothing less."

"Drive carefully and I'll see you again."

Richard picked up the guard and slung him over his shoulder and he clicked his dimensional shifter and everything went purple. He watched as Kuthanaga drove off. He wasn't upset. His wife would be pacified and he would be able to deal with Dmitri.

He had valuable information on why the Annukai were on the crust and he also knew that Kuthanaga knew about Tiamat. Kuthanaga didn't seem too bothered by the news that the drakes had a weapon which could wipe out all of the Annukai. He smiled.

Part of him was relieved that Tim wasn't going to have to suffer under his wife's hand. Realizing this he suddenly knew part of why Kuthanaga risked so much. There *was* something about the human.

Richard walked into the building and worked his way down to where Dmitri and his wife were waiting. He materialized in front of them and dropped the guard's body in front of his wife.

"What has happened?"

"Kuthanaga ambushed us. I was able to keep hold of the human and survive. My guards and the security at the doc were not so fortunate."

The guard groaned. His eyes opened and Melissa smiled as she stomped down knocking him back out.

"Well at least he didn't get his human back."

Richard nodded and watched as Dmitri began to undress and place him on the metal slab and locked him down.

"Dmitri, when you finish I want to talk with you."

Dmitri nodded and continued his prep.

Chapter 40 – Home Coming

January 1st 2012 – Bimini 6:30 am

Xanari was startled by the connection from Kuthanaga.
Kuthanaga, how goes it?
Things are good. I have Tim and am coming to you.
You do?!

She felt a tugging sensation and Kuthanaga was standing there holding Tim in his arms. Joy jumped up and ran to them.

"Tim!"

Tim's eyes fluttered a bit and he slowly opened his eyes. He saw Kuthanaga and Joy and he smiled.

"What the hell? One minute I'm on a plane heading to tortureville and now I'm waking up and everyone is here. What did I miss?"

Kuthanaga slowly put Tim down and smiled at Joy.

"Thank you Kuthanaga." she said as she hugged Tim.

"Yes, Tim you were indeed heading to a very bad place. I saw what was to happen to you and it wasn't nice. I was able to arrange to have you released. I dealt with the drake that had you personally and we came to an arrangement."

Kuthanaga, there is an aura on you, I've never seen on an Annukai. Are you OK?

Xanari, sometimes one must do things to save the ones they care about that is not morally correct. I have broken the code and will have to answer for that later. But I have learned something more troubling that would have me excited to face the council instead.

Xanari was nervous.

What do you speak of?

Young Xanari do you recall the history of the Planet Slayers?

Xanari paled a bit which Tim and Joy noticed.

"Xanari, what's wrong?"

Xanari waved it away.

We shall discuss it when the humans are asleep.

"It is nothing Joy. I am just relieved that they both made it back safely and quickly."

Joy nodded and turned her attention back to Tim.

Tim looked at Kuthanaga.

"You made a deal? Dude, there's no way that guy was gonna give me up. His wife wanted me pretty bad."

"Wife? Why?" asked Joy.

"The drake we killed in the room in Vegas."

"Yeah."

"Turns out that dude was the nephew of the guy who tried the jack move at the hospital. His wife was not too happy about her fave nephew going headless from what I could tell. So Richard was gonna let her tear me up and while at it get information from me. What kind of information I don't know, cause I really don't know much of anything."

Kuthanaga nodded and had a distant look in his eyes.

"Kuthanaga, thanks for the save man. I didn't mean to seem like I was ungrateful or anything. It's just that guy Richard didn't seem like the kind of guy you could really negotiate with."

Kuthanaga eyes narrowed a bit.

"He isn't under normal circumstances and I'm sure we haven't seen the last of him, which brings me to the next topic. Now that the Earth's Milk has shown here we can retreat back to a safer location and lay low for a bit. I'd like to spend some time with you and Joy and see exactly how you're able to do the things you've been doing."

Joy shrugged.

"Figured it was something you did."

Kuthanaga shook his head. "No, you are not supposed to be able to anything near what you're doing."

Tim nodded. "OK, so we're moving again. Where to?"

Kuthanaga thought about it for a moment and then smiled. "We're going to Atlantis."

Joy and Tim's eyes widened.

"Atlantis?"

Kuthanaga nodded.

"The seeds of my plans have been laid and now we need a location in which to wait and watch. Atlantis is perfect, since it is ultimately where we will be bringing the humans."

Tim was confused.

"Kuthanaga, I am so fuckin' lost at this point. I know you have a lot of secrets and normally that's way cool. But I'm kinda at the point where I don't really know anything. After everything we've been through do you think you could shine some light on what's going on?"

Kuthanaga nodded.

"Yes, Tim. I suppose it was just a matter of time before we had this discussion. The Earth is waking up and when she does, nothing on this planet will be the same for a long time. There was no way for humans to know this. And you populated the land far and wide. But this mass population is going to be severely diminished."

"Diminished... You mean dead?!" Joy's voice cracked.

"Yes."

"By how much?" she asked.

"Without our help? Almost all of you. You see, it's not just the Earth waking up and reemerging, but your sun is also going to contribute to this as well. The sun will be very active in response to the Earth waking and there will be lots of solar storms. The flare from the sun will be bathing the planet and your technology will be wiped out for the most part. The reemerging will be more dramatic."

"Judgment day." said Tim in an almost whisper.

"Yes in a manner of speaking. The bible and religions around the world have many truths and you have had many seers and psychics who have warned as well. Atlantis was a continent and it will be again. There are parts of it that are accessible still and it is in this area we will wait."

"So how much destruction will there be?"

"Well Tim, if we Annukai were not here to manipulate a safe area for the humans it would be apocalyptic. The Earth has a cycle and when she wakes the crust is almost completely disrupted as the other off phased dimensions crash back into focus. There is a 12 day process for the most destructive parts. The build-up will start soon enough though and we should start seeing the signs soon. When the dimension where the other Annukai are at merges with the crust, they will join with us and we will be able to maintain an environment which will sustain the humans we save."

"How many humans do you think you'll be able to save?" asked Tim.

"We're hoping for 1 billion total."

"And the rest?"

"Will have to deal with what happens."

"What are their chances?"

"Not good."

"So what about us?" asked Joy.

"What about you?"

"Are we part of the 1 billion?"

Kuthanaga smiled. "Do you need to even ask?"

She smiled weakly.

"How are you picking the 1 billion?" asked Tim.

"We had a system in place, but it seems that some tampering with nature has forced us to do things the hard way. We are judging each one case by case."

"You have 1 billion Annukai here?"

"No Tim. We only have five thousand. More than enough to handle the basic scanning. The Earth's Milk will also help us figure the rest out as well."

"Earth's Milk? What's that have to do with anything?"

Kuthanaga paused. "The milk in its native form is very pure and has many properties which are beneficial to the drinker. Energy, removes toxins from the system, etc. But if tampered with it will change its structure to something darker. When people are exposed to the tampered liquid other effects will materialize. Imagine all the drugs in your world and combine them with all their varied effects and make the addiction a hundred times more intense. That is what will be potentially flowing around the world soon."

"Wait. You mean we just released a super drug into the world?"

"No, we introduced a special liquid that if left alone and shared freely would alleviate almost ever disease on the planet as well as rejuvenate the human body. The proverbial fountain of youth. If people steal it or try to sell it the liquid will shift and have some negative consequences. Furthermore if people attempt to modify and change the liquid to turn it into a product that can't replicate on its own…"

He shrugged and put his hands together.

"Yeah, but come on. You know it's not up to the people. The corporations will get to it and do whatever it takes to control and sell the liquid."

Kuthanaga nodded and turned to face Joy.

"Yes Joy, I am aware that that is the most likely scenario."

"Is there a cure for the tampered milk?"

Kuthanaga nodded.

"It's the pure milk right?!" asked Tim.

"Yes, if you find an individual with a very strong will and an exceptional mind they will understand you and heal themselves with the pure Earth's Milk. That is the purpose. You see when it gets closer to the evacuation time we shall push out the information of the pure milk and where to get it. This will lead the chosen to us. The others will be too far gone to be of concern by that point."

"But won't good people be hurt by the mega addicts?"

Kuthanaga looked down for a moment and thought about the massacre in Mexico.

"Yes. A lot of people will die from this."

"And you're cool with that?"

"Yes, Tim I am. You see, in a manner of speaking you were all going to die anyway. So if a few die during this period it's necessary. The survivors have to be strong because there is a judgment which happens to all the chosen. Annukai society can only exist with people of certain ethics. Each and every Annukai has been judged. Those who are not strong enough are cast out into the wild to fend for themselves. There will be a great many of you who will be outcasts. But even as outcasts at least you will have survived the great Convergence and will have a fighting chance in the new world."

"What are my chances?" Tim asked.

Kuthanaga shrugged. "I do not know. I see strength in you and in Joy. Will you be among us after the judging? It will remain to be seen. I also will have to be judged again for the things I have done since coming to the crust. Do not be concerned with these things now. We will collect Rachel and get samples of the Earth's Milk from here and will make our way to the border of Atlantis. It is abandoned and will take some getting used to, but is the safest place on the planet."

Tim hugged Joy and she squeezed him. She could feel his heart pounding in his chest. Kuthanaga paused and glanced at Xanari and walked away. Xanari smiled weakly at Tim and Joy and followed after Kuthanaga. A few steps away she paused and turned back to face them.

"Do not be concerned. The great Convergence is very destructive but when the dust settles, you will see things which will amaze you. The judgment is nothing to be worried about as well. I have a feeling we'll all be together when this is all said and done."

Tim nodded and Joy just held on to him tightly.

Xanari could feel their emotions and she empathized with them. She followed after Kuthanaga and when they were out of earshot of Tim and Joy she asked.

"Are you mad?"

"You do not agree with me telling Tim and Joy the truth?"

"No, the truth is fine, but using the Earth's Milk as you described?"

"Ahhh I see. Yes, that is against the teachings. But in all honesty are we truly getting the best 1 billion? By my estimations we will have over 4.5 billion which will be suitable. How do we further trim that down to 1 billion?"

Xanari knew he spoke the truth. She had been coming across many people who met the basic requirements and to get deeper would require more time. Time which they did not have.

"But Kuthanaga. There will be much death."

"There has been much already and there will be much much more. Xanari, I am sorry to disappoint you, but my time here on the crust has made many things apparent to me and one of those is the nature of human beings is not far removed from our own nature. We strive to be as close to perfect as the Maker has asked of us, but the humans with their short life spans do not have the time needed to perfect themselves in the same manner. We share the same emotions as they. We needed a way to make sure we could find the absolute best of the best and in this way I feel the Earth's Milk was the best method for determining this. Do you have an alternate suggestion?"

Xanari thought for a few moments and she realized that Kuthanaga was bearing the full weight of his decision and she shook her head.

"No, I do not know of another way. I am sorry to have offended you."

"Do not be. I value your council and apologize for not sharing the details with you sooner."

She nodded and then looked at him.

What of the Planet Slayers you spoke of earlier?

His shoulders sagged just a bit for a moment.

Yes, that was a topic I had hoped we wouldn't need to discuss. It seems our friends the Draconians and Quinuks have discovered that the Planet Slayers may have noticed us after all this time. If that is indeed the case we may be doing all of this for nothing. We have no way of escaping them if they lock their gaze upon us. We managed to fool them once, but it won't work again I fear.

So the drake told you this?

Yes and I know he told the truth.

What are they going to do?

We didn't discuss it further.

What do we do?

Nothing. We stay on task and continue with the evacuation. If we find out later that the Planet Slayers have found us one of two things will happen.

Which are?

Enslavement or total destruction of the Earth. I am hopeful for the second option. I was a child when we escaped to the Earth but not before they marked me.

Kuthanaga shifted back to his normal shape and turned and revealed his back. There were two large scars that ran from his neck to the base of his spine.

Even though I was a child they marked my family and I with this. The Quinuks were able to remove the devices they had implanted in us. I was very lucky. Many of the Annukai home world Dimathruel were worked to death in the mines and as test subjects. The Draconians were enslaved as military fodder and were controlled in a similar manner.

Shifting back to his human form Kuthanaga shook his head.

If they do find us, my hope is for a quick death although I fear they would have other plans for us now.

Xanari nodded slowly. She had heard stories of the old world and what the Annukai had been put through but she had never seen the bondage marks. She was sure her father also had the scars though she had never seen them herself.

Kuthanaga, I am scared.

As am I.

Kuthanaga walked up to Xanari and placed his forehead on hers and took three deep breaths which she matched. With each breath she felt a wave of calm soothing warmth pass over her. By the third breath she was calmed back down.

Thank you.

You are welcome.

What now?

Now we find Rachel and head towards Atlantis.

Chapter 41 – Decisions

January 1st 2012 – New York, Ellis Island 8:01 am

Richard was amazed in a way. The guard-Tim was exactly the same as Tim. He cracked jokes was defiant and managed to survive many of Melissa's best techniques before finally cracking. It took longer than he thought it would and his wife was genuinely satisfied with her plaything. What was more amazing to Richard was the amount of information he was able to gather. It seemed to him that Kuthanaga was uninterested in hiding anything and it was also very apparent he had not shared much of the upcoming Convergence with Tim.

Dmitri seemed detached and bored with much of the procedures and when Melissa seemed sated and Richard content with the information he had gathered, Dmitri was anxious to strap guard-Tim into Tiamat.

Melissa looked at Richard and smiled. "I am happy husband. I would ask for more time, but seeing as he was completely broken I will gain no more satisfaction in torturing him. You may throw the scraps to the dog now."

Dmitri was not offended at all and actually smiled when she insulted him.

"As you wish wife. Where are you off to?"

"I'll be heading home to get some work done. And you?"

"I'll make sure everything is cleaned up and then will take the information and report to the council."

"Sounds fun. Enjoy." with that she sauntered off silently.

"So I may have him now?"

"Dmitri, there's something I need to tell you."

"What? That this is not the Tim you went out for?"

He smiled when Richard just stared at him.

"How long did you know?"

"When you brought him in the sensors in Tiamat lit up slightly. He is 'almost' an exact copy. His blood has shifted slightly to match the Tim you were after. Annukai did it?"

Richard smiled and nodded.

"Yes. Kuthanaga himself."

"Really? He is very powerful that one."

"Yes he is. Which is what will make it so much better when I finally kill him."

"I'd like to watch that."

"I'm sure you would."

"You know Kuthanaga messed up though."

"Why is that?"

"Messing with this guy the way he did he left a very distinct fingerprint on him. A kind of energy signature. I'm almost positive I could use Tiamat and using the imposter here blast our friend Kuthanaga into another existence."

"No! You will do no such thing. I will have the honor of dispatching him at a later time."

Dmitri smiled. "I figured as much. As you wish. May I use him?" pointing at guard-Tim.

"I don't care. Use him as you wish, but you will not mention this to anyone else and you will not use Tiamat on Kuthanaga."

"I hear and obey."

Richard flashed him a warning glance.

"Do not mock me Dmitri."

Dmitri got serious and nodded. "I meant no disrespect."

Richard waved it away and nodded. "None was taken old friend. What of the Earth's Milk? Seems important to Kuthanaga for whatever his plans are. Do we have any idea what it is for?"

Dmitri nodded. "Seems to be perfect for lack of a better explanation. The healing properties of it are phenomenal."

"And it self-replicates?"

"Yes. It just needs another liquid and it transforms it. The most amazing thing I have ever seen."

"Can we modify it so it can't self-replicate?"

"We're looking into it. It may not be possible. The liquid is alive and the self-replicating is part of its biology. If we were to kill it and extract elements from it maybe. We could also limit it's replication to work maybe with just another liquid compound."

"Well, when you are done with Tim here, please jump back onto the Earth's Milk. I have to go meet with the council and look into contingencies regarding the Planet Slayers."

Dmitri paled a bit when he heard the name and he tried to quickly regain his composure.

"Are the stories true?" he asked.

"No, they are not."

Dmitri weakly smiled a bit.

"They are no words to describe the horrors they inflict. Anything you can imagine barely scratches the surface of their cruelty and depravity."

Dmitri nodded and watched Richard walk away.

When Richard was gone Dmitri locked the lab down and regarded the man on the metal slab. He approached with a scalpel and placed it gently on the man's throat. The pulse on the surface of the neck was visible and he knew with a quick flick of his wrist the man would be gone. He paused and put the scalpel down.

"I've got plans for you my friend…"

Chapter 42 – Atlantis

January 1st 2012 – Bimini 9:37 am

Tim had spent a couple of hours coming to grip with the fact that the world as he knew it was going to end. He worried about his sister and her family. He wondered if he asked Kuthanaga would he put a good word in for Tim's family. Joy's family was all gone as far as Tim knew. She never spoke of anyone important and as he glanced at her he saw she was off in her own world same as he was. The sun was up and a gentle breeze was blowing. Wisps of her hair danced around her pretty face and he was relieved that he had her by his side. He realized that if anything happened to her he wouldn't care if he lived or died.

"Hey you." he said to get her attention. She snapped back to him and smiled softly.

"What?"

"Penny for your thoughts."

"I was just wondering how it'll be when this Convergence is done."

"Yeah. Just when we were comfortable with dragon killers and aliens we learn that the Earth is gonna wake up grumpy as shit."

"Yeah. I'm numb in a way. It's like all the stuff we watch in movies is kinda real. I mean what the hell? What else is gonna happen?"

"Who knows, but you know what?"

"What?"

He pulled her close to him and stared deep in her eyes with such intensity that she was momentarily taken aback.

"I really don't care as long as I have you with me."

She kissed him and for a brief moment was lost in eternity with him.

"How are you doing that?"

Startled Tim and Joy spun around to see Xanari staring at them with her mouth slightly opened.

"What?"

Tim looked around and noticed that the area around them was scorched and blackened.

Joy was shocked as well and she noticed a slight reddish glow fading from her and Tim.

"Whoa... We need to be careful Tim."

"Well shit. I was just kissing you. I didn't know that was gonna happen."

Xanari crouched down and placed one hand on the ground and one hand on her necklace. Chanting silently she closed her eyes. The blackness faded from the ground and the grass grew back quickly.

"Wow." said Joy

"I wonder how you are manipulating." said Xanari.

"You need the necklace to do things?"

"Yes, and the chant. Only the elder Annukai can manipulate with will alone. And here you are manipulating inadvertently. How is this possible?"

"Got me." said Tim.

"I was just getting my mack on with my wifey. Maybe we're just hot stuff!"

Joy jabbed him.

"Tim, be serious will you? Xanari is concerned."

"Yes I am. What if you have a nightmare and lash out in your sleep?"

Tim hadn't thought about that. He hadn't needed to. This was the first time something like this had happened.

"Well usually we have to think real hard to make it happen." Tim said with his best redneck imitation.

"That's true. Tim's had a hard time making things happen. But there was the time I got shot."

"Well I was freaked the fuck out. I thought they had wasted you. I didn't really think. It just happened."

Xanari nodded. "So you manifest when you have strong feelings for Joy?"

Tim shrugged. "Got me. Isn't there some tests that Kuthanaga can do or something?"

"We'll see. You may ask this of him. We are preparing to leave. I didn't want to interrupt you. But when I saw the flames..."

Joy smiled and started walking with Tim at her side.

"No worries Xanari. Where to?"

"We are to meet Kuthanaga and Rachel by the beach where the Earth's Milk has appeared."

They walked on in silence for the next fifteen minutes and as they got nearer to their location they noticed a huge crowd all sampling the liquid as it gently crashed against the shore. The troops which had been along the beach had moved their operations to a platform out on the water a few hundred yards away from the shore almost directly above the center of the white liquid. There were hundreds of people on the beach and someone wise had ordered the soldiers to stand down and let the people grab what they wanted.

On the outer ring of the mob were Kuthanaga and Rachel in a very animated discussion of some sort. As they got closer Rachel stopped and turned to face them.

"So have you guys heard yet?"

"Heard what?"

"Where we're going?"

It was obvious that Rachel was very excited.

"Yeah we've heard." said Tim.

"Isn't it amazing? According to Kuthanaga it's been there all the time, just kinda hidden from us."

"Hidden?"

Kuthanaga nodded.

"I'll tell you more in a moment. There are too many people here and no telling if there are Drakes. So I'll make this brief. We'll continue walking along the beach. When we're clear of all the people walk into the ocean but make sure you do not go further than 100 yards from me."

Tim was fine with the instructions but he could see a look in Joy's eyes.

"Babe, trust me. If the man says something just do it. It'll seem a bit weird but trust me you'll be fine."

She nodded. She was sure if Kuthanaga had a plan it would be fine. They walked a little ways and when Kuthanaga was confident that there wasn't many people nearby he focused on the group and suddenly there was a slight whooshing sensation which covered them all and a slight chill filled Joy and she realized the warmth of the sun was gone.

She glanced at Tim and saw he had a slight shimmer around him.

"What the hell?"

Tim grinned.

"Kinda tickles."

Joy could barely hear him.

"What?!"

"I said it tickles!"

She nodded. Kuthanaga started walking into the water and Tim followed.

As they came in contact with the water Tim was expecting the cool water to soak his shoes and clothing. Instead the water passed around him and he noticed that there was a thin barrier between him and the water. Joy caught up to him and she noticed the same thing.

"So weird."

"At least you can breathe." Tim thought back to passing through the solid walls in New York and the painful sensation that accompanied it.

She nodded and took his hand and she noticed for a brief second it was hard to grip his hand. They continued walking and a few seconds more and they were completely submerged. They didn't have to fight the current and swim. They just walked and there was a slight effort on their part as they made their way deeper and deeper. Soon it was getting hard to see.

"Kuthanga?!"

He stopped and after a second nodded. He closed his eyes and a brilliant light surrounded them which more than illuminated the area nearby. A few hundred yards away they saw a few sharks which seemed interested in them for a moment and then swam away quickly.

Tim glanced at Rachel who kept holding her breath and then gasping and quickly grabbing more air.

"Rachel!"

She turned and looked at Tim.

"Relax. You can breathe!"

"It's scary."

Tim nodded.

Actually you don't even need to speak. You're not really able to hear each other anyways. I've been conveying your thoughts with each exchange. Just think towards the person you want to speak with. Kuthanaga's voice was loud in Joy's head.

Hey can you turn the volume down?

Interesting. Am I too loud for the rest of you?

Tim and Rachel shook their heads.

I will tone it down for you Joy.

Thanks.

So how far is it to Atlantis?

Roughly 1,466 miles.

Are we walking that? asked Tim.

No. There is a transporter about 12 miles out.

Transporter?

Kuthanaga smiled.

You'll see.

Tim shrugged. He was so overwhelmed with everything that he was unshakable. Soon they started seeing large stone slabs on the ocean surface and Tim wondered if these were roads or just some natural occurrence of rocks which looked like a road to him.

It is a road Tim. There is much under this ground which will be revealed soon enough. The Atlanteans were a marvelous group of Annukai who stayed on the crust while the bulk of us left to the outer dimension. They kept an eye on the humans for a while. When the crust shifted the landmass dropped under the water. When the Earth wakes and slumbers the land mass shifts and changes drastically. After this Convergence you'll be one of the first to see the new Atlantis.

Swell, will we still have Playstations and the Internet?

No, not exactly. There are things we have which should replace those distractions. Trust me Tim. It's not as grim as you fear. True in some ways things will be very different but overall things could be much worse.

Yeah, I could be dead.

Exactly.

The walking was getting harder and Tim wondered if it was the current picking up around them. He wondered if they got separated what would happen.

It's not good. Stay close.

They continued on for a few more hours and then suddenly Kuthanaga stopped and motioned for everyone to be still.

Tim looked around and didn't notice anything out of the ordinary and scanned the area to see if there was anything that he might have missed.

Kuthanaga raised his hand and suddenly the area around them shimmered slightly. Barely visible on the ground were railroad looking tracks that glowed a dull bluish. A circular platform appeared under their feet and Kuthanaga sat down.

Everyone please sit down and make yourselves comfortable. In fact sleep if you are tired. I shall wake everyone when we arrive.

Tim and Joy sat down and Tim decided he was pretty tired. He laid down and Joy snuggled up against him. Rachel sat near them and was too excited to even think about sleeping. Xanari sat and closed her eyes. Kuthanaga closed his eyes as well and suddenly the platform began to slide slowly at first as if it had been slumbering for a very long time and needed to wake up. It slid with no sound and started moving faster and faster. Rachel was amazed as it slid along kicking up sand from underneath it. The landscape was bland and barely visible. She had no idea how fast they were going. Every so often they would startle a shark or a dolphin. At one point she heard the sounds of a whale song and she couldn't actually see it though she felt it was near. She got nervous that even sitting that perhaps they might come to close to something and she might get knocked off the platform and fall out the range of Kuthanaga's protection.

Relax Rachel. The platform is protecting you now. I still have my wards up around you, but nothing can come in contact or near us while we are on the platform.

She smiled and nodded. She laid back and noticed there was no real sensation to the platform. It just felt solid under her. She closed her eyes and listened. There was no sound; there was no sensation of movement. It was just still. She wondered if a sensory deprivation tank was different then what she was experiencing as they slid effortless along the ocean floor.

Tim was asleep in a few seconds which was no surprise to Joy. She on the other hand was having a difficult time sleeping. Her mind was reeling and filled with so many questions. Her fear and anticipation was barely controllable. She was worried about Tim. Was it him or her that had caused the burn out on the beach? She wanted to keep an eye on Tim and make sure he didn't lash out and cause any problems while he slept. She had been a sleep for a long time and had not slept since Tim was taken and yet she wasn't tired. She didn't understand what was happening to her and Tim and that was the other issue which prevented her from sleeping. She watched Tim snore away and she was envious. He never had a hard time sleeping while she would spend hours at night obsessing over the many details of her life.

Kuthanaga meditated and focused on Tim and Joy. Tim was asleep and dreaming of eating Twinkies of all things and Joy was wide awake mind racing with dozens of thoughts coming at her from all sides. Kuthanaga wondered how they were able to manipulate universal energy so easily when it took Annukai thousands of years of training. What was he missing? Something was different. He had to rule out the manipulation of the rings since they would only allow them to communicate with Kuthanaga and also allow for a recall of what happened to them if they were to die. They were not powerful enough to allow them to shift and control as they were doing. His mind suddenly rested on the milk. The milk had been known to only a handful of Annukai as it was discovered by Quinuks when they first arrived on Earth. The Quinuks meddled with it and went mad and eventually fell under Annukai blades. Kuthanaga's father had returned the milk to the place where they had discovered it and the council ordered that no one ever tamper with the milk again. Kuthanaga realized there were many rules he was bending ever so slightly to achieve the goals he had laid before him. He silently hoped that these rules wouldn't break under his subtle pressure. The Annukai were very clear in their laws and if broken there were dire consequences.

He continued speculating if somehow the milk had inadvertently mixed with the Annukai energy that Kuthanaga had placed in Tim and Joy's rings. He would have to spend time with them to determine their capabilities.

Suddenly he noticed Xanari shudder.

What is it?

Death, one of my mirrors just died… crushed… hard to maintain the others.

Breath and focus!

Kuthanaga noticed a small trickle of blood from Xanari's nose. He focused on her and healed her gently so as to not interrupt her concentration. She was deep in focus now.

Pull your energy into your core and focus on stability.

Another of my mirrors has died.

Where are they at?

San Francisco.

Pull the mirrors closest to them to you now.

Xanari did as she was ordered and discipline and training took over. She washed away the fear and regained her composure. She pulled the mirrors which were closest to the ones who died away and was horrified to see buildings collapsing.

Xanari, do not be concerned. It was an earthquake. When we get to the main city of Atlantis we'll learn more I'm sure.

His calmness eased her slightly and she nodded.

Meditate now and heal yourself.

They both returned to their sitting position and closed their eyes.

They traveled on for another two hours and they were surrounded on all sides by darkness. Rachel had fallen asleep as had Joy and Tim. Kuthanaga opened his eyes and Xanari stood up.

"Wake them gently Xanari, we're here."

Tim and Joy woke quickly. Rachel took a few more moments to compose herself and she stood slowly.

"Where are we?" Rachel asked sleepily.

"Atlantis."

Kuthanaga closed his eyes and held his necklace with a firm grip and said a single word which Tim forgot the moment he heard it.

The platform they were on shifted slightly and then it started to drop down into the ground. It moved quickly but not too fast where anyone felt like they were losing their footing. After about four minutes a slight glow illuminated the tunnel they were in. Tim got close to the edge and could see light streaming up towards them. The tunnel they were in was almost glass smooth and it had a slight shimmer to it.

"It looks…"

"Alien." Kuthanaga said with a smile.

"Yeah."

"Because it is in a way. When the Atlanteans were here they had to make sure it was livable because at that time the Earth was still very cold. They used some of the remainder of the technology we had with us to carve out tunnels and used a lot of energy stored in this location. They discovered an energy source on this continent which was unique to the planet. Using crystals harvested from deep underground here they manipulated energy even when the Earth was sleeping. The shimmering you see there is fine dust of the crystals. As we get closer to the main city the energy will grow. I think you're going to like this Joy."

Joy stood next to Tim as the light grew brighter, so bright that they momentarily had to shield their eyes as it reached its full brilliance. Joy gasped as Kuthanaga pointed.

The platform stopped and they were looking at a city easily three times the size of San Francisco. It had towers made of crystal and smaller buildings all arranged facing the central pyramid. The pyramid was made of pure gold and it reflected the light coming from the crystal structures that surrounded it. The city was in the bottom of a giant pocket of crystals. Crystals of all shapes and sizes hung from the ceiling of the grand chamber.

"A pyramid?" asked Tim pointing at it.

Kuthanaga nodded.

"Yes, the very first one, the most powerful one. This pyramid was a channeling mechanism and also allowed the Atlanteans to flee this area once it was swallowed by the ocean. Their population was too much for this city to sustain, so they fled the crust after we did and have been waiting for the Convergence for a long while. They will return to the city once the Convergence is over. Atlantis will rise again and all you see here will resurface as well."

It was a surreal experience. There was air and the tunnel they had arrived through was barely visible lost in the maze of crystals.

It was warm and Tim noticed that it was slightly breezy.

"Wow feels like the beach."

"The heat is from nearby magma tunnels. These crystals keep out all the dangerous elements and create a livable environment. I've spent a few hundred years in here off and on studying the environment and I can honestly say there is no other place on the crust that can match this."

Tim thought he heard the faint sound of music.

"Is anyone else here?"

"Sadly, no. The few that decided to remain died a long time ago. The music you are hearing is the crystals. They sing. Some have speculated that the crystals are aware."

Tim strained and the music sounded like feminine Gregorian chants.

"It's beautiful."

Kuthanaga nodded and closed his eyes. The platform again began to move. It slid silently towards the pyramid.

"Where we staying at?" asked Tim.

"The pyramid."

"This place is huge."

"Yes, it is the capital city. There are twenty more chambers similar to this one but this is the crown jewel."

"Wow, so Atlantis is big."

Kuthanaga nodded. "Yes, it's very large and there's two main continent pieces connected by tunnels. This is the western continent. The eastern and larger of the two is just west of Portugal. There are twin pyramids there but they aren't made of gold."

"And gold is important why?"

"It's an ore from the Earth which allows for easier manipulation of universal energy. As we get closer to the Convergence, normal humans will be able to do incredible things with gold. The more gold they have the more they can tap into. But there's also a risk to those who don't know what to do with the energy."

"Oh shit, imagine if Mr. T was still wearing all that gold."

Joy laughed and slugged Tim in the shoulder.

"Can you go more than ten minutes without some wise ass joke?"

"Nope."

Joy stepped past Tim and got closer to Kuthanaga.

"Will they be able to do what we do?"

He shook his head. "Doubtful."

"Well what will they be able to do?"

"Read minds, project thoughts, basic transmutations of one thing into another. Nothing like what Tim did."

Joy nodded and looked nervously at Tim.

"Well at least here we won't have to worry about killing anyone by accident right Xanari?" joked Tim.

Xanari considered this and nodded.

They got closer to the pyramid and when they came upon it they all realized just how massive the structure was. There were hundreds of thousands of gold slabs in place and they were smooth as glass. Tim wondered how they were able to make the bars so smooth when he smiled to himself.

"What is so funny Tim?"

"I just figured out how they built this."

Kuthanaga leaned closer. "How"

"With their minds. They just willed it a certain way and the gold did what they wanted."

Kuthanaga smiled. "In a way you're right. When you meet the Atlanteans you can ask them for a demonstration."

Tim nodded.

"So what's the deal with the pyramids? I've seen em everywhere and had a friend of mine who swore it was like one of the symbols of the Illuminati."

"Illuminati?"

Kuthanaga seemed at a loss for a moment and then laughed.

"Ah yes, well your friend is right. The pyramid is a holy symbol of the Draconians. We found that their symbols hold great power on the crust and so there was a melding of cultures between our three races. I believe the Drakes still use it as markers. They influence a great deal on the crust and I'd imagine they have their claws in damn near everything by now."

"Do you think they are nervous about the Convergence?" asked Joy.

"No, if I know them, they have multiple contingencies in place. Plus with the Quinuks helping them, there is no doubt they will hole up somewhere and ride out the chaos."

The platform rose to the top of the pyramid and the top was opened wide enough to allow the platform to slide down into it.

"Well this will be home base for the next twelve months."

The chamber opened up into a very wide room with several hallways. The décor reminded Tim of fancy rich modern art airy lofts with lots of wide open spaces. Wild angles jutted this way and that. There was a huge crystal in the center of the room and many cushions were positioned neatly around it. There were several larger cushions also pointing towards the central crystal.

"What's up with everything pointing towards the big crystals?" asked Tim.

"You sleep with your head at the top. That way you share dreams with your mates."

"Mates?"

Kuthanaga nodded. "They are Annukai, but they have different cultural beliefs than we do. While we mate with only one, they have several mates at the same time. The royal family had nine men and nine women and they all belonged to each other."

"Wait you mean they were swingers?"

"Swingers? They were interested in increasing their population and when you live for more than 30,000 years you tend to want... variety? That is how it was explained to me."

Tim thought about that.

"Yeah I can see how Joy would get sick of me after a thousand years or so..."

"More like fifty years!" she jabbed him.

"Damn, you're a cold piece you know that?"

Kuthanaga walked to the main crystal.

"Tim lay down on that bed there."

Tim shrugged and did as he was instructed.

Kuthanaga ran his finger along a crystal ring which ran along the outer edge of the large crystal and it vibrated and hummed slightly.

"Cool." said Joy.

"OK, Tim prepare yourself for something a bit different."

Tim was about to say something when his eyes focused on something that Joy couldn't see and he blurted out.

"Wait… go back!"

Kuthanaga ran his finger back for a brief moment.

"Holy fuck?"

"What?!" asked Joy.

"I think I'm watching the news and there some bad stuff going on right now."

"Such as?"

"Earthquake."

"What? How are you seeing? I wanna see."

Joy went to an adjacent bed and laid down. She felt a wild vibration at the base of her skull and a few feet in front of her an image materialized. She could see a young pretty newscaster and could hear her speaking.

Rachel copied Joy and she also took position on one of the beds. Xanari closed her eyes and waited. She had experienced some of what they were seeing and she had no desire to revisit it.

"We are reporting again live from downtown San Francisco that an 8.0 earthquake has hit central Daly City and has devastated much of San Francisco and outlying areas. The first quake hit at 7:25am and lasted for twenty seconds. It was followed an hour later by a 7.9 earthquake which lasted fifteen seconds. Fires can be seen everywhere and there is major structural damage and collapses…"

"Jesus." said Tim with a solemn tone.

The camera man panned the area and Tim and Joy both shuddered as they saw their old apartment complex completely obliterated.

"Man, that's our old place. If we were still there we'd be…"

Tim couldn't finish his sentence. He was suddenly aware he was supposed to be dead many times over and he was beginning to think he was cheating death.
Tim sat up and the image faded.

"What the hell man? I thought there was twelve months before the Convergence."

"Yes that is true. But it doesn't happen all at once. An event happens here and an event happens there. Recall the earthquakes in Japan and Chile those were examples of what will come. All gaining in intensity and destructive nature until it culminates with the fusing of all five outer dimensions onto the crust. The Earth is waking and she will move much more before the full Convergence. This is just the beginning."

Tim was scared and relieved at the same time. Scared to see what was going to happen and relieved that he was with Joy and Kuthanaga.

Chapter 43 – Contingency Plans
January 1st 2012 – New York 8:59 pm

Richard watched the news and saw the city by the bay burning. He wasn't shocked, he knew it was coming. He and the other Draconians had long removed all vital personnel from red zones and knew there was nothing of importance lost in the disaster. He knew also that the earthquakes would continue for at least a week and would cause much more destruction after the fact. Projected death toll was well over a million residents and that number also was to rise as time went on. The only thing which was of concern to Richard was the timing. The Convergence was going to affect many things and he had read all the reports from previous merging but the time-line on this seemed accelerated somehow. The Quinuks had predicted that the large earthquake along the San Andreas Fault wouldn't go until the end of first quarter. This was three months ahead of schedule. If there were off by so much with this event what of the others?

Richard stood up and walked from the comfort of his over-sized chair and wondered silently if the preparations the Draconians had spent trillions on was going to be sufficient for the Convergence. He shrugged and retrieved his phone. Dialing a number he waited. A single ring and he heard Dmitri's voice.

"Yes Richard."

"What does our Quinuk friends have to say about the quake?"

"They are somewhat indifferent in their answering of my questions. I pointed out their time-line was off by a large factor and they simply replied that their estimations are just that, estimations. They are using data from previous Convergences and as you know each one was different from the previous. This is the first Convergence where all the planes will come in contact with the crust."

"I understand that. My question is a bit more urgent. Do they still think the underground bases will handle the Convergence?"

"Yes, they made sure that these locations were safe from the displacement that other areas will face when the planes collide with the crust."

"And what of the polar shift? The crustal displacement?"

"Has also been factored in. The bases are like giant sealed containers. Regardless of what happens above them, we should be safe."

Richard nodded. Something in Dmitri's voice told him that the man had been over these specific details many times and was completely satisfied with them.

"Good. I am relieved to hear this."

"Yes, and Tiamat 2 is already secured and loaded in our location. Have you been down there yet?"

"No, I haven't. Been too damn busy to take the trip. You?"

"Yes. It's pretty amazing really. Ours is large enough to hold a quarter million. That's including the animals, food storage, equipment, etc."

"How much supplies have they packed away this time?"

"Enough for a couple hundred years if we need it. That doesn't take into consideration the food and crops we could harvest on our own if we needed. A bit of an overkill in my opinion."

"Well the last few times these Convergences have occurred the landscape wasn't useful for a while and it was uncomfortable. They want to make sure this time things will be covered. Just in case."

"I see. Was there anything else you needed?"

"No, I just wanted to double check, as I know there will be questions and I like having the answers."

"I'll let you know if anything else pops up."

Richard hung the phone up and paced a bit. He was feeling a bit nervous. He wasn't sure why, but he was trembling slightly. Fear was a normal feeling even for drakes but what he was feeling was far more intense than anything he had ever experienced. It wasn't the Convergence. Conflict wasn't the issue either. He cherished the thrill of battle and savored the thought of facing Kuthanaga again. The Planet Slayers he realized was what was bothering him. He recalled the look on

Kuthanaga's face and he knew that even the great Kuthanaga himself was terrified of the potential of being found by them. He glanced at the television again and watched the newscaster as she showed horrific pictures of buildings on fire. The sky was filled with darkness and people were walking around with dazed confused looks on their faces. His phone rang and he glanced down. The caller-ID revealed it was Melissa.

"Yes?"

"So what's the latest? I'm watching the news about San Francisco. Isn't this early?"

"Yes it is. But I've been informed that all the preparations are in place already. If you would feel more secure, you can take the boys and head to the bunker."

"Do you think it wise to go so soon?"

Richard paused and considered.

"I think it wise to prepare for an early transport. You know the events will get wilder as time goes on. Considering this earthquake is a few months early I wouldn't object if you took the kids within a week. I wouldn't wait longer than a month all things considered."

She paused.

"And what of you husband?"

"I'll join you before the final lockdown."

She sighed.

"I shall instruct the boys to go into the bunker and will wait with you. That way I can make sure that you make it before lockdown."

He chuckled at that.

"As you wish."

"What are you doing now?"

Richard paced the room more.

"Thinking."

She could hear a tone in his voice which concerned her.

"About?"

"After the Convergence we'll be visible to them."

She knew what he was referring to and she took a slow long breath.

"Do you think they will find us?"

"I can't see how they couldn't"

"Is there any way to defend ourselves?"

"No."

She paused and felt her heart race a bit.

"What if we fled?"

"There's no place left to hide. This planet was special. We have no time and very little options."

"But there are options?"

"Yes. Potential options."

"Such as?"

"Tiamat... And something rumored to be in the possession of the Annukai."

"How could Tiamat handle them?"

"It won't work until the last possible moment and would require a lot of modification and luck. The device that the Annukai have is a remnant of the old technologies. If used with Tiamat there's a slight chance we could stand against them."

"If we were successful what would it mean?"

"More time. The victory would be short lived. It would give us a few decades to plan our next move. It would hopefully take them that long to get their weapon close enough to us to attack again."

"You do not sound optimistic."

"Because I am not. We are running these scenarios based off of our last encounter which occurred thousands of years ago. Who knows what advancement they have made in that time. The variables are too many to account for. That prevents me from optimism."

"I understand. I'll check in with you later."

She hung up and Richard felt slightly better discussing his fears with his wife but the fear lingered on.

Chapter 44 – Corruption

January 19th 2012 – Atlantis 9:46 am

Tim had been watching the news daily after arriving in Atlantis and was amazed at the damage the earthquake had caused. Not just on a local level, but on an international level. The stock-market crashed at levels never seen before and the destruction was epic. It was so powerful it was reported that it had slowed the Earth's rotation and the shaking was felt as far away as Texas. Hundreds of aftershocks rocked the Bay on a daily basis and it was apocalyptic in visage and sound. Joy would join Tim and they would observe most of the news in somber silence. They wondered what else was to come. They had been informed the earthquakes were just the tip of the iceberg and worse events were coming.

Kuthanaga had been quiet and Xanari spent much of her time deep in meditation. Rachel was deeply depressed and spent much of her time sleeping and jotting notes in a journal she had.

Tim wondered about his sister and her family. Joy took his hand suddenly and he snapped back and smiled weakly at her.

"Hey you. You cool?"

He squeezed her hand and nodded.

"Yeah. Just thinking about Judy. I can't help but wonder what might happen over there when things get bad. I haven't asked if they are gonna be protected or not."

"I'm sure Kuthanaga will get them to safety with us."

Tim nodded.

"But what if it's better to just pass then go into the collective? I mean everything is going to be completely different. We have no idea of what to expect. Plus there's the test that we all have to pass or else we're on our own. Who knows how crazy that might be. I don't know. I guess I'm just kinda scared is all."

Joy nodded. She liked the new Tim. The old Tim would've just put up a front of what a bad-ass he was and she would've just had to guess to how he felt.

"I know. I'm scared too. But at least we'll be together."

He nodded and realized it didn't matter how weird or bad things could get. He could handle anything as long as Joy was by his side.

"Thanks baby-doll." he said as he held her firmly in his arms.

"No worries. You want me to ask Kuthanaga about Judy and them?"

"Nah. I'll ask later."

Tim was interrupted by a soft yet distinctive moan.

Joy looked past Tim and saw that Rachel was deep in her sleep and it was obvious that she was having a bad dream. Neither one of them were surprised as she had been having them almost on a daily basis since arriving in Atlantis. Something was different this time though. She was clenched tightly and her moans increased. She got so loud that Xanari entered the room with a puzzled look on her face.

"What's going on?" Xanari asked with concern growing on her flawless face.

"Got me! She's having another dream, but this one must be hella bad."

Xanari closed her eyes and concentrated on Rachel. A brief moment passed and the world went vertigo with prismatic colors which shifted to muted grays and blacks. Thousands of people were clawing and battling with each other. They attacked wildly with no real focus. Savage beastly attacks at each other until one would fall. The victor would then set his sight on another and begin an assault anew. The streets were covered in blood, which ran like thick dark crimson rivers mixed with bits of flesh here and there. The sky too was dark and black, filled with angry clouds which saw no end. A hot wind brought the foul stench of death to Rachel's nose. She stood there watching the carnage continue unabated for what seemed like hours to her. Grunts and wails of anger filled the air and she tried to close her eyes but they would not obey. She felt waves of nausea and anguish wash over her like a cold wet blanket being pulled through her core.

Rachel, relax. I am here with you. You are dreaming. It is just a dream.

"No Xanari! This is no dream. This is what will be!"

270

What caused this?

Rachel pointed to a small bottle drenched in blood. The label read 'Potential X'

"This liquid is the vehicle of destruction. Delivered to us by Kuthanaga..."

Xanari paused and watched as Rachel picked up the small bottle opened it and started to pour out a milky white liquid. Several people who were fighting saw Rachel pouring and immediately were upon her pummeling and tearing at her. A few of them dropped to the blood soaked ground and started licking away feverishly at the spots where the milky liquid had splattered. Rachel screamed one last time and fell silent.

Joy was holding Rachel and Tim stood nearby. Xanari opened her eyes and she said nothing.

"What the fuck was all that about Xanari?" asked Tim.

She stood there processing what she had seen. Was this part of Kuthanga's grand plan? Did he plan on the death and destruction of that magnitude to help the determination of the billion they would shelter? She shook her head.

"Xanari, what was she dreaming about?" asked Joy.

"Horrible. Let her rest. I must speak with Kuthanaga first before saying anything else." she turned then and left the room.

Tim looked at Joy who simply shrugged as she set Rachel back down in her bed.

"Dude, that last scream kinda freaked me out."

Joy nodded as she looked at Rachel who was deep in sleep snoring gently.

"Me too. Wonder what that was all about. Xanari seemed upset."

"Horrible."

"What?"

"She said horrible."

Joy nodded slowly as Tim continued his thought.

"After the shit we've seen. Horrible is a scary ass word for her to use. I mean the quake was horrible to me... And she didn't even seem faded by it. So what the fuck is horrible to her?"

"Let's let Rachel rest."

Tim nodded and followed Joy out of the chamber into their sleeping area. When they were far enough away Joy took Tim's hand and stared deep into his eyes.

"I love you."

Tim was taken aback by the sincerity and tenderness in her voice.

"I love you too baby. What's wrong?"

"Nothing. Just want to let you know is all."

"I know. OK, so what do we do now? Watch more depressing ass news on the Bay Quake? Hunt down Xanari and find out what exactly is horrible to her. Or explore this place more?"

"I vote for exploring."

Tim nodded. "Yeah, that's my vote too."

Joy took Tim's hand and they walked on.

Xanari hardly noticed them as they passed by her as she stood patiently in front of Kuthanaga who was deep in meditation. She silently cursed under her breath. She knew better than to disturb an elder Annukai but she had broken many rules thus far and it seemed so had Kuthanaga. She focused gently on him and said his name once.

Kuthanaga.

He opened his eyes and focused on her. He could see something was weighing heavily on her. She had tried to mask her anxiety when she interrupted his meditation but he felt it as clear as if she had hit him with a block of ice.

"What troubles you Xanari?"

"Rachel has had another dream."

"Really?" he could hear a slight tone in her voice as she struggled to control that which was fighting to be blurted out.

"Yes. She saw some... troubling things and have made some serious allegations against... you."

He stood and nodded.

"I was wondering when she would see the effects of the Earth's Milk."

"You knew the level of it?"

He nodded solemnly.

"Yes, the addictive properties would cause them to do some pretty questionable things. Stealing, fighting, etc. All

272

meant to aid us in the discovery of the humans with the strongest moral foundation."

"Are you sure you know what you are speaking of? What I saw was not someone who was addicted just trying to get more of the drug. What I saw was barbaric... pure evil."

Kuthanaga could hear the fear and disgust in her voice. In the time Xanari had been on the crust and been observing he knew she had witnessed many horrific acts which humans had inflicted on each other and he knew she must have learned a great deal of the nature of addiction. Something was not right.

"Can you please share with me what you saw?"

She nodded and closed her eyes. Kuthanaga closed his eyes and witnessed what she showed.

He was stone-faced and silent. When she finished his eyes snapped open and he shook his head.

"That is far worse than anything that the Earth's Milk is supposed to do. That was modified in extremes so far that the humans become nothing more than mindless wild animals. The Milk is alive and if freely shared has great healing effects and increases the bond between those who are sharing it. If someone were to steal it or sell it for self-gain the liquid becomes tainted and the effects are different. They still will seem quite beneficial but the drinker of the tainted milk will become ill and suffer withdrawal effects until they are given some freely and shared with the natural Earth's Milk. Whatever the Potential X version of the milk is, it is something far worse than anything I ever intended or even feared. The only question on my mind now is who would do this? Rachel blamed me for this potential atrocity for which I will shoulder the blame since it was I who released the milk in the first place. But I did not plan on it getting this far out of hand."

"Do you think it was the Draconians?"

"I do not think it was them. While I do think they would like a version that was addictive to help them control and enslave the humans again, I do not think they would allow something that destructive out since they would fall victim to it as well."

"Then who?"

"Possibly the humans by accident will do this..."

"Or?"

"Or we have another player for who we have not been aware of all this time. It is possible that other groups have infiltrated the crust while we were off phased. Or something else for which we have yet to see. I'll have to look into this. Were you able to gauge when this scene you saw actually took place?"

"No. I am sorry. The scene was too chaotic and the only thing which stood out was the skyline. It was dark and ominous like the sky itself was enraged."

Kuthanaga nodded.

"It matters not. It seems we won't be able to just wait it out here. We'll have to venture out and try to prevent this from happening."

Xanari nodded.

Kuthanaga didn't let Xanari see the concern he had. With everything they were facing and everything that could possibly go wrong the last thing he wanted was another major obstacle. He had a very bad feeling about the modified Earth's Milk. He would have to work quickly, since he had no idea who was responsible for the tampering.

Chapter 45 – Potential
January 23rd 2012 – Mexico City Mexico 12:46 pm

Victor Menendez sat in small ergonomic gray computer chair his long jet black hair pulled back into a tight ponytail. He was slim and tightly packed muscle wise and his skin was a deep bronze in color. His eyes were sunken in and the skin on his face seemed pulled very tight making his features seem exaggerated and chiseled. He wore a light gray suit and wore no jewelry. He was sitting in a warehouse control room with old wood surrounding him.

There was stillness around him and a stale dank smell permeated the air. The room was silent except for the small humming sound of the computer in front of him. He was reading a news report about the great quake of San Francisco and he grinned slightly. There was a slight buzzing noise and he glanced down at his cell phone. There was a text message waiting for him that simply read 'It's done.' He put his phone away and continued reading, with a grin spreading even wider.

Victor took a deep breath and stood. He closed the lid of his laptop and walked out of the office. He closed the door behind him and it squeaked slightly. He continued down a long flight of stairs and the warehouse appeared completely empty. He turned and went into another room and the sound of heavy machines and automated systems were barely audible and as he passed though each door the sound increased. After walking through several doors he entered a large room which had dozens of workers busy unloading large crates and setting up complicated machinery.

One man in the chaotic symphony of workers was standing still at a small table with a microscope and several glass beakers filled with white liquid. His name was Enrique Sanchez. He was tall and bit heavy set. He had very skinny thighs and legs which were exaggerated by his heavy upper torso.

Victor walked over to the Enrique and nodded at him.

"It works?"

"Yes, see there?"

Enrique pointed at a small glass case which had eight rats in it.

"They have been given a very potent dose of PX and you can see they are very active."

Victor watched as they ran around in the case very excited. They were interacting and everything seemed normal with them except the speed which they were moving.

"Now I'll introduce the trigger."

He opened the cage and took a small dropper and put it near one of the rats which drank as he squeezed the liquid out.

"How long does it take?"

"It's almost instant." he quickly pulled his hand out of the cage and before he could close the lid the rat started squeaking. It dropped down and was in obvious pain. It slowly stood and the other rats quickly moved away from him seeming to sense there was something wrong with it. The angry rat stood and crouched and attacked the closest rat with savagery that Victor had never seen before in a rat, systematically attacked and killed all the other rats in mere moments.

Victor smiled.

"Perfect."

Enrique nodded. "Yes, we will get the gringos hooked on PX and then once we unleash the trigger we'll ransom the cure and make trillions."

Victor smiled. "Yes. The cure works?"

Enrique nodded and took out another dropper. As he opened the cage he put the long dropper through the crack and slowly slid it down to the agitated crazed rat. The rat sniffed around and attacked the dropper and quickly drank as each drop poured out. With each swallow it calmed down. After a few seconds it curled up and slept.

"It is exhausted from everything and will sleep for nearly a day."

Victor nodded.

"How much liquid is needed to counteract the trigger?"

"Depends on the subject, but typically one tablespoon for a large adult male."

"Will the cure replicate?"

"No. It is genetically modified as well."

"Good work Enrique."

Enrique smiled satisfied with the compliment.

"Well if you had not provided us with the stolen documents from the Americans, I'm not sure we would have been able to find the right sequence to modify. But once we knew what we were dealing with it was relatively easy."

Victor nodded.

"How soon until we can start to smuggle this across the borders?"

"We just need a little prep time to get the liquid modified in large enough quantities and packaged up. Maybe a week at most, but we have a few hundred we can start with now to get people exposed to it."

"Do it. I want this going full speed by the end of the week. We can use the distraction of the quake as a window. While the Americans are stretched thin still dealing with that, we will be able to get this into their system before they even know what's happening. "

"I understand."

Victor walked away smiling to himself. Enrique was talented and Victor was happy with the progress he had made with the modifications. His plan was coming along nicely. He knew he had a small window of opportunity before the Annukai and Draconians caught wind of what he was doing, but by the time that happened it would be too late for them to do anything about it.

Chapter 46 – Investigations
January 27th 2012 – Atlantis 4:50 pm

Tim knew something was going on and he felt like a child whose parents were hiding bad news and were trying to shelter him from it. It aggravated him to no end. Joy could feel it as well. Rachel had become almost mute not talking very much and she avoided discussing the dream.

They were all sitting around a large crystal slab eating fresh seafood and drinking a liquid, which was very sweet. Joy was drinking her Earth's Milk and Tim was as well, Rachel avoided it like it was the plague and Xanari and Kuthanaga barely ate or drank most of the time so nothing seemed out of the ordinary, yet there was a tension so obvious it could be touched.

"OK, what the fuck?!" Tim blurted out.

Kuthanaga glanced at Tim and Joy and then looked at Xanari. Rachel seemed to not notice or care about Tim's outburst.

"Yeah guys!" added Joy.

"Seriously what's going on?"

Xanari looked down and Kuthanaga sat a bit stiffer and rolled his shoulders stretching.

"We have some new developments."

Tim nodded.

"Developments?"

Kuthanaga nodded slowly and stared at Tim squarely.

"You mean like, besides the Convergence?"

"Yes."

Tim threw his hands up.

"What is it this time? Giant comet going to slam into the Earth? Zombie invasion? What?"

"Zombie invasion. Interesting choice of words."

Tim looked at Kuthanaga and did a double take.

"W-What?"

"Not literal like the zombies of your movies, but the similarities are there nonetheless."

"Are you fuckin' kidding me?!! Zombies?"

"More like violent crazed homicidal addicts would be more specific."

Joy looked at Tim and then back at Kuthanaga.

"How?"

Rachel pointed at Joy's glass.

Joy stared at the glass and then back at Kuthanaga.

"She's kidding right?"

Kuthanaga shook his head.

"No. It would seem that someone is going to modify the Earth's Milk and the consequences are dire."

Joy pushed her glass away.

"What about our milk? Is it going to do anything to us?"

Kuthanaga shook his head.

"No, that's the source. It is pure and you didn't steal it. It was given to you."

Tim stood up with his hands in the air.

"Wait, you mean to tell me, that somebody has the milk and is jacking it up just to turn people into psycho zombies? What's up with that? Is it the drakes doing it?"

Xanari smiled when Tim asked the question.

"I asked the same question," she said.

Kuthanaga shook his head. "No as I told Xanari, I doubt the Draconians would do that. They want slaves not animals. From what we saw in Rachel's dream, the people were completely out of control. That would be of no use for the drakes. I would imagine at this junction they are more concerned about preparing for the Convergence and reintegration of the outer planes then enslaving the humans."

"Well if it isn't the drakes... Who the hell is it?"

"We are trying to figure that out right now."

Tim sat down and allowed his shoulders to roll and droop.

"So that's what you meant by horrible Xanari?"

She nodded.

Joy thought for a second.

"Who has the milk now? We know the Drakes have some. We know there was some in Bimini. Where else?"

Kuthanaga answered, "There were three locations. Canada, Mexico and Bimini. Canada is locked down. I have already checked everyone involved with that location and for the time being it is being hidden. Mexico was being spread quickly but the town was massacred and the Mexican government has sealed up the whole area and put up a metal container around the area to prevent outsiders from being exposed to it. They are examining it and have lots of scientist working on it. Bimini is similar. Government controlled. From what we are seeing on scanning people involved, everyone is in analysis mode. They know the liquid is special but so far no one we have come across has actually done any form of modification to it yet."

Joy nodded.

"Massacred town? By who the government?"

Kuthanaga shook his head.

"No, a drug cartel came in and wiped out the town and took a large amount and left with it."

"Well there you go." Exclaimed Joy.

"Hell yeah!" added Tim.

Kuthanaga looked at Joy.

"What do you mean?"

"That's the only group who you haven't really checked. It must be them."

Kuthanaga nodded.

"Yes, but the odd thing is. Every one of the men who had attacked the village is now dead. We don't know where they are. There were 63 men. All killed. Someone went out of their way to make sure it would be hard to locate them. Fortunately, I had a watcher there during the massacre and he was able to get some information from the attackers. I will be working with him today."

Tim shook his head.

"Wonder why they would want to make crazed addicts? Is it because the people couldn't get their fix? I mean where's the payoff on killing you customers? You wanna get em hooked and then keep on the line as long as possible, bleeding every cent out. If you customers start killing each other, it doesn't make any sense."

Kuthanaga nodded.

"I thought the same thing. The only other options I can think of is eradication of your enemy, or ransom."

Tim nodded.

"Yeah if you had a shitload of crazed junkies and sold the cure to the highest bidder you could make a lot of money."

Joy shook her head.

"That makes sense, but doesn't feel right. Something just feels weird about this whole situation. All the governments have it and they can barely make sense of it, but the drugman gets it and can make super drugs with it that turns the user into a crazy zombie? Something isn't right about this."

Xanari nodded in agreement.

"I don't have your logic to support my feelings, but I do feel something is odd about this situation. Kuthanaga you mentioned the Quinuks had discovered the milk long ago and they modified it. Their modified version drove them mad. That level of addiction seems to be what we saw in Rachel's dream. Wouldn't you say?"

"True it would seem that way, but the Quinuks are very fragile and a few Annukai had tasted their modified version without experiencing the same level of addiction. I'm basing my expectations on what the Annukai experienced since humans are more closely related to Annukai and not Quinuks."

"What about them?" asked Joy.

"The Quinuks?"

"Yes. Would they have any reason to want to wipe us out?"

"Not really. They actually enjoy humans. Humans make the Quinuks feel superior, and if you want to endear a Quinuk to you, make him feel superior. I will look into that regardless though."

"What can we do to help?" asked Tim.

"You can help us by monitoring the systems and compiling the incoming data so we can sort through potential leads."

Tim grinned. "I meant is there anything physical we can do to help?"

Kuthanaga shook his head.

"Not at the moment. The drakes think you're dead and I'd like to keep it that way."

Tim shrugged.

"Cool, whatever. I just am pretty bored here and would love to do something other than exercise, eat and sleep."

Kuthanaga nodded.

"You will be in service again soon I fear, but for now, just monitor the news and let me know if you come across anything. I will be working with Reshnogga to follow up on the Blood Cartel. Xanari, keep working with your mirrors and continue what you are doing. Rachel, I know you're angry with me. But if you have any more details in your dreams please let us know."

She simply nodded and took another bite of fish.

Kuthanaga stood and excused himself from the table while Joy and Tim finished their meal. Xanari simply closed her eyes and focused on her mirrors.

Kuthanaga retreated to his quarters and sat down. He focused on Reshnogga and after a few moments, he could feel the presence in his mind.

Yes Kuthanaga?

Reshnogga, how are you doing?

I am well. The markings are proceeding as I expected. I must tell you though. I am growing tired of human weakness. There are many who obsess over trivial things like clothing, favorite sports teams and sex. For every one human I mark in my heart I feel only every tenth one will actually make it through the tests. All this work may be for nothing Kuthanaga. Many Annukai will not like the integration of humans among them.

I appreciate your honesty in this matter. I know things will work themselves out in the end, but for now I need you to help me look into something that you may have seen during the massacre.

Kuthanaga could feel the mixture of anger and resentment from Reshnogga.

I do not wish to revisit that experience Kuthanaga. I would remind you that you have volunteered to take it upon yourself. I would have you do so now and look into it yourself than waste another moment of my essence there.

Kuthanaga was disappointed in the young Annukai, but at the same time understanding. Kuthanaga had felt the same way watching events like Nazi camps, great purges during the building of the pyramids and other genocides. While these events were horrific to be party to, they offered a glimpse into base human emotion, which Kuthanaga felt, was also that of undisciplined Annukai. Many Annukai were arrogant and dismissed humans as short-lived barbarians, where a small minority saw humans as beings with infinite potential worthy of being preserved. It was obvious that Reshnogga did not want to learn from the experience and Kuthanaga was obligated to do as he promised.

Bring me to your location.

Kuthanaga felt the slight tingling sensation of his body being pulled and a moment later, he was in a tower overlooking a small town. Reshnogga was monitoring his mirrors from the top of an old church.

"Kuthanaga."

"Reshnogga, are you ready?"

He nodded and Kuthanaga stepped forward and placed his hands on his head. He took a deep breath and scanned until he got to the day of the attack. He could see Reshnogga observing and even scanning some of the attackers. Kuthanaga focused and pulled the memories free and then placed them into his mind as if they were his own. He had done this procedure only once before and it pained him daily to revisit those alien memories. No more than two seconds had passed and Kuthanaga was finished.

"Kuthanaga, I cannot recall any details of that day and for that, I thank you."

"No, I thank you for doing your duty and going above and beyond. I shall now leave you to your task."

Kuthanaga focused on his mirror he had left at Atlantis and a few moments later, was in his sanctuary.

Reshnogga, I would have you do one more service in addition to marking.

What would that be?

Seek any additional information you can on a group called the Blood Cartel

As you say, it will be done.

He felt the presence of Reshnogga fade from his mind. He sat there in silence for a long while building his composure. He looked at the memories and slowed each down to a snail's pace so he could focus on all the details and extract all the information he could. All the while he also had to force out Reshnogga's emotional reactions to what he was seeing which was proving to be difficult as Reshnogga was not prepared for what he was experiencing and the emotions were both profound and powerful.

After spending twelve hours on the event, which took four, Kuthanaga had managed to extract a great deal more details than he had previously had. He stood up and looked for the others.

Xanari was deep in focus on her mirrors; Rachel was sound asleep as was Joy. Tim was awake and viewing the remote crystals. He was doing research on the internet.

"Find out anything Tim?"

Tim was startled.

"Yeah, there was a lot of information online about the Blood Cartel."

"I've learned a great deal as well."

"The guy we want to look at is some guy named Victor Menendez."

Kuthanaga nodded.

"Yes, his name came up many times within their memories."

"Well did their minds tell you that this guy is rich? I mean like fuck-you rich. The kicker is this guy's family has had money forever. So why mix up in the drug trade when you're that loaded?"

"Yes, I learned that as well. As to why he entered the drug trade I do not know nor do I care. I know where he is though and I'm going to go there to ask him some questions."

"Sweet. Do you know for sure he's the guy?"

Kuthanaga nodded.

"How do you know?"

"Because he knew where the liquid would be and he sent the killers a few days before the liquid showed up."

"So?"

"So only I knew roughly where the liquid would show up, and even then I didn't know exact locations until it started to emerge. My point is, there is no way a human could've known that unless he had some sophisticated equipment and knew what I was going to do, or he had help."

Tim had a chill creep in his spine.

"So what exactly are we dealing with here?"

Kuthanaga shrugged and then smiled.

"I don't know but I'm going to find out. I don't think I'll need any help but stay alert in case I need to pull you to me."

"Wait? You mean you could pull me to you before?"

"No. But, I've been watching you lately and want to try something with you. It may be uncomfortable and may not work but I'd like to try."

"Sure thing. What is it? Another barb or something like that?"

"No this is a bit more... involved."

Tim shrugged.

"As long as you're not putting anything painful in my junk, go for it."

Kuthanaga stood over Tim, placed one hand on Tim's chest, and began to chant a low grumbling guttural set of phrases. Tim felt a wild burning sensation, which passed from the location Kuthanaga was touching to the furthest reaches of his body. The pain was mild at first and then escalated to white searing agony, which seemed to fill Tim's whole existence. How long he was in that state, he had no idea as he slowly blacked out.

"Tim..." the sound came from a million miles away.

"Tim..." the sound was much closer now.

"Tim!" he opened his eyes and saw Kuthanaga there.

"Oh fuck man. What did you do that for? That was the worst yet. What the hell did you do?"

"Made us more... compatible."

"Compatible?"

"Yes, now we'll test to see if it worked."

Kuthanaga walked out of the room and Tim sat there still feeling very dizzy.

Tim, can you hear me? this time the sound was more intense in his head and he could *feel* Kuthanaga.

Yeah.

You may feel a tugging sensation, if you do just relax and let it take you.

OK.

Just as Kuthanaga said, there was a strong pulling sensation that Tim allowed to pull him and the next thing he knew he was standing next to Kuthanaga.

"Fuck me! That was weird. My hair is tingling."

Kuthanaga smiled.

"I knew I did right in picking you Tim."

"How were you able to do that?"

"In time Tim. Rest now and do not mention this to Xanari. You may discuss it with Joy but please make sure to not bring it up with Xanari."

"Sure thing. Whatever you want."

"Also, Tim. You may start to hallucinate. That is also part of this thing that I have done. Do not be alarmed. What you will see isn't real. They are kind of like walking memories. Kind of a side effect of what I just did. You will know what they are when you see them. Again do not be afraid."

Tim nodded and felt completely exhausted.

"Now go sleep. I'll call on you if I need help."

Tim nodded and walked to his room and plopped down next to Joy and fell instantly to sleep. Kuthanaga nodded to himself and then closed his eyes.

Reshnogga.

Yes, Kuthanaga.

I need you to bring me to one of your mirrors near this location. Kuthanaga revealed where he wanted to go and Reshnogga nodded.

I have a mirror 5 miles from there.

Kuthanaga felt the pull and a moment later, he was standing next to a mirror of Reshnogga. He said nothing more as he began to walk.

Chapter 47 – The Hunt
January 28th 2012 – Mexico City, Mexico 6:41 am

Victor was growing impatient. He had shipments going into America and more than 10,000 samples of the PX were already floating in the market with new customers popping up daily. Even though the United States was deeply entrenched in an economic depression, the market was very receptive to PX and the dealers couldn't keep it in stock. The dealers were ordering more PX than all the other drugs combined and since there were no adverse side effects whenever a transport was intercepted the shipment was eventually allowed to go through to America, as upon inspection the liquid just seemed to be plain milk. That was Enrique's idea and the modification worked. It passed all the base inspections and customs couldn't stop legitimate looking imports from coming into America. It had cost Victor millions of dollars to get the infrastructure right, but he spared no expense to make the project work.

The first major shipment was on its way to America as well as Canada. Over a million bottles of PX was on the move. Everything was moving according to plan. Victor was about to make a call when he sensed something. He paused and smiled.

"Ah alien. I know you are here. There is no need to hide. Come out and let's talk."

Kuthanaga was amazed. The man before him seemed to be human and yet he discovered Kuthanaga too easily. Kuthanaga focused on the man and noticed his aura shifted constantly. As he tried to read Victor, he realized that he couldn't get anything out him. His mind was sealed solid.

"I can feel you trying to read my mind. Not very polite. Now I know which type of alien you are though Annukai. And I think I even know which one you are... Kuthanaga."

Kuthanaga was amazed.

"Come now Kuthanaga. Let's talk shall we?"

Kuthanaga examined the man and then revealed himself.

Victor regarded Kuthanaga and smiled.

"I have to thank you, you know."

Kuthanaga kept a safe distance.

"What do you mean?"

"The milk. If you hadn't gotten it I wouldn't be able to do what I am doing now."

"How exactly did you learn of the milk?"

"Ahhh I see. Full of questions eh my friend?"

"Just a few."

"Well by all means, ask away."

"Why are you modifying the milk? You do know what will happen yes?"

"Yes, I do. As to why... Well that would spoil the surprise."

"How did you modify it in the first place? That is no easy task."

"Well let's just say I am fairly intimate with it, a long history with it."

"I'm afraid that is impossible. Humans have never seen the milk."

Victor smiled. Understanding came to Kuthanaga in a flash.

"But then you're not human."

"Ahhh was wondering when you'd figure that out."

"What are you then?"

"Not yet friend. When next we meet you'll undoubtedly will have more answers to your questions. Good bye for now."

Kuthanaga stood in amazement as Victor faded away. He had a sinking feeling in his stomach and knew this wasn't a good thing. His mind reeled. What was it that he had just seen? There was something familiar that he couldn't quite put his finger on. He walked around the building and examined the workers. No one knew what Victor was. Not even the main scientist who thought he had broken the code on the Earth's Milk. Enrique didn't know that Victor wasn't human and from what Kuthanaga could tell the plan was to get the PX to the general population and then release a trigger which would kick the addiction through the roof. Once it was firmly in effect, they were to ransom the antidote to the highest bidder. Kuthanaga saw the logic there and knew it would work. But when he considered the cryptic answers Victor had given him, he realized that whatever he was, he had more sinister plans in order for the humans. Kuthanaga took a sample of the PX as well as antidote and trigger and then focused on Atlantis. A few moments later, he was back standing in his sanctuary.

Tim and Joy were up although Tim looked worse for wear than Joy. Xanari stood nearby watching and listening.

Tim smiled weakly at Kuthanaga.

"Did you find out anything?"

Kuthanaga nodded.

"Yes, I did Tim. Yes, I did."

Tim nodded slowly. "So, what's up?"

"I wish I knew. I ran into Mr. Menendez. Turns out he's not human."

"Drake? I knew it," said Tim.

Kuthanaga shook his head. "No, he's not Draconian or Quinuk. I am sure he's not Annukai either. I don't know *what* he is."

Tim and Joy were silent for a few seconds.

"What about the Planet Slayers?" asked Xanari.

"What the fuck are Planet Slayers?" asked Tim with a crack in his voice.

Kuthanaga slowly nodded and turned to face Joy and Tim.

"I told you how we were on the Earth, but I didn't tell you why. Long ago, the Annukai, Draconians and Quinuks were on the verge of complete slavery. The race that was attempting to enslave us was known as the Valdorians. We called them Planet Slayers, a name that encapsulated their massive technological weaponry. They had the ability to take a star in a distant galaxy and cause it to go supernova and direct a precise gamma blast to wherever they wanted. They destroyed two Annukai planets before we finally surrendered. The Draconians witnessed the power they possessed during a battle with another race called the Gethonians. Half of the Draconian fleet was wiped out in that attack. The Draconians surrendered as well.

The Quinuks were the ones who convinced us to try to find help and new home worlds to colonize far enough away from them. We had thought we escaped and ended up in this universe. The Quinuks thought that because the Earth was so unique we would be able to hide on it and evade our shared enemy. We didn't know then that the Earth woke up and slept at that time. We took only a small portion of our technology to the surface of the Earth and kept most of our major technology on Earth's smaller moon. The Quinuks were paranoid that somehow we would be found. The majority of us were on the surface of the Earth, the others remained on the moon. When the Planet Slayers attacked, we were fortunate that the smaller moon was far enough away that the debris damage was minor to the Earth. The larger moon also took most of the damage. We were stranded on Earth which was also entering its sleeping stage which offered us some shielding from the Valdorians."

"So you mean you guys got stuck here?" asked Joy.

"Yes."

"We had two moons?" asked Tim.

"Yes."

Joy paused for a moment. "So if the Earth is waking up does that mean that those Planet Slayers will find you?"

Kuthanaga shrugged. "The Quinuks and drakes think so. Which is why I do not think it is a Valdorian doing this Xanari. Getting back to your original question. The Planet Slayers do not play games. They just do what they wish. If a Planet Slayer were here then things would've been much worse a long time ago. No, this is something I have never come across, but whatever he is, he is very old. He knows much about the Earth's Milk."

"So what's this guy's problem?" asked Tim.

"I have no idea. But he is definitely playing some sort of game. He was very polite and seemed to enjoy our conversation. He is aware of Annukai and he even knew my name. That could mean he's a powerful psionic or he has heard of me."

"How's that?" asked Joy.

"Yeah, what is there? Some kind of alien popularity contest?"

Kuthanaga shook his head.

"No, but out of all the Annukai, I have spent the most time on the crust. So in a way I am notorious to those who are aware of the true nature of things."

"So what's the plan now? Did you learn what he's up to?"

"Yes. They are smuggling it into America by disguising it to look like milk.   They already have a large amount being used. A million more is currently on its way. It should be out in circulation within a day or two."

"So are we going to stop it?" asked Tim his mind still reeling from news of larger problem then the tainted milk.

"I'm not even sure how to stop it. It's been delivered to several distributors already. It could take us several days to track down the major players and then the issue of cleansing each person who has used?"

Tim scratched his head deciding to focus on the problem at hand.

"How does this work? Does the PX infect and hook?"

"No, it needs to be triggered. There's a second dose that everyone would need to take."

Kuthanaga showed the two vials he had and then the third.

"What's the last one?"

"The antidote. It will supposedly reverse the triggering agent."

Tim looked at Joy and grinned.

"Well seems easy to me. All we need to focus on it the triggering agent. If no one gets it then no one will go bananas."

Kuthanaga nodded.

"I agree. Only problem is, the people I scanned while in Mexico know nothing about the trigger and so it is a mystery as of this moment. The second in command Sanchez, knows everything but doesn't make the deals. The deals are all brokered by Menendez. So far the only thing I know about the trigger is, they had over a million doses ready to go. Sanchez came into the lab a week ago and they are all gone. Menendez smiled at him and said it was all being taken care of. So only Menendez knows where the triggers are and he can't be read."

Joy shook her head.

"What the hell? Can we make more of the antidote with what you have?"

Kuthanaga shook his head.

"No *we* can't. But I know who can."

"Who?"

Kuthanaga sighed.

Tim put his hands to his face, as he already knew the answer.

"The drakes."

"Oh great. We're screwed." mumbled Tim.

Chapter 48 – Guess Who's Back

January 29th 2012 – New York City 5:31 pm

Richard was winding down his day. The meeting had seemingly gone on for what felt an eternity to him and he had reached the boiling point many times over. His phone rang and he answered quickly. "Yes?"

"Hey it's me Sam. I catch you at a bad time?"

"Same situation as usual. What's going on?"

Richard's phone vibrated slightly and he glanced down and saw that an unknown number displayed.

"Hang on; I have another call coming in."

He pressed talk again and said, "Hello"

"Hello Zygriel, it's Kuthanaga."

"Really? How interesting. Hang on."

He pressed talk again.

"Sam, I'm going to have to call you back." without waiting for a reply he pressed talk again and heard Kuthanaga.

"We have a problem you and I. A mutual problem. One that affects both Annukai as well as Draconians."

"Yes, I am well aware of the Planet Slayers. We're not going senile I hope, I told *you* remember?"

"I wish we were just discussing that issue. No this is something a little closer to home. By now you are aware of the Milk?"

"Ah yes, the liquid we found from Tim and Joy? Yes, it is remarkable. Although I do not know its purpose, it is something we are examining. Why do you ask?"

"Well another player is in town and they have managed to do some very bad things with it and plan on unleashing it on the humans."

"OK, I am officially bored with this conversation. Isn't it the Annukai who are interested in saving those mongrel slaves? What does the Draconians care about them?"

"I think this is also a threat to Draconians."

"Our biological system is different than both Annukai and humans. I don't think there is an issue here. I think you need something and are trying to establish leverage. I am still waiting to hear what you want."

"We have an antidote to the modified milk and the only problem is that we'd need over a million doses to be able to counteract what's been put in play."

"What does the contaminated version do? Kill the humans?"

"No, it turns them for all practical purposes into wild killing machines."

"Wait, so something you introduced to actually help the humans might actually cause them to kill each other off?"

"Yes."

"And I care why?"

"Well by my calculations you Drakes are probably in preparation to hibernate as you usually do when things go off yes?"

"Possibly."

"Well it seems to me, that millions of humans going wild and crazy would tend to disrupt all those preparations. A large group of the workers are human yes?"

Richard was uncomfortable with the thought of his scientist being turned into crazed killers. The first call he planned on making after hanging up with Kuthanaga was to lock his scientist down and feed them food and drink that was screened.

"Let's say I do this for you, what's in it for me?"

"Besides knowing you have the antidote in case your workers get infected? I don't know. What do you want?"

"Hmmm let me think about this for a moment."

Kuthanaga was nervous about dealing with Richard and Richard knew Kuthanaga was desperate.

"I want your word that you will never kill me."

"Excuse me?"

"Come now Kuthanaga. You and I both know you cannot wait until the day you can slay me. I'm quite fond of my life and want your word as an Annukai that you and your Annukai brothers will not kill me. Now I understand if I attack you, you may defend yourself. But you will never have the enjoyment of killing me."

"What do I have as assurance that you'll do your part?"

"I will swear with you the Draconian blood pact."

Kuthanaga knew that the Draconians would never break a blood pact. The thought of sharing his blood with the Drake who had taken so much from him was too much to even consider.

"You will swear your blood pact with another of my choosing and I need to think about your offer a bit. I'll call you back tomorrow."

Richard hung up the phone and smiled.

He dialed a number on his cell and waited a moment.

"Hello."

"Dmitri, I want you to lock our scientist down and put them in quarantine. I also do not want any outside food or drink coming into the facilities. Make sure they are under constant surveillance."

"As you wish."

Richard wondered who the person was who had Kuthanaga by the balls and was a bit unnerved that someone other than himself was able to unnerve the great Kuthanaga.

Kuthanaga was frustrated. Tim and Joy were sitting nearby and Xanari was standing next to Kuthanaga.

"So what did dragon-man want?" asked Tim.

"He wanted my word to never kill him."

Xanari looked down. She knew that what the drake asked for was a price too high for what he had done to Kuthanaga.

"I will kill him for you Kuthanaga," said Xanari with coldness in her voice that made Tim shiver slightly.

"He was specific. Neither I nor any other Annukai associated with me would be able to kill him. We'd be allowed to defend ourselves but never kill."

"So that is a bad deal?" asked Tim.

Kuthanaga nodded. "Yes. He killed my wife."

"What?!" Both Tim and Joy said at the same time.

Tim looked at Joy and imagined what he would do to anyone who killed her.

"Dude, fuck that! If he killed your lady he's fuckin' toast."

"That was a long time ago."

"Shit, I don't care if it was before the big bang!" Joy smiled at Tim.

Kuthanaga nodded. He had to weigh it out.

"I learned a long time ago, what is, is."

"What is that? Some Zen shit? He has to pay! I mean if he killed Joy..."

The thought angered him and suddenly the area shifted. He saw a beautiful woman hugging him. She had warm lips and her skin was softer than silk. He was in love with her. They did everything together and she knew him as well as he knew her. They shared thoughts and barely needed to speak.

The images shifted again and Tim could see her beneath the blade of Richard. His cruel words echoing all the while her moans of pain amplifying. Tim was suddenly on his knees holding her. His tears would not stop; they flowed as freely as a river running wild.

He screamed out one time and the world came back into focus. Tears were still running down his face as Joy was holding him. "Babe are you OK?"

"Ye-yeah. What happened?"

Xanari studied Tim and then quickly looked at Kuthanaga.

Kuthanaga smiled softly.

"You just experienced some of what I went through all those years ago."

"How?"

"Perhaps your ability. I'm not sure. But in any event you see my dilemma."

Tim was sad and his heart ached deeply.

"Well if we take your concept of what is, is... Then we should do nothing right? Because acting on it is trying to change what is."

Kuthanaga smiled.

"And for that matter, why even try to save us in the first place?"

"Because Tim, most of this is our fault. Our DNA was merged with humans, making you what you are today. The Earth's Milk, which I unearthed, is being used to cause pain on humans. We have an obligation to try to fix that which we have imbalanced."

"Well I'm not convinced. I mean, you have nothing to do with the Convergence. That would have happened with or without you. So, the way I look at it, if you really truly believe what is, is... Then we should just pack it up, chill, wait, and see what happens. Me? I'm of the opinion that we make our fate and we shape the things that are important. I say screw the deal and let's find another option. I'd like to be there when you kill Richard."

Kuthanaga thought long and hard.

"I swore an oath to get one billion humans to safety. My personal desires come second to that. I will make the deal but I cannot do the blood pact between Richard and me. I have a favor to ask of you Tim. He will swear to hold his end of the bargain up as long as I swear my part. The Draconian blood pact is the most honor bound oath a drake can make. I need you to make that pact with him."

For some reason Tim felt such anger and resentment to the request.

"I'm sorry Kuthanaga. I can't do it! Anything but that."

"I'll do it," said Xanari.

"I'll make the blood pact with him and if he breaks it then I will not be obligated to fulfill my part of the bargain you make with him. I will kill him."

Kuthanaga nodded.

"I shall make the arrangements. Thank you all."

Tim rose up and walked into his bedchambers and Joy followed behind him.

"Babe? What the hell is wrong with you? You told Kuthanaga no? I thought you'd do anything he asked?"

Tim nodded. "I don't know. That request was like 'Hey Tim I want you to kill Joy...'"

Joy smiled.

"Wow you're pretty fired up over this. What did Richard do to you? Must've been pretty bad."

"No, not really. Not compared to what he did to Kuthanaga's wife."

Joy hugged Tim and they stood there for a while.

Kuthanaga sat in his sanctuary and Xanari was there by his side.

"Are you sure you know what you are doing? I do not think this is the right choice."

Kuthanaga stood before Xanari and hugged her. She was taken aback by the gesture.

"Kuthanaga are you OK?"

"Xanari, I have been alive a long time. Seen many things. I will cherish the day when I can finally pass on. I have felt this way long before even thinking about the great Convergence. When the discussion of the humans arose, I took the cause as my own. I decided I would do everything I could to help them. So please understand why I do these things I do."

Xanari fought the tears back. She had no idea that the legendary Kuthanaga was so utterly broken. She was honored that he trusted her enough to share with her.

"Kuthanaga. I had no idea."

"Of course not. When you've lived as long as I have you learn to protect yourself."

He grinned at her and she smiled back.

"Why do you tell me this Kuthanaga?"

"I tell this to you, so that you understand choices I have made along the way and choices I will make moving forward."

She nodded and slowly walked away leaving him with his meditation.

Chapter 49 – The Deal

February 3rd 2012 – New York City 12:08 pm

Richard was starting to think that Kuthanaga wouldn't agree to the terms he had laid out. He silently cursed under his breath when he thought about the possibility of blowing the deal. What if what Kuthanaga had said was right? The Annukai were many things, but one thing they were not was paranoid pessimists. They were realists to a fault. They dealt with the reality of things and their assessments were usually fairly accurate.

Richard stood and walked around his office when a faint noise caught his attention and he spun. He felt the icy touch of a blade on his throat and a small familiar beautiful face was staring at him with a controlled rage so potent his breath was caught in his chest. Behind her was Kuthanaga.

"Hello Zangriel."

Richard smiled weakly realizing he should have added security to his office.

"Hello Kuthanaga. Mind having our friend here lower her blade just a hair. I can feel the trickle of my blood and I don't like it."

Xanari fought the urge to push the blade deeper and she hissed. "You betray Kuthanaga and you won't see me the next time we meet."

She pulled the blade just barely off his neck and Richard nodded.

"Point taken... Literally."

Kuthanaga walked closer to Richard and their eyes locked. Richard was taken aback slightly when he saw a hint of fatigue in Kuthanaga's eyes.

"What troubles you Kuthanaga? You seem not in the moment."

Kuthanaga nodded and put his hand on Xanari's shoulder, which was tense and solid. She felt his touch, relaxed a bit, and lowered her blade to neutral.

"Because what troubles me is above you and I Zangriel."

Something in his composure and tone bothered Richard. He had stood before Kuthanaga many times in the past and the Annukai warrior had earned not only Richard's respect as a valued enemy but also his admiration at surviving whatever the situation he had found himself in.

"So this is something that you consider dangerous enough that you would come to me for help?"

"Yes."

Normally Richard would have been thrilled with the situation and would have cherished every moment. But, to have his greatest enemy need his help in such a way seemed unfitting.

"The terms which we discussed are agreeable?"

Kuthanaga nodded.

"With one minor change. The blood oath you will swear will not be with me. Xanari will perform the ritual with you."

Richard glanced at Xanari and winked at her.

"Why not, since she seems to want my blood anyway."

Xanari fought the urge to say what she felt and just bite harder on her lip.

Richard shifted suddenly and Xanari took a cautious step back as he did. He stood in his true form and she took a breath as he snarled at her.

"Well then, let's get to it then shall we?"

He held his mammoth hand out and pointed where Xanari should cut. She placed her blade against his hand and he gripped it firmly and slid down it until blood started to drip. He opened his hand and began to speak in Draconian. Kuthanaga understood and listened as Richard swore his oath. As he did the blood pooled onto the ground into a small ball. To Xanari it sounded like a series of low growls. He pointed to the ball.

Kuthanaga explained softly. "Xanari, pick it up and place it in you left hand."

She made a motion and her blade faded. She reached down and grabbed the small ball. It was warm and soft to the touch.

Richard walked close to her.

"This is an oath I swear to you Annukai warrior. I shall make the antidote as you ask in the quantity you require. In return, none of you shall slay me. I need to make a small cut on you. You will then know if I betray you. When I open the wound, you will place the ball on it. Understand?"

Xanari nodded. Richard gently placed a claw on her right palm and pressed. The blood flowed quickly but bled no more than the small pool. Xanari placed the small blood ball in the pool and it mixed with hers and slowly it filled the cut and the cut faded into a small pink scar.

"It is done Kuthanaga. I have made the blood oath and I accept your word as Annukai that you shall not slay me."

Kuthanaga nodded grimly.

"Give me the antidote."

Richard shifted back to his human form as Kuthanaga handed him the small vial.

"How will I contact you when I am done?"

Kuthanaga handed Richard a small crystal.

"Speak into this while picturing us. We'll hear you."

Richard nodded.

"It'll take me a few days to get it started and once I have an idea how long it'll take for the mass production, I'll contact you."

"We'll be waiting," was all Kuthanaga said as he faded away. Xanari paused for a moment and held her gaze with Richard's and then she too was gone.

Richard examined the liquid and glanced at his hand, which was still dripping. He closed his eyes and took a deep breath. The wound closed and he retrieved a small towel and wiped his hand clean. He took out his phone and dialed a number. A few moments later Dmitri's agitated voice answered.

"Hello Richard. What can I do for you?"

"Who do we have working on the Annukai milk?"

"That would be Raymond Ignacio."

"Is he good?"

"Yes, the best. Why?"

"I have something else I need him to work on. Could you make sure he gets here as soon as possible?"

"I'll make sure he's there by tomorrow. Is that soon enough?"

"Yes. By the way, all the scientists are being supervised correct?"

"Yes. As instructed they are being fed from food reserves on site and all are locked down until we are done with them."

"Good."

"Is there anything to be concerned about?"

"I'm not sure yet. I'll let you know when I know more."

"OK."

"I'll let you get back to your project."

"Thank you."

Richard hung the phone up and examined the crystal communicator.

Xanari and Kuthanaga returned to Atlantis and Tim was waiting.

"Hello Tim."

"Hey Kuthanaga. How did it go?"

"As I expected it would. Xanari did the blood pact and we gave him the antidote."

"Hey man. I just wanted to apologize."

"For what?"

"When you asked me to do the whole blood pact thingy, I kinda lost it."

"I understand."

"You do?"

Kuthanaga put his hand on Tim's shoulder and smiled.

"More than you know. Tim, do not be concerned. We have done what we needed to do and in a few days we'll be able to deal with the situation at hand and then continue the preparation for the Convergence."

Xanari saw the conversation was going to be a while and walked off glancing down at her hand as she did.

"Cool. I just don't understand why I felt the way I did."

"Just know you may see more visions and things that seem odd to you will make sense later. Just trust me."

"I do man. If it weren't for you, Joy and me would be dead. So I just want to let you know I still got your back."

Kuthanaga smiled.

"I appreciate that. I have a question for you."

"What's up?"

"Have you and Joy still been practicing with your abilities?"

Tim looked a bit nervous at the question.

"Why?"

"I'm just curious is all?"

"Well yeah. In fact I kinda blew up a building yesterday."

"You did? Which one?"

"The small crystal tower at the far northern end… The one by the fountain."

Kuthanaga shook his head.

"Oh Tim. That was a shrine."

"It was?!"

"Yes. Fortunately for you, it was a temple to honor my father."

"Your dad? I thought he was still alive."

"He is. We don't have to be dead to have shrines dedicated to us. Sometimes a deed is so momentous that a shrine is erected to commemorate it. That one was for when my father helped tricked the Planet Slayers initially. There are some here even for me."

"You?"

"Yes, but those are stories for another time. How did you destroy the shrine? What specifically were you doing?"

Tim shrugged.

"Me and Joy was goofing around. I told her I could create a ball of fire like in the Street Fighter… It's a video game, and she was like 'go for it!' And I did, but after I created it I didn't know what to do with it and I kinda panicked and it flew out and hit the shrine melting it to a slab."

"Interesting."

"What?"

"Well you created what you thought was fire."

"It was."

"No Tim, fire wouldn't hurt the shrine at all. The shrines here are made with the crystals, which we call graxlacos. It is twice as hard as diamond and has to be shaped by the usage of two Gak-lua-kuun by elder Annukai. Normal diamonds are resistant to heat of almost 4,000 degrees. Graxlacos is resistant up to almost 9,000 degrees. Fire burns around 800 to 1,200 degrees. So your flame had to be hotter than 9,000. You felt nothing?"

"Nope. Joy didn't seem to notice the heat either now that you mention it."

Kuthanaga smiled.

"It seems your abilities are still growing. I don't know how but that may not be a bad thing. I wonder if the elements around us here are amplifying them. We'll have to examine them once we are done with Victor."

Tim nodded. He hadn't even broken a sweat with the fireball. He actually felt a slight release when he let it out and he wondered just how large an explosion he could create if he tried.

"Well now we wait. It will take the drakes a few days to get back to us."

Tim shrugged.

"So there's nothing else we can do?"

Kuthanaga shook his head and started to walk towards the courtyard outside the pyramid they lived in.

"No. Just wait and ready ourselves."

Tim turned and headed to his room where he had left Joy earlier and scratched his head irritated.

"I fuckin' hate waiting…"

Chapter 50 – Trigger
February 6th 2012 – Atlantis 3:01 pm

Tim felt as if he was going to scream. The waiting was driving him crazy. He and Joy had finally investigated the western portion of Atlantis and discovered all sorts of interesting things, which were fun at first but soon bored the both of them. He would have killed for a double cheeseburger and he realized it had been months since he had a coke. The Earth's Milk tasted like anything he craved but the texture was always the same and he craved something of substance to munch on. They were eating a diet, which was comprised mostly of fish and some odd vegetation that grew all over Atlantis.

He had discovered that he could tap into any video stream on the internet no matter how secured the system was. This was fun for a couple of days. After a while, the free movies were boring him as well. He finally found a few exercise websites, which caught his interest. He and Joy would take viewing crystals to the courtyard and then watch the routines and every day for an hour, they worked out. His favorite was a program called Insanity by a trainer named Shaun T.

Tim and Joy had been working out hard for over four weeks and they were showing results.

They were in the courtyard, the routine was over, and Tim was drenched in sweat. Joy was exhausted as well and they high-fived each other.

"Good job!"

Joy smiled at Tim and he took a deep breath.

"Wanna run?"

He shrugged.

"Why not. Nothing else to do."

They jogged for a bit and even after being in Atlantis for over a month the architecture still amazed them.

"Babe."

Tim glanced over to Joy.

"Yeah."

"Not trying to scare you or anything but I'm late."

"Late? For what?"

She flashed him a look and understanding hit him like a lightning bolt.

"Oh shit. You mean your monthly friend?"

"Yes."

Tim jogged on for a moment thinking.

"Doesn't working out and stress cause that to kinda go nuts sometimes? Remember when we thought Marco was gonna shoot us?"

Joy laughed and was amazed that Tim even remembered the whole Marco situation, as he was so high and messed up that he was off in his own world through the whole horrid ordeal.

"You remember that?!"

"Hell yeah, right when I was coming down you told me you were knocked up."

"Well it's really late."

"We could ask Kuthanaga or Xanari to check. I'm sure they could find out for sure for us."

"You seem mellow about it."

"Well we are married and we do have sex. It was only a matter of time something would happen from all that practice."

Joy laughed. She was relieved. She was scared to even mention it to Tim for fear that he would be upset.

Tim stopped running and pulled Joy to him.

"If you are pregnant, then I am very happy. If you're not, then we'll just have to keep working at it until I get it right."

She hugged him and he kissed her softly. She was afraid of having kids with the dark specter of the Convergence and the uncertainty of the Planet Slayers, and yet something powerful drew her to the thought of it. Something beyond a motherly desire to have children gripped her to her deepest core.

"I love you Joy. Nothing would make me happier than us having a baby."

"I know. But, what about the Convergence? Probably not the best time to have a kid. Right?"

Tim shrugged. He put his hand on her stomach, which was flat and ripped. She had put a bunch of muscle on since they started training. Suddenly his world shifted again and he was in a room with vibrant orange material hanging from the roof. The beautiful woman he had seen before was there smiling at him.

"Are you sure?" he heard himself saying.

"Yes." she replied with a smile.

"We are blessed."

"Yes we are."

He kissed the woman and she held him close.

"I'm scared."

"I'm not."

"But we're going to be on the crust. Isn't it going to be dangerous?"

"No. After all, I will protect you the whole time. We're just documenting."

"Why you love the crust so much I will never understand. But where you go I go as well."

The room darkened and Tim snapped back and focused on Joy who was staring at him.

"Tim what just happened?"

"I saw the woman again and she was pregnant."

"Which woman?"

"The one who Richard killed in my vision the other day."

"What did Kuthanaga say?"

"It was something from my abilities? I don't know. I think this is what he was telling me about the other day. He told me I would see stuff. I think it has something to do with what he did to me. Remember I told you about it?"

Joy nodded. Something weird was going on and it made her nervous.

"Well anyways, not a big deal. Felt so damn real though. I think the more important thing right now is to find out if you have a bun in the oven."

Tim started jogging back to their living quarters and Joy followed him. A few minutes later, they were back in the pyramid and looking for Kuthanaga. They saw Xanari and Joy pulled Tim.

"Let's ask Xanari."

Tim shrugged.

"OK."

"Xanari!" as Joy called out to Xanari, Tim saw another shift in colors and this time the woman was standing beside him and another woman was there. Tim realized that they all were

Annukai and he wondered how he could have missed it from the first few visions. The beautiful woman for who he loved more than life was so filled with excitement. He realized her name was Sani. The other woman had a large crystal, which she held over Sani's stomach, and an image materialized in front of them. Two small images were visible.

"Twins?"

"A blessing indeed!" said the woman.

Tim leaned close to the woman. "Speak this to no one. This is our news to share when we deem it appropriate."

The woman nodded.

"As you wish Kuthanaga."

Tim snapped back and saw that both Xanari and Joy were both staring at him.

"What about Kuthanaga?" asked Joy.

Tim shook it off and smiled.

"I think we should have Kuthanaga here too. Let me go find him. I'll be right back." Tim hurried off before either Xanari or Joy could say a single word. He suddenly realized who the woman was and what was going on.

Tim found Kuthanaga meditating and he gently tapped Kuthanaga on the shoulder.

"Kuthanaga."

Tim waited and no response from the Annukai.

"Kuthanaga, I need to talk with you."

Again, there was no response.

Kuthanaga! It's about Sani.

Kuthanaga's eyes popped open and he fixed his gaze on Tim.

"What did you just say?"

"Kuthanaga, I am seeing visions of your wife. But it's like she's my wife. I can't explain it."

Kuthanaga stood and was amazed. He knew Tim would see visions but nothing this profound.

"What were you doing when you saw her?"

"Talking with Joy about…"

"A baby?"

"Yes."

308

"Tim you know something that only one other person knew. My wife was pregnant when she died."

"With twins."

Kuthanaga fought the wave of anguish, which tore at his core.

He simply nodded since he couldn't make the words come out.

"I don't understand. Why am I seeing this?"

"Because you walk a path that paralleled my own path. You know for sure that Joy is with child?"

Tim shook his head.

"No, she's just late. We don't know for sure. We were going to ask you or Xanari to check."

Kuthanaga nodded. "Where is she?"

"Over in Xanari's spot."

Kuthanaga started walking.

"Did Xanari see you have the vision?"

"I think so why?"

"Please do not mention what you know to her."

"What's with all the secrets dude?"

"Tim, this is important."

Tim put his hands up. "OK, nuff said."

They walked over and Xanari was standing over Joy who was lying on a long crystal crying.

"Babe, what's wrong?"

She smiled and wiped a tear away.

"Sorry! I couldn't wait. Tim."

"What?"

Kuthanaga examined Joy and his mouth opened.

"We're going to have babies."

Tim grinned.

"A baby?"

Joy shook her head.

"No Tim, we're going to have babies. Twins."

Tim looked at Kuthanaga who had a bewildered look on his face.

"That is a blessing indeed.," said Xanari.

Tim nodded and he sat down on the floor, as he felt dizzy.

"Babe, you OK?"

He quickly waved it away and took a deep breath.

"Yeah, I'm fine. Just caught me off guard. I was ready for the thought of a single baby. Twins just kinda tripped me out is all. What about you? Why you crying?"

"I don't know. I'm just so happy, scared, excited... All at once."

He nodded.

"Yeah, that makes sense."

Tim stood up and held Joy's hand.

"Well I guess it's good we have Earth's Milk huh?"

Joy looked at him with a questioning look.

"Cause if you crave some crazy ass shit, it'll have you covered."

She laughed and nodded.

"I didn't even think about that. Speaking of that... Kuth, do you think there's any reason I shouldn't drink it?"

He shook his head. "No, it will provide you all the prenatal nutrients you'll need. I would caution one thing though."

"What's that?"

"Be very careful with your abilities. Also, I'd like Xanari to keep a mirror with you on at all times to make sure the children do not manifest abilities while they grow in you."

"Why?"

Xanari nodded.

"Yes, I was thinking the same thing. If they were to manifest abilities while inside you, that could be dangerous for all three of you. I will be near you until the babies are born."

Joy swallowed. "OK, if you guys think it's that important."

Tim nodded. "Yeah, let's play it safe babe."

He hugged Joy and he looked up past her and Rachel was there with an odd look on her face.

"Hey Rachel guess what?"

She nodded. "Yes, I know of the babies. I have for a while. But I'm sorry there's something I must interrupt the news with."

Kuthanaga stepped closer to her.

"What's wrong Rachel have you had another vision?"

She shook her head.

"No, it's on the news. It's started."

Kuthanaga linked everyone into Rachel's memory. She had been watching the daily news and reports of killing sprees were coming in from Texas, California and Arizona. All of the killers had been ultimately killed by law enforcement. Early reports speculated that this was the result of some new terrorist attack by Al Qaeda but they all knew what it was. The trigger was being distributed.

"So it's already begun." Kuthanaga said sternly.

"So what do we do?" asked Joy softly.

Tim was the first to break the silence.

"I wonder why only a few outbreaks have happened. From what you told me this was going to be fuckin' epic."

"I was wondering the same thing." Kuthanaga closed his eyes. "Let's find out." Tim felt a vibration deep in the base of his spine, it quickly spread outwards, and the environment began to shift violently. Vertigo filled his mind and suddenly he was standing next to Kuthanaga in a desert.

"What the hell?" Tim fought the nausea that almost overwhelmed him.

"Where are we Kuth? Where's everyone else?"

"They are still in Atlantis. I needed to have you with me."

"Why?"

"It doesn't matter. Suffice to say I need you with me."

Tim shrugged.

"Where are we?"

"Arizona."

"Why Arizona?"

"Because this is between California and Texas. I had my mirrors in a few locations, which I suspected would be logical. Somewhere remote, yet logistically viable for distribution. Arizona was one of the locations. "

"Hey can you connect me to Joy so I can tell her not to worry?"

"I have had her connected as well as Xanari since we left."

Yeah Tim, glad you were concerned.

"Oh snap. OK cool. I just didn't want you to worry is all."

I know.

Tim sighed and smiled. He was still reeling from the thought of being a father. Twins. The thought overwhelmed him. Twice the responsibility.

"Tim, you can think about that later. I need you to be alert."

Tim looked around and for as far as he could see there was sand and rock. There were some clouds gently floating high overhead which offered brief moments of shade. The heat was overwhelming compared to what he had become accustomed to in Atlantis.

"Alert for what? There's nothing out here."

"I would not be so sure of that."

Kuthanaga pointed towards a large bundle of boulders. "Rocks?"

Tim wiped his forehead, which was starting to sweat.

"I was afraid you meant something more dangerous."

Kuthanaga flashed Tim a warning glance that brought Tim to full attention.

"Look closer." he hissed.

Tim squinted and the waves of heat distortion danced on the horizon and as he focused, the rocks rushed closer to him as if he was looking through a zoom lens. He could see a small structure with two men crouched on both side armed and alert.

"Oh shit! I see em. Can they see us?"

"No."

"You think that's the place?"

"I'm not sure. My mirror came across this before and I wasn't sure if it was a military location or if it was our friend."

"So are we going in?"

Kuthanaga shook his head.

"No, we need to make a phone call."

"A phone call? Hope you have signal out here. Can you hear me now?"

Babe, I think you need to kill the jokes.

Tim nodded. "Sorry. Just nervous."

I know, Tim was glad Kuthanaga had Joy hooked in. It helped him calm down.

Kuthanaga took out his phone and pressed a single number and a rapid series of beeps gently chirped out. A few moments passed and Richard's voice answered.

"Yes Kuthanaga."

"Do you have detailed files on US military facilities?"

"Public and Private. Why do you ask?"

"If I tell you coordinates could you verify for me?"

"Yes. Why?"

"I may have found the main distribution site. Did you see the recent news?"

"Yes I did. It seemed fairly small outbreak though."

"I agree. I'd like to see if this is the location and if so deal with the threat itself."

"Yes we're still a few days off on the antidote. Tell me the coordinates."

"35.990372,-112.123353"

"Got it. Give me a second."

Kuthanaga waited a few moments.

"Hmmmm. That's not a military facility."

"OK, that's what I needed to know. You said a few more days for antidote?"

"Yes."

"Hopefully we'll be able to gain a few more days with our actions now."

"Well then I'll let you get to it."

Kuthanaga put his phone away and looked at Tim.

"Tim, we're going to go in there. Any thoughts?"

Tim looked at Kuthanaga and wondered why he'd ask Tim.

"Well I think we should go with stealth and get close and you do the whole mind reading thing. How close do you need to be for that to work?"

"I have to be about 100 yards away. How close do you have to be?"

"Who me?" Tim looked around quickly to see if another Annukai had joined them.

Kuthanaga smiled.

"Yes you. You were able to see them pretty clearly from here. Why don't you try to read their minds?"

Tim shrugged.

"Whatever man. I can try."

Tim stared again at the clusters of rocks and saw that the two men were both over six feet tall and had paramilitary gear on. The man on the left was large and his skin was weathered and tanned. He focused on him and realized all at once that the man was named James.

Amazing. Tim heard Xanari's voice for the first time and it caught him off guard.

Xanari, please. said Kuthanaga

Apologies.

"Now Tim, gently press in. Not too hard or you could cause damage and alert them of our presence."

Tim nodded.

Images of memories flooded into Tim's mind and they were all jumbled randomly into tiny ghostly floating slide shows.

"Good Tim, very good."

Tim focused on his breathing and fought the urge to push harder. Finesse was never his strong suite so the effort to be gentle was very difficult.

The images passed by like videos on fast forward until one snippet caught Kuthanaga's interest.

"There he is."

Tim paused the clip and reviewed it as all the other clips disappeared.

"That is the man I saw. Victor."

Tim realized that James was afraid of Victor and sensed something not natural about him. The money was good and he was a seasoned pro who had worked for all kinds of clients. The job was easy. Just guard a bunker and it would be an easy $80,000. Not a bad payday for a weeks' worth of work. The client had showed up to show the location and gave the men a schedule of when trucks would arrive and how long they would stay there.

Tim focused more and found out that the bunker was only two levels deep and was the size of a football field. There were ten men there guarding the facility. There was only a single pickup from the bunker. Another two trucks were due to show up later that evening.

"Doesn't look like your guy is inside." said Tim.

"But looks like stuff is definitely stored there. What's the plan?"

"We wait for the trucks and take them out further away. I want to get information from the drivers and find out how they are going to distribute. This may not be the only location. If we can just stop the deliveries and give Richard more time we can slip the antidote into the main supply chain and let them distribute harmless liquid."

"So you think there is more than one spot?"

"Don't you?"

Tim nodded. It made sense. Why keep your stash in only one place. Better to split it up in different locations. If they could figure out how the trigger was being distributed they could use the same supply lines to get the antidote out.

"I'm concerned about timing on this."

"What do you mean Tim?"

"The trigger seems to act quickly. Why would they even bother with the antidote?"

"They don't know it's the antidote. They have a wild hunger for more liquid. The liquid we'll provide is the key to breaking it."

Tim nodded and hoped it would work.

Don't worry babe, we'll get it done.

He nodded.

The heat was amazing.

"Hey Kuth, is there anything we can do about the heat?"

"Why are you asking me to do something that you are more than capable of handling yourself?"

Tim gave him a sideward glance and smirked.

"Yeah yeah yeah. OK."

Tim took a deep breath and imagined a cool breeze. Suddenly the area around him dropped in temperature so drastically that he shivered slightly and frost surrounded his breath.

"A bit too cold eh?" said Kuthanaga with a smile.

"Yeah a little."

After a few more attempts, Tim was comfortable.

"So we just waiting here for the trucks?"

Kuthanaga sat down and closed his eyes as he nodded.

Well if we have time, do you want to discuss names?

Tim sat down on the warm sand and tried to ignore a small scorpion as it avoided Tim's zone of cold.

"Why not. I like Isabella if it's a girl and Xavier if it's a boy."

Bella and X. Not bad.

Tim smiled and glanced at the sky

Chapter 51 – Contingency Plan
February 6th 2012 – New York 4:45 pm

Richard wondered how Kuthanaga was doing and laughed aloud. A tech was startled and glanced for a moment at him and then returned to his work. There were thirty-five men and women working in shifts on the antidote. Dmitri was overseeing the project and he was tired. Between the new project and the existing accelerated timeline, he had little time for sleep. It was moments like that that he appreciated being half drake. His specific genetics allowed him to push harder than any human could ever dream and with specific augmentation courtesy of the Quinuks, he could even out last purebloods. But, even with all that going two weeks with no sleep was wearing thin on him. Dmitri glanced at Richard with an inquisitive glance.

"Sorry, I was just thinking of the irony."

"Of?"

"Working with Kuthanaga."

"Why?"

"You know I have fought him many times?"

"Yes I have heard."

"Did you know I killed his wife?"

Stunned silence answered him.

"He had a wife?"

Dmitri knew much about Annukai and one thing, which never made much sense to him, was the single mating that they practiced. Rarely would an Annukai take another mate.

"Yes. And she was with child."

Suddenly it was very clear why Kuthanaga had wanted to kill Richard. Dmitri understood full well what lines Richard had crossed and now was wondering why the man before him was still breathing.

"You are wondering how I am still alive?"

Dmitri nodded. "Yes and also why you share this with me."

Richard shrugged. "I don't know. Perhaps I am nervous and need to vent a bit. I have a blood oath that he cannot have his vengeance. In fact, no Annukai can. This in return for this science project we're working on."

Dmitri considered the information.

"I don't understand why they would make such a deal. Does the humans mean so much to them? With the Convergence coming so soon, many of the humans will die anyway. They can't save them all."

Richard nodded.

"I think it's guilt."

"Guilt?"

Richard nodded. "Yes. You see he introduced the liquid to the world. Someone corrupted it and now he feels obligated to fix it."

"Annukai honor?"

"Yes, Annukai honor. Not all Annukai are as honorable as Kuthanaga. He is almost the last of a dying breed. I do respect that though."

"As do I. But it does make him vulnerable."

Richard nodded.

"Yes it does. But, I still don't trust him. Blood oath or not. I have a feeling he's not done with me yet. Kuthanaga is many things and one thing he is not is an idiot. I need to make sure we take appropriate precautions. I have done the one thing that I regret. You see I didn't know until it was too late that his mate was with child."

"Would you have acted differently?"

Richard shrugged. "You know, I've asked myself that question thousands of times, and sometimes I answer yes. Other times no. I don't speculate any more since what's done is done and cannot be undone. But still I do regret it."

"What do you want to do?"

"I need a back-up plan in case our Annukai friend suddenly doesn't follow his code of honor."

"I'm listening."

"I need you to take the trigger sample."

Their conversation was interrupted by Richard's cellphone.

"Hello? Yes. Send it to the lab."

He hung up the phone and turned his attention back to Dmitri.

"What's coming?"

"Blood samples of humans who were affected with tainted liquid and trigger."

"What do you wish me to do?"

"I want you to find a way to intensify the taint and make it strong enough to affect Kuthanaga. And then an antidote to calm the effects but not remove them."

"Won't he just heal it away?"

"That may be a problem. Put your big brain on it and see if you can trigger it by him manipulating universal energy."

Dmitri nodded.

"I'm on it and the human antidote? Should it work the same?"

"No, I want that to do its job. I swore a blood oath after all and I am honor bound to do what I promised. I want the tainted for Kuthanaga just in case."

Chapter 52 – Supply and Demand
February 6th 2012 – Arizona 10:12 pm

Tim shivered and suddenly shifted his temperature to warm himself as the ambient temperature around them dropped. He glanced at the structure and saw two trucks loading up crates.

"Well looks like they are almost done. What's the plan?"

"I'll follow one truck and you the other."

"So wait we're splitting up?"

"Yes."

"What am I supposed to do?"

Kuthanaga put a hand on Tim's shoulder.

"Just ride along and learn as much as possible. Once you get to the location where they start to actually distribute the triggers do what you feel is necessary."

"And if Mr. Bad Guy shows up?"

"Do not engage Victor. Avoid him. There's something about him that doesn't feel right to me."

Tim nodded. He had butterflies in his stomach.

Wow, babe. You're going solo…

"Hey will Joy still be in touch with me?"

"Tim you can do the same thing."

"I can?"

"Tim, I am unable to read the mind of a person who is unwilling and untrusted who is further away than 100 yards. You read that man's mind from five miles away. I'm sure you can stay connected to Joy."

Kuthanaga smiled.

"Trust me."

Tim nodded.

Joy can you hear me?

Wow turn it down studly!

How about now?

Much better.

Kuthanaga?

Loud and clear.

Relax honey. You got this.

Tim nodded. *Yeah, no problem,* he thought to himself.

OK, let's head out and intercept the trucks and see what's rocking.

Tim started walking and Kuthanaga followed.

The trucks started up, the engines groaned, and the area lit up as their headlights blazed ahead of them.

Kuth, how do you go invisible?

Actually, that is the wrong way to look at it. You don't make yourself invisible; you just don't allow anyone to see you. You just push out that you're not interesting and typically, humans will just not register that you're there. As long as you don't hit them, make an obvious noise or draw attention to yourself you'll be invisible.

But what about cameras?

You'll then need to camouflage yourself as we did in New York. That requires more effort to maintain. Another option, which I haven't tried, is to change your physical form into a transparent gas. That is completely possible but I have not attempted it. You shouldn't have a problem as long as you maintain your concentration.

Great. I'm not really known for my attention span.

I don't think you'll have any problems.

If you say so. Here we go.

Tim focused on not being interesting and stood to the side of the truck and when it was passing him he jumped up and grabbed the side rail. The driver didn't seem to notice the soft thud as he landed. Tim glanced back and watched Kuthanaga get on the second truck.

Good luck.

Tim saw there were two men in the cab of the truck and two men in the back with the crates. All were armed. Which wasn't a surprise to Tim. The trucks rolled together for an hour and then when they got to a main road split up and went in different directions. Tim learned his truck was heading to Las Vegas and Kuthanaga learned his was heading to Texas.

Heading back to Vegas? Looks like Vegas loves you babe.

I know right. What the hell?

Kuthanaga was silent for the next few hours which unnerved Tim a bit.

Hey you. You still awake? Tim was relieved to hear Joy's voice.

Hell yeah. Scared shitless. Fear is keeping my ass up. What you doing up still?

Just worried about you.

Nah, don't be. I'm chillin'. You should get some rest.

Can't… I feel amped up. You learn anything good from those guys?

Yeah, they work for some cat named the Chef. He's the distributor they're meeting with in Vegas. I guess homeboy owns a restaurant and a couple clubs where he has some bomb ass food. These jokers are making bank. There's not one of em who isn't making at least fifty thousand. Crazy.

Ha, maybe you'll need to renegotiate with Kuthanaga when everything is said and done.

Nah, what good is the money gonna be anyways? I wonder what it'll be like when this Convergence happens?

Silence answered Tim's question. He rode along for a while and wondered why his arms weren't getting tired. He wondered also how he had so much energy. He rationalized in his head that fear was keeping him on his game but something inside of him; a little voice told him that he was different now. He thought back to Kuthanaga's experiment and wondered what he had done to him. The visions of Kuthanaga's wife dying kept haunting him.

Tim kept probing until they arrived in Vegas a little after 6AM. He had more than enough information to see where the deliveries were going and who they were meeting with. Their relationships to each other and even their favorite foods. He marveled at how easy it was to get the most personal private information from each of the men. Joy had finally fallen asleep and Tim silently disconnected from her. Kuthanaga was also silent which left Tim alone with his own thoughts. He was happy to see the strip and couldn't wait for the ride to stop. He wanted to stretch his legs and was impressed that the drivers had driven the whole way without a single pit stop. He knew they needed a break and were anxious to drop the truck off with the Chef.

Twenty minutes later, they were standing at the rear of the truck waiting. An anorexic looking tall man walked out the main entrance and laughed a high-pitched weasely laugh.

The driver nodded at him and grinned.

"Yo, what's up Chef?"

"Nadda man. Just waiting on you guys. You have my stuff?"

"Yes sir."

"Any problems?"

"Nope."

He handed each a heavily filled envelope.

Each quickly tucked theirs away and smiled.

Chef walked to the back of the truck and glanced inside. He saw the crates and nodded.

"Sweet sweet. OK, the other truck is at the regular place. Pick it up tomorrow and bring the last batch here."

"Hey is there gonna be any more work after this?"

"Yeah should be a lot more. Right my man?"

"Oh yes." said a voice walking out the door.

Tim's heart pounded so hard in his chest that he thought everyone there could hear it. Victor, the man Kuthanaga had warned Tim about was there in front of him not more than twenty feet away.

"This is just the first batch. This is the small stuff. I have ten more locations across the country and some that should be landing in Europe and Asia even as we speak."

Victor looked at Tim squarely and the men looked in the direction he was looking.

"What is it man?" asked the driver as he pulled out his Glock.

"Oh nothing to be concerned with. Just a pest."

He continued and Tim froze. *Did he see me*? Tim wondered.

"So yes, one more shipment from the Arizona location and then I'll need you to go to the California facility."

The driver put his pistol away and nodded.

"Sounds solid man. If we're cool we're gonna head out and get some rest."

Victor nodded and smiled.

"By all means. Thank you again for doing such good work."

The driver nodded and walked away passing just inches from Tim.

The Chef went back into the building and when he was gone Victor looked squarely at Tim and grinned a toothy grin.

"Amazing."

"What's that?" Tim said.

"You."

"Me?"

"Yes. I never thought I'd actually see a human possess the power you have."

"You can see me?"

"Yes, I can see all of you."

"All of me?"

The man looked past Tim and then back at him nodding.

Tim looked behind himself quickly and saw nothing.

"Dude you're trippy. What the fuck is your game? What are you?"

Tim tried to read the man and there was some force blocking his thoughts.

The man stopped smiling suddenly.

"You are stronger than the Annukai that is for sure. I'm sorry but you can't read me. I cannot allow it. Not yet. The reveal is so perfect. I wish I could see your face when it happens. Perhaps I will. I'll spare you. You are special enough to warrant that. So I allow you to leave Tim."

"You know who I am?"

"Yes you and your wife Joy."

"Dude, what's to stop me from waxing your ass right now?"

"Nothing. You're welcome to try. However, I assure you, you cannot kill me. You'll cause all sorts of damage and massive loss of life. But I'll still be standing."

Tim he speaks the truth. I told you to not engage him.
Why not?

"Because dear boy, you can't read me, but I can read *you*. I now know your plan. Very elegant to counter my trigger. But it won't matter."

Kuthanaga, I'm sorry man.

Don't be. Take out the shipment and leave.

Just what I was about to do.

Victor smiled and motioned, the ground opened, and the truck fell into the wide gaping hole and exploded violently sending Tim flying back.

"What the fuck?!"

"You were about to do the same, so I just wanted you to know it doesn't matter. The result will be the same. In fact let Kuthanaga know I'll be at the Texas location he's going to and we can continue this conversation there."

"Wait!"

"Farewell Tim."

And just like that, the man was gone.

Kuth. I guess he's heading your way.

I heard. I'm going to pull you to me.

OK, is the truck still moving?

Yes.

Tim felt the tugging sensation and he didn't resist it. He faded just as the Chef came running out. Blinding light surrounded Tim and then he was free falling. He felt a strong hand grab him and pull him up. He grabbed the truck and stabilized himself.

What is that guy?

Kuthanaga shrugged.

I'm still trying to figure that out. We should be arriving at their location in about ten minutes .

El Paso?

Yes with distribution into Mexico as well.

So do you think he'll be there?

Yes.

What's the plan?

See what he has to say and then destroy this shipment. We need to buy time for Richard to finish the antidote.

Tim nodded.

The truck slowed down and entered a warehouse where a large group of men were waiting, and standing there among the men was Victor with a wide grin on his face.

Tim cursed silently and looked at Kuthanaga with a mixture of anger and fear in his eyes.

Relax Tim.

The driver stopped and got out and showed the cargo to the distributor who was standing next to Victor. After the standard exchange of money, the man sent everyone away and when the three of them were alone in the warehouse, he faced Kuthanaga.

"Hello again Kuthanaga."

"Hello."

"Tim."

"Yeah. So again what the fuck dude?"

The man shook his head and smiled.

"Such language. Kuthanaga you surround yourself with such interesting people. It's a shame those around you die. Must be painful."

Anger flared in Tim. "Hey fuck you man. What the fuck is that? Watch your fuckin' mouth!"

"Or what human?! You'll kill me? You can't! I can't die. But you... You surely can. Don't press me."

"Then show some fuckin' respect."

He nodded. "OK, I'll respect that. I am after all in the presence of the great and mighty Kuthanaga. Slayer of Saqqara, Conqueror of the Tanguts and Macedonians, student of Aristotle, etc. etc. etc." he did a deep sweeping bow as he recited the titles to Kuthanaga.

"You seem to know a great deal about me, and yet I know next to nothing about you. What are you?" asked Kuthanaga with great interest.

"As I told your young sidekick here, that's all part of the great reveal. You're soooo gonna love it. I know your plan and it was a good one. So go ahead and destroy this shipment. You needed to stall me for another three days while your Draconian ally makes the antidote. That's fine. I'll hold up the distribution for another week to allow for any SNAFUs. And then my Annukai friend we shall conclude this dance of ours."

"You are aware of the destruction your trigger will cause aren't you?"

"Yes I am. Yes I am." the smile on Victor's face was so wide he reminded Tim of the Cheshire cat.

Kuthanaga closed his eyes for a moment and the truck imploded into a sphere of metal with liquid pouring from small cracks.

"Nice touch. One week gentlemen." he turned his back and walked away fading with each step.

"Well at least he gave us the time. You think he'll wait."

Kuthanaga nodded slowly.

"Yes he will. Something about him troubles me. He knew many things. Many things which even my kind are unaware of."

"Such as?"

"Do you know your human history well?"

Tim laughed and followed Kuthanaga as he walked out of the warehouse.

"Um only if there was a movie or TV show about it. Why?"

"To understand humans better there were many times when I would try to help by uniting large groups together to undermine whatever the Draconians were doing at that time."

"OK so you were some historical figure?"

"Actually several."

"Like who?"

"Alexander."

As Kuthanaga mentioned the name images flashed into Tim's mind and he saw battlefields littered with bodies and rivers of blood.

"You never lost a battle…"

Kuthanaga examined Tim and saw the images flash in Tim's mind.

"Yes."

"The Drakes were trying to regain control and you stopped them."

Kuthanaga nodded. "Yes with the help of the humans. I did this numerous times, which sometimes were revealed. Most of the time it was kept a secret. There were only a handful of people who knew who I really was. When I laid siege to Tyre, Richard's grandfather was there and we fought. After that, I made sure their Egyptian control was broken as well. Some of the troops witnessed some healing I had done and I had to play upon their superstitions that I was a god. Once there was a way for me to exit I did and the rest is as they say history. Victor knew this and much more."

"You were so savage." Tim saw images of Kuthanaga slaying hundreds of warriors.

Kuthanaga looked down.

"Yes, I embraced the human condition and allowed myself to bask in it. To understand humans I had to be as close to them as possible in the good and the evil. It was these dark chapters where I learned the duality that lives inside of humans. I saw that extreme in you as well… You reminded me of a human I encountered named Simon Bolivar in the early 1800's. Your spirit is the same as his. I have committed great atrocities and great advancements for humanity. I take full responsibility for my actions and do not try to defend them."

Tim nodded. "I understand. I know everything you did was to help us. I don't have the right to even try to pass judgment considering all the shit I've done. I mean shit, we do the best we can with what we have right?"

"Exactly."

"So what now?"

"I think we should get some breakfast for you. I know you must be tired of the milk and Atlantean food."

"Yeah, even though the milk tastes the same as what I want, the consistency isn't quite right. Hey, I have a question for you…"

"Yes."

"You weren't Hitler right?"

"No, that was a human who was being manipulated by Drakes."

"OK, just curious, cause that dude was a real douche."

Kuthanaga laughed and smiled.

"Yes he was."

They walked on for a few more minutes before Kuthanaga added.

"Which is why I had to kill him."

Tim was shocked and didn't speak again until he was ordering food at a nearby diner.

Chapter 53 – Devil's Due
February 12th 2012 – Atlantis 7:15 am

Tim had been pacing so much that Joy had joked that he had singlehandedly carved a path in crystal in their living quarters. It turned out the antidote took longer than the drakes had anticipated which bothered Tim but not nearly as badly as the fact that Victor had kept his word and not released the trigger. A week had passed and the drakes had massive shipments ready to go from all along the United States, Europe, Asia and the Middle East. The drakes had spent billions in the preparation and Richard reminded them every time he spoke with Xanari.

Kuthanaga spent much of the week deep in meditation and Tim waited patiently for news to come from the drakes. With each delay, he became more agitated. Joy was the only relief he had. He shared with her what the strange man had said and the information he had learned from Kuthanaga. Joy was somewhat a history buff and when she learned that Kuthanaga was Alexander the Great she flipped out. She had so many questions for Kuthanaga but held them back as she respected his time in meditation.

"Man this waiting is killing me."

Xanari was there with Tim and Joy. She was never too far from Joy and she obsessed over Joy to the point where Joy started calling her 'Mom'. Joy thought that by calling Xanari 'Mom' it would cause her to chill a bit but it had the reverse effect and more than ever Xanari was checking on Joy and bringing her special drinks and bestowing decorative necklaces upon her which were supposed to be helpful in a peaceful pregnancy.

Joy regarded Tim who was fidgeting.

"So we're solid on those names?"

"What?"

"The names of babies."

Tim nodded quickly.

"Yeah I like Isabella and Xavier."

"Maybe Isabella and Alexander?"

"Alexander?"

Tim shrugged.

"I suppose it's a good name. Maybe Alexander Xavier Christenson or the other way around. We have plenty of time to finalize."

Joy nodded and noticed he had stopped fidgeting and pacing.

"How are you feeling babe?"

"Yes, how are you feeling Joy? Are you comfortable?" asked Xanari.

Joy rolled her eyes.

"I'm good guys! Mom! I promise if there's anything out of the ordinary I'll let you guys know."

Xanari nodded and sat down a few feet away from Joy.

"So any weird cravings or any of the pregnant madness yet?"

Joy shook her head.

"No seems like normal. Like I'm not even pregnant."

"Cool, well maybe it'll be an easy one for you."

"Yeah let's hope right? It's not like we have a hospital or anything here."

"Do not be afraid Joy. I am more than capable of helping you deliver your babies. I have done this many times before."

Joy nodded.

"I know Xanari. It's just going to be totally different than anything I am expecting."

Xanari nodded.

Tim it is time.

Tim jumped up and spun around. Kuthanaga opened his eyes and stood.

"Dude, was starting to wonder if you'd ever get up. So did you figure anything out while you were meditating?"

"Maybe. We shall see. I hope my suspicions are not correct."

"Care to clue us in?"

"No, I don't want to voice my fears just yet. Let's just focus on preparing. We know California is one of the main distribution spots. I am nervous about that region as it is due to have another series of quakes before too long. When we are there stay close to me and be alert. If it starts to go we abort immediately."

Tim nodded.

"We going northern or southern Cali?"

"Southern. Downtown L.A."

"You think he's going Hollywood on us?"

"Yes."

"OK, let's get going. You gonna be cool Babe?"

"She will be perfect," answered Xanari.

Rachel walked in and looked pale.

Kuthanaga approached her and stared at her.

"Rachel how are you?"

"It doesn't matter. The dream continues repeatedly with no deviation. I don't think we're going to be able to stop this from happening."

"We can try."

She nodded and he put a gentle hand on her shoulder.

"I know you blame me and I do have some part in this. But this was never my intentions."

She nodded. "I know. Good intentions and all that. I've seen some of the Convergence as well so I know the good you are doing. Be careful, I've had mixed dreams of another earthquake. It's the big one."

Kuthanaga nodded. "As I feared. Tim we should go now."

Kuthanaga walked to Tim and closed his eyes. Tim felt the familiar sensation and instinctively he added an effort to the shift and after a brief flash they found themselves in an ally in downtown Los Angeles.

"Much nicer trip that time." Tim commented.

Kuthanaga nodded.

"Because you did it."

"I did it?"

"Yes. I envisioned it, and you pushed us through."

"Sweet."

"Yes. Now let's head to the main street something feels wrong."

Tim noticed it as well. There was a huge sense of stillness and silence. No cars driving, no horns, nothing. Just the faint sound of the wind.

"What the hell?"

They walked out to the street and looked around. There were cars lined up in the street as if all the drivers suddenly just abandoned their cars.

"Where'd they go?"

"They're dead," said Victor with a matter of fact tone in his voice.

Both Kuthanaga and Tim spun around to see the man standing behind them.

"What?"

"I wanted us to have some private time, and you know how the humans are in their crowded cities. Can't have a decent private moment with all that damn noise."

"So you killed them?!"

"Yes just a few thousand. The rest fled pretty quickly. A few thousand are being triggered right about… Now."

Faintly in the distance screams echoed out followed by gunshots.

"Why?!"

"Come now. By now, you must have some clue Kuthanaga. Don't disappoint me. You know who I am?"

"Yes."

"Well don't keep the human in suspense."

"In New York when I inserted the Earth's Milk into the vein there was a guardian."

Victor smiled and nodded.

"Yes please continue. I can't wait to see his face!"

Tim looked at Kuthanaga.

"Guardian?"

"Yes, the guardian wouldn't let me insert the liquid unless I swore an oath to repay the favor."

"And that time is now my Annukai friend. The favor you owe us is due now."

"What is it?"

"Do not interfere with your antidote. You will not use it. If you do we'll kill all the humans."

"Wait! I don't understand. Why would you do this?" cried Tim.

"Why? Why?! We've watched for thousands of years as you humans have destroyed our mother. She was sleeping so peacefully and you have repeatedly raped and scared her with your wars, your weapons and your poisons. If it were up to us we'd wiped you all off of her. She is compassionate though and had forbidden us from interfering directly with you. But, when Kuthanaga came along and took all responsibility for anything that the milk would do, it gave us the opportunity to inflict our revenge on you and cause you pain. It will not kill all of you but it will hurt and it will interfere with the Annukai's rescue effort. Maybe the ones of you left will remember why you are being punished and learn from it. I doubt it but at least there is some justice being dealt out."

Tim stood there in silence for a few moments and Kuthanaga stood there with his shoulders rounded forward. The weight was heavy on his back. This is what Rachel had alluded to but not vocalized. She didn't have the heart to tell Kuthanaga that his actions alone had put the humans in harm's way. He was torn. He had promised the guardians a favor and the favor in front of him was directly in conflict with his oath to save a billion humans. He weighed the options and then nodded. The movement looked like it took all the strength he had.

"I will honor your request."

"I won't." said Tim.

"I'll stop you!"

Victor shifted his form to the being that Kuthanaga had seen before.

"You can try and you will die. Tim, I see the potential in you that Kuthanaga has seen in you as well. Do not be foolish and throw your life away. I can kill you easy enough and you will see me die shortly for violating the Mother's wishes. The trigger is already being used."

Tim realized that by the killing the people, the guardian had broken rules and he was going to pay the ultimate price for that and he didn't seem bothered by it all.

"I thought you couldn't die."

"Not by your hand, but by hers I can and I welcome it. I did what I did for her and I will die happy knowing I dealt out justice in her name."

The ground shook violently and debris fell to the ground.

"My brothers come for me. They know of our agreement. If you break your word Annukai they are allowed to extract my final wishes of complete eradication of the humans. Oh the look on your faces alone are worth dying for."

Tim looked at Kuthanaga and his mind was reeling. There had to be something they could do.

"There is nothing Tim. We can only move faster to save as many lives as possible that haven't been tainted. I fear this area is a lost cause anyways."

"Why?!"

The ground shifted violently upwards and Tim fought to maintain his balance.

"The Mother is angry with me and my brothers are here."

The ground exploded and three beings stood there.

"Goodbye Tim. Goodbye Kuthanaga."

The three simply put their hands on Victor's body and he started glowing brightly. A few moments passed and he was no more.

"Kuthanaga we have witnessed the crimes of our brother and the agreement you made still stands. What do you say in regards to the agreement?" The harmonic melody the three voices made as they spoke was hard on Tim's ears.

"I understand and honor the pact. I will not interfere. Nor will anyone I have influence over. I cannot speak for the Draconians. They have the antidote and will still try to use it."

"We understand. We will help you hold up your part of the agreement."

"How is that?"

"We will prevent the antidote from working."

"What?! How?" asked Tim.

"We are part of the Earth's Milk. Our life force is the base essence of the liquid. The modification was not chemical in nature but more of an emotional change. Our pain and anger that we held in check was allowed to manifest in the liquid you call tainted. The antidote is nothing more than a chemical treatment.

335

We will tell our brothers to ignore it and continue sharing the pain and anger with those who have consumed it."

"Wait you mean the milk is alive with... you?" Tim suddenly thought of Joy.

"Do not be concerned Tim. The milk your wife drinks is pure happiness and love. The majority of us are love. It's only with the suffering that some of us were tainted. The pure essence is synergistic and helpful. It is meant for healing. The reason you humans crave it so badly is that you have been wounded and hurt by the tampering of the aliens. The milk can heal to a point but humans are ultimately broken. The tainted milk amplifies this fact and turns them into savage animals."

"So there's nothing we can do?"

"We are sorry, but the agreement has been made. To break it would result in the death of all of you. The Mother is sorry, but the deal was made."

The ground violently shook more.

"We need to leave now Tim."

Tim felt utterly hopeless and defeated.

"We have to find a way to stop this."

The three began to fade.

"Tim, sometime things are what they are. Go now to your wife. The deal is done."

The three guardians were gone. The world around Tim began to explode in different directions and he could see building topple as he saw a brilliant flash. Suddenly he was back in Atlantis and he could see Joy, Xanari and Rachel crying.

Kuthanaga walked into his quarters and sat down. A single tear ran down his face and he sighed deeply.

"I am sorry." was all he said.

Tim stood there and quickly went to the observation crystals. He watched as news helicopters showed Southern California burn and split. He watched in horror as water rose around it and the left half of the state was submerged. After three hours, the area from San Diego to Redding was gone. The great city by the bay was no more as was its glamorous sister, the city of angels. The loss was so devastating that he couldn't fathom it. It numbed his mind, his heart sank, and he knew this was only just the beginning. With the tainted allowed to run rampant he didn't know what was going to happen.   All he knew was over 35 million people were dead and suddenly the full gravity of the Convergence weighed on him. He dropped to his knees and cried. Joy held him and in that moment, he felt another presence there among them. He looked around and couldn't focus on it. A moment later, it was gone.

Chapter 54 – A Deal's a Deal
February 12th 2012 – New York 3:20 pm

Richard watched the news on the computer screen and glanced at Dmitri with a look that spoke volumes. Dmitri shifted uneasily and cleared his throat.

"Dmitri, what the fuck happened?"

"I've consulted with the Quinuks and they are as surprised as we are. All indications were that the fault line was strong but not strong enough to cause that."

Images streamed on the screen and showed the newly formed coastline which was littered with explosions and smoke.

"And yet, there it is. The whole western side of California gone and the rest in shambles? Oregon is devastated as well. What caused this? The Convergence causes damage and shifting. We expected quakes and other extremes. But this? We've never seen anything like this before. Come on!"

"Yes, all data suggested no greater than an 8.1 maximum. The Daly City quake was thought to be close to the maximum."

"What were the measurements on this?"

Dmitri was silent for a moment.

"10.2 from early reports."

"Anything else?"

Dmitri nodded. "Yes, there were multiple epicenters that triggered all at once. It almost seemed intentional."

Richard turned and looked him square in the eyes.

"What? Multiple?"

"Yes ten. There were measurements of the exact same force from all along the San Andreas Fault as well as the Cascadia Subduction Zone. The resulting tsunamis are going to be destructive as well. Reports indicate that it will cause massive losses in Hawaii, Alaska, Japan, Philippines, Australia... It goes on and on."

"Projected death toll?"

"37-38 Million."

"Of our people?"

"Luckily most of our kind has already taken to the shelters. One of our Primary west coast shelters were in

California. We've not heard from them. The Washington site is still reporting. So early estimates is 200."

"Was there any reports of explosions to trigger these?"

"No, that's the odd thing. They all triggered at once with no warning. No explosions. I can't explain it."

Richard nodded. He wondered why he hadn't heard from Kuthanaga.

"Any word from the Annukai?"

Dmitri shook his head.

"Did you have a chance to finish the special trigger I asked for?"

"Yes, but I don't have an Annukai to test it on. So I'm not 100% sure it'll work as expected."

"It doesn't matter. Even if it does nothing more than just distract him long enough for me to gain the advantage. I am not even sure I'll use it. It's just safer to be ready."

Dmitri nodded.

Richard took the communicator out and focused on Kuthanaga. A moment went by and he heard a low guttural growling voice.

"Richard."

"Kuthanaga, I am calling to discuss the antidote. Everything has been ready for hours and we haven't been told where to distribute it. Obviously, the west coast is a moot issue at this point. Where would you like us to start?"

"Do not concern yourself. It will not work."

Richard was taken aback. "What do you mean?"

"It will not work on the tainted. You are free to try. We are in a different position. We are now speeding up the transport of the chosen ahead of the Convergence."

"Why is that?"

"The quakes were not part of the Convergence. They were unleashed on us."

Richard suddenly had a cold chill shoot down his spine.

"The Planet Slayers?"

"No, the planet *itself*."

"What?"

"More specifically the guardians who serve her. They were making a point."

"So our friend was not one of us or human?"

"No, he was a guardian."

"A guardian? Our deal still stands?"

"Yes. It was not of your doing and you fulfilled your part of the deal. It stands as agreed upon. No Annukai will harm you unless you attack first. And I will not kill you."

Richard couldn't help but smile.

"I'm glad to see the honor is still intact after all these years."

"I bet you are."

"In any event we will still attempt to distribute the antidote to verify this for ourselves since we have invested a great deal on this. Crazed humans running wild would be very problematic. I'd rather not have to kill them."

"As would I. I fear that may not be an option for either of us though."

"Well then that concludes our business then?"

"Yes."

"Farewell Kuthanaga."

"Good bye Zygriel."

Richard glanced at Dmitri.

"Seems our antidote may not work. Have the SAR team armed with darts that have the antidote and find out what happens when we treat the tainted humans."

"I'll have it done and report back to you when I have data."

Richard nodded and sat back down to watch more footage of the new coastline of California as it was ravaged.

"Remarkable."

Chapter 55 – The Crack in the Darkness
May 25th 2012 – Atlantis 12:15 pm

Three months had passed fairly uneventful for Tim and Joy. She was starting to show and Xanari was focused more than ever on scanning the twins on a constant basis. Rachel had barely uttered a word since the trigger was unleashed. Tim and Joy had tried to cheer her up but she seemed so deeply saddened by the events that they just couldn't understand fully. Kuthanaga had barely moved from his meditation chamber and other than Xanari, Tim and Joy felt alone.

"Man, I can't believe everything that's happened," said Joy. Tim nodded and rubbed her belly.

"I know. I'm numb. I'm kinda scared but happy at the same time. Does that make sense?"

Joy nodded and placed her hands over Tim's and smiled at him. "We've been through a lot and looks like we have a lot more coming. But, for the time being seems like we're safe here. At least we'll be able to have the babies here and with Xanari around, I feel completely at ease. She has taken such an interest you'd almost think she was having the baby."

Tim smiled.

"Yeah she's something else. Has she scanned you today yet?"

"No not yet, but she'll be here soon. Where were you earlier?"

Tim shrugged.

"I went for a run."

"How far did you get?"

"Two laps around the perimeter."

"Wow!"

"Yeah, I barely broke a sweat."

Joy was impressed. The perimeter of the city was at least 25 miles.

"How long did it take you?"

"Just under three hours I think. I was deep in thought. These memories keep flooding in. It's getting hard to tell which is mine and which is his."

Joy nodded. She had also noticed a distinct difference in some of Tim's mannerisms and his mood seemed more reflective and somber. Truth be told, all of them had taken a morality hit. Questions hung in the air heavy with uncertainty. The only thing giving hope was the twins and their impending birth.

"Have you spoken to him?"

"Not in months. I think he's taking the tainted really hard. I know why he did what he did and I know there was nothing he could do, but it was messed up how it all turned out regardless. I'm sure he'll snap back. I just wish he'd let me know what he's doing so I could help."

"He will in due time Tim," said Xanari in a warm tone.

Tim wasn't surprised that Xanari was there. He had heard her approach and felt her presence a few minutes before she was behind them. Joy was so fixated on her conversation with Tim that she hadn't noticed Xanari.

"He's accelerated his timeline to factor in the tainted and I suspect you'll have your wish soon enough. He's had all of the Annukai on this mission change our tactics. We've revisited those who were marked and planted in a powerful suggestion for them to head to designated safe areas. These will then have to be collected and stored in preparation of the Convergence."

"Stored?"

"Yes, we have decided the best course of action is to place them in a deep sleep and slow their vitals to a level where they will need little nutrients to survive. There are far too many to try to explain and care for during the Convergence. Once the Convergence has ended we will wake them and reintroduce them to the new world."

"So we won't be having guests then?"

"Perhaps a few which seem qualified for leadership roles to help in the transition. But, no more than a couple hundred or so."

"Out of a billion?"

Xanari looked down for a moment and then fixed her gaze firmly to Tim.

"We're not going to be able to get a billion are we?"

She shook her head.

"There is too much chaos now. With the tainted growing exponentially we'll be lucky to get half that. The governments are taking extreme measures and purging the areas with the highest number of tainted. I take it you have not been keeping up with current news?"

Tim and Joy both shook their heads. "No, we're trying to be mellow and not add too much stress on Joy. Bad for the babies."

Xanari smiled and realized Tim had been doing lots of research into pregnancy.

"I suspect your babies will be fine regardless of the stress considering your midwife is always keeping a watchful eye on them."

Tim grinned.

"Thank you Xanari. I really appreciate you keeping an eye on things. I don't know what we'd do without you."

She blushed slightly.

"It is an honor to be of use. Especially to you my Tashquella."

"Your what?"

Xanari looked embarrassed.

"Kuthanaga has not explained to you about being a Tashquella?"

Tim shook his head.

"No. What is that?"

"I just assumed as I saw his memories from time to time in you that he had explained to you."

"Xanari, he hasn't said anything to me. What's going on?"

"It is not for me to say. I have said too much and I am sorry. There is nothing to be concerned about. It is a great honor and what he did with you very few Annukai ever do, and as far as I know never with a human. Trust me when I say it is not a bad thing. I can only assume he is overwhelmed with directing the others that he has not had time to break away and explain everything to you."

Joy squeezed his arm and he glanced at her and relaxed. He hadn't realized he had tensed up so intently.

Tim sighed and tilted his head.

"Fine whatever. Let's do the baby check-up shall we?"

Xanari nodded and followed Joy into her living quarters. Joy laid down relaxed and took deep breaths as Xanari had instructed her to do many times before.

"Tim you'll like to see as well?"

"Of course."

She nodded and rubbed the fifth slab of gold on her Gaklua-kuun. It glowed slightly and suddenly in the air images of the babies materialized and Joy smiled. Her eyes watered a bit and she noticed Tim also was getting misty eyed.

"Man that never gets old. How are they doing?"

Xanari focused on all the organs and called them out. "There's the heart beat for Isabella and there's the heartbeat for Xavier." The image showed how both the babies were lying inside of Joy and it almost seemed like they were staring at each other.

"Can they see anything?"

"I don't believe so, but their eyes are open."

Joy rubbed her belly and smiled.

"Hello my babies." she said softly.

The image showed both of the babies responding to her voice and they moved. Isabella kicked then and Joy giggled.

"Looks like Isabella is the active one huh?" asked Tim.

Xanari nodded.

"Yes. Seems like it's a bit crowded in there and she wants more room."

Joy looked a bit concerned.

"Is it OK? Is it too small in there?"

Xanari laughed and smiled. "No, they are fine. More than enough room. Sometimes they just want to stretch is all. Do not be concerned."

The image showed Isabella turning her head as if she could hear Xanari's voice and she was suddenly very still.

Xanari stopped smiling and a look of astonishment filed her face. "By the Creator."

"What?!" asked Joy in alarm.

"Your baby just scanned me."

"What?"

"Isabella just reached out and scanned my thoughts."

"What?! Are you serious?"

"I would not jest about such a thing. It is not possible. And yet, I swear to all I hold dear that it happened. It was not gentle either. But something else."

"What is it?"

"They are growing mentally at an accelerated rate. They have full cognitive abilities and are aware. Communication is not there yet and yet she conveyed a thought to me. A very basic but straightforward thought."

"What was it?" asked Tim.

"Safe."

"Safe?"

"Yes she wanted me to understand she was and is keeping you safe."

"She's keeping me safe?" asked Joy in amazement.

"Yes as far as I can tell. I have noticed some interesting energy fluctuations around you but dismissed it as something you were doing subconsciously. I'd like to try something if you don't mind. There is a small amount of pain but shouldn't be more than a bee sting."

Joy looked at Tim who shrugged.

"OK."

Xanari pulled out a small blade and motioned for Joy to lift her hand. Joy lifted it and Xanari took it gently and slid the blade across her finger. A small cut started to bleed slightly.

"Ouch! More than a bee sting!"

Xanari said nothing as they all watched and the cut closed up and the only remaining mark was a faint pink line.

"Wow. Did you do that babe?" asked Tim.

Joy shook her head.

Xanari grabbed Joy's wrist firmly and swung the blade down. Before Tim or Joy could say anything Xanari was thrown across the room and the image of the twins vanished from the air. Xanari stood and smiled.

"What the fuck?!" yelled Tim.

"I was curious as to just how aware the twins were. I needed to know if they were able to do what Isabella suggested."

"Isabella did that?"

Xanari shook her head. "No. Xavier did. Isabella healed you. Xavier defended you. They are aware of you and your environment. I do not think it necessary for me to keep such a tight watch on you anymore. It seems you are in safe hands. Small but capable hands. I am sorry if I alarmed you."

Joy shook her head and smiled. "I trust you Xanari. I know you would've fixed whatever you might have done."

Tim was slightly irritated.

"Yeah well, I'd like it if you'd be a little more careful."

Xanari nodded.

"I apologize Tim."

Tim waved it away and grinned. "Damn they are little bad asses huh?"

Xanari nodded. "Yes they are powerful now. I am curious how they will be when they are grown."

Joy was nervous.

"Do you think they'll be normal? I mean I kinda feel like a freak now and I don't even know what we're doing most of the time. What if they come out and want to rule the world or something like that? I mean we were messed up before Kuthanaga came along and I don't even want to think what we could've done if we had power back then."

Xanari nodded. "Let me pose a question to you. Since you've gained your abilities have you done anything evil?"

"Well no."

"Have you hurt anyone for the joy of it?"

"No."

"Then it seems like you are no longer walking the path of darkness. We all experience the darkness at some point just as you walk through the night at some point in a single day. Whether you decide to live in the darkness is up to you. I have scanned millions of humans and the one thing that never ceases to amaze me is the duality that exists in you. The ability to do great good or great evil and then swing around completely in a different direction sometimes with little effort in a short time is in your nature. Some of you call it redemption and others call it corruption. Raise them with what you have learned and they will be just and righteous."

"You seem pretty confident."

Xanari nodded.

"It is said among my people that we are born with what we are supposed to be. Our roles are determined before our birth. Your children are healer and protector. They will do great things for Human and Annukai. When I was scanned by Isabella I could feel her essence and when Xavier attacked me the same. They are good. Keep them in the light and they will grow to be legendary. Teach them the ways of the light so if they are ever surrounded by the darkness they will be able to pull from their memories of the light and seek it back out. I know you both and I am confident you will do fine."

Xanari walked back, put her hand on Joy's belly, and smiled.

"I am sorry little ones if I startled you. Your mother is safe."

Joy felt a warmness fill her from the inside and radiance emanated from her skin.

"Damn babe, when they say you're glowing you really *are*."

Rachel walked into the room and smiled.

"May I say hello to the babies?"

Joy nodded.

Rachel came over and placed her hand next to Xanari's and she smiled.

"Hello again little ones. I can't wait to meet you on your birthday."

Her smile widened and she looked at Joy. "They are miracles."

Joy smiled back.

"Thank you Rachel. Are you OK?"

She shook her head. "No. But, I'll be fine. Those babies represent something real to me."

"What's that?"

"Hope for a brighter future. They speak to me in my dreams. They promise that they will help heal the world."

Rachel nodded and walked away with a peaceful smile.

"Well today was special huh?"

Joy flashed Tim a look. She knew he was about to drop a joke when he surprised her and said nothing. He just put his hand on Joy's belly and rubbed it gently.

"I love you guys."

Xanari walked away and seemed in better spirits.

Chapter 56 – Collection
July 18th 2012 – Atlantis 9:05 pm

Kuthanaga sat deep in meditation. The mental link he had with all the Annukai required his complete concentration. To handle all of the input and conversations going on and keep his communication outwards clear and precise was something that never got easy. The complication of the tainted made it even more difficult.

The plan had shifted greatly, he was coaching, consoling, and caring for his Annukai, which were doing the best they could. Xanari was handling the task she had before her splendidly and he was grateful and impressed. He was growing weaker by the day and he knew he needed to have all the pieces in place. Once the Tashquella between him and Tim was completed, he would need Tim's help more than he knew.

He silently cursed himself. He had not been this brash and foolhardy for thousands of years. He reflected to his time as Alexander and smiled briefly. Some traits died hard he decided.

He checked the status with his Annukai and one by one, they checked in and were ready to send the marked humans.

Send them and protect them watchers.

Was all he said and then he opened his eyes. It had been months since he had used his physical eyes and they were sore and sensitive to the light. It took a few moments for them to clear and he scanned his sanctuary. There was the presence there again and he tried with all his effort to get a solid fix on it. He felt a brief moment of warmth and then it was gone. It frustrated him that he couldn't figure it out. He heard Tim coming and he smiled as he turned.

"You're up. Great. So what's the plan my man?"

"Has Xanari been keeping you up to date?"

"Yes. She mentioned something about getting half a billion of people into some kind sleep mode to ride out the Convergence."

Kuthanaga nodded. "Yes, that is correct. We will place them in locations that we know are going be affected the least by the Convergence. With a few watchers there to protect them things should be fine."

Kuthanaga could sense something was troubling Tim and nodded to himself.

"You are aware of the Tashquella?"

"Yeah Xanari kinda let the cat out of the bag but didn't explain exactly what it was. She said it was some kind of honor."

"And a curse I'm afraid."

"What do you mean?"

"Tim, I have chosen to move on and have decided when I will rejoin the universe."

"What... You mean you're going to die?"

"Yes. I know roughly, when it will happen. I have chosen you to be my Tashquella."

"What does that mean?"

"It means that I have been alive for over 35,000 years and I have learned many things. That knowledge is best served by someone who will use it for the betterment of the human race as well as Annukai. I have given you all my memories and knowledge. As time goes on you will understand more and more. It will take a few years for you to gain a full grasp of what you have now."

"Why me?"

"Because you are a good man Tim. I knew it when I first encountered you. I also know you have a larger role to play in a destiny which I do not yet understand."

"Dude, I'm a douche."

Kuthanaga laughed.

"No, you are not."

"How do you know?"

Kuthanaga placed a hand on Tim's shoulder.

"Because Tim, I just know."

"Man you're nuts you know that?"

"Maybe." Kuthanaga wanted to tell Tim everything but he didn't want to alarm him. He decided some things were better left unsaid. Tim would in time learn everything anyways. So, he patted Tim on the shoulder and changed the subject.

"How are the twins? Xanari reported the news of their rapid development. How are you and Joy handling?"

Tim grinned. "Yeah they're awesome. They do some really wild crazy stuff. Sometimes they prank me. Other than scaring the shit out of me they're solid. Joy is really happy and excited about the birth."

"When is that supposed to happen?"

"Middle of November."

"Interesting."

"How so?"

"The Convergence begins full swing around November 15th. The timing is interesting is all. Well at least the twins will be born and ready for when things shift."

"Yeah that's what I was thinking. It would have sucked if she had to give birth right when it was all going crazy. What is it going to be like?"

"The Convergence?"

"Yeah."

"Hard to explain. There is pain. Then there's a distortion to the perceived world around us as the dimensions come into focus. The air will change and get heavier as well as have a richer smell. The skies will change and you'll see your old moon again. The process will be similar to being born."

"Lovely."

"We go through it when we shift planes. It's unpleasant but it also has a cleansing effect. You'll feel alive."

"OK, well we'll see how it is when it happens. How long does it take?"

"The Convergence lasts for almost a month, during which many large scale disasters will happen. If we didn't intervene these events would have more than likely killed all human life. The crust goes through a lot of shifting and as the Earth wakes, it gets worse. In America Yellowstone will erupt and the air will be filled with smoke and ash. The sun will be blocked out and the Earth will seem to enter a nuclear winter. Once it happens and the crust is back its normal size the other dimensions will start materializing and once they are all in place the Earth will heal itself. She will then look after life and adjust what needs to be adjusted to support it on the crust. The outer crust will remain full of life and energy until she sleeps again."

"When will that happen?"

"35,000 years. When that happens, humans need to be off the planet. We will need to be as well. This is the great Convergence. When we arrived, originally there was always a dimension on the outside of the crust. We suspect when all five dimensions are joined on the Earth and she goes back to slumber those dimensions will tear off and the crust will quickly become a frozen wasteland again. I don't think that will be a good thing."

"Well I suppose we have time then yeah?"

"Yes I suppose."

"How do the animals survive?"

"The Guardians I suspect."

"Oh snap. The guys who sank California?"

"Yes. I think they protect that which pleases the Mother."

Tim nodded. It made sense in an odd way to him.

"So what's my part in the next chapter here?"

"I'll need you to help me get around to the various locations to make sure they are accurate. I trust my watchers but many of them are young and inexperienced. I need to double check and help where we can."

Tim shrugged.

"No worries as long as I make it back to see the kids born I'm all yours."

"We should be done well before then. I also need you with me for your protection."

"Me protect you?"

"Yes a cruel side effect of the Tashquella. Much energy was used to do the transference. While you are learning, I am weakened. So I may need additional support from you from time to time."

"Say no more. I am glad to be able to help you."

Kuthanaga smiled and nodded.

"Let Joy know we leave in the morning to check on Xanari's location first."

"No problem."

Kuthanaga walked away towards the gardens. As he walked outside their living quarters, he felt a slight breeze and smiled. The Atlanteans spared no details in their city. The wind had a faint smell of flowers, which reminded Kuthanaga of Hawaii in the spring. He took a deep breath and sighed. He knew the end of this journey was coming and he relaxed and let his shoulders droop forward a bit. He was tired and he missed his wife. He hadn't been with another Annukai in hundreds of years and had learned long ago that mating with humans was nothing but heartache due mostly to their short life spans. His mind drifted to Xanari and he smiled. She was so full of life and he knew she had feelings for him. But, he also knew who her father was. Their relationship would not be tolerated and with everything Kuthanaga had done, he doubted he would make it past the trials of truth. He sighed again and gently shook his head. He sensed a presence and he stood tall and strong.

Xanari appeared from down the path and her eyes were fixed firmly on Kuthanaga.

"Xanari, I was just thinking about you. How are you?"

She walked to him slowly and held his gaze.

"I am fine Kuthanaga. How are *you*?"

The emphasis on her question was loaded.

He relaxed his posture a bit. "I am tired."

She stopped in front of him and she nodded softly.

"I would imagine so. After all the Tashquella does take a lot out you."

He nodded.

"Yes, I found out from Tim you know."

"I have known for some time now. Tim is many things but he is not a trained psychic. His flashes were very distinct and loud."

Kuthanaga nodded.

"I am sorry I did not inform you of my decision."

She shook her head and he could not help but notice her long neck.

"It matters not. It is yours to give to whom you choose."

"Even a human?"

She shrugged and he noticed the muscles flexing along her shoulder.

"Tim is much more than a normal human, though I do not pretend to understand how he and Joy do what they do."

Kuthanaga nodded. "It is the Creator's wish."

She nodded.

She stepped closer until she was pressing against him. She could feel his heart beating heavily in his chest. She laid her head against his powerful chest and relished his strong breath.

Kuthanaga embraced her and held her long and firmly. He inhaled and her hair smelled perfect to him.

"You are going to join with the universe when we are done?"

He swallowed hard and questioned himself.

"I am ready Xanari."

She looked up and stared deep into his eyes and her eyes watered. He saw the waves of blue swirl wildly in her eyes. She reached up and gently, yet firmly, grabbed the back of his neck and pulled him to her. She kissed him and for a moment time stood still. The electricity he felt from her kiss shot though him like a bolt of wild energy.

"I'm sorry Kuthanaga, but I am not."

She took him by the hand and led him away from the main living area until they had found a secluded area. He lay with her and they made love as lovers who knew they might never love each other again. In the morning, he gently kissed her and smiled at her.

"You know what we did…"

She silenced him with a kiss and a tear streamed down her face.

"Was mine to give. Do not be troubled."

Kuthanaga stood and she marveled at the power that radiated from him. His aura was almost blinding to examine. He simply nodded and walked back towards the living quarter to gather Tim. He knew they were about to leave the heavenly confines of Atlantis and see the hell that he was responsible for.

Tim was standing there hugging Joy. He rubbed her belly, crouched down, and spoke to his twins.

"Daddy's gotta go work now. I'll be back soon."

Joy hugged him again and kissed him long and hard. She was scared. Tim had power and Kuthanaga was going to be with him but something scared her.

"You be careful. Make sure you are safe. Kuth, keep an eye on him."

Kuthanaga nodded.

"He will be fine."

"Well you be careful too."

He was touched by her concern.

"I will. We will return very soon."

Rachel came out and she had deep dark circles under her eyes as if she had not slept in some time.

"Rachel, you need rest."

"I have slept but the dreams are relentless. I sleep but do not rest."

"Any new dreams?"

"None, except the dream of you and the Drake."

Kuthanaga nodded. He wondered why the one dream kept reoccurring. He knew in his heart that there was still closure that needed to be had between him and Richard.

"Tim, are you ready?"

Tim nodded and Kuthanaga took him by the shoulder and envisioned Xanari's mirror. Tim focused and flowed energy through Kuthanaga and Atlantis was no more. Replacing it was a dark melancholy sky. A faint rain was drizzling around them. Xanari was standing there and Kuthanaga smiled.

"Where are we?" asked Tim

"Utah." answered Joy.

Tim looked up the mountain range and scanned the area. The rain made a faint sizzling noise as the water hit the sandy slope he stood on. There was a faint smell of ozone in the air and he felt goose bumps rise up along his forearms. Tim turned and saw smoke in the distance. Large billowing clouds which cast an almost crimson tone to everything around them. The sun tried to peek from small cloud breaks but couldn't fight its way through. He stared at the city from their location and his vision zoomed in. There were next to no one on the streets and there were National Guard tanks in various locations with a few soldiers keeping a watchful gaze on the area. There were areas where the ground was blood stained and Tim shuddered when he realized what had caused such a large stain.

Kuthanaga interrupted Tim's thoughts.

"Xanari, please show us the area you have prepared."

Xanari walked on and as he approached the mountain, Tim noticed part of the wall shimmered slightly. Xanari walked through it and they followed close behind. They were walking down into a long shaft, which extended as far as Tim could see. After walking for about twenty minutes, it opened up into a grand chamber, which opened upwards and outwards.

"Damn, that's huge!"

Xanari nodded.

"It took some effort to dig this out."

"You did this?" Tim was amazed.

"Yes."

"Wait you were with us most of the time. When did you do this?"

"I had three mirrors here working around the clock."

She motioned and nearly half a mile away Tim could see two more Xanari mirrors digging with telekinesis.

"How many are going to be here?"

Xanari looked at Tim and he noticed a touch of sadness in her eyes.

"We will have 630,000 people in this location."

"Out of how many possible for this region?"

"23,427,781 People. From Utah, Nevada, Arizona, New Mexico, Colorado, Wyoming, Idaho, Oregon and Washington."

"So what is that? Like less than 5%?"

"Closer to 2.7%"

"Fuck me. 2.7%... Is that the average?"

Xanari almost couldn't contain her heartbreak.

"Yes the tainted outbreak and containment measures are causing massive loss of the chosen."

"So will we even get the 500 mil we're shooting for?"

Kuthanaga sighed.

"We are now adjusting to an optimistic 3% worldwide."

"Which means how many? Sorry, I suck at math."

"Roughly 200 million."

Tim nodded slowly. He was numbed by the numbers. To go from one billion people to 200 million was horrific, but at least humanity would continue.

"Will the chosen from this region all fit in here?"

"In their modified state they will all file in and be condensed. Their mass will be shifted slightly and yes they will fit."

"And when the Convergence is done?"

"They will file out into the open area and the human leaders will help them adjust to the new world."

"So how will the leaders be chosen?"

"We watchers have been marking and the most exceptional humans bear the leadership marks."

Kuthanaga walked around a bit examining the area. He scanned the rocks and calculated the structural integrity.

When he was finished, he looked at Xanari.

"I think it is ready. You've sent out the message?"

She nodded.

"And a few mirrors will be escorting the groups as they start to form larger clusters to keep them safe from the tainted."

"How long until they arrive here?"

"Some will show up today and the last should be here within three days."

Kuthanaga nodded.

"Well we better get this ready. Tim I need you to stand with me and channel for me."

Tim took position next to Kuthanaga and watched as Kuthanaga chanted something barely audible and saw his Gak-lua-kuun glow a brilliant blue. Tim focused and pushed energy towards Kuthanaga who exploded outwards until energy snaked around the large chamber. It filled the entire area with a shifting pattern of blue energy. Kuthanaga dropped to the floor and slowly stood. Tim was breathing heavily and his head tingled.

"What is that?"

"That, Tim, is what will sustain them until after the Convergence."

Tim stretched and took a deep long breath.

"How many more of these do we have to do?"

Kuthanaga also took a breath.

"319 more locations worldwide."

"Oh fuck."

"Ready for the next location?"

Tim shrugged and watched as Kuthanaga closed his eye.

Chapter 57 – Challenge
September 12th 2012 – New York 3:11 pm

"So Dmitri how are things? Are we ready to head out?"

Dmitri nodded. There were no new disasters other than the tainted to slow the progress of his personal research and 90% of the Draconians had been dispatched and reported that they were in the underground facilities worldwide.

"Yes everything has been completed ahead of schedule. And, in perfect timing. With the collapse of everything remotely civilized there's nothing left for us until after the Convergence. We simply ride out the storm now."

"Any news about Annukai activity?"

Dmitri considered lying but curiosity got the better of him.

"There are some oddities. Lots of localized energy bursts and sustained anomalies across the globe. The first we registered happened in Utah and quickly spread to other states and then abroad."

"Do you have a map?"

"Of course."

Dmitri showed a map with the areas clearly marked.

"Anything else?"

"Yes there is large human migration to those areas as well."

"What?!"

"It was small groups and then larger clusters."

"What happened to them when they got to those locations?"

"Unknown. They arrive and then they seem to stay."

"Do you have thermals of the areas?"

"We have limited capabilities all things considered. But there is one location we still have active equipment."

"And?"

"The heat signal is maintained and then fades out."

"What could cause that?"

"If they go far enough underground, then that would cause it."

Richard smiled.

"So they have underground bases of their own to protect the humans?"

Dmitri nodded. "It would seem so. Why does this matter?"

"It doesn't matter to me. However, it does matter to him. Can we still fire a nuke?"

Dmitri nodded.

"When was the last energy signal?"

"Three hours ago."

"Where?"

"Australia."

"Do we have any local nukes close to any of the energy sites?"

"Yes, five of them."

"And would those areas affect any of our locations?"

Dmitri worked on his computer for a couple of minutes. "No."

"Detonate one of them on an area least important to us."

"As you wish."

Dmitri brought up a command console and put in a series of passwords.

"I need your voice print authorization."

In Draconian Richard simply said "Authorized."

"It's done."

"Where was it?"

"Tennessee."

"Now we wait."

Chapter 58 – Challenge Accepted
September 13th 2012 – Australia 5:17 am

Tim was lying on the ground snoring away. He had collapsed after the final location was completed and Kuthanaga did not want to disturb him. The Watcher known as Yeruth stood near Kuthanaga.

"He seems exhausted."

"He is. He has done much for his fellow humans."

"So we wait for the chosen and guard them?"

"That's the plan."

"How many do you think will pass the trials?"

"Perhaps 10%"

"All this work to bring 2 million humans into the collective?"

"They need our protection."

The young Annukai stood there with Kuthanaga and they studied each other. Kuthanaga realized this Annukai had no love for the humans.

"Tell me Kuthanaga, what will happen to the other 90%?"

"They will have to survive on their own in the outlands away from Annukai."

"Do you ever stop and think maybe they are dangerous? I have seen what this human can do. What if they all start to manifest? You know how destructive they are. If they were to unleash that kind of energy at us they'd be worse than the Draconians."

"I do not share that belief. Tim has done nothing but good with his abilities and has been a good friend."

"Understood. But what if others are not so inclined?"

"I suppose we'll have to…"

At that moment both Annukai felt a searing pain and loss of connection to the Watcher Lahoko. Kuthanaga was still standing but Yeruth collapsed and screamed.

Tim startled by the sudden outburst jumped to his feet.

"What the fuck man?!"

Kuthanaga raised a hand up to calm Tim.

"Something bad just happened. We need to find out what."

"Where? Back in the United States."

Kuthanaga tried to reach out to watchers in the area and there were none. He scanned neighboring states and realized many of the watchers were injured and dazed from what had happened.

"What happened?"

"We were attacked somehow."

"By who?"

"I do not know. We need to find a way to get there."

"How?"

Kuthanaga closed his eyes and kept probing. Finally, he was able to get a Watcher in the neighboring state of Alabama. He focused and Tim felt the connection and he pushed through.

The watcher was dazed still and had blood running from his nose. Kuthanaga healed him quickly and then bolted out.

Tim was hot on his heels as they got outside Tim froze. To the south, he could barely make out a mushroom shaped cloud.

"Is that?"

Kuthanaga nodded.

"Yes it is."

"Who would do that?"

"I have my suspicions."

"Isn't that one of our spots?"

"Yes."

"Was it full?" Tim's heart was racing.

"Yes." Kuthanaga answered with rage welling within him.

"How many?" Tim was almost too scared to ask.

"550,000."

"Damn."

Kuthanaga looked at his cellphone and there was no signal.

"No way to check at the moment. We need to get to Atlantis and use the Quinuk system there to reach out with."

Kuthanaga closed his eyes, Tim pushed, and they were suddenly back in Atlantis. Without missing a beat, the two walked into the main crystal room. Kuthanaga pulled out a crystal orb and placed it on his forehead. A few moments went by and Tim heard a displaced familiar voice.

"Ah Kuthanaga I wondered how you'd get in contact with me. I wasn't sure if your communicator would work the other way around."

"Did you do it?"

"Yes I did if you're referring to the nuke."

"Why?"

"To get your attention. I have all the locations."

"What do you want? I've already swore the oath to not kill you."

"Yes I know. I realized though, that out of all the Annukai that my family has ever encountered only you have beaten us. Time and time again when it mattered most. When my great grandfather almost had Egypt, you came along and messed that up. And, I don't even want to remember the whole Babylon thing. I should have finished the job all those years ago when I killed your mate. A mistake I need to fix. I can't really allow you to live. So, I issue this challenge to you. We'll face off again before the Convergence is done and I'll leave the rest of the humans alone."

"That's not going to be a fair fight. Especially since I can't kill you."

"Yeah that's a bit unfortunate but I don't have anything to do with that. It's your honor that dictates to you how you'll handle the combat. The holy day of the arrival is coming up at the end of October. I think the arrival location is fitting for us to fight our last battle."

"So to be clear. I am honor bound to not kill you or have any of my Annukai kill you. If I do not fight you, you'll kill the humans I have marked?"

"Yes."

Kuthanaga nodded and anger welled inside of him.

"When I am done with you Drake you'll wish you were dead. I accept your challenge."

"The location is agreed upon?"

"Yes. The Barringer Crater is acceptable."

"No one but you and I in the center. Everyone else stays outside?"

"That is fine."

"October 21st?"

"Yes."

"Splendid. You are my greatest enemy and I cannot wait for us to end this once and for all."

Kuthanaga put the crystal down and looked at Tim.

"Dude, are you fuckin' serious?"

"I had a feeling it would come to this. I had hoped it wouldn't. I want you to be there Tim."

"You couldn't keep me away."

Xanari and Joy had heard their voices and hurried into the chamber.

"You're back?" asked Joy.

Xanari was barely on her feet a small trickle of blood ran from her nose. Kuthanaga helped her and gave her a solemn look.

"OK, what happened?" asked Joy confused.

"We just got jacked again by fuckin' Drakes." said Tim as he hugged her.

"Kuthanaga, what does Tim mean?"

He closed his eyes and shared everything that had happened with Joy and Xanari.

"He means to kill you. You can't trust him." said Xanari.

"I don't."

"You will kill him?"

"No, I swore I wouldn't. But I will bring him as close to it as possible."

Xanari smiled knowing full well what Kuthanaga was capable of.

"What about the rest of the chosen?" asked Joy.

"They are all protected and ready for the Convergence."

"What's next?"

"We get the leaders and bring them here to prepare them." said Kuthanaga as he walked out of the communications chamber.

"Well we'll finally have company." said Joy trying to lighten the mood.

Tim walked along quietly.

Chapter 59 – the Stage is Set
October 19th 2012 – Atlantis 12:11 pm

Tim stood within the group and greeted each one by name. One hundred fifty humans from all walks of life stood in amazement as he explained why they had been chosen. Xanari and Kuthanaga demonstrated enough technology and magic to make the most skeptical of them believers. It took many of the humans days for them to come to grips with that fact that many of their family and friends were dead or would be dead. There was anger, sadness and finally acceptance. Tim was amazed at how well they adjusted and accepted their fate.

That is part of the reason they were selected. said Kuthanaga to Tim.

They all have mental strength, which makes them more than capable. Their moral foundation is solid and unwavering. They are the highest level of civilized humans on your planet.

And then there's me... A former junkie with supernatural abilities...

Tim, you consistently do not acknowledge your worth.

Dude, I used to rob old people just to get fuckin' high.

We have all done things that we are not proud of. The greater the person the greater the deeds, good and bad they have done. Forgiving yourself and moving beyond the bad and doing the greater good is ultimately what defines you as a villain or a hero.

Well I'll keep pushing forward and will do everything I can to make this second chance worthwhile.

How is Joy doing?

She's fine. I think the twins are getting anxious though.

What do you mean?

They kinda told me last night they're ready to be born.

Kuthanaga looked at him.

Excuse me?

Isabella said she wants to come out.

Do you think they will?

I reasoned with them telling them that there's a reason for the long pregnancy.

And?

*They're *considering* it.*

Kuthanaga grinned.

I do not envy you Tim. Your children are going to be something else.

Yeah, tell me something I don't know.

How are you feeling?

The memories are coming faster. I can speak over fifty languages now.

That will be useful when you help lead them.

Kuthanaga nodded at the humans who were speaking amongst themselves.

Lead who?

Them. You will be the voice for humanity.

"Ha!"

Tim couldn't help blurt that out which startled a few people near him.

"Sorry."

Me?! Dude, seriously. I'm starting to wonder if you're OK.

You'll know about my people and you know about your people. In addition, your abilities will make you the obvious strongest leader. Once your children are grown, they will undoubtedly take up after you.

You've given some thought to this.

Yes I have.

I will do my best and will see how things shake out after the Convergence. I'm not sure I want the responsibility of leading them.

Your fate is yours and your destiny will lead you where you are needed most.

You ready for your battle to the death… or near death for him?

Yes.

You scared?

Yes. Richard is powerful and has a force of will that is legendary. He never quits. I once had a force of a few thousand that laid siege to a small city he had. The siege lasted over a month and when we finally gained control, he nearly killed a third of my force by himself. When word got to me that the city had a dragon I entered and we fought. I barely defeated him before he fled. Every battle I've had with him has been close.

Don't worry. You'll kick his ass and be home before you can say Genghis Khan.

Ahh, I see those memories are flooding into you?

Yes.

I am sorry for some of the more colorful memories.

Dude, no worries. I have a few of those myself.

Once Richard is dealt with we should be fine to wait for the Convergence to run its course. Atlantis will rise as will its sister city Lemuria and that event in and of itself is very traumatic. When it begins, the city will darken. Do not be afraid, that is normal. It is basically redirecting energy to keep the interior safe. That will last for about thirty minutes and once the surface is reached the light will shine down. The cities won't rise until a week before the Convergence is over. That means there is still a danger of wild weather and waves. Make sure to stay within the buildings and you will be fine.

Why are you telling me all of this?

Just in case I don't win.

Dude, you're not going to die so cut it out.

I always make sure to cover all my bases when I can. Either I tell this to you or Xanari will after the fact. I'd rather be the one to tell you all of this.

Tim nodded.

OK, fine.

In the event that something happens to me, you must retrieve the Gak-lua-kuun from my body and wear it. When the Annukai elders approach you, simply say to them the Creator has blessed us, we come to be of Annukai.

And then what happens?

They will help you and any injured and set up the trials within a year. It may be pushed off for two years with the changes that they will have to adjust to.

What are the trials?

It's nothing more than a test to measure your moral soundness.

If we fail?

Then you are outcasts and will need to make your own path.

Tim shrugged.

So, what will the Earth be like?

Different. Much of what you came to know as normal will be gone. Most of your technology will not be of use, and the landscape will appear alien and new. In addition, the laws of physics are different. While the Earth was asleep, the basic laws of the universe were followed with a few notable exceptions. When all the dimensions are sitting on the crust, the astonishing is normal. You will see things you never thought possible. Your crust was so bland and dull. When the Convergence is completed, the world will literally be a brighter place.

How about the buildings, cars and stuff like that?

Some of that technology will work for a while. But, eventually the cars will run out of gas and the houses electricity. You'll need the basic survival tools and knowledge, which are stored in my memories. You'll need to teach your people the way of the land and they in turn will train their children.

So if things do go bad, is there anything special you want me to tell Xanari?

Kuthanaga eyes widened a bit and then he smiled.

You know?

Dude, it's quiet as hell here. Plus, it's soooooooooo obvious that you're into her and she's madly in love with you.

Kuthanaga felt silly.

I am not sure what to say to her if I fail. Maybe no words are better than clumsy words which are unable to convey the weight of how I feel.

OK, gotcha.

Tim, if things do go badly for me, I don't want you to risk yourself at all. Do not try to fight Richard. He is too strong for you to engage.

I understand I won't try to fight him.

What will you do for the next couple of days?

Work with the leaders and spend time with Joy.

Kuthanaga nodded locked arms with Tim and he hugged Tim and walked away shoulders pulled back proud radiating prestige and purpose.

The group parted as Tim passed through them and he could feel their anxiousness eyes on him as he did. He continued and came upon Rachel who was sitting and reading a book.

"Hey Rachel how are you doing?"

She glanced up and held his gaze for a moment.

"I am concerned."

"About?"

"Kuthanaga."

"What about him?"

"I was angry because of what he did with the Earth's Milk so I didn't say what I've been dreaming about lately."

"Which is?"

"Kuthanaga is going to die."

"No, he's not."

"It's been the same since your encounter with the guardians. You are watching him as he battles the Drake in a huge crater. The battle looks like it's decisively Kuthanaga's but then the Drake cuts him with a silver blade. Kuthanaga is weakened and as the battle continues, he slows and the Drake takes his head. You are running with all your might and get to him and Richard says something to you and then leaves. You kneel and the ground is soaked with blood. You pick up the large necklace from Kuthanaga and begin to cry."

"No changes in the dream?"

"No."

"Why do you tell me now?"

"Because maybe you can do something about it."

"Why haven't you told Kuthanaga?"

"I have."

"What?"

"He just smiled at me and said 'we'll see'."

Tim was irritated. Now the whole conversation with Kuthanaga made sense. He was at peace with dying and knew he was going to die.

"Thank you Rachel. I'll see what I can do."

"I'm not mad at him anymore. I forgive him. I know why he did what he did and I know he was just trying to help. I'm sorry I didn't say anything sooner."

Tim waved it away and gave her a small smile. "Don't worry about it Rachel. The fact of the matter is you told me. I'll do what I can."

Tim walked on and saw Joy in the window of their living quarters. She was leaning back her hair dancing in the faint breeze. She was radiant.

"Hey you!"

She glanced down and gave him a smile that was so perfect it was permanently etched in his memory. He jogged up the stairs and hugged her.

"How's my baby mama?" she laughed at him and pushed him.

"More like how's my goddess."

"Goddess?"

"Yes." she flashed him a look and he grinned.

"Fine my goddess. How are you?"

"Tired. I am so friggin' huge. I can't find a position to be comfortable. At least they try to reposition inside to help me get comfortable. They are so sweet. Look at what they did on the wall."

Tim looked at what she was pointing at and the wall had an images of him and Joy. Two small children stood at either end of them. There was wild prismatic colors in the sky and it was one of the most beautiful things Tim had ever seen.

"How? I don't understand."

"Isabella likes to leave the womb and travel. She calls it stretching her legs. Sometimes Xavier does as well. They said the sky will look that once the Convergence is done."

"Holy shit. Are you serious? They talk to you?"

"Kind of. It's weird. It's not words. It's like feelings and images."

Joy looked serious.

"Xavier wants to know why you're sad."

"Just got done speaking with Rachel. She's been dreaming a lot lately."

"Oh yeah about what?"

"Kuthanaga. She's pretty fired up and knows that he's going to die."

"Did you talk with him?"

"Not about that specifically, but from the way he's talking, sounds like he's OK with it. I don't know what to do. I'm scared. He said I'm supposed to lead all these folks. Why not you? You're way smarter than me. I'm a fuckin idiot."

Joy stepped up and stared at him hard.

"Yes you are!"

He was shocked.

"For saying what you just did you are an idiot. I wouldn't have married you if you were. You are caring and full of love. Oh!"

"What?"

"You've pissed off the kids. They are not happy with you. Why would you think so little of yourself?"

"Babe, come on. You know what I've done in the past."

She shrugged and sat next to him.

"Yeah, so what? It's the past. And hello, news flash, that world is about to end. The world is going to be reborn fresh and new. A new beginning! You have your future to live. Stop dwelling in the past."

Tim nodded. She had a point. By the time the Convergence was done, it was very doubtful that anyone Tim had harmed would even be alive and if they were the things he had done would be just a pale memory compared to the changes they'd be facing. He smiled.

"Well I guess you have a point. I mean shit, I can speak over fifty languages at the moment."

"Yup and you always make me smile."

"I'm just scared. I don't know what to do. I don't have a plan. I don't know if I can handle the responsibility of leading the human race."

"Just go with the flow baby."

He smiled.

"Go with the flow?"

"Yes."

"Damn you are truly wise babe."

"So whatcha gonna do now?"

"Just wanna lay here and spend time with my family."

He laid down and Joy laid next to him. He hugged her and rubbed her belly. He felt warmth pass up from her belly into his arms and he was filled with a sense of well-being.

"Thanks guys." he said as he dozed off.

Chapter 60 – The Fix
October 20th 2012 – Arizona 11:11 am

Richard was kneeling, grabbed a handful of sand, and watched as it trickled out through his fingers. He was in his natural form and it felt good to be unrestricted. There was no one around. The sun was high in the sky and it warmed his scales, which almost shimmered in its light. He inhaled deeply and smiled to himself. He pressed the tiny earpiece in his ear and waited a moment.

"Yes?"

"What is the reception like?"

"Loud with a little distortion. But, fine all things considered. Your wife has called again. She wants to know why you're not in here with us."

"Tell her I had some unresolved issues to deal with. Dmitri, I want to thank you for all the hard work you've done over the years with me."

"What's this shit? Are you kidding me? Sounds like you think he may actually kill you. With all the odds stacked in your favor I can't see how he could win."

"The time bend is the only thing I'm concerned about."

"It's a non-issue. The equipment you brought with you will negate it. Plus once you hit him with the trigger that should give you the distraction you need to be able to finish him off. There should be no interference either; as long as you have the perimeter rigged, no one will be able to get near you. You can always abort."

"No this is long overdue. He needs this as much as I do even if he won't admit it. I killed his family and for that, he'd chase me to the end of time. Call it guilt, but I fell I owe it to him to at least kill him with honor so he may join them in the universe."

"I still think it foolish. There is nothing to gain."

"I disagree. There is closure."

Richard started jogging and broke into a full sprint after a few laps around the inner ring he took a deep breath.

"Are you ready?"

"Yes."

"Will you need me to monitor tomorrow?"

"Yes I'd like that."

"I will keep the com open and record it all."

"Thank you."

Chapter 61 – Closure
October 21st 2012 – Arizona 12:00 pm

Tim and Kuthanaga arrived at 12pm on the dot near the top left ring of the crater. Kuthanaga saw that Richard was waiting for him in the center.

"Kuth, I spoke with Rachel."

"I know."

"Are you sure about this? You know it's a trap."

"Yes."

"And you're still going down there?"

"Yes."

"Why?"

"Because I need to end this. I need to move beyond Sani if I hope to have a future."

"Future?"

"Yes, Tim."

"So you don't have a death wish?"

Kuthanaga smiled. "I have some things that are keeping me here for a while. I'd like to see my brother's children grow to help lead the humans."

"Brother, huh?"

Kuthanaga nodded and stripped down to just a long black silk-like pants. He shifted to his native form and his tattoos shifted wildly across his flesh making a distinct pattern. He flexed and muscles Tim had never seen before bulged and constricted. He motioned and a long silver blade materialized in front of him.

"It's been a long time old friend," he said to the blade.

"Well then go down there and fuckin' whoop his ass so we can go home."

Kuthanaga nodded and began walking the distance to meet his greatest foe.

Richard waited patiently as Kuthanaga walked closer.

Tim watched, as Kuthanaga got closer and closer. Tim kept his focus on him and his vision zoomed to keep everything in clear sight.

Good luck man.

Thank you Tim.

When Kuthanaga was just ten feet away Richard bowed his head and saluted him as was traditional for Draconians. Kuthanaga returned the salute.

"Finally, after all this time. No tricks, no Annukai magic. Warrior against warrior."

Kuthanaga nodded. He had dreamed for hundreds of years of this moment.

"Kuthanaga there is something I need to say before we begin."

"What is that?"

"I've thought long and hard about that fateful day when I took your mate. I've often wondered if I would do things differently and never could come to a clear answer. Now in this moment I now know for certain what I would do if I had known she was your mate and with your child."

The blood was flowing in Kuthanaga and pain and anger welled in him.

"What would you have done?"

Richard smiled a cruel smile.

"The same thing, but would have drawn it out longer and made her suffer more!" With that he sprung at Kuthanaga with his blade which was twice the size of Kuthanaga. Kuthanaga brought his blade up and easily deflected the attack.

Kuthanaga stepped to his left and brought his blade up and it bit deep in Richard's thigh. The roar of pain was loud enough that Tim heard it half a mile away.

"You'll pay for that Richard; I will deal a thousand cuts to you."

"We'll see!"

Richard swung a wide arc and Kuthanaga barely dodged. A large swath of his long hair floated to the ground freshly cut by the swing. He answered with a rapid series of slashes that cut Richard's forearm from his wrist to his elbow. Eight razor thin cuts started oozing and Richard growled.

Richard swung his tail deep into the earth and flung dirt into the face of Kuthanaga who leaned and swung most of it away. Richard pressed his advantage and swung his blade down lighting fast. Kuthanaga saw there was no way to avoid the swing and focused and attempted to bend time to give him a better chance to dodge. Suddenly he felt a searing pain in his head and a moment later, he looked to his right side, saw that Richard's blade was five inches deep, and had severed his collarbone. He screamed in agony and time seemed to slow around him. He saw the blade was coated with a milky liquid and it mingled with his blood. He reached up and grabbed the blade holding it in place as Richard attempted to pull it free to swing again.

Tim screamed as he saw Kuthanaga fall. He realized something was wrong.

Kuthanaga kicked hard at the base of Richard's sword arm at the elbow connecting solidly and snapping it. He stumbled back and freed the blade from his shoulder. He tried to focus on his wound and again the searing pain as well as something different. His vision was shifting and he found it hard to focus. He dropped to his knees.

Tim continued to scream so loud that Richard heard it.

"I'm sorry Kuthanaga. I wish there was a way we could have fought on equal levels. But your damned Annukai magic. I had to find a way to disable it. I couldn't allow you to heal from your wounds as you have done so many times in the past. The irony is your Earth's Milk was your ultimate downfall. That and your honor. Let me ask you a question?" Richard retrieved his blade and stood over Kuthanaga who was weakened to the point where he could barely move.

Tim noticed the presence again and wished so desperately that there was something he could do the save his friend.

"Whatever the fuck you are please help me!"

Tim felt an energy flow through him like a wild uncontrollable bolt of electricity. Suddenly he was glowing brightly and his skin burned. He focused on Richard and the anger and pain that Kuthanaga had suffered all the years was suddenly raw and fresh as if it were his own pain.

"What is your question fiend?" hissed Kuthanaga through waves of pain.

"If you had bested me would you have honored your vow to not kill me?"

Kuthanaga sensed the mysterious presence again and tried to focus on it. The confusion was numbing his senses. He smiled at Richard and nodded.

"I swore an oath to you that I wouldn't kill you. That no Annukai would kill you..."

Suddenly a blast of energy struck Richard in the chest sending him flying 300 yards. He screamed in agony as he crawled to his feet. Tim was standing there engulfed in wild blazing energy.

Tim's voice was distorted and deep. "He swore that he and the other Annukai wouldn't kill you... I... Am... Not... Annukai!"

Another blast shot forth from Tim and Richard raised his blade to try and block and it disintegrated instantly. Richard could feel his body being blown into large pieces. He could hear the pieces thumping heavily to the ground. He fought to get his breath and nothing came. He looked down and saw his burnt and broken form.

"Richard! Richard! Who is it? Who is that?"

"It... was... the... hu... Tim..." and the last breath left him and Zygriel was no more.

Tim dropped to the ground and felt like he was going to black out. He fought to stay conscious. He crawled to Kuthanaga who was lying in a puddle of blood that was growing wider with each breath.

The presence was gone and Tim held Kuthanaga in his arms.

"Kuth, damnit don't fuckin' die. Come on man you can't die on me. I need you. I don't know what I'm supposed to do."

Kuthanaga looked at Tim with fading eyes and smiled softly.

"Be what you were destined to be."

Tim shook Kuthanaga keeping him conscious.

"Kuth! Stay with me I'm going to bring us home. Hang on."

Tim focused on Atlantis and suddenly a searing pain tore through his mind, and he pushed on.

Memories flashed in his mind.

All the bad things he had done.

The people he had hurt.

The beloved family he had hurt.

All the pain became a tangled web of razors he saw a faint light in the darkness which was overwhelming him. He saw memories of Kuthanaga of Joy and Xanari and his babies.

He screamed a mighty scream and the web of pain shattered and white light surrounded him.

He arrived in Atlantis and was holding Kuthanaga so tightly that his hands ached.

"Destined to be… be…"

Xanari was there suddenly and she was crying.

"Kuthanaga!" she immediately placed her hand on his Gak-lua-kuun and began chanting.

"Why isn't it working?!" she screamed.

Kuthanaga grabbed Tim and pulled him close and stared deep in his eyes.

"*Hero!*" and he collapsed back and his breath faded. Tim couldn't let go, he sobbed so hard he felt his breath would never come to him. Xanari focused and pushed and nothing happened. Joy walked in and saw the bloody mess. She ran to Tim and held his arm. She felt energy pass through her and it snaked into Tim and passed from him into Kuthanaga who gasped a violent single breath. He lurched up eyes wide open and he screamed once and collapsed.

They all stood there holding their breath waiting for a sign. Any sign. After twenty seconds which seemed an eternity Xanari sensed a faint beat in his heart and she worked quickly to bandage the would he had. His breathing was shallow and he was still, but he wasn't dead.

"Will he be OK?" asked Tim with a wild look in his eyes.

"Tim?!"

"Hang on a sec babe!"

"Tim?!"

"What babe?" he turned and saw that Joy was bent over in pain.

"They're coming!"

"What?!"

Xanari was overwhelmed. She lifted Kuthanaga and placed him on a bed. She turned to face Joy who looked pale and was breathing heavily.

"Xanari! I need help."

Xanari sprang to Tim's side and the got Joy to a bed across from Kuthanaga. Xanari focused and saw that indeed the babies were coming. She caressed her Gak-lua-kuun and started chanting as Tim held Joy's hand. Joy's grip was so strong that it hurt. He spoke softly to her, caressed her face, and kissed her gently on her forehead.

"You're OK babe. Hang in there, you can do this." he coached.

Joy was glowing and she did as was instructed by Xanari and after three sets of pushing Isabella was born. Xanari motioned, a faint glowing platform appeared, and she placed Isabella on it. Tim stood nearby as Xanari continued. Two sets later Xavier was born. There was complete silence as they entered the world. Xanari motioned and the cords were cut. Another motion and the platform pulsed with a whoosh and the babies were cleaned up and smelled of flowers. They cooed and Tim noticed they were both holding hands.

He stood over them and they were staring at him intently.

Bring us to him.

He pushed the platform near Kuthanaga.

The twins closed their eyes; energy flowed into Kuthanaga, a black liquid poured from his eyes, and his breathing deepened. The bandage that Xanari had hastily placed over his wound seemed to move and shift slightly. Tim pulled it back and saw the wound healing.

Bring us to mother please.

Tim did as he was instructed and Joy sat up, grabbed her babies, and smiled weakly.

"You did it babe. You are amazing. You did it." said Tim

Tim turned and saw Xanari standing over Kuthanaga. He opened his eyes softly and stared at Xanari.

"Kuthanaga." she kissed him and he smiled. He sat up and chanted gently and the rest of his wounds healed. He walked to the foot of Joy and knelt before her and the children. Isabella and Xavier stared at the room and their eyes seemed to smile.

"Thank you." was all Kuthanaga could say.

A great shifting shook everything for a moment.

Tim looked around and groaned. "What now?"

Kuthanaga laughed gently.

"It is a precursor to the Convergence. It will begin in a few days in full force but it is building. This is expected."

Chapter 62 – Rebels
November 25th 2012 – Salt Lake City 3:13pm

Diane was sitting on the small bed staring at a photo of her son Jeff. He had been missing for months. She cried heavily again as was her routine every day. She couldn't understand how he was gone. Who could have taken him? She was terrified that maybe one of the crazies had gotten him. The police were no help, as the remaining police wouldn't do anything unless they were paid. She had no money and with the crazies randomly attacking and killing people, the police had more things to worry about than a missing person no matter his age. The area she lived in had been barricaded and secured by many of her armed neighbors and he neighborhood was almost a fortified prison to her.

Sheba her cat wrapped herself around her ankle and purred. Diane didn't have the strength to shoo the cat away. She was numb and hollow. She barely ate and was a shell of her former self. A sound startled her. A faint thumping noise from outside the window. She stood and approached all the while hoping it was him. She flung back the curtains and looked outside. There was nothing there. She saw hail falling outside the size of oranges. Each one thumped the ground and the wall. And, just as quick as it began it ended. She gazed up at the sky as the clouds broke and a beam of light hit the house and illuminated the small room.

The sky was shifting colors and she wondered to herself why she had never noticed just how vibrant the colors were? She went to close the curtain when she thought she saw a feminine figure standing by the trees across the street. She looked again and saw it was nothing. Glancing back up at the sky she paused and noticed the faint white outline of what looked to be the moon, but this moon was broken and shattered. The shimmering in the sky intensified and she thought she saw a Pegasus fly by. Closing the window, she sat back down on the bed and regarded Sheba.

"I think I'm losing it for sure. I just saw something that isn't there…"

Sheba purred and hopped up next to her as she began to sob again.

"Diane, do not be sad. I'll bring you to your son."

Startled, Diane jumped up and stared into the eyes of one of the most beautiful women she had ever seen. She looked at the woman who had her hand stretched out before her.

"Who are you?"

"My name is Xanari and I am here to help you."

"You have my son?"

"Yes, he is safe. Let's go."

You know she's not marked…?

So what? We've broken so many rules so far. What's one more?

Kuthanaga laughed a long hard laugh. As they walked out the house with Sheba in tow, the Earth began to shake and the sky illuminated brighter than anything any human had ever seen before. Xanari picked up Sheba and then held Diane close.

"Your world ends now, the world is being reborn. Its future depends on the choices you make going forward. Change is never easy and with this pain maybe something profoundly good will happen. Your destiny awaits you."

They walked on and as Diane glanced back, a huge wave of water crested the Wasatch Mountain range and she gasped as the world went dark.

Epilogue

January 1st 2013 – 1:05 pm

Joy smiled softly at Tim who was bathing Xavier.

"Well how did it go with the council?"

Tim sighed a deep sigh and shook his head.

"Could've gone better. There's a lot of Annukai who don't care for us."

Joy gave him a sideward look as she powdered Isabella. Lifting Isabella gently into her arms she sniffed her neck and giggled while tickling her.

"Well overall how'd it go?"

"It went good. They are still intent on putting Kuth and Xanari though the Trials of Judgment. That could end up being a really bad situation if it goes south. Kuth admits to the things he's done and he's so stubborn about the whole honor stuff…"

"Which is why we love him."

"Yeah I suppose. The refugees are settling into the new way of life and so far, things seem pretty good. The Earth has finally settled down and Kuth wasn't lying when he said it was going to blow our minds. You know what I saw earlier as I was walking back from the council?"

Joy laughed.

"What?"

"Honest to God, I saw a fuckin' Jackalope."

She flashed him a look.

"OK, so maybe not a Jackalope per se, but it sure looked like one."

He opened the curtains and they stood there looking out the window to the world, which was alive, and thriving. The sky was a mixture of reds and purples and there were multitudes of flying animals, which Tim had never seen before. The air was fresh and he saw human and Annukai living together working and building.

"I think we're gonna be OK babe." he said with a smile.

Millions of light-years away a man dressed in a dark metal uniform with perfect build and features examined a monitor. Excitedly he stood and walked down a long corridor with glass cages filled with bodies and blood. His footsteps echoed softly as he opened a large door, which groaned in protest at being disturbed.

A tall man with equally perfect features sat on a throne made of tiny childlike skulls plated with a gold-like material. He glanced up at the anxious man.

"Yes what is it?" he asked with an air of boredom.

"I have detected Annukai, Quinuk and Draconian technology."

The man on the throne snapped to attention.

"Are you sure?"

"Yes and the planet they are has shifted from an M class planet to an A class planet."

A wicked grin played across his face.

"How very interesting."

"What are your orders?"

"What they always are... Enslave them."

The man nodded, snapped his heels, turned, and walked away.

Below, you will find a list of people who have supported me during the writing and publishing of "CONVERGENCE 2012". This is the list as of the current publishing. The website: http://www.convergence2012.com will always have the latest list.

THE MARKED:

Irene Ricks, Angelica "Angel" Ricks, Maile "Momo" Ricks, Zachary "Zach" Ricks, Tony Ricks, Mita Ricks, Darrien Ricks, Elijah Ricks, Barbara "Bobbie" MacKeon, Scott MacKeon, Luz Alfaro, Conrad Alfaro Senior, Conrad "Junior" Alfaro, Gilbert Alfaro, Chris Alfaro, William Manera, Stephanie Manera, Kayla Manera, Brayzeann Manera, Rhianalei "Analei" Manera, Colin "Advances" Preston, Jennifer Coke, Rod Sias, Ajah Sias, Asiah Sias, Lola Love, Cyrus Nooriala, Norma Nooriala, Megan Nooriala, Kristen Nooriala, Mike Pierson, Janayla Pierson, Tim Pierson, Sean Pierson, Alex Castillo, Rebecca "Becca" Castillo, Dakota "Koty" Sharp, Nate England, Rukiya Piersion, Joe Morici, Pearlena Sarono Stone, Gilberto Rivera, Chris Hatch, Georgia Hatch, Stephen Lytle, Debbie Griffon, Steven Griffon, James Lin, Telaya Gaudette, Nate Jorgensen, Allan Young, Cynthia Young, Earl Crawford, John Broklebank, Tari Hoyt Anderson, Tirzo Ruelas, Lionell "Max" Pasamonte, Carter Lipscomb, Clint Rogers, Merih Turkdogan, Luke McDowell, Josepha "Josie" Cox, "Her Tortured Embrace", Keenan Yazzie, Kenneth Keoki Whitehead, Lisa Bell, BJ Heinley, Dane Karr, Danny Franco, David Hawkins, Miko Marks, Ronald Brooks, Nerissa Olaes, Pat "Mac G" McGraw, Phil Burns, Shana Miyahira, Vanessa Olaes, C-Lee Silorio, Cynthia Silorio, Ron Silorio …

www.ingramcontent.com/pod-product-compliance
Lightning Source LLC
Chambersburg PA
CBHW061922170626
46813CB00006B/2272